I0818200

COMPROMISED

This book is dedicated to all the dangerous women with a sharp tongue, who don't take shit from anyone. You are loved my girl.

CHAPTER ONE

A decision,
so heartbreaking.

A gun,
so close.

A pain,
so sharp.

A diamond,
so perfect.

A beginning,
so right.

CHAPTER TWO

WORST VALENTINE'S DAY EVER

I can't stop it. Can't stop the vigorous breaths coming from my mouth. Can't stop my chest from rising and falling in panic. Can't stop my head from spinning.

What did I do? What did I do? What did I do?

I have long since washed it all off—the shower lasting almost an hour. Long since have been relocated, but somehow, I can still feel the slick stickiness of his blood coating my skin. Still have the faint flowery aroma mixed with the metallic stench of blood and the musky aftermath of fallen rain lingering in my nose... like a curse.

What. Did. I. Do?

I'm not supposed to feel this way. No remorse. No regret, and yet... Damn it! If I had known, if I was properly informed, I *never* would've gone through with it. But I'm free, and that's what I've wanted all along. Right? Freedom? In the moment it was all I could think about, that, and protecting the tiny scrap of my past I had left. But now... why now is my heart pounding?

I shake my head.

No. I did the right thing. I did the right thing. It was the only way. My only way. And besides, he broke me first. Screw that look he gave me. The one that tells me everything he's feeling. Everything I'm supposed to be feeling too. Screw the shiver that went down my spine. Screw the guilt, if it's really even guilt I'm feeling.

Maybe it's just shock.

Yeah, that's it, it's just shock. I just left the world I've been a part of for years. Got left by the person who was supposed to love me, and was dropped off in some small town with only two bags and new id's. It's just shock. I can pull myself from shock. That's easy. Guilt, not so much. But good thing what I'm feeling is just shock.

I shakingly breathe in and out then straighten, my hands still gripping the rim of the porcelain sink. My reflection stares back at me. The broken girl who has always had something to prove. The broken girl who has just been shattered even further, which I didn't think was possible. But shit happens. I guess...

No. Not guess. I know.

Shit happens, and you have to deal with it. I have to deal with it, now, or I'll fade into a ghost. A slight laugh tickles the back of my throat at my choice of the word 'ghost'. Not a fond laugh though. It's more of the dry laugh that you can't help when thinking of something that irritates you to your core. Terrible timing, but maybe that means I'm starting to feel better about everything.

Something in my stomach clenches, telling me the opposite. The sudden ache forces me to bend forward. I release a hand from the sink and grab my stomach, holding it as if I were just shot. It's all in my head, but when I glance down and my eyes catch my empty ring finger, the pain triples.

A tear rolls down my face, despite my protest. I violently wipe it away—wipe away any trace of weakness—and then stare at myself again. The broken girl who needs to change and grow... without him.

"Pull it together!" I unevenly shout while pushing my fist into the glass, the thought breaking through my every safety wall.

I breathe in. I breathe out.

"Hate him."

Slowly I retreat my fist from the mirror and uncurl my fingers, still staring at my own face. The blood dripping down from my knuckles doesn't seem to matter as much as it would a normal person. Neither does the heavy throb starting in my fingers. All I focus on is the glass that now shows the true me.

It's cracked into four pieces, disturbingly in the shape of a heart with my blood staining its middle.

Perfect.

Happy Valentine's Day, I guess...

CHAPTER THREE

Brooklyn, New York

3 YEARS LATER...

My phone rings, playing 'Girl on Fire' much too loud. I snap my eyes open, yet it takes a minute for me to remember where I am, and admittedly, even who I am.

As the song plays on though, my mind clears. I reach for my phone, stare at the bright screen with blurry eyes then groan at the time, and who's calling. With a thumping chest I quickly clear my throat—desperately trying to take sleep from my voice—yank out the charger, then slide my finger across the cold surface.

"Hello?" I answer with still a bit of dryness.

Shit. I'm dead.

"Were you still sleeping!? Elle, I'm on my way to your place right now, so get up and start getting ready!"

I hang my sweating head and sigh. "I know you're frustrated. But can you please yell at me much *much* quieter?"

Lazily I push off my elbows to sit up, Rebecca continuing to berate me the whole time.

"No! Get your ass up now Michelle Hannigan or so help me—"

"Muy bien, relájate, me estoy lenvantando ahora."

(All right, relax, I'm getting up now.)

A sudden wave of tiredness hits me. I try to fight it off as I rub my middle finger on the bridge of my nose. I'm *not* a morning person, which means I have to give myself a second to process all of the energy being thrusted at me through the phone. Energy that doesn't let up considering she starts talking again, but this time, I pretty much just put my brain on autopilot while I sluggishly get up. Really, she distracts herself with all of the talking she does. Whether I'm listening or not.

"Please don't cut me off in a language I barely understand. You're lucky I got an alert from The Steam Bean about their deal on two for one vanilla caramel lattes. That just bought you twenty minutes."

"Uh huh," I mumble.

Flinging the warm blankets from my legs, I swing them over my bed then hunch my shoulders as I grip the edge of the black sheets. Immediately the cold of February hits my damp skin. I've lived in Brooklyn for two years, and have had the same routine, because as I learned the hard way, routine is good. Though today—today I'm not practically fond of the feeling I'm getting by just being in my own home.

I'm used to my dampness being there from the nightmares, but this time the chill of them looms over me. Like they followed me into reality. After last night, I don't need anything more to worry about. Despite my best efforts though, it seems I don't have control over that anymore. Temporarily. Angering, yes, but right now I need to focus on getting ready for my day job.

Even that has me looking towards my bed.

I want nothing more than to get back in and just shut the world out. Have a moment to gather up the broken pieces of my brain. Any possibility of that fades when I tune Rebecca back in and quickly get ready to respond, as if I've been actively listening.

"—but you know Shane," she laughs dryly, "so I guess just make it twenty-five minutes then."

"Alright. I'll be ready to go."

"Ready as in in front of your building ready Elle. I mean it."

"Pero por supuesto mi amor," I say, dramatically rolling my last R.

(But of course my love.)

"Ha. Don't try to sweet talk me. I'll see you soon."

My lips curl into a small smirk. "Bye."

I toss the phone aside then plant my feet onto the heated wooden floor, slowly beginning to stretch, hoping it'll help my body relax. A breeze travels up my back as my oversized Batman shirt rides up, exposing my lady boxers to the chilled air. Another groan leaves my lips as the morning sun peeking in through my curtains beats down on me. I loosen my shoulders and breathe slow.

Deep breath in.

Deep breath out.

Just like always, as I go through my routine, those steady breaths calm an old part of me. Though this time, not completely. I straighten and tightly shut my eyes, waiting for the blood to rush down from my head. Unexpectedly, instead of the flashes of dizzying colors I usually see, a still image of 'his' face creeps into mind. What tranquillity I had going for me doesn't last much longer. I've dealt with the nightmares before, but I haven't been able to shake them off as quickly as I used to for a while now. It causes all of my internal warning alarms to go off. The very ones I put around the walls I created the first time those dark dream reminders caused me to wake up in rapid breaths and tears.

Every day though, textbook feelings of paranoia spread themselves throughout my brain, and in some desperate hope I choose to listen to that voice that's telling me everything's only in my head. The night terrors have already taken up an undeniable amount of my sleep. I'll be completely fucked if I let it interfere with my day.

Trying my best to dismiss it and move on, even when I know it'll wander around my mind, I focus all my attention on the other obstacle in my way. My nine to five soul crushing job.

I'm not particularly excited to sell office supplies today—or any day for that matter—but seeing that it's Friday, my brain pushes the annoyance aside. After one final stretch, I let out my 'I don't want to go anywhere' groan, and then strip off my bulky shirt and drop it onto the floor.

The freezing air stings my skin immediately, making my steps to the bathroom become much wider. I've always hated frigid weather, no matter where I am, but today it's colder than any I've faced before. It's almost haunting.

The chill lingers, and for a minute I could've sworn I was on that bloody pathway again. The craving for warmth glazes over the memory. It doesn't completely wash away all of the remaining dream fragments, but it's a start. I wiggle out of my boxers, start the shower and then jump in.

I try to relax, absorbing all the heat I can. Fiery water always feels so comforting on my skin in times like these. Moments when I need to restart my brain. I stand directly under the shower, eyes closed, head up, with my infuriating hair becoming heavy. I dismiss the weight, like I have for the last two years, and just listen to the water. The sound of it repeatedly hitting the bottom of my shower puts me in a trance. I sigh, taking in the rain like tune while wrapping my arms around my waist.

I flinch slightly. Sometimes it still takes me by surprise when my fingers graze my thighs. I'm much more filled out than I used to be, forcing myself to eat whenever I got the chance. It's become a hobby of mine for the last month, to cope with the stress of having two jobs now. Maybe I should go easier on the donuts, but with the amount I sweat each night from the nightmares, if I didn't cram baked goods in my mouth, I'd lose the weight and go back to being slim. Too slim, which wasn't healthy, for so many reasons. 'Him' being one of them.

This time, when the image of his face breaks through my walls, it's my fault. That, and the wave of memories I'd rather forget. Yet, despite protest, they start to surface from that place I dare not go. The place that begins in my heart, travels up to slightly grasp my throat, then forcefully seeps its way into my head. I slowly begin to get wrapped in the same cold that swaddled my night, but as disturbing as the chill is, my mind only continues to play tricks on me, as I feel another set of hands steadily slide down my hips and gently pull me backwards. Like I'm not in here alone.

It mimics an all too familiar touch.

Everything in me flinches. I swiftly open my eyes to shake the thought, and whatever I just felt, but slightly lose my balance in the process. My hands shoot out and grab the glass surrounding me before I fall, and despite the racing in my chest, I only focus on spinning around to reject the deception my brain caused by showing my eyes that no one had joined me. The hot water blurs my vision, forcing me to control my breathing. I drag both hands across my face to see clearly. But even that doesn't stop the memories from circling inside my head.

A buzzing sensation overwhelms my entire body, to the point where my legs begin to wobble. As if I don't remember how to stand on my own. Gripping the opaque glass now, I push out a deep breath then let the water run down on the back of my neck.

I hate this. I hate every single thing about this. It's like no matter how hard I try, how hard I want to move forward, the plague of the past keeps worming its way back into my present.

I don't want the burden anymore, especially not when that past includes a version of me I don't recognize. Or at least that's what I taught myself to believe. Yet even that line hasn't been a straight one in the sand for a while. My whole life has been a series of unknowns and risks forced to be taken. But I've been given a chance to change that, and the more responsible part of me knows that that's what I have to do.

It's amplified that little voice in the back of my head to an almost shouting nag, telling me I'm overreacting. Annoying, yes, but it does help to purge that entire history from my mind. And as I do, I think to myself, *no more distractions. No more brief moments.*

If I keep moving, I can move forward. A plan that unfortunately has me interacting with the world, whether I want to or not. I've already made that choice by getting out of bed. So, after one last glance around me, I let myself picture 'his' face once more before speeding up my morning routine. The image then fizzles away, back to that dark corner in the back of my mind.

I stand in front of my massive body mirror, the entirety of my room in its reflection. Flint grey walls with gold trim, a white headboard attached to my Queen-sized bed with black sheets, one white dresser and a matching nightstand. Simple. Almost boring. I stand in front of my mirror, blurring out my almost boring room and lean into the glass, only a finger gap away from my face touching it.

"Pull it together," I harshly tell myself.

Slowly my paranoia starts to drift away. The only thing that remains is the numbness of past emotions. It's not exactly what I want, but I've done this authoritarian method enough to know that that's the closest I'm going to get to soothing the rest of the memories still lingering in my head. For now, that's all I need. I tighten my towel, slide my closet open, and then stare at my collection of bland clothes. Every grey, black, and white piece I own.

My lips perk up into a smirk as I become dryly amused at the irony that's only now come to pass. My amusement only continues while picking out an outfit, still thinking of the fact that no matter what kind of person I try to be, shades always seem to play an important role in my life. It may not be as funny as I think. It's probably just my mind cracking under the pressure.

Despite my late epiphany, I quickly pull something together. It comes down to a slim business jacket and pants that are a blue dark enough to be mistaken for black, a smoke grey turtleneck that cuts off at my elbows, and classy black suede boots. And just to class it up a bit more, I pick out a necklace with a single black pearl dangling in the middle and matching earrings. Jesus, if the old me could see me now, I'd get the world's highest eye roll just for the matching blue purse with a scarf tied to the handle alone. But as I step back to get a better view, I *am* proud of how the outfit turned out, which is the only thing that matters now anyways. The old me be damned.

"Not bad Michelle," I say almost sarcastically. "Not bad at all."

Now comes the hard part, my hair. I wish I could just chop it all off to the length it used to be, but presentation is a large part of the routine. So, all I can do is sigh, grab my brush, and let it hang down. It may not be ideal, this whole 'routine is good' crap, but it is something I have to do. Especially since it's been the only thing keeping me on solid ground since—my phone buzzes, ripping me from the thought. *Thank god.* I drop my blank stare to read the text, already knowing its Rebecca. I roll my eyes and smirk.

'I know you're not downstairs, so I'm giving you a 2 min warning. Tick tock... my love.'

God, this chick is even more tightly wound than me, and that's saying something. I love her to death, but she needs to lighten up. I could never tell her that to her face, given the character I'm cast myself as, but seriously someone needs to mention it before she pops. Though since I can't bear to see that happen, I quickly brush out the rest of my mulish hair, grab my trusty black scrunchie and reply while walking out the door.

'Becca... r u texting and driving young lady!?'

'...no,' she answers back.

By the time I emerge into the black and grey hallway—overly decorated with paintings of random lines in my opinion—my phone goes off again. This time it's Shane.

'Elle if you care for me at all you'll get downstairs now! I'm begging you. She's got her crazy eyes. S.M.S!'

Rebecca and Shane live in the same apartment building, which means he gets the first face time with her, the poor guy. And given her tone earlier, she's still stressing about her big presentation today. Honestly, I've never met someone so dedicated to their shitty job, but at the same time it did create a certain respect for her. I appreciate loyalty, and no one has more than my best friend Rebecca Taylor.

As for Shane, well, he's been friends with Rebecca way before I came along, but we bonded immediately when I asked him if she ever relaxed. The answer was an unprecedented no, and since then, we've had a lot of fun teasing her about it. When he texts 'S.M.S' though—Save. My. Soul—he means it. Just when I'm about to text him back with my normal 'don't worry', I get distracted by the sound of the elevator doors opening down the hall.

"Shit shit shit," I mumble as I speed walk to catch it.

By the time I get there, the doors start closing, but, right before I'm screwed, a familiar hand sticks out to stop them.

Oh god, I forgot she's back today. I guess hurrying was a waste of time, because like she never left, like clockwork, here she is. Slowing up on each step I take, I quickly alter my facial expression from skeptical to friendly while I ascend upon the doors. And as I come face to face with my downstairs neighbour Theora Salano, in the back of my mind I painfully roll my eyes.

Oh, the peace I've felt with her being out of town for the last couple of days was unreal, but I guess all things can't last forever. It's not that I don't like her, it's just... there's something about her just always seemed off. I look past my annoyance, like I do every time she pops back into my life, then finally step into the elevator, beginning our little scripted conversation with obligatory kindness.

"Oh hey, Theora, it's nice to see you're back. Thanks for holding the doors for me... again."

The word 'again' comes out much more suspiciously than I meant, though she doesn't seem to notice it in my tone. And considering that it's actually been over eighty times in the last two years, I let it hang in the air for another minute. I found it odd around the first three times, because as I know, routine is good. So, on that third ride down it got me thinking, *am I a part of her routine?*

Now, she hasn't given me any sign that I am, though I've been keeping an eye on it, despite that foggy voice telling me it's all paranoia. Either way, Theora's excited 'Elle Woods' type voice almost makes me jump when she speaks. Her rosy face lighting up with joy, and I swear I can literally see her bubbly personality spread throughout her petite body.

"Of course, anything for my favourite neighbour. I bet you missed me and our elevator chats while I was gone, huh?"

Not even a little.

"You have no idea. Actually, I was just about to text Shane," I tell her, trying to change the subject, and she bites.

"Oh, I can't wait to see him. I missed him *so* much!" she squeals, her voice somehow goes higher.

How long is this elevator ride going to last? I mean honestly, I can only stomach her personality for a certain amount of time until I want to smack her. Yes, I know how it sounds, but Theora is that type of person I can't stand sometimes. And as the torture continues, I mainly focus on not letting my friendly facade break. Fighting the burning urge to clench my jaw, I keep my smile on like its duck taped to my mouth, and just watch the numbers count down while I patiently continue our conversation.

"How was the Bahamas with corporate?"

Theora lets out an airy laugh. "That's classified missy."

A dark cloud suddenly overtakes my kind demeanour at the choice of her words, and that chill from earlier returns. Goose bumps start to form on my skin as I side glance over to her and ask coldly,

"What did you just say?"

First, she says nothing, and from where I watch her, it's only her eyes that change in any sort of way. They fill with something, but I don't have the time to read what it is, as she switches them back to playful. "So serious Elle. I'm just joking silly," she chuckles.

Taken back to my mirror, what I had ordered myself to do, I try to calm down. Things can't get out of hand because I had a long night and bad dreams, I'm better than that. Although, as I'm about to pick up my friendly mask and put it back on my face, by the time another chill leaves me, the silver doors slide open. Theora doesn't move. I can feel her eyes on me, but a perfect distraction comes to my rescue.

Standing in front of us is Shane in a light brown suit—no tie of course—his ocean eyes slightly dilated with excitement as he comes forward, and Theora runs to him. *Sweet freedom.* I let out a much-needed sigh and thank Shane in my head. I could've handled it, but I *really* didn't want to. I'd much rather have him take over, and given the way I watch him greet her with open arms and a passionate kiss, he seems glad to. Shane's always been a different person with her, one that's not a complete asshole. Honestly, I couldn't believe he found someone crazy enough to date him, but that non-belief was trumped by the non-belief that that crazy girl lived so close to me.

I mean I'm all for making certain coincidences happen, but I don't particularly believe that they ever occur on their own. With Shane and Theora though, I try not to think about it too much, especially not when they're still making out and it's making me—as well as the other sprinkle of people in the lobby—uncomfortable. So, for the good of all, I clear my throat and step forward. Theora giggles as she draws away from Shane, who then finally acknowledges my existence.

"Oh, hey Elle," he says, and then hungrily looks back at Theora. "Sorry. I didn't see you there."

"It's fine. But don't you think you should be in the car with Becca?" I ask with a bit of annoyed uncertainty.

"She was making my eye do that irritated twitch thing," he laughs dryly while raking a hand through his cinnamon hair, then glances to Theora's lips and gushes.

"Plus, I needed to see this sexy lady as soon as those elevator doors opened."

My stomach literally flips at his comment. Sure, Theora is a stone cold ten, but I can't stand cute couple talk. I'd much rather get hit by a car, and I've been through that before, so that's really saying something about my stance on the matter. Yet despite my low scoff, Shane and Theora only start to suck face again. After another second though, she lightly pushes him away and giggles like before.

"Boo bear stop, we're in public."

Wincing at her girly attitude, and that *sappy* nickname, I'm more than eager to get away from their lovey-dovey relationship. Just before I turn from them however, from the corner of my eye, I watch Shane's demeanour completely change as he obeys. His broad shoulders slightly loosen, his head tilts to one side, and his eyes dip to her glossy lips. That only lasts about, oh I don't know, ten seconds before they're back at it.

I can't take this anymore.

I move past them, the clicking of my heels on the marble floor the sound I choose to focus on, but soon my attention goes into doing my usual morning check. Rebecca is already on edge, so I'll have to make it quick this time, just a second or two less than my usual routine. I look around, my eyes barely moving. Still aren't a lot of people in the lobby, of course there never really is, which is what I like about this place.

It's a fairly nice middle-class apartment, pre-war, but completely remodelled to have a more 'modern feel', and the owner doesn't micromanage the place. It's not interesting enough to be a target for crime, the residents are nice simple people who more or less keep to themselves, and it was easy for me to adapt to the surroundings. Once I figured all that out, it was also easier to know the kind of potential problems I'd have to deal with, and with whom. I know all of the residents, the amount of children to each family, where all of the cameras and exits are, and when frigid Amy at the front desk takes her breaks and when she's not working, which means friendly Antonio takes her place.

Details comfort me, help sooth any paranoia resting in my bones, but today—today there's a detail that I'm missing. Something that's out of place. Maybe it's just because Theora is back, which would temporarily force me to recalculate things, but as I walk out of the building, something suddenly shifts. The mood, the mellow morning, it changes, not by much, but just enough. I freeze in my tracks, glance from side to side, then shift my eyes to the glass doors and do the same. There's nothing and no one around to be giving off this unsettling chill. One that's recently crept under my skin and makes me jumpy.

I'm not supposed to feel jumpy. But, despite my hard stare and alert behaviour, when Shane's phone blares with his Seinfeld theme ringtone I flinch. It yanks me back from falling into myself, that part that wouldn't stop until I put my unease to rest. I sigh and loosen my jaw, then turn towards Shane. His swollen lips are downturned into a frown while looking at his phone. His left eye starts to twitch *ever-so-slightly*. Well, I know who's calling.

When he answers, I slowly shake my head, swallow back the laugh that starts up my throat, then return to my mission of getting to Rebecca's warm car. Though as I get closer, I slow up on my steps, seeing the phone to her ear and the pissed look attached to her face. No way I'm getting into that car to be left alone with her, even if it's only for a millisecond. Especially not when, from where I am, I hear her voice from both directions when she yells.

"Now!"

She's much scarier than I give her credit for. So much so even I pick up my pace. And as I take wide strides across the sidewalk only now do I realize how cold it is, even with the sun shining down. It plays tricks on me every year with that clear blue sky from my bedroom window, but really it's so icy that a street cat would freeze in mid stroll. A biting cold that has me practically teleporting into the car with Shane and Theora immediately following. Before I can apologize for the delay—still not completely sure why I'm feeling off and trying to figure that out in the back of my mind—Rebecca is already giving all three of us her evil eyes. Oddly at the same time.

Now, I know my best friend, which means I know that—despite her attitude this morning—she almost never gets upset. It's something I've always found a little troublesome, but in the rare moments she does get mad, or frightened as one horror movie night has taught me, she'll hold her breath until she's ready to speak. Or yell, which is more likely in this case. We sit in silence for half a minute, not moving an inch, all too scared to tell her to breathe. Then, when she finally lets out a breath, she twists around to Shane in the back and raises her voice. And not in her normal joyous tone.

"What the *fuck* took you so long? I knew I shouldn't have let you out of the car."

Uh oh, she's swearing. I should probably calm her down. With the twisted look of anger on her face though... maybe it might be better to just let her get it out of her system.

Which she does.

"All the fucking time, holy shit. Look, today is not the day to piss me off! You're acting like I don't have that huge presentation on our sales this quarter. One that has my job and promotion hanging in the balance!"

Okay, now I should calm her... but still something tells me to wait.

"You seriously don't think that that dick weed won't fire me in a second? You don't think that he cares if—?"

In an odd turn of events, she stops herself mid-scream and takes a deep breath. She then pulls the car out of park, jerks the wheel, and then zooms down the street. Her focus starts on the road, but when the morning traffic stops us, she turns back around and continues her furious rant in a softer irritated tone.

"I swear if I'm even a bit late, it's your ass. And your *ass* can take the bus next time."

"Why do you keep looking back at us?" Shane innocently questions, genuinely sounding confused by her anger.

I try to shut him up but Rebecca answers him before I can open my mouth, her tone creeping back into the same anger as earlier. "Because *boo bear*, you two are the ones who have the disturbing primal urge to crush your faces together every time your eyes meet!"

"First of all, don't call me that, ever again, even sarcastically. And second, so what? You're saying all this like I hold you up every day. I haven't seen my *girlfriend* in a week!"

"I. DON'T. CARE! What part of my tone is not making that clear Shane!?"

Now I have to intervene. Calm her so we don't crash. Knowing Shane like I do—that information taking up a special corner of my brain—he'll try to say something that'll piss her off just to get the last word in. Maybe today he'll opt to keep his mouth shut, given how much Rebecca's screamed at him already. His choice would definitely help my day go smoother, but he chooses the opposite.

Just great.

"What's wrong Becky? You seem... stressed," Shane mischievously snickers.

"You're such an asshole!"

I spin around in my seat, my fingers curled into a loose fist ready to inflict just the right amount of pain, expecting him full well to understand why. Rebecca isn't one to mess with when she's stressed, he knows that, but for some reason he's not making it easier for himself today with his extra... Shane-ness. My fist colliding with his arm will snap him out of his own stupidity, though before I make contact, I have to stop myself mid-swing, because Theora beats me to it. A small 'ouch' comes from her boyfriend.

She raises her voice. "Hey, that's enough. Don't be a dick, alright? You know our boss isn't exactly friendly. Rebecca has every right to be flipping out, so be nice."

"Thank you, Theora. It's nice to have you back." Rebecca smiles at her, then sticks her tongue out at Shane.

After he returns her gesture with a sharp middle finger, everything mellows out. The line up of cars finally starts to move in front of us, and Rebecca sighs. Work is only ten minutes away, but with the traffic at this time it's going to be at least twenty-five, and clearly she's figured that out. According to her time sheet—the one that's burned in my brain—we're already three minutes off. I for one know how important timing is, normally. Except today it hasn't been a priority.

The thought of why crosses my mind as we sit in silence while Rebecca drives, and the memory of last night starts to ring in my ears and plaster over my vision. It was strenuous, just like every night this month, but the lingering nightmares, and the sudden memories of 'him' that followed... I definitely wasn't expecting all of that. And now this strange gut feeling is telling me—well I don't know what it's telling me. All of this is the last thing I want to be thinking about before work, which the quiet is forcing me to do that. Luckily though, when Rebecca sighs again, my attention shifts towards her.

She has on the outfit we picked out for her big presentation a couple of days ago. Her 'boss bitch ensemble' as she called it. The mahogany jumpsuit, showing just enough cleavage, the black plaid button long sleeve blazer, and matching leather boots with a gold necklace and earrings. Even her hair is in the style she said she liked when I was just playing with it, a braided crown with two of her twists draping around her smoky eyes.

I wonder where her readiness for the presentation had gone. I've been helping her to prepare for weeks, and she never seemed stressed when it was just us. To be fair though, our boss is a little man who thinks that him being the manager of a mid-level office supply company gives him the right to be this egocentric, ill-mannered pitiful asshole that makes everyone's blood boil.

Especially Rebecca's.

She hates the man. Almost every day she tells me how hard she tries not to choke him with his own tie. Personally, that wouldn't be my choice of murder. I'm more of a 'use what they love' kind of girl. But that's just me. Now, considering I had him figured out from the start, when I shook his hand a little too tightly and he flinched, I know he'd be a beggar. It's always so much more entertaining when they—I stop myself from going further into detail and wipe the unknownst smile from my matte rouge lips.

My heart starts to race with excitement and an uneven breath silently blows out from my parted lips. I try to control myself before anyone notices; staring out the window, watching the brownstone buildings and sleeping trees pass by. It helps, but only for a few seconds, because then Rebecca's voice cuts into my thoughts and I turn again to be met with her semi-frustrated expression.

"So, what's your problem? Why are you so quiet today?"

I think she's going to stop there, let me answer before she starts prying, but that was my mistake. She only goes on with a smirk. "You look like you're trying not to look like you're thinking about something that's bothering you. Which also happens to include that staring-out-of-the-car-window-music-video vibe."

Last night must've really screwed with my head for me to actually be showing my frustration and not notice. It's bothering me more than usual, and I don't understand why. Really, I don't want to, since I still feel off about it. But Rebecca asking me what's wrong... I can't seem to think of anything to counter with. I'm normally very good at thinking on my feet, except today I'm tired. More tired than I've been this month alone. I don't have it in me to bullshit right now, so instead of answering right away I reach for the strong scented latte and take a sip. The hot liquid slides down my throat as I think of a response, and everyone is a new kind of quiet. The suffocating kind.

Shit. I haven't been acting that differently, have I?

I take another gulp, my tongue whaling from the heat, and try not to gag before speaking in my most convincingly confident voice. "I'm fine. I just have a lot on my mind today, that's all."

Silence.

"Well, *that* was reassuring," Shane mumbles, breaking the barrier of soundlessness as he reaches for his and Theora's drinks, glaring at me while he does.

After forcing down another swig of coffee, I lightly breathe in and out. *Relax,* I think, *just relax.* The mantra begins to work on my nerves, that is until Shane opens his mouth again with more BS coming out. It's like he's deliberately trying to make me hurt him.

"What can you possibly have on your mind Elle?" He takes a sip from his drink, puts it down, and then starts using his fingers to list off things in my life.

"You have the most boring job. You do live in an oddly nice apartment, but it's so quiet that it's boringly normal most of the time, and you hang out at the same place after work almost every day."

Slowly closing my eyes while holding down my coffee, I tuck back a strand of hair from my face and open my eyes while snickering at his last comment. "Shane... we have the same job, your girlfriend lives one floor down from me, and you're one of the people I hang out with at the same place after work almost every day."

He shuts up for a minute and grabs his cup, as if only to regroup the thoughts in his shell of a brain. Watching the way his face changes, it's like scrolling through the emojis on my phone. I almost laugh, but then, right before he puts the drink back up to his mouth, his expression seems to settle on sly asshole, and he raises a finger and continues.

"You still didn't answer the question though Elle. What's bothering you?" Shane tosses back more of his brew, then lets out a huffy laugh. "Because if something is bothering *you*, this much, well it must be something pretty big—"

"Shane proposed to me last week!" Theora blurts out.

The car slightly swivels as Rebecca does a double take, then turns to face them while at the same time we shout, "What!?"

"Can you not kill us today please!?" Shane yells.

Rebecca straightens the wheel, locks eyes with me, and then in one quick widening motion I know exactly what she wants me to ask. Though given the fact that I didn't detect an engagement ring on Theora's finger, I'm guessing that my line of questioning will only make the two parties uncomfortable, and or upset. Either way, I'm just glad that the focus is officially off me. And when I work up the nerve to lock eyes with Shane, or at least his forehead, I awkwardly ask,

"There... there was a proposal? Like a marriage proposal?"

His face turns a tomato shade of red while he grips his cup tightly. "Is there any other kind?"

"Business proposal," Rebecca remarks.

"Investment proposal," I say.

"Promposal," Theora cheerfully adds.

"Alright! I get it." Shane turns his attention from me to Theora, with nothing but seriousness lining his frowning features.

"I thought we weren't going to say anything."

"I know."

He scoots closer to her, as if trying to make sure I don't hear what he's about to say, but despite the effort, I still make out every innocently optimistic word.

"So does that mean you're saying yes?"

"Wait, you didn't say yes!?" Rebecca shouts then looks back at Theora with a hint of evil in her eyes.

Her shock is more than justifiable. Given the way they always act around each other, I would've guessed she said yes too, with or without a ring. I know what it feels like to be in such a loving relationship, or at least I thought I did. I'm not really one to take advice from on the love front anymore, and as I rub my thumb on my empty ring finger, my mouth opens, and my internal response accidently slips out.

"Saying yes doesn't guarantee you'll both stay the same forever."

My suddenly glossy eyes dart up from the silence surrounding me, and I'm met with a look of sympathy and confusion from Shane. Nothing has felt right since I got up this morning, and him staring at me now only reminds me of who I used to be. There's no way I can go back to that person, not when the biggest piece is missing, and especially not when I can't put it back. And if I think Shane is anything like me right now, then Theora not saying 'yes' must be eating at him. I guess that's why he's been acting like more of an asshole than usual.

It's not my place to ask Theora why she's torturing Shane like this. Really, I don't want to get involved and make it worse. But the choking silence that has spread itself throughout the car is no doubt because of what I had said, which shouldn't have been said at all. That lingering chill returns, though I push it aside, along with the memory of 'him', then speak up before anyone can ask about my "experience" in the matter of marriage.

I clear my throat and let the world spin back into motion. "What I meant to say, is that maybe she's just scared that their lovey-dovey relationship won't last forever."

The seat belt on my neck seems to become tighter when no one talks but their stares stay glued to me. *You're an idiot*, I think while twisting forward, forcing my eyes to focus on the coffee cup in my hands. It's still very hot, warming my fingers and the thigh where it sits, but as for the heat circulating through the rest of me... it's not the coffee. Why am I acting this way? Why can't I stop thinking of—Rebecca takes over my questioning before I plummet further into uncertainty. I never thought I'd be so happy for her nosey nature, yet now I find myself wanting nothing but for her to poke around.

In someone else's business I mean.

"Regardless of Elle's unusual little side comment, and the fact that she thinks your love will die before it really grows, what I wanna know is why you didn't say yes."

She parks the car, barely looking behind her. Her eyes are narrowed in on Theora in the rear-view mirror, waiting for her to answer. And while *I* actually look back, so we don't hit someone's car, I see Theora shoot Shane a 'help me' glance. But with the mood he's in, I doubt he wants to move on without her explanation as to why she's temporarily broken his heart.

"Is it because of the traveling?" Rebecca asks while turning off her car.

Another cycle of quiet passes, and we all sit and wait. When Theora finally realizes that Shane's going to be no help here, she lets out a deep sigh and glances to me before answering. There's a stone-cold look in her eye, like she wants me to say something, yet nothing comes to mind. She's the one who brought up the proposal in the first place, and I guess that clicks somewhere in her head when she abandons her mean girl stare, then looks to Rebecca.

"It's not the traveling. It's—"

Two distinct buzzes interrupt the reason even I'm on the edge of my seat for, but once that sound cut in, Theora's answer never comes. It completely shuts down the conversation, and her attention dramatically shifts from Rebecca to her phone. Her quick motion even catches me off guard, something I thought couldn't happen until today. But despite that, I do find it impressive how fast she went from care to couldn't care less. A little too impressive. And by the forming look of irritation and hurt on Shane's face, I assume he knows who it is on the other end of that text.

"Seriously T?" he asks, bordering on angry.

She brings her gaze to him and tries to sympathize. "I'm so sorry, but I need to take this. It's Wes with the details for my next—"

"Trip. Yeah, I know. But what I don't know is why you can't answer the question as to why you didn't say yes."

"It's not like I said no either," Theora pleads, "I'm just—"

Her phone goes off again, and this time she looks to Shane with a more sincere expression before answering it, now fully blocking all of us out. Hurt stretches further across Shane's face before he leaves the car in a huff of frustration. A scene that's well deserved, but also one that's not going to go without an entire angry scene later.

It's going to be a long day.

Before Rebecca can steamroll her with questions, Theora practically jumps out of the car without so much as a word, leaving just me and her. I can almost feel her annoyance with Theora rippling off her, and something tells me that that's going to be projected onto me. Given that I never really answered her question from earlier. My day hasn't gotten off to a great start—hell, my night was shitty too—and I don't think I can take feeling my emotions right now. I need to get out of here before things get too... touchy feely. Just as I'm about to leave the car next though, Rebecca takes that choice away when she quickly locks the doors.

"What's going on with you?" she questions with both concern and haste.

"What... nothing," I lie while turning to face her. "I'm fine."

For a minute I think she believes me. Except, given the fact that I don't believe myself, I know the words came out much less sure than I wanted them to. She narrows her eyes, looks me up and down but only sighs, and then says demandingly,

"Bullshit. Get out of my car."

She unlocks the doors and without another word, surprisingly, gets out, and I follow behind knowing that this conversation is far from over. Her tone alone has me dreading our after-work hangout, and that 'long day' comment rings even louder in my ears.

CHAPTER FOUR

It is said in history to never ride in an elevator with a stressed out and frustrated Rebecca Taylor. But since today is already not going my way, I take the risk, because why not. My mind feels like it's melting from lack of sleep, last night's task has me so sore I have to remember to walk without groaning, and now I think I just pissed off my best friend. I did have some help on that front, except those two people have already taken the elevator ahead of us, so I'm the one who gets to hold the Taylor daily talkie baton. And honestly, despite loving this girl to death, I'm not in any kind of mood to deal with anything. That doesn't seem to matter though, especially not when she loops her arm into mine and pulls me so close to her hip we basically become Siamese twins.

"So... do you wanna talk now and give me some peace in knowing that you're at least moderately fine before we get inside? So I won't worry about you during my presentation? Because you know that if I worry it'll inevitably screw me up, right?"

"You're not giving me a lot of choice to say no then, are you?"

Her demeanour switches so quickly I almost flinch when she tilts her head then intensely stares at me. "I'm being serious Michelle."

"I know. It's just..." my words stumble over each other as I contemplate whether or not I should answer with the truth.

A lot has been happening this last month that has me regretting most of the life decisions I've made, which is way more than usual. And it's getting tiresome. My sour behaviour and slightly askew mannerisms hasn't exactly all been about me. That fact alone only makes all of it worse. I've tried everything to make myself feel better, and the one thing I've enjoyed not doing is the one thing she's asking me to do. Talk about my feelings.

A slight grin does come to my face though, and I drop my eyes from hers as familiar warmth starts to form in my cheeks. I know I shouldn't appear to be laughing at the look on her face, but it's been such a long time since someone has cared for me the way she does. I guess I don't know how to react. It's an odd feeling. Two years and it's still odd. I became so accustom to the chill of loneliness during that first year on my own, yet this, her, it's nice.

No matter how many times this happens, I'm not used to someone refusing to believe me when I tell them I'm fine the first time. Part of me feels weakened by that, but that's not supposed to matter to me anymore. Except, in an attempt to regain some control, I let my smile fade, and with a deep sigh return Rebecca's stare. I try my best to explain while mixing in an element of truth that will appease her for the rest of the day.

"It's just my brother," a faint pain surges inside my chest, but I push through it. "He's been a bit of a handful lately, so I've had to deal with that. But I do know what will make me feel a little better."

Her face lights up with both sympathy and intrigue. "And what's that?"

The sound of a light ding is the demoralizing reminder that we've reached our floor. It creates a pit in the bottom of my stomach. And as the metal doors open to our slice of hell—a tight beige and black hallway that smells of forgotten dreams and dull memories—I force myself to have some cheer in my voice. For Becca's sake, and mine.

"The Steam Bean after work, and then maybe we can binge 'The Good Fight' at your place?"

A happy squeal comes from her, though before she can use actual words to express her joy, we turn the corner that leads to our grey office door and find Shane and Theora blocking our path. They whisper to each other at an arm's length in the brightly lit corridor. It doesn't seem like they're having a pleasant conversation. Shane leans against the wall with his arms folded over his wide chest, eyes glued to a frustrated looking Theora. As much as I wish I was here to see them actually have an argument, the question as to why they're outside in the first place comes to mind. Rebecca is the first to ask it, completely shifting her attitude from happy to purely annoyed in seconds.

"Why are you two are still out here!?" she yells in a whisper.

Glancing away from Theora, Shane looks to her and pushes off from the wall while reaching for the door handle. "We were waiting for you guys."

She throws her hands in the air, ignoring the slight brokenness in his tone. "Why!? I was counting on him yelling at you first so my being five minutes late would mostly be out of his system."

"Wow Becca," Shane gasps with amusement, masking his sad voice, "I'm glad to see you're starting to relax a bit."

"Wait, I need a new game plan!"

Shane swings the door open, I'm hoping because he didn't hear her, and a gruff sigh escapes Rebecca as she rolls her eyes. I don't think it'll be that bad. It's only five minutes. If anything, I can just blame the whole lateness on myself so Rebecca will take less of the shit stick's wrath. But, as soon as the door opens, all four of our fates are sealed.

There our boss Mr. Roderick stands, already waiting right in the entry way, and he doesn't look like a happy little shrimp at all. After a couple of seconds of us standing quietly, he finally addresses us with what I'm guessing is all the disrespect he can muster from that tiny body of his.

"No, please, go ahead, finish your conversations. I wouldn't want your *paying* jobs to have any impact on how long it takes the four of you to get to work on time."

I can't stand this dick.

Not one of us speaks, even when I know we're all thinking the same thing, like a mentally linked message board. There aren't a lot of ways I see this going, considering Roderick is all bark and no bite, but that doesn't stop Shane from trying to piss him off further. He draws in a deep breath, glances back at Roderick, and then speaks with a dangerous amount of sarcasm in his voice.

"I guess we'll just have to dial back our *uncontrollable* socializing until later guys. When we're only among friends."

A smirk creeps onto my face at yet another connection between Shane and me. We never know when enough is enough. I mean, *I've* learned how to keep my mouth shut when it comes to superiors one doesn't like, simply because it only makes things worse in the long run. But Shane—looking at him now while wiping the smirk from my expression—it's clear that he hasn't learned that lesson yet. And judging by the deep frown on Roderick's face, and the way his glare shifts from Shane to Theora, he's about to witness that his words can have consequences for others around him.

"I know for a fact that you physically have somewhere else to be Ms. Salano, so I suggest you make your way there," Roderick brutally remarks, making sure we all hear the ego in his tone.

Theora's body shrinks, almost down to his size as she timidly answers, "oh, y-yes. Sorry Sir."

I have to commend him for identifying Shane's weak spot, but that doesn't make it okay to stab at, especially when bosses are supposed to lead by example. Not use their status to control or win a pissing contest. A subject I know about all too well. Though instead of ignoring the situation by taking another stroll through the mine field I call my memories, I watch this play out, purely to make sure I know when to shut it down. And that moment seems to be approaching soon, as Roderick crosses his arms then says something I'm sure he'd soon regret.

"I don't want your apology Ms. Salano. I want you to go sort out the details for your trip, then get as much work done before you depart," he looks up at a fuming Shane for a brief second before barking out, "now!"

At his last command, the office around us comes to a halt, and all eyes are on Shane. I don't even have to look his way to know his expression resembles the traits of intending murder. But, when he takes a step towards Roderick it grabs my attention, and I twist around to stop him from ripping his face off. Theora though, already has me beat. Her small hand is on his chest while she stares down at our boss in shame. Then, when she looks back to Shane, there's something in those jade eyes I've never seen before. It borders on mischievous and wicked, but just as sudden as it came, it fades as she calmly speaks.

"It's okay Shane, just relax," Theora glances back at Roderick and then continues coldly, "I'm going."

I can't have been the only one who felt the icy breeze coming off her words, but before anyone can point it out, she lightly grabs Shane's collar and pulls him down to her face. It doesn't take me a second to figure out the angle she's playing at, and it's genius, given the current single status of our boss. Except, this theatrical display isn't in her nature. I've known Theora for two years, and in all that time she's never seemed like a 'payback' type of person. But with the way she's gazing into Shane's eyes with hunger, and how she roughly crushes her lips against his, I might have to re-evaluate what really is or isn't in her so-called nature.

Everyone from accounting to sales abandons their work and the office erupts into cheers and whistles as their kiss deepens. Beside me Rebecca laughs like she can't believe what she's seeing. Roderick on the other hand, knits his brows together so tight it creates ugly wrinkles in his forehead, and his frown returns. This time with the added motion of his jaw moving back and forth. And that irritated expression only sinks deeper within his face when he shouts.

"Alright, that's enough!"

Now, me, I've seen them make out more than I can count, yet here, watching Theora slowly pull away from Shane, his mannerisms are almost as if he's not used to her taking the lead. That's what finally makes me smirk, his slumped over posture and the absent glimmer in his eyes. But when Theora turns her attention to Roderick, my smile fades as she glares at him.

It lasts long enough for everyone to calm down, and with a satisfied look lingering on her upturned lips, she casually strolls over to her space at the back of the office. However, before she walks through the door that separates us, she waves to me and Rebecca, like her 'fuck you' kiss didn't just happen in front of everyone. We quickly steal a glance at each other, both our expressions a combination of 'what the hell' and 'well... okay,' then we stiffly wave back. And when she disappears behind the opaque glass door we're left standing in awkward silence.

My attention doesn't gather back towards Shane until after I've glance around at everyone, who is either staring at him or Roderick. Their shock and amusement doesn't last much longer when Roderick twists his melon head around the room. He then breaks into the silence by clearing his throat, and within seconds everyone has eyes on their computers again.

"Mr. Wendell," Roderick impatiently calls to Shane.

He doesn't answer. I'm pretty sure he's still trying to piece together what just happened to the girlfriend he was arguing with minutes ago, but that doesn't stop Roderick from calling him again.

"Mr. Wendell!"

I lightly elbow Shane to help him find his way back to the present. He shakes his head, like waking himself from a daydream, causing his neatly brushed back hair to slightly become the mess it usually is. And once he decides to answer Roderick, he speaks as if he had no clue what was going on before Theora had kissed him. Almost kind, yet with hints of lingering disbelief.

"Yeah?"

Roderick gestures his hand in the direction of Shane's desk, as if helping him to remember where it is. "Your desk Mr. Wendell."

He doesn't say another word and walks off towards his area, which now leaves Rebecca and I alone to endure this dip shit's temper. Part of me—a large part—wants to pretend I can't see him. I almost laugh at the thought, but I reframe and wait for his coming rant to be over. When he directs all his focus on Rebecca I fix my stance towards her, readying myself to defend her, though to my surprise his furious demeanour melts a bit.

"You have twenty minutes to prepare Ms. Taylor. And not a minute more," he says with relaxed rage.

He then retreats back into his cave without her response. Once the door is shut Rebecca looks to me and huffs out, "I think I'm going to need that drink after work more than you."

"Yeah," I agree as I widen my eyes for emphasis, "me too."

CHAPTER FIVE

THINK FAST

The pathway is lined with its usual red carpet of blood, but when the sweet reminders of who we used to be suddenly start to flood my mind, things shift into a new scene entirely. Everything around me morphs into the memory I thought I buried deep within myself. One that has him and I at our best. And despite my efforts, there's nothing I can do but let the scene play out. He comes up from behind, wrapping his thick arms around my waist, and plants a kiss on my collarbone.

My breath catches in my throat, and I close my eyes as my body goes from a stiff block to melted butter in seconds, all because of that single kiss. I hate that he can do that, make me tingle everywhere and melt inside at the same time, yet I let it take me over until I feel that old flame that used to burn between us. It's so familiar, so warm that I sink into him. I don't want to fight, I just want to stay like this, but then his hold on me starts to tighten, and soon the honey scented air quickly turns to the petrichor smell from that night.

I lift my now throbbing head from his shoulder—a place I hadn't even noticed I settled it—and start to struggle to get away. His grips doesn't let up though, even as I'm clawing at him. But in my defence, part of me is still trying to pull myself from the pocket of his warmth that I lingered in for too long. Stupid. Stupid. I'm *so stupid*! This isn't who we are anymore. This isn't who *I* am anymore, and as I remind myself of that, his touch goes cold. I stop moving. He stops tightening his grip. Then, as we stand motionless in the black that is my mind, he leans down to my ear and whispers in a voice that's darker than I remember,

"You did this on purpose, didn't you?"

Immediately tears fill my eyes, and my response catches in my throat. I know what I did, maybe not while I was doing it, but if I had—no. No. It was the only way for me to be free. For me to finally protect him. To *finally* protect both of us. Yes, it came with a cost, one I thought I'd never have to pay, though plans got changed along the way. At least this version of him had the momentary luxury of not knowing who we are out there. Of not knowing the sad truth that we're no longer a 'we.'

Something that's his fault.

But, as his hands are now wrapped around my neck, it's more than clear that his perception of us is up to date. And while my lungs begin to burn for the need of air, I'm stuck staring at the face he wore on the night we officially broke. Then, to add insult to injury, his words from our last conversation resurface, as icy as his fingers at my throat.

"You're too broken. And I tried, but I can't—I'm not the one that can fix you."

That sentence, that broken, and cruel, and heartless, and hateful sentence cuts deep into my heart. Just like before. And despite his hold on me, I shake my head and let the tears fall onto my cheeks as my thoughts echo around me, sad and hollow.

This isn't real. He could never really do this to me... right? Am I the only true monster here?

I don't get the answers. Or at least I don't accept the ones I already know are true. It's getting harder to breathe, but with each gasp of air I take, the thought to just give up seeps into my head. It wouldn't matter if I did, and it's not like I haven't before. Maybe death will be easier than life. However, before I get to test that theory, before my vision goes black, a grossly familiar face forces its way into my eye line. Right behind 'him'. Like a ghost.

Confusion presses up against my skull, rage starts to bubble in my stomach, and that smug smirk on their face coats my tongue in the taste of intended murder. Hate and the tang of prunes always comes to me naturally whenever I see that face, and those haunting blue eyes. But why are they here now? I don't get the chance to explore that question further however, not when a sudden thunderous bang resurrects me back to reality.

I gasp for the air I thought I lost as my eyes snap open. The first thing I see is a blurry hand on a stack of folders. Every instinct I have tells my body not to react, but the command comes too late. Within seconds I grab the hand, pull it towards me, and then stand while twisting it up against the person's back. A wail of pain follows which finally shakes off the rest of my nap. When my vision clears, I gasp at who I've got pinned down. Quickly, I let go of him, then back away with both hands in the air.

"Mr. Roderick! I'm so sorry Sir," I say, only partially meaning it, but the disappointment in my voice, I completely mean that.

Fuck. This is why I need to get sleep. So I don't accidently break my boss's arm.

I'm still trying to pull myself from the dream, still trying to take his hands off my neck so I can breathe. It wasn't real. It wasn't real, I keep telling myself, but that doesn't stop my heart from racing, my palms from becoming sweaty. The only aspect I seem to be able to control is my face, which, despite every memory playing in my head, I keep firmly locked in anticipation.

Everyone around us is quiet as Roderick says nothing. He's not even looking at me. He only rubs his shoulder in the silence the office has fallen into. I stare at him and go through every possible scenario, so I know what to say or do. No one laughed or gasped, which might've eased some of the tension, but no. We're just at a complete stand still. Maybe it wasn't as bad as I think, yet when my eyes wander to Rebecca and Shane, whose mouths are hanging wide open, I think again.

Shit. How am I going to play this?

I take a breath to relax the thundering inside my chest, then slowly step forward, ready with another apology. Before I talk though, Roderick does first. A clear hint of frustration and embarrassment in his voice.

"Get back to work Ms. Hannigan, now. Or I'll start to doc your pay. You're not here to sleep."

"Of course Sir, and again, I apologize."

He ignores my apology then turns to Rebecca with more demand set into his stance. He then clears his throat and starts to straighten his tie, as if desperately trying to regain control. All I do is swallow down the rest of my fading nightmare and try not to look too relieved when the office springs back to life. My worry begins to dissipate, but Roderick's slightly rude tone towards Rebecca slows the process.

"Ms. Taylor, your presentation begins now," he orders while dropping his arm. "I don't need to remind you of its importance, do I?"

"And yet you are," Shane mumbles rather loudly under his breath from across the room, but Rebecca quickly stands, throwing Roderick off before he can reply to the comment.

"No Sir. I'm ready," she says.

"Good. Let's go."

They start their journey towards the conference room, and as I step out of the way I give Rebecca a thumbs up. She returns it, with a little less enthusiasm, then disappears down the hall. As soon as I can no longer see Roderick, I drop my stiff limbs down into my chair and let out a deep sigh. My hair falls into my face like the pest it is, but I sit there with it as my curtain for a minute while I curse myself endlessly.

How could I have been so unable to keep myself in check? I don't even remember falling asleep. That could've been *way* worse than it was. I could've broken his arm. I could've fractured his shoulder, or worse, I could've taken the pen from my desk and jammed it into his—no. No. I can't let myself go there. None of that happened so I'm in the clear. Mostly. I just have to act like it wasn't a big deal that's all. Easy. I can do that.

Calm down. It's not like he fired you. He barely looked at you.

By the time I cool my nerves, I move my waves of brown back behind my ear, fully expecting to be alone, but there's Shane. He sits in Rebecca's chair and leans on her desk. I didn't even hear him coming, let alone see him. Impressive. But then again, I'm not exactly all here yet.

"Remind me to *never* wake you up. God. I mean I know you're not a morning person, but damn Elle," he laughs.

I mimic his easy-going behaviour, despite my mind racing with thoughts as to what that tyrant was doing in my dream, and let my body relax.

"Yeah, well, I guess those karate lessons I took as a kid are finally kicking in."

"Ah, a fellow karate kid I see," he then points to himself and declares with pride, "black belt."

I smirk at his excitement, and the other more graphic images that parade through my head. Honestly, I don't think a coloured belt is a big enough warning or representation for what I can really do. But either way, I play along with the lie I spat out to keep my other best friend happy and distracted.

"Brown. But only cause I missed the transition ceremony," I dryly snicker.

"Well given that performance, you're an honorary black belt in my book."

The smile on my lips widens. "Thanks."

For a while I let Shane hold my attention, as I listened to his reasons why he wants to marry Theora. It was actually pretty sweet, until his tone went dark when the topic of her travel advisor Wes Black and his partner—some guy named

Jasper—came up. After that, he excused himself to sneak away to talk to her about it, leaving me to my game of solitaire.

It's been almost an hour since then, and now, looking up from the firework display on my screen, I see Shane coming back from Theora's side of the office. He appears much happier than he did when he left. The rosy shade of red in his cheeks and the smirk of male pride on his lips is answer enough for what happened back there. Well, that, and the pink shaded lipstick he so swiftly wipes from his mouth. By the time he sits down next to me again, I just manage to hide my smirk at the sight of his messy hair.

I try keeping my stare on my computer, which becomes difficult when Shane's eyes start to pierce a hole in the side of my head. I have nothing to say to him. Nothing except that his fly is down, though that isn't something I want to tell him.

He'd probably happily describe what happened back there if I did, and I don't need those images in my head anymore than I need a bullet. But of course, my stand-offish behaviour doesn't make my dear cocky friend leave. The minute I met him I figured out he tended to make himself feel at home, and that's exactly what he does now.

He sits down again, making it clear he isn't going to be doing any more work, which leaves me with the rest of his undivided attention. And it gets awkward. For a full minute he simply stares at me with a smirk that I'm pretty sure was designed to get people to talk to him.

Why am I friends with you again, because I can't remember.

It's kind of making me uncomfortable. I let my hair fall into my face, it tickling my cheek as I stare down at the scrunchie on my wrist and sigh. Long hair sucks. It just gets in the way most of the time, but since I'm kind of using it for that purpose at the moment I dismiss it and focus on ignoring Shane's odd refusal to speak first. He catches on and finally looks away. But does he leave? No.

Instead, he takes my jar of paperclips, creates some sort of lasso, and tries to catch my hand every time I click on my mouse. And just before he tosses it again, it gets caught in his hair and I can't help but snicker. I guess that's what he was waiting for, because then he finally talks, his voice filled with compassion.

"What's wrong Elle?"

Oh yeah, a secret sweetheart That's why I'm friends with you.

I appreciate the question, even though I've been asked it way more than I'd like for today. Either way, I do love him for his concern, but there's just too much going on in my life right now. Situations I can't explain that are *more* than private. And even though he pulls out the innocent doe eyes, I keep everything to myself. But, before I can answer with the usual 'I'm fine,' a light vibration rattles my skin.

Quickly, I steal a glance to the gadget strapped to my ankle, and from there, everything becomes a second thought. A serious switch immediately goes off in my head but I keep my expression level. He still has his eyes on me, waiting for me to say something.

"I'm good, Shane, really." I tell him, tucking my hair behind my ear and giving him the warmest smile I can muster.

He pulls a hand through his hair and sighs. "I want to believe you, but that felt very rehearsed."

My heart skips a beat at the sound of the small threat in his tone. As much as I'd like to, I don't have time to go back and forth with him about how *I'm* feeling. Luckily, and I use that word very lightly, Jim Bobick stalks up beside my desk and interrupts our conversation.

The tall 'average Joe' looking man acknownledges Shane first, calling his name is a douch bag like hauler. "Psycho Shane! How's it hanging, bro?"

Glancing over to me, Shane smirks with a simple plea in his water-colored eyes. I roll mine as the form of approval to mess with Bobick he's just asked for, also using the opportunity to remove myself. I get up as he answers back in his most mocking douche bag tone while I gather up a random stack of papers to head to the copier.

"Jim jam. It's hanging low bro," he starts but when I begin walking away his attention shift solely onto me. Something I don't need.

"Elle, wait. I—" He starts to get up from the chair, slightly reaching for my arm. I take his in my hand first and lightly push him back down before he can stand.

"It's fine, just stay here. I'll be right back."

I give him a quick smile then turn away from him, right into Bobick, who is leaning down mere inches from my face.

"Mmm, Michelle Michelle," he says, low and with a slight hum, a voice I assume he thinks is seductive.

It's not.

"How you doing this *fine* afternoon, sweetheart?"

Getting up, swiftly knocking my phone into my purse, I move to go around his massive body, yet he only draws closer. Any other day I would've played along with him, just to amuse myself and keep up appearances, but not today. Today, instead, desperate, I look to Shane for his help to get this sack of meat with a pebble rattling inside his brain away from me.

Now it's his turn to roll his eyes. "Hey Bobick, you see the commercial for the new Jet bike? The one with those—"

"Those *fine* tight-ass jeans?" His head snaps back to Shane, and that's my cue. But I don't go before giving Shane a playfully disgusted once over. He only winks and then shrugs.

Leaving the two of them at my desk without another word, by the time I get to the copier their conversation sounds so far away. I tune them out completely before looking around, then click the top of the device that mimics a pen and watch it transform in my hand.

The end half of the narrow stick folds over onto itself and then rises so the small slit embedded along the side has room to open. It reveals a hidden screen that quickly slides down to connect to the gadget's other half.

Now the once pen looking object has converted into what appears to be a phone, which can easily be mistaken for the one I normally use. On it a message from someone that isn't supposed to contact me during the day lights the screen. A message that only contains four words, yet still makes every part of me tense up.

'You're on call. Tonight.'

My heart starts to race faster and faster with all my attention on the message, which doesn't help with letting my earlier paranoia go. All these sudden intense emotions, lingering dreams and signs can't just be coincidences that don't tie into what's been happening this past month. Like I said, I don't believe in coincidences. Something must be very wrong if I'm feeling more uncertain than I have in years.

Despite my desire for a good report, this message is most likely an introduction to bad news. Staring down at it my mind goes over all the explanations as to why the urgency. But I can't seem to focus on just one. A problem I've had in the past. One I thought I had figured out after the 'wrecking ball incident', but apparently not. Though this time I do something much harder to pretend never happened.

I'm so wrapped up in the mesmerizing yellow-ish glow of the device and its message, that by the time I smell the hazel nut coffee—Evan's favourite—it's too late. I bump into him, hard, and from there everything in my head slows. Despite my mind's objection, my body decides to go against me and react. Sliding the device down, I use my ring and pinkie fingers to hold it against my palm while using the others to catch his mug before it hits the carpet. The stack of papers that he and I dropped I catch with my other hand in a zigzag pattern. Then right before I force myself to a halt, I give Evan his coffee and lightly place the papers on the copier.

Shit! Why'd you do that? I yell inside my head.

To me, all of that lasted about a minute, but the realization that it was much shorter than that comes when I finally look up and see Evan staring at me. Eyes wide with his coffee in one hand and the other held out like he still has the papers in it. In my defence, I was preoccupied, but that excuse won't explain what just happened.

I drop my gadget, to make it seem like what I had just done wasn't flawless. Not the best plan, but it does shake him from his awe. He lifts his jaw up off the floor, and as he bends to pick up my "phone", I look around to see if anyone else had seen my cat-like reflexes.

All I'm met with is the top of heads. No bulging eyes or dropped jaws. Thank god. I whip my head back to Evan as he hands my "phone" to me, his eyes filled with amazement.

I viciously curse myself, bilingually, because just English wouldn't capture how stupid what I just did was. Even letting him touch the quick stick communicator makes it worse, but I slow the stream of swear words flowing through my head. Just enough so my face presents no sign of worry.

I let my expression melt into a mellow calm, and then softly but quickly take the device from his hand. Still, he doesn't speak. I see it as an opportunity to get ahead of whatever he's starting to think about me.

Especially after what happened with Roderick in combination with this. Praying my new amused attitude will do the trick, I simply take my papers from the copier and scoot past him.

"Sorry about that Evan," I say, meaning it, while hiding the desire to leave from my tone. "I guess all those waitress jobs I did in college paid off," I joke.

I didn't go to college. I did have a job as a waitress once upon a time, so not a total lie. But that doesn't matter. What matters is that he believes me, which he does, because he has no reason *not* to.

"Ha," he huffs a laugh, "yeah, I guess."

"Excuse me."

He moves aside, his purple-ish eyes locked on mine, following me as I walk by, like still trying to comprehend what he had just witnessed. As flattering as I feel by his shock, I only continue to act like it wasn't a big deal and go about my business.

When I get back to my desk, I'm glad to see Shane and Bobick have taken their leave. I push up my chair, exit my game, then start to pack up for the day while the message scrolls across my mind. A ghostly feeling starts to lurk in the air around me. The words I understand, I always do, except I can't help but think, *is it something that urgent?* That one thought breaks the dam, and the rest of the possible problems start to pour through.

No. I just need to focus on something else. Anything else. Yet for some reason, I can't seem to shake the feeling. It's already made me forget how to act twice now. I'm can't do anything that stupid again. For now, at least. I have to pull it together. I'm better than this.

Deep breath in.

Deep breath out.

Without even realizing my temperature had risen, my body proceeds to cool itself down as I go back to logging out for the day. Only two minutes left before we're officially off for the weekend, but I have a feeling that it's going to last much longer. If I get lost in my head again there's no telling when I'll be able to—

"I got it!" Rebecca speed walks up to my desk and interrupts with perfect timing.

I take a second to thank whatever god did this then stand to give her a hug. When she squeezes me back I practically feel her heart racing with excitement. I draw away, deliberately move into the coming conversation of her tale of triumph.

"Congratulations, Becca. I knew you'd kill it."

"Thank you. I—" her sentence comes to a hard stop, and I follow her eyes to what has grabbed her attention.

The trail ends where Shane stands with a goofy grin on his face. "You got it?"

"I got it!" Rebecca shouts again.

He takes three wide steps towards her and strong arms her into a hug. First she fights him, but eventually she gives in and accepts his affection. I swear sometimes I forget they're like brother and sister. It's moments like these that I find so sweet, but at the same time it also rips out my heart. Family is family. Either the family you're born into, or the one you make, and you hold on to that. No matter the cost.

It's the one important lesson I learned from my shitty parents, but also the one I couldn't seem to get right. Looking at them though, I know I'm at least starting to get the hang of it, even when that should've begun a long time ago. The bitter memory of my past and the person I used to be threatens to invade my mind, seeping in like spilled ink. But as Shane lets go of Rebecca it catches my attention and I simply breathe.

"You deserve it," Shane happily remarks.

Rebecca jokingly bows in his direction. "Thank you, thank you. Honestly, I *deserved* it six months ago, but I guess the little monster came around."

"Well, it was only a matter of excruciating time," Shane then uses his thumbs to point to the back of the office, "and I would love to hear what happened in there, but I gotta go get Theora. After we head out though we can go celebrate your rise above the grim reaper and his band of soul collectors."

As Shane tip toes to the back of the office I silently laugh and finish getting ready to leave. The quick communicator is the last thing I take from my desk. I stare at its blank screen for a minute before shoving it in my coat pocket. That message means I'll have to duck out from the celebration early to get to my other job on time. It's not for a couple of hours, so, until that happens, I'll have to try and relax. I don't want to ruin Rebecca's moment by acting like something is wrong, more than I already have today.

"So, anything interesting happen while I was gone?" Rebecca asks while we walk towards the front.

A quick re-cap of my little performance dances across my mind, but it's nothing I want her to know about. Having one person witness it already caused enough suspicion for one day, and that's a level I'm not even comfortable with. Her knowing too would only draw more attention to me, and with everything I have to focus on I'd rather direct the spotlight onto anyone else.

I realize I've been thinking about her question for too long when I turn and notice her patience starting to dim. I find the words just as Evan strolls by, his eyes scanning over me like I'm some kind of super human. I quickly let a friendly smile come and go, then, as he slowly continues to walk by I answer her as dryly as possible.

"No. Not really."

CHAPTER SIX

DUTY CALLS

The second we enter The Steam Bean, I figured the rest of my day was going to be almost as long as work was. Getting here is always the easy part, Rebecca's road rage being an advantage, but after that, it's just a test of patience. So far, in just the sixty seconds of being here, I've stepped on a napkin with something green on it which I'm hoping is *just* kiwi jelly, the place smells like burnt muffins, and it's so crowded that I can't see our regular booth. I'm used to the swarm of people since this is exactly the time when all the other offices in the area get off work too. But that usually means that this cute little cafe turns into a war zone. And just like in war, nothing is guaranteed, especially not our table. So, Rebecca and I get into formation.

She hands me her purse, shoves the hair in her face behind her ears, and before stepping into the battle royale, we both sharply nod to each other. Then, once she disappears in the sea of suits and briefcases, I swing her purse over my shoulder to free up the use of my elbows, and then follow in the small gap she's made. When I get a few steps in, I swiftly glance over my shoulder to make sure Shane and Theora stayed close. They tail behind me like we practised, and once Shane nods to confirm he still has his wallet I quickly spin back around to watch my front. When the crowd slightly thins I find Rebecca waving us over and we practically run to her.

As we finally arrive from our long journey, the only thing on my mind is to sit and enjoy our spoils of victory. Yet, about to slide in next to Rebecca, I notice a sign taped to our table winnings.

'DO. NOT. SIT. Needs strong cleaning.'

Before any part of me touches those brown cushions, I stare at her and speak with hesitation. "Umm Becca, I really rather not have to deal with any kind of gross bodily fluids today."

While she rips the sign off, from the corner of my eye our usual waiter Taron coming over. As he approaches, Rebecca responds to my concern in her greeting.

"Hey Taron, thanks for holding our table," she rips the paper in two. "Good sign by the way."

Taron's face becomes red as he tries not to look at me. "Thank... thank you. It was no problem, Becca, really," he stutters out while glancing at the ground and brushing the blonde hair from his face. Then he finally turns his attention to me.

"Hi... hi Michelle."

I slowly smile at him as I sit. "Hi Taron."

Our waiter Taron is probably the sweetest seventeen-year-old boy anyone will ever meet. He's had a crush on me since I started coming. It was weird at first, but I've gotten used to it. Except for moments like these, when he stares at me like he's day dreaming. I raise my hand to snap him out of it, though Shane's loud clap outshines me. Taron promptly turns his way with his order pad out and ready to go.

"What would you like today, Mr. Wendell?" he says in a smooth rush.

Shane and Taron didn't exactly get off on the right foot, given that it was actually Shane's right foot where he had dropped a tray of dishes. Any sane person would think the twenty-eight-year-old man would be the grown up and forgive the kid, but Shane hasn't gotten over the fact that he fractured three of his toes. I can't believe he's still acting like such a baby. I've had way worse broken by people without a sweet bone in their body like Taron, but no, Shane can't let it go. Sad that Taron is still trying to get Shane to like him, especially since it's been a year.

Theora narrows her eyes at Shane, giving him that 'don't be an asshole' look. He takes in a sharp breath, as calmly as possible then runs off all our usual orders. I'm not particularly in the mood for food. I'd rather have an empty stomach when over thinking about my life. And considering that my night job has had me do work more on the running side lately, I'd prefer not to be caught any more off my game because of the bad pairings of tomato soup and salted caramel donuts. That wouldn't be a pretty sight to see. I did tell myself to fully enjoy this time though, which includes a human participation aspect.

"Can you believe how long it's been since we had to bully a group of strangers to tears to finally declare this as our spot?" Rebecca reminisces as she lets out her hair. "And now we get to celebrate my rise to the mid-level top, and you two getting—" she stops herself from finishing and presses her lips thin while looking at Shane, and then Theora.

For god sakes, she *really* knows how to make things go from moderately fine to awkward and tense real fast. Sound somehow seems to cease to exist around us as Shane's eyes switch to a glare, almost as fast as I moved at the office. Rebecca's expression melts into an 'I'm so sorry' and an 'I'm so stupid' look all at once. It kind of makes me feel bad for her. Part of me wants to see how all of this will play out between Shane and Theora—hell even Shane and Rebecca—but the more practical part that knows I have more pressing matters to deal with later, wins. It wouldn't be good to have the guilt of gas lighting this toxic behaviour on my mind. I better say something or else—

"Alright, I have your orders here Taron proudly announces and gives them out. "Oh, and Theora, I completely forgot to say this, but it's great to have you back."

"You can just put down the food and leave Kingsmen, thanks."

As he slides the last plate over, Theora smiles and tries to dispel the hurt look on Taron's face.

"Thank you so much, sweetie. That was very nice of you."

Without another word, Taron only gives a shy smile before he leaves. When he's completely out of sight, and earshot, Theora's demeanour shifts, and a hint of sharp attitude becomes present in her tone as she glares at Shane.

"That was rude. He was just happy to see me."

"I'm really not in the mood for this Theora, and besides, he has nothing to be happy about. You'll be gone soon anyway. Like you have been almost all month."

"Well, I thought my promotion was something to be happy about, but maybe it's just me who thinks that now," Rebecca mumbles while grabbing her food.

I lightly elbow her in the side and place a finger on my lips while Theora glances at her, but she ignores her comment. Despite her disregard though, I swear I notice her starting to get upset.

"That's not fair. You know I don't control that. I know it's been a little crazier this month, but we both agreed that me doing my job wouldn't interfere with our relationship."

"And yet here we are, having that same conversation," Shane snaps.

"I..." Theora trails, not bothering to finish her sentence only lets out a frustrated huff.

This needs to stop. The sour look on Shane's face could peel the black paint right off the walls. And by the slight shift of his foot, he's about to stomp off. I bite on my tongue—shoving aside my bad morals—and swiftly intervene.

"We should just enjoy the time we have with Theora right now."

I turn to Shane and lean my elbows on the table to support my tender tone. "You should've seen how happy she was at the mention of your name in the elevator this morning. I say just let it go for today and be together, because before you know it, in the blink of an eye she'll be gone."

They all stare at me, frozen in place, but I ignore them and grab my bisque. I said what I said because it's the simple truth. From me It's much more direct than they're used to, but I can't possibly care less. I have shit to do later. Shit that requires me to not have more on my mind than I already do. Relationships are complicated, I get that. No one gets that more than me. But given my most recent—to put it lightly—problems, I'd rather not hear about their 'basic' issues.

I'm being harsh. I know. But I need this piece of normal before my night shift. It may be a tad selfish, yes, though I'm also helping two friends so their relationship doesn't die in this coffee shop.

"She's right," Theora sighs then takes Shane's hand in hers. "We shouldn't be arguing about this now. We can discuss it later."

For a minute he doesn't seem like he'll be as cooperative about changing the subject, and in that minute, I don't blame him. With the unanswered proposal and her brushing him off this morning in the car, his tantrum would be justified. I hope just he lets it go for right now. If not for the sake of the mood, then for himself, because if not it'll eat away at him all evening and into tomorrow. I don't think he's capable of resentment towards Theora, but if he is, it'll spring from this moment. Watching his foot draw inwards, it tells me I know he's letting it go. For now.

"Okay. But only if you promise."

A smile slowly appears on Theora's lips. "I promise."

Rebecca claps her hands together then spreads a grin across her face. "So does that mean I can talk about my promotion now, or—?"

"Jesus Becca, fine, go ahead. But your story better include you *really* hurting Roderick's feelings in some way, shape, or form," Shane playfully demands as he lets go of Theora's hand to give all his attention to Rebecca.

"Oh trust me," she says, starting to smirk, "it does."

After a couple more over-priced coffees, decent food and Rebecca's seemingly endless story, the dishes on our table start to pile up. The last thing I heard her mention was how Roderick's face looked when she finished the presentation without a single problem, which had the added bonus of ending in applause. When my foot slightly started to bounce up and down under the table, I couldn't help but tune her out and graze a finger over the quick communicator in my pocket. It's been hours since I've thought about this morning's or this afternoon's haunted little strolls down memory lane, yet now that door is starting to creep back into mind.

The door to that dark place in my head lightly pushes open, and the blinding light that had drawn me in in the past calls to me again. A lot of things are up in the air for me right now, I'm not going to lie to myself about that, I just thought I could handle it. Pushing all of it to the back of my mind maybe wasn't the healthiest thing to do, because now I'm sitting here with my friends but they're the furthest thing from me. It's wrong on so many levels. Levels I can't even begin to explain to them, and *never* want to. That chilling thought alone forces me back into the conversation happening around me.

"Well, hey," Shane shrugs, "if the poor little guy was uncomfortable with you being so great, maybe he should switch branches," he says politely but with obvious hints of cheeky attitude.

I snicker at his comment as the communicator buzzes in my grip. It startles me. Despite the hold I've had on it all evening, but I brush off my unnecessary surprise and check the new message, blocking out everything, which is probably why a comment of my own slips from me without full intension.

"Or at the very least he should remove that stick shoved up his ass."

With sudden erupting laughter of my friends I glance up from the communicator, a little confused by their amusement, but then smirk. Rebecca wraps her arms around my shoulder, like she needs help holding herself up. It makes we want to laugh too. I feel it start up my throat but swallow it down as my eyes drift back to the message. And whatever joy I had accumulated dries up into a frown.

Great, I have to make a scene. And I was *just* letting myself not think about all the shit plaguing my life. Too bad. I take my wrapped up donuts and jam them in my purse while sliding out of the booth.

Surprisingly it's Shane who's the first to notice my sudden distress. "Everything okay, Elle?"

Playing off my already stressed state of mind, I suck in a deep breath, grab my jacket, and as I push an arm through the down fill sleeve I roughly exhale.

"I'm so sorry guys, but I need to get going. I just got a text from my uncle that my brother ran away. Again. I have to go deal with all that." Sitting back down to pull my knotty hair over my shoulder, I stuff the annoying wad into my jacket and ignore the slight bitterness in my cheeks.

Rebecca gently throws her head back and sulks. "Again?"

"Yeah, I told you about him this morning. Unfortunately he hasn't changed since then. He's a dreamer, but sometimes still acts like a naive little boy. Twenty years on this earth, but apparently in all that time he hadn't figured out his calling to become a DJ until tonight." I quickly glance down at my watch and start the countdown in my head.

"I need to find him and talk some sense into him."

You have an hour, I tell myself.

Turning back towards the table, I grab my purse and get up. Rebecca's voice from behind temporarily stops me from saying goodbye.

"He's such a handful. I'm not saying you shouldn't go—of course you should—but isn't this like the tenth time you've had to go get him, or bail him out?"

"I don't find it an inconvenience, Becca. He's my brother." My words come out much sharper than I mean. He's been a touchy subject for me. Especially this month.

I adjust my tone before it becomes a thing I need to apologize for, and because she's kind of right. My brother had always been a handful, yet I've never minded it. A crooked smile warms my cheeks at the thought of him, but I let it fade and sling my purse over my shoulder.

"What I mean, is that I've always been the one he counts on. The only one he talks to about everything. He trusts me, so it's my responsibility to find him." My eyes water a bit but I blink back the unexpected tears, then turn to Shane and Theora.

"Alright, I'm heading out. I'll see you guys later. Have fun and be nice to each other. Shane."

"Really? Me? I swear you guys plot against me," he rolls his eyes yet grins softly.

"We do. Every Wednesday," I joke.

He chuckles dryly but stops when the playful smirk doesn't leave my lips and I raise a brow.

"Okay, I can't tell if you're messing with me or not, so see you later and get home safe. Oh, and tell that little squirt that if he needs a turn table I know a guy."

Some part of me laughs at his guileless offer, but the part that knows I need to leave drops my smirk and keeps only a slight amused smile.

"Do you need a ride back home? It would be no problem, really," Rebecca offers.

"Thanks, but no thanks. I wouldn't want to interrupt. I can just get a quick taxi."

"Are you sure you can't stay for five more minutes Michelle? Last time you left Taron was giving away free muffins before they expired the next day," Theora pleads too kindly, then swings her head back in my direction after briefly looking at the display case.

All of them glance up at me, as if they're expecting me to say yes, but then the communicator goes off again, saving me.

'Now.'

The message from earlier flashes through my head. I shake it off and I slowly start walking away. "Sorry guys, I would love to, but duty calls."

I'm almost to the door when I hear Rebecca and Theora shout out their byes behind me, and I spin around to wave before strolling out the door. As soon as I'm outside, the cold hits me like a slap in the face, and my body instantly shrinks and becomes frigid. Like I haven't been sitting in a toasty coffee shop for hours.

While cursing under my breath, I clasp my hands together to form any kind of heat, then turn to see a cab on the other side of the street. We lock eyes for a second, and then exchange an understanding nod. I speed walk over to it, hop in, and give the man my address. As he zooms off, I sit back to enjoy the warmth while I can. It's a short trip back to my place, but even with knowing that my obedience finally kicks in and I answer the message.

'On my way. Priority one.'

CHAPTER SEVEN

BEHIND THE CURTAIN

Lazily dragging myself through the front door, a rush of hot air brushes up against my face, a much better greeting than outside's frost. I kick off my boots, the relief making a small moan leave my mouth while shutting the door. With each step towards my room, a piece of clothing comes off. First my jacket, pants, then, by the time I get to my bed, only my mismatched black bra and blue panties are left clinging to my body.

Nothing is greater than getting out of the clothes I've felt trapped in lately, that reek of coffee, and what's left of my perfume. I flop onto my bed and let out a loud groan. The 'day' portion of the day was *so* long, but, as much as I want to curl up in my sheets, I can't. Since it's over, now the night half begins.

Allowing myself to enjoy just five minutes of doing nothing, I take a deep breath and slide my arms over my head, but slightly flinch back as my hair brushes up against me. I completely forgot it was there for the first time today. But while sitting up and feeling it cascade down my back, I miss my short hair all over again. It was nice not to have to worry about it getting in my way or taking up space, like it does now. Half the time it feels like it's choking me, and the other half it's like I'm drowning in a sea of dark brown waves. I glance at my scrunchie and waste no time in pulling it up.

My hand quickly gathers the thick bushel of hair and swings it back and forth until it becomes fully intertwined with the clip. And with the tightness of my high ponytail, I sigh. *Relief, oh sweet relief!* There's nothing more satisfying, and with that thought my five minutes is up, which means it's time to get ready for work. Again.

I stand, my ponytail swaying proudly as I stroll up to the mirror. Before lifting my hand to slide the closet open, I pause and slowly turn to see the light scar that runs along my collarbone. Another reminder of the life I was born into, and while tracing over it with my middle finger, it also reminds me of the life I had chosen.

Stories and lessons go with every scar I own, inside and out. A lot are from entirely different situations. Some are from very similar ones that I just didn't get right until that second... or third attempt at picking and choosing my battles or standing my ground. But, before going down *that* bumpy road, I pull myself from the alluring trance that is my imperfect skin, open my closet, and then activate my watch.

Excitement tingles at the tip of my finger as I tap the glass twice then circle the diamond bezel in a counter clockwise motion. A comforting blue light instantly begins to glow under the glass, and each hand spins rapidly until the numbers disappear behind the hologram fan inside. It creates the image of an off switch, and as I press the watch's silver crown to turn it on, my head lifts to observe my enhanced closet go to work.

The dark rainbow of clothing gets pushed to opposite sides, and the wall of shoes behind it flies upwards soundlessly. Now I'm left staring at a metallic brown door that's just a bit smaller than the closet itself. I firmly place my palm in the center of its cool surface, then, after a slight burning sensation, I remove it and wait for the door to pop out. The sound of mechanical locks clicking out of place quietly go off. I give my hand a swift shake before swinging the new entrance open, then gaze at a whole other wall standing in front of me. It's filled with a plethora of quantum touch modular lights, but when stepping up to it, I draw a complete blank on the pattern to gain access.

"Shit. What is it again?" I mumble as I tap a finger on my bottom lip.

Only a certain amount of tries can be done until the failsafe kicks in, and that amount is one. I'll never remember what was going through my head when I built that in, though maybe if I tried to, I could avoid being electrocuted to death today. Any other options would be great, especially since, for some reason, memories of the past have been following me like shadows all day. But there isn't a lot of time before I'm summoned again—with a much angrier message. Wanting to avoid the verbal harassment, I tightly close my eyes and decide to scale the wall that is my mental shield against everything I've endured that almost broke me.

Little by little, I tap into the fear behind that wall. The rage, the hurt... the shattered love. My heart pounds in my ears as the slight taste of raspberries coats my tongue. I see darkness but feel warmth—despite the icy theme my day seemed to have—and the faintest smell of sweet mint slides past my nose.

Tears sting my eyes as I let memories dance across my mind. Though in the nick of time, before I go too far and lose myself to the past, the code becomes a clear image.

I open my eyes, raise my hand to the wall and input the pattern, then release the breath I didn't know I was holding. The sigh calms some of the nerves, and already my brain initiates its purge sequence of my shitty thoughts and emotions. It may be that very purge that has a bitter laugh escape me when I step back to stare at the combination. I dismiss the uncomfortable chuckle as the dog paw pattern turns an approving green, and then walk through the splitting wall.

After fully entering, I stop in my tracks to admire the small bedroom sized space filled with my special... "accessories." No matter how many times I've been in here, the decor never ceases to amaze me. The entire extension rests in mellow white lighting that bounces from each porcelain-coloured wall. Shelves and display cases of firearms, knives, gadgets and tactical clothing items decorate all four corners of the room, working together to create a pleasing sense of security.

Amazement aside, I focus and head towards my second closet, which isn't quite different from the first. The color pallet is the same, but the other doesn't have nearly as many wigs and ammunition. Plus, this wardrobe is entirely made up of clothes I don't mind getting dirty and have better 'flexibility' to them.

Not to say the Ester & Ester mandated business casual can't keep up with my swift movements. Such was approved by my co-worker Evan. But my current uniform for the last couple of nights is arguably the best option. In agility and style.

I don a contrast mesh raglan sleeve half zip top, a shoulder holster, with cargos and a matching double leg thigh holster. All in black, naturally, body hugging, and fully equipped with the standard beretta ninety-two, eight throwing knives, and an opal ring that's elegant in its simplicity. I'm not really the jewelry type. Not unless it has a little something *'extra'* special.

I put the finishing touches on my outfit, then get a couple of my own "accessories" to complete my look. Everything in me has to stop from checking myself out. The glimpse I do get causes an ounce of pride to rise up my chest. *Damn, I look good.*

Letting the moment pass, I grab one of my many trench coats then, after locking up, use my watch to set everything back to normal. Normal being a word I've used *very* lightly as of late. I head to the front door with keys in hand while tying my coat. As I stop to lace up the high-top camo converse, I smile at the absence of hair falling into my face.

It really is the little things.

I avoid the elevator, and all six security cameras, then race down the stairwell that smells lightly of garbage and piss. I've smelled worse, but somehow, whenever I take this exit route, it's like the city is trying to prove that I haven't. Either way, I ignore the stench, twist off the ring I slipped on my finger, and then push down on what's supposed to be an opal.

A red light quickly flashes. The ring then splits, opening like a binder clip on one side in a single swift motion. Soundless. I place the adhesive bone conduction cellular device behind my ear, then tap to call the only number programmed into it. It rings once, twice, and when the call goes through I speak fast.

"Meet me at the west end location now."

Peeling the ring from my skin, when reaching the buildings side exit, I only wait for a second in the icy night before a matte midnight blue BMW i8 pulls up. It's a little flashy for my taste, and this neighbourhood. But no matter how many times the topic of a more 'plain Jane car' came up Manager never listened.

It's a good thing the meeting spot is so dimly lit because of faulty wiring and a laid-back owner. If it wasn't, questions that needn't be asked about me would be, especially since cars don't normally scan the coming occupant with a green light from head to toe. The door to the passenger seat pops up and I climb in. As it shuts, a virtual yet life-like voice programmed into this luxury vehicle echoes around me.

"Good evening, agent 401. You have an incoming call from Mr. Manager."

Great. Just what I need right now.

Before I can say ignore, which would only piss him off, the car pulls away from the curb and puts my boss through.

"This kind of car is still too nice, and the voice is different. Is it new issue?" I talk first, asking a neutral question, yet that doesn't stop him from sounding irritated.

"You're late."

"I'm not even there yet," my words come out innocent. Wrong response on my part. He confirms it immediately as he slightly raises his prickly voice.

"Exactly my point, agent, so just consider me yelling at you in advance to save some time later. If that makes you feel better," he changes his tone while addressing the A.I system. "Bethany..."

"Yes sir?"

"Please take route road runner to the winery, switching traffic lights if you must."

"Yes sir, right away," she answers.

A slight jolt forces me back in my seat, but the silent hum of the vehicle works to soothe the knot in my stomach. The city now rushes by, and Manager's voice also becomes a distraction while I swallow down an unsettling amount of saliva, and then breathe. *I knew eating that last donut was going to be a stretch.*

"What took you so long?"

"Are you talking to me, or Bethany? And what happen to Zoey? I liked Zoey," I tilt my head up, "no offense Bethany."

"None taken."

Not expecting a reply, a huffy laugh escapes me. But when Manager responds, rather annoyed, my smile disappears instantly. Because that, I expected.

"It's new issue, and don't get smart with me. Answer the question. What held you up?"

I sigh. "The *day* portion of my day was kind of bumpy, plus I was thrown off by the early message... among other things. And besides, I didn't know I was going to be summoned tonight after yesterday's task. The task I was told was merely going to be a stakeout but became parallel to a training drill I had to do in my first year."

"I told you to stay in the car. You're the one who decided to disobey my order."

"Because it was a bad call," I say defensively, crossing my arms.

"Then why are you complaining to me? You made the choice to pursue."

My words take on a slightly sharper edge. "Ese no es mi punto."

(That's not my point.)

Manager pushes out a breath before answering, which is old man speak for 'you're testing my patience.' A bad idea when I'm already late. He may like me, but not that much.

"No, agent, the point, is that you *were* summoned. You know how this project works. I call, you answer and get your ass here. On time. I thought the early message would cross your mind as 'this must be important'. I literally spelt it out for you, but I didn't know you'd need a voice reminder as well," he grunts. "Just come to me as soon as you get down here. I have an important mission."

"Yes, sir," I say obediently.

"And some intel."

My body slightly warms at the thought of what he could have possibly found out, but, quickly, I force myself to cool down. "Intel? What intel?"

His tone softens. "Not now. I'll see you soon agent."

"Call ended," Bethany declares, "and we are arriving at your destination now."

I gaze up through the windshield, and I'm met with the gigantic yet elegant sign that has the words 'Bloody Hell Winery' decorating the Ikea sized building. And while continuing to stare, the car slightly shakes as it pulls onto the auto turntable elevator. It spins a full three-sixty before it lowers itself, and when I'm even a bit in the ground, above me, a new platform replacement is already locked in. These leisurely rides always let me admire the scenery on the way down, and I can almost hear that seemingly endless informational introduction playing over the speaker when I started back a month ago.

'Welcome to Bloody Hell Winery, where the wine is bloody good! This is branch 66B. One of our more 'hidden gem' locations, though I'm sure you already know that. In fact, let's cut the tourism shit. This, is Unknown. The highly elite black-ops agency that deals with international threats and criminal organizations. You've heard of the CIA, CSIS, KGB and whatever else, but Unknown is all that combined. Founded to create peace and fair justice, Unknown...'

As an act of mercy, my mind stops the memory there. The rest was just spewed out facts I had long since had memorized when first recruited. Thank god I don't have to hear that ever again. I'm surprised Manager didn't have it play just to punish me for my tardiness. Luckily, he doesn't dislike me that much, so I get to enjoy the beguiling decor in silence.

My eyes become drawn to the thousands of shelved wine bottles and barrels that cover the curved walls. All of which are being held up by rustic beams to be aged to false perfection. The whole space resembles something of a billionaire's basement wine cellar.

Further down however, is a different story.

The billionaire ambiance remains, though as the agency's front business falls away, the other more *covert* levels start to pass me by. Each is wrapped in thick pristine glass, which invites a peek into the various different activities under way. Simulation situation training, gadget testing, combat drills, and even night classes.

All of it is amazing. The second I had seen this branch I knew it was built to have a homey feel. But, when finally reaching the command center, that feeling goes cold, and the ultramodern work aesthetic sets in.

As the car gently sets down like an autumn leaf, the Unknown seal greets me first. The large black question mark and red X pasted on almost every flat surface, displaying the perfect combination of guaranteed protection and unquestionable fear. Once the door opens, my attention shifts to the office hustle happening around me.

This is one of the busier nights, and at first, the atmosphere is a bit overwhelming. Constant chatter fills the wide interior, agents from almost every nationality rush from every direction while others sit at desks, staring at the holographic computer monitors with such importance.

So the complete opposite from my day job.

It doesn't take me long to get accustom though. I find that I thrive in chaos, and this is nothing if not chaotic. As I step into the belly of the beast, Bethany addresses me before I go about my business.

"Goodbye, agent. Thanks for the ride and your company."

"Umm... I think I should be thanking you, but you're welcome," I answer before furrowing my brow. This new automated speech recognition A.I system seems so familiar. Like talking to an old friend. And clearly that line was meant to throw me off for a laugh.

"Bethany, who programmed you?" I ask, curious.

"A Darling," she says.

Shaking my head as I step off the platform, I watch the car sink further into the ground while chuckling at Bethany's answer. Nice to see that someone still has a sense of humour around here. Even when the car is no longer in sight, I let my amusement last as long as possible, because something tells me that whatever awaits me in Manager's office will kill any kind of joy.

Plus, interacting with these younger agents requires at least a weak smile so they don't instantly think I'm going to make their lives a living hell.

I greet some of the ones I've gotten to know in the last month with just the simple 'hi's' and 'how you doing's.' Except, with the last agent I pass, I stop in my tracks and my lazy smile becomes a full-blown grin.

"Hey, Peters. I heard you got your ass kicked by a trainee yesterday."

He glances up from the communicator in his hand, and the minute his embarrassed expression falls into a smirk, I know. He's about to say something stupid.

"And I heard you had a little 'Hanna' experience last night," he remarks with such fake confidence.

"Oh, really?" I slowly rock back on my heels while rolling up my sleeves.

I start to walk towards him, letting my friendly smirk drop, and a purely terrified look springs to his face. *Priceless.* Out of nowhere, before I reach him, a heavy hand is placed on my shoulder, holding me back with little to no effort.

"Leave the kid alone, 401," Manager demands, his voice breaking into the tense silence. He lets me go, and I twist to meet his eyes, but his stare is only on Peters. "He's still sore from yesterday," he dryly snickers.

"Come on, Manager, really?" Peters pleads with a shy smile as the crowd that has formed around us erupts into silent laughter.

Manager's hefty chuckle outshines everyone's, and like a single organism, they turn their attention to him. Like they've never heard him laugh before. That might be the case, because when his amusement ends, and he orders them back to work, the room transitions into the scene that was playing when I arrived. He then dismisses Peters—who practically scurries away—and I let myself enjoy the look on his face a second longer. But, as soon as Manager glances down at me, my grin fades.

"What's the intel?" I tightly cross my arms over my chest, as if shielding my heart from any breaking news.

The wrinkled crease on the corner of his mouth falls and a serious thin lip replaces his smirk. "Mission first."

"But—"

"We'll get to it."

He nudges his head towards his office, and while we walk through the energetic bustle of the nightshift, I elevate my voice over the noise. Making sure he hears my protest.

"Fine," I respond sternly as we come upon his office that takes up almost half of the ground floor, "but I want the record to reflect that I think the intel would've made sense to discuss with me beforehand."

"Your objection is dually noted," he opens the door and lightly snorts, as if my impression of command is amusing to him. "But luckily I'm the boss here, so get in, sit down, and shut up."

I spin to face him, to challenge his snort, but there's no trace of merriment in his expression anymore. Instead, I stroll past him in complete silence. And choosing not to focus on the slightly irritated look donning his face, I switch my attention to the smell of rich leather and pine that immediately seeps into my nose.

My eyes dart around the familiar classy room filled with packed bookshelves, bottled ships, and his weird collection of scribble art as I plant myself into one of his worn out chairs. It's definitely a real "man's man" type office. Almost. The hung-up art of him as a teddy bear from his grandkid's really captures the softy he is underneath the order and standoffishness etched into his face.

The décor quickly falls away when my eyes catch sight on the glass tablet embedded into the center of his desk. Something in me starts to reach for it. For all the information it contains. I slightly lift my bottom from the cool leather. The sudden sound of Manager shutting the door snaps me back into obedience mode and I quickly sit. He comes around, suspiciously eyeing me, but as he takes a seat behind his massive desk, his glare softens.

"Now, this mission I have for you is not only important, it's also time sensitive."

"Oh really?" I cross my legs and lean forward. "So I'm not going to be strong armed into waiting for any more mysterious packages? Only to end up dodging bullets and running on top of shipping containers?"

Manager sighs and drops his stare. "Again, *you* decided to get out of the car, but no. I'm putting a pause on that. You've gathered enough info to have an agent from General Tasks handle placing tracking devices for now. The mission I have is high-priority. I need you on it instead."

"I thought unmasking this new faceless mobster who's attempting to tap into the global market was high-priority," my brow furrows as the rest of the words leaving my mouth turn into a rhetorical question. "But judging by your face I'm wrong?"

Manager's left brow rises ever-so-gently. I sit back, hoping the chair will be enough to support me when the weight of whatever he's about to burden me with falls unto my shoulders.

"You have my attention."

His tense expression relaxes. "I'm so glad, agent."

"So, what's this "time sensitive" mission I've been graciously given?" I ask with some intrigue.

The question comes out somewhat rushed, and I take in a slow deep breath, trying to keep my impatience in check. By the way he's eyeing me, Manager notices my slight frustration, but thankfully dismisses it and begins to dive right in. He activates the tablet by pulling it from his desk, and then speaks with his usual order. As if he's debriefing an entire room of agents.

"Two days ago, I initiated an agent to tail a man named Harry Hamilton. A game tester over at White Ghost Cartel

Games. The front business for our rivals I'm sure you're familiar with."

"Well considering they're our evil counterpart, yes, I'm *very* familiar," my voice takes a sharper tone without meaning to. It's just the memory of going face-to-gun with them for years, of even their ironic three ghost hear no evil, speak no evil, see no evil insignia, makes my blood slightly curdle.

Manager glances up from the glowing screen, only giving me a deadpan stare. "So I don't need to remind you of your past dealings with them then?"

"No, but what's up with this Hamilton guy? Is he a mouse or a spider?"

"Well, he started off as a mouse. There but not being seen. These game testers are so rarely detached from their headsets they're hardly—if not ever—a threat. Too busy playing the games *in* life and not playing the game *of* life."

"So what happened with this one?"

"Mouse was a mouse, until he left his house and got a DUI the day prior. And it was not his first. But, according to our sources, he didn't even spend an hour incarcerated, was *barely* processed through the system, and was back to work the next day."

"Mouse got back into the house rather quickly. Mommy and daddy rich?"

"That's one of the first things we came up with, but no. The company supplied his bail."

"A million-dollar company paid the bail of a meaningless part-time employee? One that probably comes a dime a dozen?"

"Exactly the problem. And since we know that WGCG is simply a cover for much more nefarious acts than just first-person shooter games, we've been gathering files on each of those dime a dozen employees for the past three years."

"And?"

"Harry Hamilton was an exemplary worker. Employee of the month, welcoming person, and didn't set off any red flags. Until—"

"Until the DUI. Then mouse became a spider," I say with confidence.

"Mouse became a spider. There and seen, but too scared of to be touched. After that, we had reason to look deeper, and the deeper we went, the more we found. Which led to an immediate tail."

He pauses for a brief moment before handing the tablet over to me. When he does, as I swipe through Hamilton's digital file, scanning over some gruesome photos, Manager continues to speak. Clearly showing he's memorized the document by heart.

"The company may have put up his bail, but it wasn't their own money. The money came from a collection of five different offshore accounts, all of which make up a total of one hundred point six *million* dollars. And, three out of those five banks, once decoded, all spelt out the same name. George Samberg."

"Not in the name of our Mr. Harry Hamilton. And that's *a lot* more money than a part-time game tester who frequents the bar scene would make in the span of three years."

"Yes, there's the different name and the unexplained sufficient funds, but that's not all. Out of the three that have the same name, all gained equal amounts of ten thousand dollars just last month."

My heart skips a beat as I read exactly which banks he's referring to. In a hollow tone I point it out, "It says one of those banks is in Madrid."

"I know. I had just seen that connection today, after our hacker finally decrypted Samberg's entire file."

"So you're saying he has something to do with my brother's disappearance?" I ask, my voice shaking a bit.

"Tracking your brother has been a long and tedious process, you know that. And with the amount of time he's been missing, we've been working on the assumption that he's still alive."

I try not to take offense to that, remembering he's always been the blunt type as long as I've known him. Yet that doesn't stop me from pleading my case.

"I canvassed the scene of his last location at my Abuelo's place in Toledo myself, and there was evidence that he was taken alive."

"There was a sign of a struggle, yes. That *someone* was taken, yes. But you and I both know that that doesn't guarantee—"

"When I got here, you told me that your border guy said a lot of people were shipped that day. Said that half were found and transported back, but the other half weren't. So he might've gotten lost like the others being trafficked."

Manager rubs the bridge of his nose. "I also said that given your past family history, it was unlikely he was in the sweep."

"Okay. But minus the potential mobsters and crooked police from that history and we're left with the ten thousand dollar payout to a nearby bank, and the unnerving coincidence that it was only a day after he went missing."

"I know. That's why I had the agent who *was* tailing him up surveillance."

"Was? What happened?"

"What do you think happened? This generation of agents are complete fuck ups. 607 only managed to send a shitty partial video of Hamilton meeting with a guy he described as "shady" yesterday afternoon. But the son of a bitch was later spotted by Hamilton and killed on sight."

"So this Harry Hamilton, a.k.a George Samberg is a confirmed agent for Specter, and that meeting was what, a new assignment?"

"Following your departure with the agency, for a brief period the mole extraction op you worked continued. Especially since some of our highly confidential information was still being leaked to Specter somehow. But after an anonymous tip, we decided we were desperate enough and looked into it. That's when we found all the evidence that the mole had been someone working inside the very extraction operation created to find them. Agent 601, Levon Vera."

He pauses, allowing me a moment to react, and I let myself. I knew Levon of course. Small but muscular. Smart but not cocky about it. A nice guy who I worked well with. The thought of him as the mole though? It doesn't seem to make sense. Slowly, as if hearing my last thought, Manager takes in a breath then continues in a much weaker tone.

"However, when we went to bring him in for questioning, we found him DOA from one of our suicide capsules. We figured he found out we were onto him so he killed himself as an easy way out. Since we wanted to wrap up that whole situation promptly, it was swept under the rug. After that, all espionage ceased, so the operation shut down. Case closed. At least until a couple of hours ago."

I lean back and press my shoulders against the cold chair, the tablet still tightly in my hands. "And why is this game of catch-up happening now?"

"Because at first, when I thought Hamilton had ties to your brother, that was the only reason I increased his surveillance. But, when we finally decrypted that shitty video, the only two words anyone could make out were 'Echo Delta.'"

Oh shit. This can't be good.

"It was alarming, obviously, though, since the transmission wasn't fully decrypted when handed to Commander, she found no reason to have General look into it. And, since 607 belonged to the Project, it got passed down to us. By the time we did confirm what was said, earlier this afternoon, we realized it was worse than we thought. So much so that it explains your unexpected company last night."

He stops for a moment then rakes a hand through his thick silver hair. It's a gesture I know him to only do when news he's giving is going in the direction from bad to worse.

"Now, because of that little run in, we know that whoever's shipments those were, whoever is pushing for their organization to go global, have strong ties within Specter. So that, in combination with the very title of our top covert op from years ago, only means one thing I'm praying I'm wrong about."

I know where he's going with this, and that knowledge alone causes a shiver to go down my spine. It's not something I want to handle right now. But given his serious demeanour, I really don't think I have the option to stick my fingers in my ears and pretend not to hear him anymore. Something in me almost does.

Although, with the way he's staring at me, waiting for me to ask the question, as if he needs me to draw the answer out of him to make the situation real, I slowly start to feel the suspense killing me. I want this to be false as much as he does, but we both know better than to only hope for the good without the bad. So I play along.

"And what's that?"

"That agent 601, the person we were led to believe was the mole, was merely a scapegoat, and the real one has been lying dormant within Unknown for the last three years. And since the only audible thing mentioned was Echo Delta, I'm assuming there was mention of the old agents involved, which includes you, 401. So, I thought it best you go and handle questioning Samberg."

This time both bushy eyebrows move up on his face and I read between the lines. He then stands, almost motionless, and reaches for the tablet. After handing it over, he gently clicks it back into his desk then strolls up to his narrow doorway. He holds onto the knob, dramatically waiting while I process and push down the haunted memories of my past work three years ago.

This is the very *last* thing I need, especially when Dominic is still out there, and the looming feeling of 'him' as also been grabbing for my attention. But knowing my duties here, and what I have to do, what I agreed to do, I stand to face him. In a low yet firm voice, I recite my words in a soldier like manner.

"Understood, Sir."

With a swift nod he opens the door for me, yet standing in my way is the tall bulky man with the face from my most recent nightmare. The man who used to be my boss. Supervisor.

That is, before I left.

The smile on his face shrinks smaller and smaller as his empty blue eyes meet mine. His commanding appearance somewhat fades when I don't avert my glare—like I normally would've four years back. Not anymore though. Since then, I've made my disrespect for him known, in more ways than one, yet still it doesn't feel like enough.

My face begins to burn with disgust as I continue to glare, so hard I'm hoping that he'll start to taste my bitter hate. It happens in silence, the slight shift in his facade, but, so desperate to retain an undisturbed demeanour, Supervisor catches his smile before it completely falls from his face.

"Agent 401, what a surprise."

Ignoring his acknowledgement, I turn back around to Manager. "Is it?" I say coldly.

"Don't agent. I know you two have a complicated past, but he's been helping with the investigation into the whereabouts of your brother."

"Why?" I snap, fury twisting my face into a scowl. "I didn't ask for his so-called help Manager, and that *complicated* past isn't that complicated—" I turn to Supervisor and narrow my eyes— "he was just *terrible* at his job."

"Enough, 401," Manager demands, "go handle your task, *now* please."

As Supervisor stares down at me, I see nothing but the smug look from my dream. Heat travels throughout my body that I'm sure would bear resemblance to hell. I swear a physical itch comes to my hand, specifically one that can't be satisfied until I punch him. I'd get in trouble for knocking Unknown's number two on his ass, but oh it'd be *so* worth it.

The only thing that stops me at this point is seeing Manager slowly shake his head in the reflection of the door. It takes everything in me to back away, and just when Supervisor moves from my path, he actually has the balls to talk again.

"It was great to see you, agent."

Biggest fucking lie I've heard today.

"And I'm *certain* your brother will come back to you safe and sound."

I don't answer him. I don't get the chance. Manager calls him into his office with haste. Surely noticing the way my hands are shaking themselves into fists. So much of me wants to hurt him, yet I choose to focus on my mission, which means cramming down the urge to slap the rest of that stale British accent from his mouth. I stroll off without looking back.

The heat running through my body only elevates while walking away, but with the sound of the door closing behind me I force my body to cool. Just when I start to calm down, I feel someone approaching me, and I quickly whip my head in their direction.

"Agent 401?" an operator, a mouse like girl with small green eyes, calls me with a bit of a stutter.

Realizing why, I relax my cold expression and stop my fingernails from digging into my palms. I take a deep breath and put on a friendlier face before answering.

"Yes. Hi. Sorry about that. Do I need to be briefed on how to go about this mission?"

A shy smile curls her thin lips. "Actually agent, I was told to inform you that you've been given free authorization for this mission. Mr. Manager's orders."

As the smile on her face grows, I assume this must be the first time she's been allowed to give an agent free authorization. For me, this isn't the first time I've gotten to call the shots, but it will be the first in a long while. And the fact that it has something to do with my brother is an added bonus. A wave of excitement pulses through my body as I join in with the smiling operator.

I then thank her, she gives me my target's usual Friday night location and I'm off. To peek behind the curtain and see if Michelle Hannigan can *really* keep up with agent 401.

CHAPTER EIGHT

THE ROOM WHERE IT HAPPENS

Everything in this East Village dive bar has something to clash with its interior décor. Whether it's the brick wall meshing with the mahogany floor, or the matching candy red chairs and tabletops. Hell, even the mud brown stool I sit on blends into the bar where I falsely sip a dirty martini. And as I stare blankly at the brick in front of me, I remove the frosty glass from my lips and slip deeper into my thoughts. The first to run through my mind being the usual whenever I 'worked the graveyard shift'. My brother.

The song 'The Scientist' playing throughout the room begins to fade away ever-so-slightly to the back of my mind, and the only thing I hear clearly is my own voice echoing inside my head. '*He's alive. He has to be. Dominic may be smart but he's also stubborn, and that's what will keep him breathing.*' But as that voice quiets, another one fills the void with a guilty tone. '*It's your fault he's even in this situation in the first place, you idiot. You left him alone.*'

The heart wrenching thought pushes me back into reality, and I slightly twist my head to glance at the surroundings I forgot I'm supposed to be a part of. As the dark storm of thoughts begin to clear, I'm shaken by the sudden erupting loudness of laughter from the group of guys behind me. I quickly force out a light sigh. I need to focus. I'm not supposed to be shaky, especially not in a place like this. Where the men can probably smell discomfort.

To calm the nerves, I let my plan spring to mind again, and suddenly, I'm oozing with pleasure. *I'm about to be left alone with the man who might've had something to do with Dom's disappearance.* It might not be in the clothes I wanted though. I was forced to change into more *"tasteful"* attire that fits the bar scene. Now, instead of what I originally went to the winery dressed in, I wear a short bubble-gum pink leather dress that zips in the front, but stops at the very end of my cleavage, leaving the collar—each side with a golden button—to lazily drape at my bare throat.

It has thin lace sleeves with a floral pattern traveling up my arms into one perfect rose on my back, and instead of my converse, magenta leather thigh-high boots are tied onto my feet, to match the stain of my lips. But, despite the tight outfit, that 'shit's about to go sideways' feeling fills the air. It smells of liquor, my 'purposely over sprayed' lavender perfume, and light sweat. I'm more than determined to make sure it stays there.

Just as I shift in my chair, almost too giddy with excitement, from behind I hear the squeak of the bar door. I don't turn my head though. I only glance down at the cheap watch that goes with my hoe-ish outfit, then smirk. It's exactly twelve AM. Time to begin tonight's event. I lock eyes with the bartender—my new favourite rookie, Peters—and he gives me an old fashion, specifically with four maraschino cherries. Just when he slides it over to me, a handsome yet familiar stranger takes the stool two down from mine.

As he does, I notice the way his lime green eyes seem to glow, even in the dim bar lights. Something cool travels down my back at the sight of them, like they've cut people open with a mere glance. The alarm I would be feeling though, gets traded with annoyance when I realize that those same steely eyes have not left my over exposed breasts since he sat down. He doesn't stop staring until Peters interrupts his drooling session with a cliché, but surprisingly decent, New Yorker accent.

"What's your poison?"

The man nods to a bottle of whiskey while giving me a quick smirk and taking off his bulky jacket. A grin spreads across my face, as I swallow down what feels like hot coals of rage, and a slight giggle comes from me as I let my temporary blond hair fall into my face, then shyly glance away. As soon as I know he can't see my expression anymore, I drop the corners of my mouth and watch to assure Peters continues his role without a hitch.

He slowly makes his way over to the whiskey, but just before he reaches for the bottle, I lightly swirl the martini in my hand and gently place it down next to my old fashion. Then, after shifting ever-so-slightly to have clear sight into the mirror behind the bar, I don't wait long to see the man's eyes do a double take from my drink to Peters. Seconds later he quickly haulers, his voice sounding rough like a beggar on the street.

"Oh, and an old fashion. Four cherries instead of two. Thanks."

One swift nod later, Peters goes about his business, and the minute his back is turned the man side eyes me again and continues to smirk. My hand travels up the side of my neck to flip the hair from my shoulder, presenting him with the glimpse of the smile on my face. It does the job it's supposed to, but once his drinks are placed in front of him, it's almost like I'm not even in the room anymore.

I've always found this part of the job so cliché, but work is work, I guess. In this scene the seductive trick works every time. So much so that it's just sad at a point. All men, and sometimes women—evil can come with breasts too—love to play cat and mouse. You glance, smile, flirt a little, or even drug them if you want an easy night. But either way, in my experience at least, my results always end the same.

I get the mouse.

After watching this handsome man order a couple more shots, and even stronger drinks, he changes from orderly and classy to a drunken mess. Everything about his demeanour is different, and not in a good way at all. His sleeves are unevenly rolled up, the white shirt under his blazer is now partially untucked from his pants, and his hair has somehow lost its shine. Maybe I should just let him drink himself to death. Seems like that's what he's trying to do here anyway.

I've never seen a man drink his weight that fast in one sitting without getting alcohol poisoning. He's clearly had a lot of practise. The same old fashion I ordered sixty minutes ago is still sitting in front of me, yet in all that time it's like the man's been involved in a drinking contest with himself.

He starts yelling for more shots while struggling to undo his tie, but then gives up and reaches for the glass in front of him that holds less than a sip. He guzzles it down, like he needs it to survive. A hint of hunger shines in his eyes. The same kind I'm feeling in my stomach to get my job done, but the difference is that it doesn't seem like he can control himself. It almost makes me feel bad for the guy.

Almost.

Again he tries to order another drink, but when Peters steals a glance my way, I swiftly nod. With that simple gesture, now the hard part of my night officially begins. Peters then completely shifts his cool attitude and starts to raise his voice.

"No man, sorry, you're done."

The man's face melts into fury as he shouts back at him, "I'm not done. You still got liquor, and I still got a working liver," he slams his hand on the bar, "So serve it up!"

Shaking his head, Peters snaps the rag out from his waist and starts wiping down the bar top. "No. You're done."

That doesn't make him happy at all, and everything about his new demeanour turns sour. He grunts out a couple of threats here and there, then grabs his coat to leave.

Now I get his full attention. I wrap my hand around the old fashion in front of me and bring it to my lips, taking a small sip. As soon as it looks like it touched my tongue, I wince, put it down, and push it away.

On my left a faint chuckle comes from behind. I slowly turn my head to lock eyes with the not-so-gentlemen like man who had come in earlier. A confused yet polite smile lights my face as I see his lips upturned as well, but more like a lion trying to reassure its prey that it won't bite.

It goes without saying I'd never fall for his pathetic act if I weren't here for business, but since I am, tonight falling for that act is exactly what I have to do. I swing the hair over my shoulder again then, uncross my legs, and he takes the bait and begins in my direction.

Its times like these I feel like I need more of a challenge in life. Other than just being a sexy woman with legs for days. That feeling becomes stronger as the man comes up from behind then slightly slides his hand down my back and leans his elbow on the bar.

Ugh. I'm totally regretting my decision to wear the dress with the *thin* lace back. I push aside my disgust at his behaviour, which shouldn't be a surprise given where he goes drinking, and focus up.

"A little thing like you can handle all that, sweetheart?"

His voice sounds almost just like his laugh. Void of emotion yet draws you in, wondering what he has to say. Though I already have a pretty good guess judging by the way he leans closer.

"Do you mind? This runt behind the bar cut me off," he says arrogantly.

As I'm about to answer, I restrain the urge to toss it back just to make him look like an even bigger asshole. Something I didn't think was possible, until I catch him openly glancing at my cleavage again. But when his wanting stare shifts to my drink, I twirl a piece of hair around my index finger and stupidly grin, channelling my inner Theora from this morning as I giggle and slide the drink over to him.

"Be my guest," I tell him with my voice having a sweet melody.

Without hesitation, he takes a long sip and actually tries to look at me without it being from the bottom of a glass. Once he puts it down, before he can eat the cherries, I grab them and tap it on the rim. Slowly I push them into my mouth. When I take out the stick, my pink lips part in an 'O' shape, and I can honestly say that the man doesn't have one loose muscle in his body anymore. He shivers slightly, then reaches out his hand towards me, not even trying to hide the fact he's still staring at my lips.

"Harry Hamilton," he slurs and grabs my hand.

I shake it loosely and widen my grin while speaking as if I have helium in my lungs. "Amber Daniels."

Hamilton takes his hand from mine but has to use the bar for balance. Clearly he's made my job much easier. It may have come with some strings attached, given that every time he leans in I get a whiff of his sour breath.

I hold back my gag as he goes on and on for a while, talking about himself. The only thing that keeps me from jabbing him in the throat is the fact that I'll get to do whatever I want to him in mere minutes.

Later, after I force myself to tune back into his bullshit, I have to bite on the inside of my cheek to stop from laughing. He mentions that he's a 'large investor at a growing company that specializes in virtual reality interactive gaming systems.' Honestly, that's the best way I've heard anyone describe WGCG, to the point where to my trained ear, the line sounds almost programmed into his brain.

That wouldn't be above Specter; to manipulate the minds of their own agents. The thought intrigues me enough to actually pay attention during the rest of the conversation. A conversation that seems to go forever, as if he's talking to himself. A peacock infatuated by his own feathers. But, in the brief moment he looks away trying to regain his balance, I sneak a look to Peters and nod again.

Acknowledging me sets off a chain reaction. Peters shifts his stare to an agent of ours planted in the crowd, and quickly gives him a thumbs up. My eyes drift over to the mirror behind the bar, and I watch as agent 302—a very muscular man—reaches over to the guy sitting across from him and decks him in the face. As fast as it happens, the once friendly bar scene becomes a downright brawl. Punches go flying, chairs get thrown, and curses overtakes the melody of Rock Lobster. The chaos lasts a minute, before Peters reaches for a bat and slams it on the bar. Stopping anything unexpected from happening.

"Alright that's enough, last call! Everybody out, now!"

The bruised crowd groan in frustration but file out nonetheless. Each have to wait for one person to leave through the narrow doorway. Some curse Peters on the way out, others find the need to express their anger by throwing food at the men who started fighting, but they do leave. Once everyone is gone, Hamilton is next to gather his things. I shoot my hand out, reaching for his sleeve to draw him back to me. He takes the hint and we fold back to our first position. Peters turns away.

Now, I had a plan. Keep him talking for a bit longer, flip my hair a little, giggle some more, but that goes way out the window. Because when Hamilton takes it upon himself to now use the inside of my thigh for balance, my schedule moves up. His hands are grossly hot and callous. I want to headbutt him so bad but restrain my violent instincts.

"You know..." I trail off gently grabbing the collar on his shirt and creating a hum in the back of my throat, "you don't look like a Harry Hamilton to me."

He leans closer. "Oh really? Then who do I look like? Cause I can be anyone you want me to be, sweetheart." His grip on my thigh tightens, but so does my handle on his collar. I'm so close to his neck—this pig—yet I pace myself and get back into character.

I pull him closer to me then lean into his ear and whisper. "You look like an agent for Specter named George Samberg. And a guy who clearly doesn't know when to say when."

Without waiting for him to admit anything, I cross my legs together locking his hands in between my thighs. He tries to pull himself free, but with the amount of drinks he's had, he can't be seeing straight. A smile creeps across my lips as I ball up more of his shirt in my fists then forcefully pull down. His head smacks up against the side of the bar. First when he goes down, he doesn't stay there. Though when he tries to get back up. I ever-so-slightly kick him in the face.

And balls.

For good measure.

His body goes completely limp to I stand and give myself a second to shake off the lingering feel of his disgusting touch. Every part of me is burning. I have half a mind to go take a shower before continuing. I ignore the desire and drag Samberg behind the bar then waste no time with tying this asshole up. His hands I tie to the golden pole, and when I'm finished tying his feet together I turn to find Peters staring in awe. He then looks me up and down, frozen to the ground.

"Wow. That was awesome. You're awesome."

I bite down on the inside of my cheek to stop the smirk from coming to my face. As flattered as I am, now is not the time to be accepting compliments. *Especially* not in this outfit. I don't let the deadpan look stray from my features as I intensely return his stare, searching behind his dark eyes for something that only someone as experienced as me will find.

It's small. You only get a second to pick it out. And I do. The minute he looks away, I see everything I need to. I then cross my arms over my chest and take a step towards him.

"You did better than I thought you would, surprised me, and I appreciate people who can surprise me. But you have to go now. Take the car and don't come back here."

"Oh, thanks 401, but Supervisor told me to stay until—"

Heat rises in my cheeks. "I don't care what you were told to do by Supervisor. This is *my* mission. *I* have free authorization, so *I'm* telling you to leave 202," I interrupt, stern.

I had seen so much innocence left in his eyes just then, when he stared at me with amazement. But, when he looked away, he only confirmed my suspicions. When agent's start out there's always a certain innocence still in them. Innocence that's blind to the full gravity of what's to come in this line of work. However, I also know, all too well, that that usually doesn't last long. The way I was raised, I've never had the burden of that virtue myself, but I've seen the very moment when the alteration happens up close.

It's dark. It kills a part of you that'll never grow again, and looking at Peters it's clear that that shift hasn't occurred yet. It will happen, depending on how long he's with the agency, but with everything I'm about to do, this shouldn't be his first reason why.

He's a good guy, has skills, so I don't let up my glare until he finally gives in and just goes. I watch him until he gets inside the car and only after I hear the car skrrt off do I turn back to Samberg.

Now my work can begin.

I take a second to change into something *much* more comfortable, but leave on the blond wig and caked on makeup that modifies my appearance. I'm not here to blow expose myself as an Unknown agent. We're in here alone, but if anything goes wrong and cameras see Amber Daniels walk in but someone else walk out, more problems will be added to my plate.

I vowed to myself that I'd never get involved in another police chase again. Even though it led to the best sex I've ever had in a storage unit. I shake my head, before the thought blossoms, and suck in a steady breath. Calm enough, I finish getting everything together for my guest of honour then grab a cup of ice water and thrust it into Samberg's red face. He wakes immediately, and of course the first thing he does is struggle.

They always struggle.

"Hey George, you took a pretty nasty spill there after all those drinks. You alright?" I ask sarcastically sympathetic.

"You little *bitch*! You have no idea who you're fucking with. You're dead!"

I don't have time to talk. Well, I do, but I just want to go home and sleep peacefully knowing I don't have work the next day. So, after a few strikes to his face, and body, I take a break to wipe off the bit of blood on my knuckles, then go for the hidden bag that's filled with some of my favourite accessories.

"What do you want? You come on behalf of Ricky, for the money I owe?" he begs in a rushed huff, as if his heart is in his throat.

Snickering, I don't answer. I only pull out one of my polished knives, squat down in front of him, then stare with amusement covering my face. But I let it morph into a malicious smirk while I calmly reply.

"No, George. I'm here because you fucked up in some other way," I move up towards his chest, "and I'm only going to tell you this once."

Stabbing the blade in his hip for the use of both my hands, he lets out a muffled groan as I unbutton his shirt and enlighten him. "If you cooperate with me, I'll cooperate with you. Okay? There's no reason why we can't start things off with a clean slate."

I take the knife from his hip and toss it between my hands, waiting for his answer. He only glares at me for a minute before spitting out blood and growling. "Go to hell, bitch."

"Oh, I have my ticket, but you'll be punching yours first after I'm done with you." I grin while cutting the rest of his shirt off and shoving it into his mouth.

"You know," I gently slide the knife down his left peck, noticing he's surprisingly ripped for a drunk, "I'm not really great with knives. Hand to hand combat is really more my specialty. But, I *am* a firm believer that practise makes perfect, George."

When a hint of fear flashes across his face, I don't blame him. If I had to choose between a new surgeon or an experienced one, I'd trust the experienced one not to make the wrong cuts. His panic passes, but it's too late, I had already seen it. So, I kindly inquire before continuing.

"Do you wanna tell me who you met with in New York yesterday to receive stolen information?"

He doesn't even blink, so I take that as a no, and start cutting.

Three hours, two waters and a bowl of pretzels later, George Samberg still doesn't break. He has about eighty cuts covering his entire body, all ranging from various sizes, lengths and depths. It definitely took a couple of tries to find my groove. Certain adjustments had to be made. I didn't cut so deep he'd bleed out before I really got him talking. "Persuasion" has always been a highlight for me when it comes to the job, but this? This could really open up a whole new method of "persuasion" for me.

It does involve a bit more blood, but maybe in time—no. No, this is just temporary. Manager, the project, it'll all come to an end, which is honestly for the best. I guess I'd better savour this moment all the more. The realization replenishes me, though as I'm about to continue with my practise, a plaguy vibration stumps my focus. I spin around to locate where it's coming from. When I don't find it, I furrow my brows and stare down at George.

"Is that you?"

He rolls his eyes up to meet mine with a weary look of rage plastered across his face. His shaky and weak breathing becomes his only response, which doesn't completely upset me. If it weren't for his temporary lack of speech—courtesy of my homemade gag—I'm sure his answer would've been one hundred percent crass remarks. Not one part of me wants to put myself in the position to be verbally abused anymore than I have to. So, I look away from his furious brooding as the vibration continues and I follow the sound until it leads me to the clutch I forgot Amber had brought. Inside the glittery thing is Michelle's phone.

"Damn it," I mumble.

Bringing it was a bad move on my part. I should've left it at the winery. But, since it's already here and ringing, maybe a little break would be good. I hold up my finger to George and dismissively utter, "excuse me for a second."

He kicks up his feet at me, but moves so slowly because of blood loss I only take a small step back to avoid him. His attempt is laughable, and I almost let a smirk curl my lips. I suppress the urge to chuckle and instead concentrate on holding my solemn expression while digging my finger into the stab wound in his hip.

I twist once, letting my nail scrape his flesh, and George yelps in pain. My brows lightly twitch upwards with satisfaction, then, after slowly pulling my finger out, I hover it over my lips to shush him. And while shoving the shirt deeper down his throat, I wipe the blood from my hands. Once it's off—most of it anyway—I pop the last pretzel in my mouth, turn away, and then clear my throat before swiping my thumb across the screen.

I mask my voice with tranquility and a bit of haste. "Hey, what's up?"

"Hey Elle," Shane answers, sounding half asleep. "Sorry to bother you so late."

"No, it's no problem." *I needed a break anyway.*

"Did you find your brother?"

Already having a response for him I open my mouth, but as I'm about to reply, George decides that that's the time to start screaming, despite the gag.

"Hold on for just a sec." I put him on mute before he can answer, then twist towards George and knee him in the face. His nose makes one of the worst breaking sounds I've heard, but despite my excitement, I darken my voice.

"Does Specter not teach you manners over there? Shut the fuck up."

With wishful thinking, and exhaustion getting the better of me, I bend down and remove the white shirt that's become drenched in his blood from his mouth.

"Or, if you're ready to tell me what you know, by all means, speak. You have my attention. However, if you don't have anything useful to say, I have a lot more knives, with *a lot* more serrated ends, George. But, if you do talk now, this could all end much faster for you."

"Don't give me that bullshit, all agents are the same. That information is the only thing keeping me alive right now, so *fuck you*. I'm not telling you any—"

I roll my eyes and shove the shirt back into his mouth, then take Shane off hold. "Sorry about that."

"Is everything okay?"

"Yeah, I just had to do something for my uncle."

Beside me George cuts his eyes. I don't appreciate his attitude and take a brief moment to show him that. I grab a lemon wedge from the bar then squeeze it over his legs. He yelps in agony, but his screams are much quieter, I hope because he's finally come to the conclusion that I hold his fate in my hands. And now, with the lemon, a lot more ideas come to mind, but I quickly flush that creativity from my system. I focus my attention on hurrying Shane off the phone.

"Is there something you wanted to ask?"

"Oh yeah," he pauses for a second, I assume to take in my sudden straight forward tone. "After you left, Becca, T and I thought that we should all go out tomorrow. You know, to properly celebrate Becca's promotion with alcohol? You down?"

Considering the activity I'm doing now, I don't know what the rest of my night will look like, but getting rid of Shane is my main priority. Especially since George is starting to nod out. If he does go under, I won't get the answers I need, derived from the fact that he won't wake up again. This needs to get done, for both our sakes. I quickly end our conversation.

"Of course I'll come. Just update me with the time and place." I take the phone from my ear then yell to no one, "Ya voy, solo ¡déjame despedirme!"

(I'm coming, just let me say goodbye!)

"Sorry, I didn't mean to keep you, Elle," he says sincerely.

"No, it's fine," I lazily tell him. "My uncle just always has chores for me." I then laugh dryly. "Just text me later, okay?"

"Alright, no worries. Goodnight."

I hang up and tuck the phone back into the clutch while turning my focus to a dying George. So much of me just wants to let him go to hell. Especially when the sudden information from Manager's tablet disclosing his big pay out a month ago flashes across my mind. Except, without any new information about Echo Delta, the first part of my job isn't over. With a sigh, I take the shirt from his mouth, and surprise surprise, he talks first.

"You're pathetic," Samberg sneers. "You're never gonna get anything from me cunt. Loyalty 101."

I move back and tightly cross my arms over my chest. "So, professor, what's your philosophy on blowing your cover, twice?"

"It doesn't matter now does it?" He spits blood at my shoe and snickers. "I would've gotten everything from you three hours ago. But given your unfortunate non-threatening gender, you don't have the skill or quite literally the balls it takes."

Checking my watch with only a bored expression, I take in the time and keep the jaded look attached to my face as I grab the serrated knife from my side. I tap it gently on my bottom lip, and as my mouth curves up into a grin I step closer.

"You see, it's comments like that that make you lose fingers, George," I express with amusement.

I force his hand into mine and saw off his middle finger, his blood filling my cupped palm. He lets out a huffy cry, and when I'm done, blood pooling around him, George's head bobs. I'm getting tired of his shit. Up until he said what he said, I was holding back. Swallowing down the part of me that just wants to play with his joints until each snap like toothpicks. Though now, as I wipe off my hand on a rag, I pull out my final trick to get him to spill the rest of his guts.

"I'm going to let you in on a little secret Samberg. I don't really need to keep you alive. So far, I've been having some much needed fun with you, but my job isn't to get info," my grin slightly fades. "My job tonight is to get you to confirm what your partner already came and told us."

Snapping his head up—the fastest I've seen him move in hours—George twitches with fury. "That's a lie!"

Looks like I finally hit the right nerve.

"Afraid not. Switching sides seems to be the norm these days. You two spoke recently, you told him about your little meeting, and then he told us everything. He's the one that sent the kill squad after you. Said that you need to be put down like a—what were his exact words again..."

I lift my gaze to the ceiling and furrow my brows as if trying to recall his false words. "Oh yeah, *a dirty stray dog.*"

His swollen eyes don't leave me as he glares, but I don't flinch. I only hold his stare and take the moment to think of a next resort, another way to get him to spill the information I need.

A couple of ideas come to mind—most involving more blood loss—expect I really don't have much time, which means George has none. He's good, I'll give him that, but everyone has a breaking point, and in this line of work those points can either be family, money, pain, or betrayal.

Having free authorization has its advantages. But a huge disadvantage, no follow up info, and the use of an operator to feed me facts is unlikely. I have to think for myself. Improvise. Although, with the information I've been given, and from what I've observed thus far, I can get by.

A man like George Samberg doesn't seem to need money, pain is clearly not an issue, and he trusts Specter, because they bailed him out, countless times. But family? He has no family known. No wife, no children. But there *is* one anonymous person listed in his will. Continuing to play at that angle is the smartest route, because no one has no one. Even when they try.

I come up with an approach, each lie laying themselves out on my tongue ready to go. Yet just when the bad taste of them settles in my mouth, George drops his glare, deciding there's no bluff, then slowly closes his eyes.

"If I confirm, not saying I will, but if I confirm about who I met with, what happens next?"

I look him up and down, searching his face for the answer he wants, and when I find it, I grab a cup of ice, take his severed finger and stick it inside, then set it down next to him.

"You confirm, you live George. Plain and simple. No one else was in the room where this happened. You can go back to your boss, tell him who flipped, and maybe you'll even get to take care of the problem yourself." I step back to lean on the wall, and then divulge with extreme emphasis, "*Free authorization.*"

His purple eyelids gradually open. "And if I don't?"

My hand slides down to my ankle and I pull out a 35 Beretta. "If you don't, I can end this right now. Because like I said, I don't need to be keeping you alive."

One shaky deep breath later, I see the fight in him finally go out, and then, he talks. "They go by 'Foreman,' but I don't know all of the details." Briefly he stares down at his severed finger.

"All I know is that they've had help from the higher ups within Specter for years. Friends like Overseer and Vice that have control over agents and other resources."

I try to contain my new attention towards him and his every word while wondering out loud. "And the information you received?"

"Current ops, aliases, hidden locations, and some information about a secret operation. 'Echo Delta' they called it. But when it came to that topic, they militantly said to pass along the message not to worry about it. That it's being handled."

Fuck, I really wished Manager was wrong about that. Would've made my life from here on out a lot easier. Since he clearly wasn't though, that means that if there really was a message saying not to worry about it, something more must be going on even Manager hasn't caught onto yet. I sigh and bite my tongue. Finding all this out in one sitting is a whole bombshell in itself, but I sideline my dismay and sudden exhaustion.

"Tell me about this 'Foreman' character. Did you see their face, or catch any distinguishable features?"

"I gathered they're about six feet two inches, but other than that, they had on a full-face voice modifier mask, a big enough jacket that would hide any kind of body type, and each hand was covered with standard tactical gloves," is all George tells me, before claiming up.

Shit. Of course they wouldn't go to an in-person meet up without being fully covered from head to toe. As for the rest, my mind draws a complete blank. It's a different alias than before, but I'll have to check into that later, figure out if it's anywhere in the database. The thought of sorting that all out almost has me calling it quits for the rest of the night, though I quickly get my second wind, because now it's my turn to ask about his extensive banking information.

I've been waiting all night to bring it up, but I swore to myself I'd get the intel Manager needed first. That job is complete, so I've earned my share of info. And as I stare down at George's pathetic beaten face, I decide on a tactic that'll get him to answer my other more *personal* questions honestly, which involves the joy of scaring him further. I gently push my finger up against the device tucked in my ear, and then the now familiar voice of Bethany echoes inside.

"Agent 401 recognized. Commencing call."

A ring replaces her, and then a bored male voice.

"Ready?"

"Yeah, I'm ready. Back of the bar."

The man hangs up, and I smile down at George while pulling back the hammer on my Beretta. "Thank you, Mr. Samberg, for all your help this evening."

"What are you doing? I gave you everything I know, I swear!"

"Well, not everything. The money transferred into a bank account of yours about a month back, specifically the one located in Madrid, what was it for?"

"That wasn't a part of the deal!" he shouts.

I hold the gun between his eyes and match his tone. "It is now! What. Was. It. For?"

"Alright, alright! It was just a simple grab job, but I was only the driver. I didn't see who got in and I didn't see who got out. By the time I got there the person they snatched was already in the car."

A dry laugh comes from me. "Bullshit."

"Real shit. I was told to drive from one location in Jersey to another. Told that when I got to the second location to ditch the car and get into another that was already there waiting for me. I don't know anything else. It was an off the books favour. I don't ask, and then a day later the money comes to me."

"A favour for who?"

"I. Don't. Know. They call and I answer, that's the system."

Fuck my life. Just my luck to get Specter's drunk who probably gets into so much trouble that they have his balls on a leash. They say jump and he has to answer with 'how high this time?'

It could've been anyone in that car, especially when I don't know who the favour was for. It's a reach that Specter took my brother out of the blue—they don't even know I'm back—but I'm turning over every stone.

Except, with the only lead I had completely oblivious to who was in the trunk of that car, I'm back where I started a month ago. My brother's still out there and I have no clue where, though at least this time I have someone I can work out my frustrations on.

"Alright. Like I said, thank you," I then press the gun up against his skull. "But given your crimes against this country, and many others around the world, I find you a threat that needs to be neutralized Mr. Samberg."

He doesn't say a word, like he knew this was going to be the outcome either way. I was hoping he'd beg a little, but oh well. Maybe his silence is for the best. I won't have to hear any crude last remarks. Although, as I'm about to pull the trigger, I stop myself. *What am I thinking? A gun? That's too messy.*

I remove it from his forehead, and take in a sharp breath placing it back on my ankle while watching George breathe a breath of relief. It gets caught in his throat when he sees me pull out another knife. Small, sharp and slick, and being completely done with playing games, I kneel down and swiftly slide it in between his ribs. He lets out a small groan, then folds forward with the life gone from his eyes.

After a quick sigh I get up and start to pack my kit, only satisfied with *some* of the results I got. To me this mission is incomplete. Since I joined the project, any mission without getting closer to finding Dom always feels incomplete, but for some reason this one feels extra unfinished. A giant jigsaw with missing pieces. I hate having to solve puzzles with little information. But I do know someone who does love a challenge and would do anything for me. Okay, maybe not *anything.* Not anymore, but still, I should give her a call. *That old voice in my head.*

Done packing, I leave through the back, not staying for the cleaners, then slide into the standby car I had waiting for me. As the door closes the lights dim, and I throw my head back into the cool leather seat. In less than a second my eyes flutter shut, too tired to wait until I get home. But, before I completely go under, my brows weave together and I groan.

"What am I gonna wear tomorrow?"

CHAPTER NINE

THORN IN MY SIDE

Peeling my eyelids open, ripping away the tired, I stare into the darkness around me. The memory of pulling down all the blinds surfacing as my eyes adjust to the black. When they do, the ache of being conscience spreads throughout my body, and the thought of moving only dredges up the soreness that runs deep within my bones. Last night, hell even the night before, still clings to me. It shouldn't. I know it shouldn't, yet my patience seems to be running thinner and thinner with each empty lead. But I can't give up. I won't.

After a while—a short while—I roll onto my stomach, sigh, and then bury my face further into my pillow. It's so warm, the cocoon of blankets and solace I've made for myself, but despite my desperation to lie here forever, I have to get up. The stupid world needs stupid protection, and I'd rather not be left alone with my stupid thoughts for too long.

Slowly, my arms tuck themselves into my chest, and I breathe out all my newfound stress and frustration. I can feel every one of my limbs conspiring to keep me in bed. The only reason I don't give in, is the sharp recollection of my now extended mission, which reminds me I have to make a call. And on top of that, I have to find an outfit for this evening that says, 'I didn't spend all night torturing a man to get information about who's sneaking around giving out confidential material that could threaten world security.'

Shouldn't be too hard. I'll probably just wear a cardigan or something.

The thought of actually having to go out just makes me sink deeper into my comforter and more darkness surrounds my vision. I don't fight it. My head keeps telling me that I need more sleep in order to match pace with everyone else tonight, but what I really want is to cancel. I can't do that though... at least not again anyway. Who knew having a normal life would be so tiring. Having to keep up with friends and work, then friends again?

I'm not complaining—okay, maybe a little—but back in the days, when working for Unknown exclusively, I didn't keep friends that wanted to go out and do things. Most of the time I'd work for days on end, in cities and countries all over the globe, then go to whatever safe house I had to and wait until the next assignment came my way.

I was happy with that life for the most part, and it did come with certain... perks. Yes, there was the whole 'creating peace and fair justice thing', but I also got to experience something more. My entire body tingles, and before I can quickly dismiss what 'more' was, I drift into the memories—my will power to prevent it wrapped somewhere within my sleep deprived brain, then it all comes so fast. Swirls of images of being together, of lying in bed most of the day and night just to get our strength back from the last mission, and other... activities.

I move a bit deeper into the sheets, my head completely disappearing in them, and I close my eyes, just for a second, to let the vivid pictures of us being tangled up together creep past my barriers and slide into my mind.

That lingering cold from yesterday morning begins to spill into my blood, even under my warm blankets, as my memories play like a movie. One I've seen a hundred times before. Hands woven into mine, soft kisses on my neck, and if that isn't bad enough, I could've sworn I heard the faint whisper of him saying, 'I love you.'

Springing up from my bed, practically flying through the air, the actual cold hits my half naked body like an icy wave. *No. No, I'm not going down that stained pathway again. Not anymore.* I breathe in and out, quick and deep, as the black room spins around me. The pounding in my chest is so loud it throws off my sense of direction, but I hobble over to the wall. My cold fingers graze the light switch and when flicking it on, relief that I'm alone warms me.

I stand in the middle of my room, listening to the silence, my ears and face burning as if I'm ashamed. Maybe a part of me is, for letting myself sink so deeply into the past, but there's something else. Something still connected to those memories that's telling me I should be feeling otherwise. God, how did I go from picking out an outfit to thinking about 'his' lips on my skin so easily? It's like my heart and head are in an endless battle for some hidden truth, but one is stuck in a lie, and it's getting harder to distinguish which one it is.

I've lived with so many morphed versions of my life that I called normal, except this last month is the first time nothing feels like it makes sense. Like I can't figure out who I really am, or worse, who 'he' really was to me. But it doesn't matter anymore... right? I shake my head. I don't have time to waste on thinking about the past, even though it feels as if the story of 'him' and I isn't, or has never been, complete.

Snapping out of my own conflicted trance, refusing to face my demons this early, I reach for the robe hanging from my door and toss my arms through its fluffiness while setting my sights onto my bedside table. One wide step later, I'm back at my bed, then I plop myself down and slide the drawer open. A lot needs to get done today, so before letting my mind replay my complicated life story, I put my emotions on lock for now. Completely necessary to make sure I keep at least some of the sanity I have left.

I gently run my fingers along the sides of my drawer, searching for the micro-sized button, then pop! The faulty bottom comes loose, and I use my fingertips to grab the edges and remove the extra panel. Inside is my collection of burner phones that cover the leather bottom. I go through the handful of them, and after tossing a couple aside, I find what I need.

Moving the box from my lap, I take out a black velvet case about the same width and size of each burner and rub my thumb over its smooth exterior. Jewellery really isn't my thing, but as I open the box and stare at the diamond studs in awe, this particular piece is an exception. A special gift that was specifically made for me by the very friend I intend to contact. I place a thumb on each earring and wait for finger recognition to release the backings. Seconds later a slight click sounds, allowing me to insert the jewels in my ears. And as the gadget comes to life, the old, less realistic voice of Zoey greets me.

"Hello agent 401. Who would you like to contact this morning?"

"I need you to contact agent 500. Encrypted," I answer while heading over to my closet.

"Of course. One moment please."

Encrypted calls usually take about a minute to activate, considering their nature, and especially when the call is to one of the most precautious operation analysts in the world. While I wait, I go through my closet, activate the other doors, then step into my 'special' add on. I do my inventory check, confirming that I didn't make any rookie mistakes last night by leaving anything behind. When everything looks to be in perfect shape my call finally goes through. The greeting I was expecting though... goes so far left.

"What the fuck do you want!? I can't believe you have the balls to call me after what you did! Honestly, I—"

"Minnie, it's me! 4.0.1. Jesus," I interrupt shocked.

"Oh my gosh, I'm so sorry!" she laughs loudly, "I thought it said 6.01."

"Oh," I breathe a breath of relief, but the release gets caught in my throat when she only continues to yell.

"What the hell are *you* calling me for then? It's been three years since you left without a trace, but then I hear through the circuit that you've been back in the system for a month!? And you didn't contact me!? That's just cruel."

"With your skills, you could've found any time you wanted," I slightly tease her. Not being able to help myself.

"You really are a piece of–"

"I missed you too," I cut her off, meaning every word. "And I'm sorry M. Really, I am. But are you done? Cause I have a favour to ask," my words come out calmly, as I try to sooth her and fall back into the rhythm of our old friendship.

"Yes. I'm done." She takes a deep breath on the other end, "How have you been? Or more formally, what do you need?"

I leave my pristine room, and lock back each door all while maintaining a mellow and genuine tone. "I'm sorry I couldn't keep in touch, but we'll catch up later. For now though, I just need you to look up something for me, as well as keep me updated."

The light sound of her typing on her keyboard makes me smile, reminding me of old times. And just like old times, her voice carries so much interest. "What's the challenge?"

"Look up an alias on all Unknown databases that goes by 'Foreman.' It should ping up something from my mission report last night. Project Cloak and Dagger, Alpha 401. Subtitle, operation Echo Delta."

Last night's knife practice didn't concern me much after I got into the car, but the information did in fact mean something. The alias still doesn't ring a bell. We didn't come across anyone going by it when we first started the case. But right off the bat, I knew it had everything to do with my past dealings with operation 'Extraction Detail.' Manager's suspicions were right, but it was the look of despair in Samberg's eyes before he talked that gave me a serious confirmation chill that our mole is most definitely back. It also may be the fact that that case is my one and only mission

I failed, after seven years of service, and it somehow still haunts me.

I might've walked away but it still fucking haunts me, and I hate it. And with everything else I have going on, even just getting an alias associated with all the information being taken gives me a bit of hope.

"You got it," Minnie happily replies, breaking me out of my thoughts. "I'll get back to you as soon as possible."

"Thanks M," I say, yet before I hang up, I feel the need to ask— "and just out of curiosity, what happened with 601?"

She lets out a bitter laugh. "Bad date. *Very* bad date."

"We really need to catch up, don't we?"

"You have no idea," Minnie chuckles again before the line goes quiet.

Nothing but that silence fills the void between the earrings and my ear, and I soak it in. I close my eyes, trying to stop my brain from over thinking, but the silence around me only lasts for a minute. One perfect minute before my phone rings, with a completely different ringtone. *Totally forgot I changed it last night on the way home.*

'Shallow'—a song much too accurate—plays.

I race to answer the call, grabbing my phone, then swiping across the screen.

Rebecca speaks first with so much care. "Hey, how did everything go last night?"

Something warm spreads in my chest, and part of me appreciates it. The Michelle part. Before I reply I put away my demanding agent tone, then slip back into my new normal.

"Yeah," I clear my throat, "it was alright. Some not happy parties, but otherwise I got what I needed to do done."

"And your brother, he's okay? I hope you gave him a stern talking too."

My brother, my mind wanders off. *I have to find my brother.* I did plan on giving him a stern talking too, after giving him the biggest hug ever. Memories of him flood my mind, and everything I have to apologize for quickly follows. The weight of these unsaid apologies makes me belly flop back onto my bed and stare blankly at my dark sheets. *What could he be going through right at this very moment? He could be being beaten, or starved, or he could even be—*

Rebecca bursts my bubble of scary scenarios. "Michelle?"

"Sorry, I had a long night. But yeah, he's umm... he's fine now." I feel my mouth go sour as soon as the lie comes out, because the truth is, I have no idea.

It's your fault, the voice in the back of my head echoes, making the guilt grow. Dominic is the only thing I have left of my past life, well, a part I still need, and I can't lose him too. But my life, the path I chose, has always impacted him, so it's my fault, isn't it? I need to find him. I need—*no*, I cut myself off, *I'm not doing this*. Not right now.

"So, this celebration tonight, what's the dress code?" I ask while laughing dryly, forcing myself to change the subject as I wipe away a tear.

Hearing Rebecca let out a long stretched out 'well' on the other end of the phone only gives me a sense that I didn't know what I agreed to last night.

"Let's just go with... wear something comfortable," Rebecca snickers, which doesn't reassure me at all.

Well, shit. What did I get myself into?

Hours later, after Rebecca came to pick me up—completely vetoing my cardigan—I still don't hear anything back from Minnie. I try to ignore it, hoping it's not because all of it is bad news. And that became much easier to do when my day went from cool and slightly collected, to taking flaming line drop shots. I usually don't drink, but tonight I let the alcohol slide down my throat and into my stomach. I need to ease my mind a little, and besides, normal people don't have to worry about hoarding covert sub-level government secrets. Okay, maybe not the real ones I know. And I know a lot.

This retro nineteen thirties looking bar, is the third one we've been to. Excluding the movies, restaurant and karaoke. Only one window is in the entire venue, but it's lit up like time square with all the fairy lights hanging from the ceiling. It's pretty, yet still doesn't take my attention away from the sticky floor, the loud music, or the fact that it's so overcrowded I could've picked at least ten people's pockets just on the way to the bathroom.

As soon as we walked in, I was ready to call it a night, but Rebecca promised that this would be the last stop. Since then, I've been ignoring everything else but our little group, eating chicken wings, and smiling like a good friend.

And on that happy note our shots finally arrive and I stand and raise the small glass, hoping to go home after this.

"To Becca," I say as everyone else joins me in raising a glass, "who kicked ass in that presentation, and who restrained herself from strangling that short tempered basket case we call our boss."

"Here here!" Shane chimes in.

I laugh. "No, but seriously, I'm proud of you Becca. Congratulations."

We toss back the tequila and quickly grab our lime wedges to chase. The burning in my throat slightly subsides, then a warm satisfying tingle goes down my back. I sink into the feeling; let it carry me to a brief moment of untroubled solitude. There's nothing but me, the liquor, and the muffled sound of Stevie Wonder's 'Don't you worry 'bout a thing' to aid my coming buzz.

I breathe in deeply.

"Oh Michelle," Rebecca calls in a sing-song voice.

I open my eyes—not realizing I closed them—and slowly release my breath. She's staring at me with this... look. A smirk plastered on her glittery lips and raised brows, which immediately reads as mischievous. I don't like this, especially when I notice Shane and Theora staring too. What is it? It can't be anything bad if she's smiling like that, but as she lightly tilts her head, gesturing for me to look over my shoulder, I'm mistaken.

I turn, my gaze becoming sharp, and find a man leisurely coming up from behind. He was one of the many people I had seen when I scanned the place on the way in, so I know he's *definitely* not my type. Got the strong first impression of him being the controlling kind, and I'm not a girl who likes to be controlled, in *any* aspect.

"Ehi roba dolce," the brown-haired lanky man utters, trying to sound seductive.

(Hey, sweet stuff)

"I'm sorry, I don't speak Italian," I say with a giggle, going straight for the simple clueless dame routine.

I step back, though, despite moving away, he draws closer. From the corner of my eye, Shane steadily gets up and his shoulders loosen, like he's getting ready for a fight. As interesting as that would be to see, it'd be even more interesting if *I* showed this guy a taste of what I can do. But that probably wouldn't be the best way to end the night. No matter how much fun it'd be. Shoving aside the entertaining thought, I move over to the man, to deescalate the coming situation, but then, still not reading the room, when I get closer, he slightly sniffs the air around me.

"Puzzi come se sareb beavessi per colazione," he arrogantly remarks. *(You smell like you'd taste good for breakfast.)*

Oh hell no. I had enough of this shit last night.

Slowly, a sweet smile sets itself on my face and I shyly look away. I then lean into him and lift my lips up to his ear. He smells like rosemary soap and cinnamon. Not terrible, but I'm more focused on making sure he hears me perfectly clear as I reply in flawless Italian with all the threat I can muster.

"Esci da qui prima di farti male."

(Get out of here before you get hurt.)

He backs away slowly, confusion lining his features. I turn my back to him, fully thinking I handled everything without bloodshed. However, when a heavy hand suddenly grips my shoulder my blood heats with fury, and without hesitation, I act. Turning on my heel, I swiftly lift my right arm, swinging it hard until it collides with his, knocking his hand off me. Then, not giving him even a second to react, I spin until I'm behind him, and use my left hand to grab his neck and lightly slam his head down on top of the booth.

The music is so loud that the sound of his head hitting the wood is barely audible, though of course Shane, Rebecca, and Theora hear it. They jump in their seats, but I ignore their shock to enjoy every bit of the baffled terror on this man's face. I smirk while holding him down like a bad dog, and for a minute everything washes away as I lean *down* to his ear this time and whisper sweetly, so low only he'll hear me.

"Ti avevo avvertito ragazzone. Ora chiedi scusa e poi vai via." *(I warned you, big boy. Now apologize and then go away.)*

I let go of his throat, and while he rises, slowly, he rubs his neck, then puts his hands up in surrender. "Okay. I'm sorry," he stammers in crisp English and then nods. "Enjoy your evening."

Watching him leave, I wait until he's at a distance *I* feel comfortable with, then turn back to a table full of surprised expressions. They continue to gaze at me, but I disregard them, too busy praying they didn't hear me, and telling myself that that wasn't suspicious behaviour. After quickly exiting my own head, everyone blinks at the same time, and instantly my worry gets put to rest.

"That was awesome!" Rebecca shouts, and then pulls herself to the edge of her seat.

"Total brown belt move," Shane chuckles with a hand in his hair.

"What did you say to him?" Theora snickers, very dryly, like she's annoyed.

Faintly, I feel myself laugh, not being able to help it as I think of a lie. *I should slow down... but not just yet.* The thought comes as I slide into my seat and answer.

"I told him..." I trail for a second. "I told him I'm practising abstinence, and that I didn't appreciate him touching me."

Shane spits out his drink and laughs and Theora only turns her attention from me to give him a napkin. They go off in their own world after that. Rebecca though, she slides closer to me, another mischievous smirk turning up her lips before she adds her opinion.

"Well, are you?"

I choke on nothing and furrow my brows. "W-what?"

"What?" she shrugs. "I'm just curious, considering I've never seen you with a guy, you know... intimately for as long as I've known you. To me you might as well be a nun. I mean, did you ever—?"

The rest of the words coming from her mouth sound muffled as my heartbeat becomes so loud it fills my ears.

I feel sick.

We've never talked about this before. I don't know how, but we just never have, and honestly, I've been *more* than fine with that. My dating history has been... complicated... to say the *very* least. But none of that compares to what I had with 'him.' Or what I thought I had.

Shit, I'm spiralling for no reason. I need to calm down. I need another drink. Actually, what I really need is—I hear Shane tell Theora 'hold on a second'—a distraction.

"What are we talking about over here?" he interrupts, leaning against Rebecca, smirking.

For a moment I think I'm saved, so much so that I blow out a light chuckle. But, when they both continue grinning and don't look away, or laugh with me, my smile drops. "Uh uh. No," I wave over a waiter, "I need two more please."

They nod and hurry towards the bar. I sigh, already thinking of more liquor sliding down my throat, yet when I come face to face with Shane and Rebecca again, it's Theora who changes the subject on my behalf.

"So, Becca," she scoots over a bit, placing both hands on Shane's lap while pressing her body onto him, "did you tell your parents about your promotion yet?"

The question brings all her focus to Theora, and she obviously has Shane's attention, what with her breasts practically morphing with his arm. He stares at her with so much love, among other things. I tune them all out while Rebecca answers her. Then, with all the liquor I've consumed somehow going straight to my brain, I can't help but think about what Rebecca was saying.

I hate that she's right, which is probably the most annoying thing. And now because of her, and her veracious observations, the mental nostalgia of 'him' seeps into my brain all over again.

I suddenly feel his tender touch on my hot skin, even when knowing full well that he's not next to me. But it doesn't stop the memories. Of how he'd always hold me a certain way that made me feel safe, through long days or even longer nights. And his kiss—I attempt to stop thinking but trying only pulls me deeper. His kiss could make me forget any alias at that time. Making me only want to be the person I was when I was with him.

A warm sensation, and the gradual tempo of that stocker-ish Police song, forces me back into my surroundings. Then, and only then, do I realize that my face is hot, and my eyes have started to water.

Violently shaking my head to rid myself of emotion, as I blink back the unexpected tears before they fall, the gesture immediately comes to a halt when tenseness forms in my body. My eyes are drawn to the bar. I don't know why at first, the reason getting away from me for a minute, but then the feeling finally sets in. A feeling I don't like at all. The one where I'm being watched. Like I said, a lot of people are crowded in here—it is Saturday after all—but I can still detect a specific lingering eye.

It's not like it's the first time this week, although here, it's followed by a more dangerous presents. I stagger a bit while heading over to where my suspicion remains the most, though my wobbly mission becomes stalled when I'm blocked by the waiter coming over with the drinks I forgot I had ordered.

Instead of pushing past him, I decide to shake it off and focus on celebrating Rebecca, hoping it's just my tipsy brain playing tricks to distract me. So, despite wanting to drink away my bitter sweet memories, I throw back one last drink, then cut myself off completely. Luckily though, my decision comes right when I got this really good buzz going. Rebecca however, as my eyes wander over to her, is beginning to sway. She can surprisingly hold her liquor, which isn't a good thing. To me it just means she doesn't know when to stop.

"Becca," I tap her on the shoulder and calmly suggest, "You should get some water or something."

Now, given all the drinks I've had, I can confidently say that all my senses are working pretty well. I can still smell the honey garlic chicken wings on the table. My sight isn't blurred. I can definitely taste the lime still lingering on the back of my tongue, and the cool leather under me feels amazing. So, when I hear Rebecca scoff at me, then try to take another sip from her empty margarita glass, I can't do anything but snort.

"Did you just pull out the 'leave me alone, mom' attitude?"

"Yup." She then blinks slower than usual. "I'm fine, Elle. I can even walk in a straight line if you want. See?" She gets up from the stool, but I don't even have to be completely sober to know that she's going to fall on her face.

I spring into action before she falls, catching her by the arm and pulling her back up onto the chair. I may have gotten up too fast—my vision ever-so-slightly going blurry, and my stomach flipping just a tad. When everything settles and goes back into focus, Rebecca is staring at me with confusion in her light brown eyes.

"What just... what just happened?"

I take a sip of water to flush out my last bit of wooziness. "You tried to stand to prove a point," I answer with a slight mockery on my breath.

"Yeah, maybe I should umm..." she starts to slightly slur her words, "wait, where's Shane and Theora?"

"I'm not sure I really want to know. But I think we should find them—preferably *before* any clothes get taken off—and get going."

Rather slowly, I stand and twist my head around to see if I can spot them in the sea of bodies. For a moment, everything sways to one side of the room, and I start to regret my decision to drink at all. But whichever reason I had decided on officially, clearly the drinking helped, because I can't remember why.

Focusing on my buzz seems like the smarter thing to do instead of figuring that out. I lean into it as much as possible, and then everything turns upright again. Feels a lot better, especially after I blink like a strobe light going off and let out a thin breath.

"Are we ready to go?" Theora strolls up out of nowhere, speaking perfectly clear.

I don't answer her. I don't know why I don't answer her. Maybe it's because I don't really like her. It's not that I don't like her, it's just... she reminds me of a fake persona. The persona I'm being right now, not the persona that I was being last night. The real me. Or is this new persona the new real me? Did that just make sense? I'm sure it did in a way. I get kind of lost when I drink. My mind tends to wander. Hence why I don't drink that much, or at all. Opening my mouth to answer, my brain finally decides to put together a simple sentence.

"Yeah, we should get a cab," I announce as clearly as I can.

"I left my car a couple of blocks back though," Rebecca complains and then goes to take another sip from her empty glass. I take it from her.

"We can get it tomorrow," Shane tells her.

"It's not a sweater, Shane, it's my *car*."

"Well, none of us can drive, *Rebecca*. What did you think was going to happen?"

He steps closer, starting to get a little more aggressive. He's not necessarily a mean drunk, but I know that if he feels provoked in anyway, like earlier, he can switch that very quickly. I move in between them and face Rebecca.

"We can get it tomorrow, okay?" I repeat Shane's words, but with much less attitude.

Rebecca steps out from in front of me and walks to the exit, side eyeing Shane while she does. "Fine, but he needs to get out of my face."

"I'm choosing to ignore that!" he shouts after her. Theora pinches him and grabs his shirt, pulling him towards the door.

It takes me a minute to register that we were leaving, to the point where I have to speed walk to catch up with everyone. When I do get outside, the cold is almost enough to sober me up a bit. Yet that feeling of being followed returns. I twist from side to side, examining the street, but when I find no one out of place enough to raise suspicion I get into the cab.

The drive is quiet all the way back to Rebecca and Shane's building, only the hum of the meter there to sooth my already coming headache. It's nice, and for a minute, I don't want the moment to end. Where I'm just tipsy in a cab with my friends, not a care in the world, except for wondering whether or not I'll throw up later. Where I can just watch the city lights pass me by, and drink in my mundane yet beautiful surroundings. But the moment comes to its inevitable end when we get to their place.

Rebecca turns to me. "You wanna crash on my couch for the night?"

"No, I'm good," I reassure her. "I'll get home fine."

"You sure?"

I smile. "Yes."

"Alright." She smiles back then pulls me into a hug. "Thank you so much for coming out tonight. It was fun to see you drink for the first time, and it was especially fun to see you slam that guy's face on the table," she laughs.

"No problem," I hug her back. "I'm here to entertain."

While letting her go, she playfully hits me in the arm and hops out of the cab. Shane is the next one to ask me if I'll get home alright. I give him the same answer. But, when it comes to Theora asking me the identical question, I wonder why she's leaving, though I quickly piece together she must be spending the night with Shane before her trip tomorrow. I thought its sweet she asked, yet for some reason I still have to hold back the urge to give her attitude. I keep my mouth shut, smile, and nod in her direction.

"Call if anything is wrong. And call when you get home, okay?" she adds before closing the door.

I raise my hand to my head, feeling the air pressure from the slam, and the throbbing doesn't get better when the driver practically yells.

"Where to ma'am?"

Coming to realize that he's obviously talking to me, I slowly raise my head and look around to see what street we're on before answering.

"Just drive straight till I say, please."

He swiftly nods then faces forward again, and I lean back into the cold fabric seats, staring out the window. For a minute it's like I'm seeing the neighbourhood again for the first time. All the house lights are still on, and in the window, I can see all the people just being... people. Sure, they have their own worries and fears, but underneath all that, they have their version of normal. A certainty that them just being them, living the way they are, is good enough.

I envy that sometimes, when I have the nightmares, or when those guilty voices in my head remind me of what I've done to survive. It makes me to wonder if any life will be enough for me, especially when I get excited about both types. The normal and the dangerous.

"Here's good!" I accidently shout when I rise, realizing what street we're on. *The ride didn't feel that long.*

The cab comes to a screeching halt and I hold out my hands to stop from hitting the passenger seat in front of me.

"That's twenty-four fifty," the driver more demands while sticking his hand out.

I give him the money and slide out of the car. When he drives off, I glance at my surroundings to make sure I can make my way home, but also to see if I have a stocker. I opted to be dropped off just a block away. That sense of being followed hasn't let up since I first left the bar we started at. I admit though, I probably should've stopped drinking then, but I didn't want to spoil the mood, and it would've risen suspicion between everyone.

But now, I'm alone. If anyone is following me, they won't be able to get to anyone but me. I begin walking down the street as straight as I can, and I'm pretty proud of myself considering I don't stumble once. However, my focus is slightly interrupted by a light buzzing on my earlobes. *You were expecting a call dumbass*, the rather rude logical voice in my head reminds me. I swear I'm never drinking again after this. Totally regret it, but at least I'm just tipsy. Like a responsible adult.

Reaching up to press on the diamond studs while they vibrate, I pray that Minnie is calling with some good news. I stall in answering, turning my head side to side again, checking for anyone, but nothing so far. With the coast clear, I click on my earrings, confirm with finger recognition, and the minute I'm cleared I'm already listening to the familiar voice of my old friend. Listening. Not entirely understanding though.

"Hello? Did you hear what I said?" Minnie asks, sounding a bit insulted.

"Actually, no. Can you do me a favour and talk *very slowly please*?" I whisper to her.

"Why? Is everything okay? Is someone there with you?"

"No, I'm just a little... inebriated."

"No fucking way!"

My fingers weave themselves into my hair as I grab my head in pain. "What did I just say?"

"You really have changed, haven't you?" she snickers, "I don't think I've ever even *seen* you take a real sip of–"

"Yeah, I know, and it's never happening again, okay?" I huff out but then quickly adjust my sharp tone. "Can you please just tell me what you found?"

Typing on her keyboard, every stroke slightly making me flinch, Minnie lightly laughs again and mumbles, "Wow, you're a snippy drunk, aren't you? Why don't you just take a S.U.P?"

"I—wait, a what?" I knit my brows together as I turn a corner, seeing my building ahead.

"A 'Sober.Up.Pill.'" Minnie dryly answers, still typing away. "Sorry. We make up acronyms to pass time here."

"Oh. I forgot it, I guess."

"Well, that's too bad. Anyway," the click-clacking of Minnie's keys finally comes to a halt, "I've got a big fish for you."

I begin to walk a bit slower when I see the front door to my building, then I take in a quick breath, preparing myself for what she found.

"Reel it in."

"Okay, so, I did a complete database search for the alias you gave me."

"Foreman," I remind myself.

"Yes. Now, it did ping up your mission report from last night, but that's the only mention of it... anywhere."

"I figured as much. I didn't recognize it from when I worked on the operation three years ago." I sigh. "But who would be stupid enough to keep the same alias?"

Opening the door, I give a slight smile to the security guard and nod. Immediately I regret it. Everything in the lobby starts to lean to one side, like I'm doing a cartwheel, though I'm pretty sure I'm not. The ground feels like it's not there. I widen my eyes and then stomp my foot, just to reassure myself that I'm for sure standing on the marble floor.

The feel of my heel slightly pushes my foot upwards from the force of my stomp forces me to finally get a grip. I balance myself, waiting for the elevator while Minnie continues in my ear.

"Yeah..." she says, her voice coming out hesitant, "but I just find it odd that this person is like a ghost in our system. Especially since information has technically been being stolen from the agency for a month now, and yet—"

I swallow my yell, as to not inflict a worse headache. Instead, I breathe out sharp and fast, then murmur. "What did you just say?"

"To help fill in some of the gaps that were in Samberg's statement, I went looking for exactly what information was missing. I started with the Echo Delta files, but when I got close enough, a virus tried to lock me out of the system. Programmed by some hotshot hacker with some lame phantom signature. Of course I went right through it, but when I did, I found that nothing was missing."

The elevator doors I didn't notice were open begin to close, but before they do I stick my foot in the way. And as I stuff myself inside, I wait until the lobby disappears behind the silver. When I feel like I'm truly alone for the first time tonight, I gently rub my forehead.

"I don't understand."

"It wasn't missing because—as the backdoor metadata shows—it was only copied so no alarms would go off, which is what the virus let the user do. Now, it wasn't done with a USB, thank god, so I managed to trace the IP address that the copied info was sent to, and that led me to one of Specter's WGCG offices in Tokyo. I'm not even sure if Manager or anyone knows this yet, but yeah, given the dates, Specter's been receiving copied classified files from the mole for a little over a month. They just haven't used any of it until three days ago, which was a tip off about some shipment."

Her words do go in one ear and get processed, but the only thing I grasp, to make sure I heard correctly is the time frame. I slowly step out of the elevator, my expression and tone ghostly as I repeat, "A little over a month? But that's..."

"Approximately how long your brother has been missing, I know. And the deeper I go, the more I notice that pretty much all of this started a month back. The implanted virus that allowed the mole to copy and send information, your brother's disappearance, and your somewhat *clandestine* reinstatement into the agency."

My feet move without me giving them the okay, walking towards my apartment, to my bed. The one thing I'm able to control is the flustered look that seems stuck to my face, and in the moment, I've never wished so much to be sober more than right now. Only about half of what Minnie is saying is getting through to my brain, which causes questions to which I have no answers, to run through my mind.

Does any of this factor into my brother going missing now? How does Manager or any of the other higher ups not know about any of this, and who is the leak inside Unknown? Oh god, I swear my brain just slapped me for trying to think, and for officially killing my buzz. I need a minute. *You need sleep, the logical voice echoes somewhere in my mind. I shake away my fear and confusion.*

"Okay, here's what I'm going to do M, I'm going to sleep. I mean..." I squeeze my eyes shut, then fix my wording, "I mean I'm going to sleep *on this*. But I think it's best you update Manager about everything, and *only* Manager. I trust him. I'll contact you tomorrow as soon as I'm up."

"Alright, I'm on it. But are you okay? This is a lot, even for me. And I know you didn't talk about your brother much, but from what you've told me about him—"

"I'm fine, thanks," I politely cut her off. "I just need a minute."

She sighs. "It's no problem. I'll check in with you later."

She's the one to hang up, but I find myself slowly raising my hands to my ears anyway. I touch the diamonds in my earlobes, and I don't blink for a while, afraid I might forget everything she just told me if I do. That sounds crazy, but it makes me feel better. Something has to make me feel better about all this, because if not, well then, I'm screwed. Screwed in so many ways that I don't even know where—I try to relax and go over what Minnie said again. And only when I'm one hundred percent sure I've remembered everything do I finally blink and let my arms dangle at my sides.

Deep breath in.

Deep breath out.

I come back to reality, and briefly close my eyes to steady my heartbeat while reaching for my keys. The lock seems so far away from me. I don't know how, but I manage to get the jagged thing into the tiny slot. And as I turn my key, I hear every spring and driver pin click. I quickly force the door open to make it stop. It swings with my body on it, and an overwhelming smell of sweet hits my nostrils.

Great, now I want chocolate.

Ever-so-softly I close my door, and upon locking it, I drop my coat from my shoulders, gently take off my shoes, and let my bag fall from my arm. The warm in my apartment welcomes me home, and the sweet smell reminds me of a scent I can't place, but it's nice.

I want chocolate, I think again.

I ignore my sudden craving and spin around to toss whatever's in my hand onto the kitchen counter. But, as soon as I turn, my body goes numb. The sound of my keys dropping from my grip does nothing to faze me. Not even the icy shiver going down my spine or my stomach dropping to the floor can move me from my state.

How is this... this isn't... oh my god. My eyes are practically out of their sockets as I stare out at what's in front of me.

All I see, all that fills my vision, is a sea of red roses.

Holy shit. He found me.

Everything in my soul tells me to run, but my feet are stuck to the ground with my eyes still surfing over all the red. There must be over two hundred. Two hundred red roses standing tall as they cover my living room floor and lead into my hallway.

I scan over each and every one of them until my gaze finally lands on a white card sitting on my couch. That's the only thing that manages to get me moving again. My breath catches in my throat, the sweet smell still invading my senses. As I reach the couch, I cautiously grab the card.

I want chocolate, my mind says to me for a third time.

Sudden rapid breaths help me build up the courage to open the card. While disregarding the somewhat soothing candy air again, I violently shake as I look it over. It's in 'his' handwriting, making all this *so much* worse. I read it over and over again, to the point where I almost hear it in his voice.

Roses are white, violets are blue. Though my rose is red, and it bleeds because of you. Hi Kitten. We need to talk. ☺ P.s. You look great. Xoxo, E.

No. This isn't happening. I...

My mind goes blank as I black out for no more than half a second. My mind repeats its comment on the sugary aroma, *it smells so good in here*, but then my stare shift to the roses littering my floor. They go from the flowers to the card, and I gradually lift my suddenly heavy head.

"Oh fuck," I slur as I only now comprehend what the un-located intoxicating smell is.

Without even realizing it, my body has become completely relaxed and my eyes start to go in and out of blurriness. I push my dizzy body towards the door, trying to recall how long I've been inside, but it's too late. The roses masked the chemical just enough for me not to notice. And now, one by one, all my senses begin to shut down, giving in to the chloroform I've been breathing into my lungs.

I shouldn't have drank. My mind tends to wander when I drink.

Feeling myself tip over, I try to grab onto anything to brace my fall. Finally submitting to the heaviness, my eyes close and I still experience myself dropping. For some reason I never hit the ground. And the last thing I hear before completely blacking out, is the whisper of a familiar voice.

"Such a thorn in my side."

CHAPTER TEN

WHAT DOESN'T KILL YOU

"Shit," I groan.

A deep crease forms in my brow as I raise a hand to cradle my pounding head, but the motion only causes a sudden fiery pain to come to my wrist. I open my eyes, feeling the weight of every slow blink I take, and everything is a blur. The ache around my hand is enough to distract me from the haze though. I lift my head to locate the source of the sting.

As my vision comes back into focus, the sight of my right hand tied to my bed post makes me flinch back. My heart races as I struggle against the tight rope, every movement causing more pain. I force myself to stop, coming to grips that I'm making things worse, then attempt to calm my nerves.

"Okay relax, just relax. Don't struggle."

Okay, well that's not helping.

The redness I see forming around my wrist is the only reason I stop moving. I need to stay calm, to think of what to do next without hurting myself more than I already have. I take a breath, and it starts to work, but it comes out in an uneven shake when all of last night's events start to dance around my memory. Going out, drinking, Minnie's information, the red roses and... 'him.' With that memory resurfacing, immediately I feel his touch lingering on my skin, like he's still holding me, and that shiver returns twice as cold.

What if he's still here? What if he—no. No, this isn't the time to spiral. I need to find him before he finds me. Again.

Fuck. How stupid can I be? I should've followed up with my suspicions on Friday.

"Okay, wait," I grumble, hoping to make thinking about him come to a screeching halt.

My neck swings from side to side, my hair following as I look for anything to cut myself loose, and so I'll have a fighting chance if he's still here. I let my free hand glide along the beam that holds up my bed until it snags on a pea sized switch. When flipping it, a side panel opens, revealing just a few weapons and small gadgets nestled into a foam tray. *This is a perfect time to be thankful for my paranoia.* I grab what looks like a simple tube of lipstick, but when popping off the lid and twisting the bottom, instead of the waxy cosmetic, I hold a CO2 laser in my hand. One careful slice later, I free my bruised wrist from the coarse rope and jump to my feet.

That was a bad idea.

The room spins in small circles, and my knees slightly give out, but I manage to grab onto my bed before completely falling over. I tightly close my eyes to let the spinning run its course. Then, when it's over, I carefully get up, desperate not to make the same mistake I just did. And as I start to get some of the feeling back in my legs, I take the Glock seventeen from the panel and grip it until my knuckles turn white—both from fury, and forcing down my nausea as I tip toe out of my room. The sweet smell that led to my downfall has vanished, and coming into the hallway, I'm surprised to find not a single rose. In fact, my place looks much cleaner than how I left it.

He's still a clean freak.

I stop myself from smirking at the thought, not wanting to remember any little detail about him, especially one that I loved. Instead, I focus on the deep feeling in my gut that wants to hurt him while searching the rest of my apartment very thoroughly. No one is here—not anymore at least. I let my arm drop down to my side, but never loosen my grip on my gun.

Not wasting another second with rage, memories, or the question of why I'm still alive, I race back to my room. I push past all my security measures and hidden doors, change from last night's clothes, and then grab the bug out bag labelled 'BREAKAWAY PROTOCOL 2'. There's no telling how long I'll need to run, but before I go, I need to find out how the hell this bastard found me.

By the time I get downstairs and into the underground parking garage, only when I come upon my car and see my reflection do I notice the dim light coming from my earrings. I didn't get the chance to take them off. It flashes quickly in Morse code, repeatedly blinking the same letters. M.E.S.S.A.G.E. I don't stop to listen to it yet as I place my hand under the car handle and wait for it to scan my fingertips.

The door pops open and I jump in and throw my bag into the passenger seat. The layer of dust inside forces out a deep cough from my lungs. But, considering it hasn't been driven it almost a year, I disregard the grime. As I drive off, a new level of determination circulates through me, and I use it. All of it. Channelling it towards hating him and getting to the Winery to find out what the hell is going on.

The upgraded car takes the wheel as I sit back and listen to Minnie's message. Every red light that causes the car to roll to a stop gives me slight road rage, each slowing me down from finding out the truth.

Deep breath in.

Deep breath out.

I relax—to an amount I'm sure is the best I can do—then play Minnie's message.

"Hey N, I hope everything is okay. You didn't pick up, but I just figured you're sleeping off all those drinks. It's probably not the best idea to leave a voice mail, even on the encrypted earrings, but I'm going to risk it considering the information I found is important." The sound of typing fills the void of her silence, then, she speaks again.

"So last night I stayed late to find out as much more as I could, but then, only an hour after our conversation, I got an alert from our backdoor server security system. Someone tried to access more files again, including some from Echo Delta through another virus. Now, I managed to fire wall their asses, but before I could find out whose user Id they're using to access the non-corruptible files, in our supposably secure hard drive, they scrubbed their tracks."

A deep sigh comes from her before the rest of her words are done in a whisper.

"Look, this *Foreman* person is definitely someone within the agency, but the viruses they're using seem much to advanced. They must be getting help from a very skilled programmer on the other side. I'm going to keep digging on this end, but you need to stay safe. This isn't only about Echo Delta, but I'm sure that whoever this 'Foreman' person is, they're just getting started with trying to eliminate anything or anyone that has to do with it, or the agency for that matter."

The message ends as I pull up to the winery. My mouth hangs open. Everything's becoming more cluster fucked than I thought possible, especially when I never got back into this world to find a mole. All of this is for Dominic, but the longer I stay, the more I'm starting to realize that the two *may* go hand in hand.

I pray that that's just my paranoia acting up. I sit quietly while my car spins down into the office, allowing myself one moment to think about the questions I've tried not to ponder all morning. *Why didn't he kill me last night? And how long has he known my whereabouts?*

"Esto es mucho para mi," I think out loud and sigh.

(This is too much for me)

I can't let it get to me. Not when people I care about still aren't safe.

Reaching the ground floor, I hop out of the car while it's locking into place and ignore everyone and everything. I move in a brisk strut to the first free computer I see and tell the people sitting next to me on both sides to get lost. They timidly scurry away, and when I'm sure I'm free of prying eyes, I tilt my head up and try to think of what to search for first.

A thought comes and my head drops down to the glow of the floating screen. It's not the best idea, but it's necessary. My hands slide across the keyboard, typing in log in information that's not my own. No. I enter the system using a password I... acquired during my meeting with Manager. A silent alarm goes off, but luckily no one is around to hear it.

Damn. I forgot about the facial recognition.

"Agent 401, you are attempting to sign in using a superior's identification. Would you like to continue, knowing that this superior will be informed?" the male voice asks, as if I'll gladly answer yes.

Quickly, I call Minnie. When she picks up, I speak fast. "I'm on a computer at the winery, and I need you to buy me some time with using a superior's log in."

She answers me just as quick. "Who is it?"

"Manager."

"Alright," she types on her keyboard at a new kind of speed. "I can buy you ten minutes before the server's security blocks me out. Starting now."

The screen in front of me glitches once before displaying a picture of Hello Kitty made of ones and zeros on a multi-coloured split screen. Then, when the image straightens out, I'm seeing Manager's desktop. "Thank you," I swiftly mumble.

"Ten minutes N," Minnie warns and then hangs up.

Dragging my finger across the screen as fast as I can, I go to the main file search engine and type in one name. Mine. The system springs to life as file after file pops up. It may have been too broad of a search. I narrow it down by typing my name and a specific date. The day after I left the agency.

What comes up takes all the air from my lungs as I gasp. There are logs on everything I've done for the last two years. But even above that—only a month after I retired—the agency started keeping tabs. A lot of the time stamps were way off, some were very close, but ultimately it makes me shake.

Just as I'm about to lose my shit, a picture labelled 'most recent' catches my eye. It's a snapshot in time I vividly remembered. It's me, in front of my apartment, just two days ago. I stand up, a jolt of fear and anger springing into my legs. This is the exact same day I started feeling 'off' and I couldn't shake it. The same day that that cold began to linger around me, and the same day I thought about 'him' more than I have in the last two years.

I thought he stopped; thought he gave up. But he's been searching for me all this time?

I didn't know why, but now, it's all so clear. That chill I felt was his eyes on me from Friday, and like an idiot I just wrote it off as paranoia, trying to make myself feel better. I dip my face closer into the screen, like I could go back to that moment and fix my mistake. But then, when I notice a familiar van in the background, slowly I sit back down.

'Two minutes,' a text from Minnie reads in my ear, so I hurry.

Zooming into the picture, I see 'him' in a black four by four about five cars down from me, but I shouldn't be able too. He's in the picture. He's not supposed to be in the picture if he's taking it. I zoom closer until I'm seeing directly into the slight reflection of the glass door to my building. And then, all my attention turns to the van across the street. I've seen it before, here, on one of the storage floors when passing through the underground levels.

It's an Unknown van, but why are they following me, and how did I not realize it? Heat rises in my cheeks, and my body slightly begins to shake, but I keep it together. I can get more answers, more recent ones regarding my apparent surveillance. Just as I'm about to deepen my search, I get another text from Minnie.

'Ten seconds left. Log out now!'

"Damn it," I curse while my fingers move across the keys. Then, when the holo-monitor vanishes, I'm left staring into the empty air.

Nothing but my reflection stares back at me, as my gaze falls to the metallic polished desk, and the world around me seems to melt away and turn into my worst nightmare. But this time, I'm awake.

My feet are planted on the same pathway I've been on a million times, and the scent of freshly spilt blood invades the air around me once more, completely drowning out what would've been the sweet smell of white roses. It's a bitter thought.

A loud bang takes my attention. It doesn't rattle me, but I do stand ready to fight. The right choice I'll find out soon. For now though, as he pokes his head out from the damp house, I fall for his innocent face for just a second, but no longer than that. I was a much more ruthless killer back then, back before I settled down and left that world behind.

But prior to getting out of the game completely, there was one more. One last job I had to take care of. It was going to be hard to leave it all behind, especially with the rush I was about to feel, but I was done. And I knew it was going to break him, leaving, but then again, he broke me first. In our line of work none of this should've happened in the first place. Falling in love was just as dangerous as pulling a trigger, and with what we do, it was worse when it came to family.

But I swear I didn't know.

Not until it was too late.

When I realized who my last target was—after my curiosity got the better of me—I didn't tell him. I couldn't. He wouldn't have understood, even when I know he knows that your life becomes nothing when you piss off the wrong people. Even with that knowledge, he wouldn't want to hear it.

In the moment, I was brutal, I realize that now, I didn't then. Honestly, the original plan was to finish the job fast. No blood or mess, but he wasn't going down without a fight. So, in the end, it did take spilling red to finish my job.

I took a breather to admire the beautiful white roses blooming all down the stony pathway. But next to his body, a full patch was covered in his blood. Red roses. There was something poetic about it, like both of my worlds colliding. I leaned over to pick one of the blood-soaked flowers then tossed it on his body. Though little did I know, that that small gesture, the last sweet tribute to my past, would show me the truth. It landed perfectly on his chest, right next to something peeking out of his inner pocket.

That's when curiosity took over, and then horror quickly followed. His wallet, and inside of course was a driver's licence. It was next to a worn-out picture, but not so much that I couldn't recognize the boy he had his arm around. Now though, he was a man. The same man that had taken my heart, only to break it just hours ago.

Oh god, I thought, what did I do?

I knew though. Just like I knew I couldn't fix it. It was the first thought when I heard the slight shuffle of feet from behind. Turning, I had wished it was not who I'd been thinking of all day, but that wish did not come true.

It was him, mouth wide open in shock. I looked him up and down, trying to find a way to apologize, yet just the sight of his face again, after all he had said to me, to break me, only a cold stare replaced my regretful gaze. Even as I began to walk over to him—his eyes pulling me in—it stuck to my face. Before he could pull me in all the way though, my earpiece came alive.

My feet stopped short in the stone as I reported my mission's completion, then gave the coordinates to the cleaners. In all that time, my stare stayed in his direction, and his eyes stayed glued to mine. As much as I wanted to look away I knew I couldn't. Because if I did, I never would've made it out alive.

We stared for what felt like forever, that is, until he made the first move. I put my hand on the gun I hated to use, but only because he took out his. Instead of firing at me though, he removed the clip, popped out a single bullet, and placed it on the ground in front of him.

I knew exactly what it meant, and a small part of me respected it. The business part. But the part that used to love him, the part that was engaged to marry him hours ago, broke in two all over again. He slowly backed away, never taking his eyes off me as he did, then disappeared into the night. All I could do was walk my separate way. My heart thumped, as if trying to tell me to go after its other half, but I ignored the pain. All of it wouldn't matter in a couple of hours anyway, because I'd be gone by then. Never to be found again. Especially not by him.

It was my time to go. I was done.

The sense of someone falling into step behind me pulls me out of the chilling memory, and I spin around while drawing my gun. My chair falls back, the quick motion causing it to bang loudly onto the floor, and the threat of tears sting my eyes. One by one, like violent waves rocking a boat side to side, the emotions from that night hit me, hard. The affection, the rage, and the heart stopping sadness.

It all comes back, clouding my judgement, even as my gaze lands on Manager, who stands unafraid in front of me. I have no idea how long he's been there, just staring, with the most disapproving look engraved into his features, but I couldn't care less. The memory still lingers yes, yet my rage isn't from that dark display. It's much more recent than that.

"Whoa, agent, it's just me alright? Put the gun down," Manager officially announces himself, but I don't move a single muscle.

Fury oozes from my voice as I blink back more tears. “What the fuck is happening here!? I saw everything Manager, every file. He’s still been looking for me all this time, and you knew? *And* you had people following me too!?”

Seeing his eyes drift to the other guns I know are surrounding me, my anger only grows. “No! You don’t look at them, you look at me!” I yell. “What. The hell, is happening Manager?”

He slightly shakes his head, gently raises his hand, and then gestures for the agents and security behind me to lower their weapons. He then takes a step forward.

“We can talk about this calmly, but you need to put the gun down. Now,” he demands, his coarse voice threatening yet soothing at the same time.

Another step forward and I still don’t act, my head partially stuck in the old memory. My old mistake. My shock. The only reason my hands don’t shake is because I was trained too well. My finger isn’t even on the trigger. I have no intention of shooting him. Something I’m sure he already knows. When I don’t lower my weapon though, Manager’s face shifts from disapproving to pissed as he keeps coming towards me.

Honestly, I need him to take the gun from me, because with everything floating around in the air, I can see myself making a bad decision real soon. Manager, after one wide step, stares down the barrel of my gun for about two seconds before grabbing it from my hands. He then forcefully takes me by the arm. His grip practically drags me along, like I’m a child being taken to the principal’s office, but I shake him off when we get inside.

“Sit your ass down!” he sternly mutters.

As I collapse into one of his worn leather chairs, Manager slams the door shut, and I’m left to face his frown and fuming stare.

“What the fuck is the matter with you!? You—” he cuts himself off, sighs, and then drops his head into his hand.

"Look, I know you're pissed and frustrated about your brother, but that doesn't mean—"

"This has nothing to do with my brother!" I interrupt.

He snaps his head up to face me again. "Watch your tone in my office, agent," he says with that raw anger I haven't heard since we first met, and it's just as intimidating.

I sit up as straight as my back will allow, feeling like the teen I was when I first started at the agency. The one who made the wrong first impression by falling out of a window—after getting into a fight with one of the other recruits, and landing on top of his new car. Back then I didn't know better, but now, seeing me straighten, Manager takes in a sharp breath and lets out a light curse before addressing me again, this time with a little more patience.

"I'm assuming that you're referring to one of our teams tailing you and keeping tabs?" he nonchalantly discerns. Though before I can share my opinion on the subject, he swiftly raises his finger and stops me from protesting.

"All cards on the table—choosing to overlook you impersonating a superior to obtain that information—you were flagged the minute you became reactivated, given your past work with operation E.D."

"Why would I be flagged if the operation was considered closed? And the missing information wasn't discovered until *I* had Minnie dig deeper and send it over to you."

"Don't flatter yourself. It was just a precaution considering at the time the mole we *supposedly* caught came from Echo Delta, and the possibility of an accomplice was discussed. We had everyone involved watched. But, when you came in and told me about your brother's disappearance, I chose to take you at your word. Others, however, weren't convinced. Said that it was too 'out of the blue.' Now, despite their protest, I wanted to help, so I suggested that we keep an extra eye on you to prove that you can be trusted like before."

I open my mouth to speak, but his finger stays in the air.

"Soon after though, I got word that the same vehicle was showing up at some of our watch sights, and it was confirmed that agent 404 was following you. We didn't—I didn't warn you, because one, no harm befell you, and two; I know you can take care of yourself. Plus, if I did tell you, our team would've been made."

"You know our history?" I ask, averting my gaze and swallowing down my sharp tone. "Agent 404 and I? You know all of it?"

He sighs. "Yes. I do. And despite my better judgement, I intervened when necessary. But you know how our line of work operates. Not informing you was a call that had to be made. However, now that you know, it'll prove useful, won't it?"

"No, it won't. Because he already got to me first Manager. This—" I pull up my sleeve to show my rope burn, "—is the result of that. Of me not knowing. Of you not warning me," I tell him, making my voice as calm as I can.

He says nothing after that, probably deciding whether or not to react to my tone, and I sit in the silent room, filled with rage. I do understand why I was flagged at first, but who didn't I "convince" about Dominic going missing? Everything seemed fine when I came for help. Well, minus the missing information, but none of them knew about that yet. So why not trust me?

I've proven myself time and time again, especially this past month. But apparently that doesn't matter, not even right now, because it feels like Manager's leaving out information that might lead me to some truth someone doesn't want me to know.

A lot of these thoughts are ifs based on my anger though, which is slowly making me go insane. I'm not going to let that happen—not today at least. I get up to leave.

"I know you're frustrated about all this, but I've been on your side since day one, because I *do* trust you. So I'm trusting that you understand why? Why I couldn't tell you?" Manager combs a hand through the silver strands of his hair. "And as for him getting to you first, well, what doesn't kill you makes you stronger, agent."

I hated to admit it—so I wasn't going to—but I do understand. Either way I look at it though, it's still fucked up. I let my eyes drop to the carpet floor, then glance up at him and say hoarsely,

"I need some air."

I shouldn't be here, sitting on an icy bench in some empty park. I should be running, or at the very least hiding. But I'm not. Instead I'm here, letting my suffocating hair blow in the frigid February wind. My face slowly turning into an icicle. I ignore it to the best of my ability and try to let my ill temper heat me up. Occasionally, one or two people walk by, but other than that, I'm completely left alone with my thoughts.

My jacket starts to sing 'I Will Survive' to me, or rather the phone that stole away in my pocket does. I must've changed the song last night, though the irony doesn't amuse me in the slightest. It almost makes me not pick up, but I do fish for it in my pocket, just to have something warm on my face.

"What," I answer.

"Hey Elle, I didn't mean to bother you, I know you're probably still a little hung over," her kind voice fills my echoing head, but I don't adjust my snippy tone.

"What do you want Rebecca?"

"Oh," her playful voice dips at the sound of my attitude, "I was just wondering if you wanted to hang out at The Steam Bean later."

I shouldn't, but I have to at least say goodbye. I owe her that much. "Yeah, sure, just text me when and I'll meet you there."

"Alright, but, are you okay Michelle? You sound like something's really bothering you." She's trying to comfort me.

I don't want comfort.

"I'm fine. I gotta go. Bye." I take the phone from my ear but still hear her voice.

"Okay, well—"

I hang up.

I'm going to be explaining that one later. I already feel bad about it, but with everything on my mind, I let myself not care right now. I shove the phone back into my pocket and lift my head, only to be met with a new amount of rage filling my gut. Across the street in front of me—clearly trying to get my attention—a dark van with no licence plates sits. It revs up its engine, and the headlights turn on, but, when I get up to let off some steam by killing whoever this fucker is, they speed away. Watching them drive off, I have half a mind to run after them. I could use the chase to warm my numb thighs.

My feet shift in the snow, but I abandon the thought to follow when someone lying in the street catches my eye, right where the van had been. I ready myself for a fight, but when they don't move, I step away from the frozen bench and cautiously strut over.

The closer I get, the more I start to see the blood in the snow pooling around them, and something of pity forms in my already heavy chest. So sad how people get into situations like this, though of course that depends on if they had it coming or not. A dark thought, but a true one. I should call the cops, have them deal with this. I certainly have more pressing matters to worry about, but whoever dropped this person off made a point of me witnessing that they did, and honestly, something is drawing me towards this person.

When I reach the body and turn it over, at the sight of his face, I freeze, and everything in me stops. A breath catches in my throat, my heartbeat becomes the loudest thing in my ears, and the world falls away. Slowly, my mouth widens in shock and my eyes shortly follow suit.

He's a ghost, my brain tells me, finally starting to work again. I can almost feel the colour draining from my face. The cold around me is something of the past as I stare at him, but when he slightly shifts in the light blanket of snow, relief passes through me, and control of my body returns. And as if this was all happening in slow motion, I drop to my knees and lift his head off the ground then gently place it on my lap. Every feature is swollen, but despite his purple eyelids and busted cheek, there is no amount of beating that would stop me from recognizing my baby brother.

CHAPTER ELEVEN

LOST AND FOUND

I don't think. I don't allow myself to think about anything, not when I'm cradling my little brother while he bleeds in my arms, clinging to life. I rock his barely conscious body back and forth. I need to get him out of the open, to get him safe, but I can't carry him in this fragile state. Everything in my mind clouds when he shivers—the fog only showing me the little boy I was supposed to protect all those years ago. But that was then, when I didn't take more than a minute to think about that decision. Here and now though, I can help him. I force my mind to stop from spinning into that dark place, stare down at him, and hold on tighter as an idea forms.

"Hold on Dom," I whisper.

Like a light switch, my mind goes into complete agent mode. I scan over the area. Still alone, good—that gives me more options for extraction. Part of me wants to call in every favour I can think of. That would get me a helicopter and bikes to chase down the van, security to escort Dominic and I to the closest hospital, but no. The only thing that needs to happen—the simple thing—is me making a phone call. I take a breath, then remove the ring from my finger to behind my ear and tap. Thankfully, it only rings once before picking up.

"Agent 401, what can I do for you today?" Bethany asks.

"I need a car. I'm only ten minutes away from the storage location. Use my conduction device to create a tracker beacon with your server to get to me. When you do, I need you to take me into the winery, but above level. Crate C," I rush out my orders as my brother goes completely limp. "Hurry, please."

"On my way."

I can't do anything now but wait, and somehow, it's so much worse than not knowing where he was just minutes ago. The cold silence doesn't help with not panicking while I stare at him, trying to assess all his injuries as an agent, not a sister. Something about that calms me a little, yet with every minute that passes, my eyes become glossed over with tears, and my calm disappears once again.

A rough breath gets pulled in through my nose as I try to focus only on Dominic, and not my own ache. But he just looks so helpless with all the bruises and blood covering his face. *It can't possibly be worse*, I think, looking him over, but my eyes stop at the sight of his hand grabbing his side. Gently I move it to see why, then gasp. My hand clasps onto my mouth as I stare at the long cut that runs down from what looks like under his armpit to his waist. I bite my tongue to stop the tears from running down my face.

"I'm so sorry, Dom," I cry. "I'm so sorry."

This is all my fault.

My heart continues to pound, and with each heavy beat the light feeling I'm having a heart attack creeps into my chest. It slightly rocks me back and forth, like it's trying to sooth me as well, but it's not working. The pain only grows, so much that at first, I don't notice the car that pulls up in front of us.

The back door quickly slides open. "Get in."

I waste no time and carefully pick up my brother, carrying him like fine china while sliding him into the back seat. The door closes before my hand even touches it, then, on the other side, the opposite swings open. Without thinking of Bethany taking control of the wheel, I get in and carefully rest my brother's hot head in my lap.

"Buckle up," Bethany calmly instructs before driving off.

"Can you do a full body diagnostic?"

"Increasing heart rate, sweating, shortness of breath, and—"

"Not me, Bethany!" I shout.

"Sorry agent," the car drifts as she starts again. "Dominic R Castillo, civilian. Minor cuts and bruises, severe concussion, dehydration, two fractured ribs, and a major laceration along his left side. I would recommend immediate medical attention."

A light snort comes from me. Her recommendation is already one I've made myself. The normal thing to do would be to go to a hospital, but given the particular situation, bad idea. The doctors at the winery will help, and with very little questions, plus I'm not going to risk a long drive to the hospital, where I wouldn't be able to stay by Dominic's side. Bringing a civilian in, even one that's family, isn't exactly Unknown's drop and drive protocol, but this is a different circumstance. Or at least that's the story I'm going with.

We pull up to the Winery—the front door opening enough to swallow the car, then, as we roll into crate C, Bethany opens the doors.

"I have contacted Doctor Eric, your preferred physician, and he will be here in exactly five minutes and ten seconds."

As I pull Dom out from the backseat I breathe heavily, almost choking on the overwhelming smell of isopropyl in the air. I ignore my slight dizziness, then place him onto one of the clean beds to make him as comfortable as possible. "Thank you, Bethany, really," I say, my voice breaking a bit.

As soon as I'm finished with the car, Bethany acknowledges my appreciation then drives off, leaving me alone in the empty med bay with my brother.

I pull up a chair next to him and cup my hands around my mouth while hot tears roll down my face, but I never take my eyes off him. And for exactly four minutes, I allow myself to cry for him, let the blame replay in my head over and over again. He looks so small lying there, exactly like when Mamá brought him home and handed him to me. Except this time, I see all the pain he's in. Even through the rested expression on his face.

The cold from outside has made some of the swelling go down, letting me notice the young man he's become without me in the last three years. He's so handsome, just like Papá when he was young. Yet noticing the resemblance only makes this worse, as I think of us. About everything we've been through.

Dominic, despite our parents, was the good one. The smart one that *always* tried to hide it, wanting to be tough to please them. I went through that phase to, without an older sibling, which was rough, but it helped me realize that they were the worst. Both as parents and people. It's no wonder we turned out the way we did. Or at least *I* turned out the way I did. More the bad seed than Dom.

That tends to happen when your parents are always off dealing with the 'family business' instead of spending their time with you. A business, that was—as I remember it in simple terms—loan sharking to posing deep pockets. Crime lords, mobsters, CEOs, and even a couple of cops. Not exactly a nurturing environment to raise children in. Most of our childhood, and the better half of my teenage years, I was shielding Dominic from all of that. The bloody bodies, cut off limbs, dirty money, and drugs.

When it came time to leave for school though, after raising enough money on my own with doing some odd jobs, I got recruited early on and didn't look back. At first. I couldn't see him during year one, what with probation. But after that, I'd visit him off the books as often as I could between training and missions.

When our parents died, Dominic's plans for university became sidelined when Abuelo decided to take him to 'have a better life'. Yet he failed to mention that that better life would completely uproot Dominic to Spain. Still, I should've been there, I would've been, but then everything happened with leaving the agency, and in that moment, I chose to protect him by steering clear. It hurt, so much, yet not nearly as much as it does right now, looking at him suffer because of me.

I hear the elevator ding, and as I find Dr. Eric coming out from the elevator—a doctor I trust—I quickly wipe my face. My final thought before he reaches my brother is *I never should've left you there, with them.* Dr. Eric simply nods in my direction then gets to work, and still, my eyes don't leave Dominic.

My leg bounced impatiently the entire time. But after an hour of watching the back of Dr. Eric's head as he worked on my brother, performing the regular bodily check for trackers or bugs, then patching him up, he finally gives me the all clear and packs up his kit. I catch him before he leaves, and lightly push him off to the side.

"Is he going to be okay?" I whimper.

"I'm not going to lie, he's in pretty bad shape. The person who did this clearly wanted to send a message, but the good news is most of his injuries were just for show." He gently places his hand on my arm.

"He's already a tough one for making it this far. He'll be alright."

I give him a weak smile. "Thank you."

He nods as he lets me go then shifts his foot towards the elevator. His exit comes to a stop though when his stare follows mine as I glance from the pen in his pocket back to him.

"No agent."

"I need to borrow that Doc," I slightly demand.

"He's *not* ready to go through that," he stresses. "He needs time to—"

"You and I both know that this is prime time. I need to get it done and over with, so please, I need to borrow your pen."

He sighs heavily while slowly unclipping it from his pocket. "Alright. But you need to be careful not to make him too upset, so he doesn't further aggravate his concussion or open his wounds. And if anything goes left—"

"I'll give you a call, yes. I understand how this works."

As I take the pen, Dr. Eric clenches his jaw and his shoulders slightly twitch upwards, but he does turn to go without another word, which is completely understandable. No one likes to stay for these moments. Hell, even I hated them from the experience of being on both ends of the stick, but it needs to be done. The fact that it's with Dominic only makes me feel worse about it. He doesn't deserve any of this, though I plan on making it up to him for the rest of my life.

"And Doc?" I plead out just as he reaches the elevator.

He twists around to me. "Yes?"

"This encounter with my brother and I never happened. So, feel free to call the last hour a coffee break."

"That's a bit of a long break, don't you think, agent?"

"Add in a little bit of lunch too," I tell him and turn back to Dom. When his eyes begin to flutter open, I completely ignore Dr. Eric's presents.

But, as I hear the elevator ding, everything in me has to stop from turning around to see if he's going to agree with my request. It doesn't feel like the hardest thing I'll have to deal with anymore though, as Dominic's stare finally finds me. I sigh with relief, and my body loosens when seeing his familiar hazel eyes, and then I hear Dr. Eric say from behind,

"You're welcome."

Some tension leaves me, but when Dominic starts to speak with a rough voice—a voice I haven't heard in years—that unease returns, knowing I now have to deal with my new brutal task.

"Am I dead?" he groans out.

My heart becomes coated in dread as I start to play along, hoping to ease into things. "Why is that your first question?"

"Cause you're here, and to make myself feel better when you didn't come to see me anymore, I told myself you died."

A small chuckle escapes me, but I find nothing funny. "Still so dramatic," I say.

"That's your takeaway? You've been gone for three years Sis, three, and what? In all that time you hoped I'd become less dramatic!?" He violently coughs then looks away.

I lower myself into the chair and hand him a cup of water while softening my voice, shaping it the way I would when he was little. "Lo siento. Pero tienes que relajarte o abrirás la herida."

(I'm sorry. But you have to relax or you'll open your wound.)

He takes the cup from me, and between desperate gulps he laughs bitterly. "¿Ya me estás diciendo qué hacer?"

(Are you already telling me what to do?)

"Dominic..."

"I'm fine. Just a few cuts and a *massive* headache. I'm more surprised they found a number to get you here."

"And where do you think *here* is?"

Waiting for his answer, I hold the pen under the table and lightly rub my thumb on the end cap, getting ready to click, though a big piece of my heart is praying he'll surprise me. But judging by the slight condescending obviousness in his tone that prayer immediately gets stone walled.

"The hospital? Where else does a person go after getting in a motorcycle accident?"

"You were on a motorcycle!?" I shout, but watching him flinch back I calm down and remind myself that that's not the biggest problem here. Especially since it's only a fabricated lie.

Shit. I figured I'd have to do this—I knew it—although now that he's actually awake and looking at me with his cute eyes, I'm dreading it even more. It's bad enough that something inside me already wishes he remembered everything. Not the pain, not the fear, just the information I need to help avenge him.

Unfortunately though, I've done this before, so I know that when it comes to deprogramming, all that suffering comes back ten times worse. And given the fact that I'm still not absolutely sure *why* he was taken, or exactly *how* he got back to me, I have to put my being his sister away for now and be the agent who needs answers.

I clear my throat, pull the chair closer to him, and stare intensely into his eyes as I begin to bring back his hurt. I click the pen.

"Dominic, we're not in a hospital, because you weren't in a motorcycle accident. You were kidnapped, remember?"

I click the pen.

"What are you talking about? I just told you I was in an accident. Why would I lie—?"

I click the pen again, but this time faster, and while hitting the tip against the chair in a steady yet unrhythmic pace.

"No Dominic, you were kidnapped, remember? You've been missing for a month because you were taken. Remember?"

He twists his head from side to side. "Where is that noise coming from?"

I ignore his question. "Dominic, listen to me, you were kidnapped."

"No. Stop! I was... I was in a motorcycle accident," his chest starts to rise and fall unevenly as his brow furrows. "I was in a motorcycle accident, right?"

I continue to click the pen while making a fist with my other hand. *I hate myself right now*, I think before slamming it down on the table. Then, I lean forward, my eyes still completely linked to his.

"No! You were kidnapped Dominic! You were taken!" My heart pounds in my chest as I yell, holding back tears when seeing them form in his own eyes.

Anywhere else. I wish I could be doing this anywhere else. He deserves to be in familiar surroundings, it'd work faster that way, but—I bite my tongue and follow through. I raise a hand to him, and he shrinks back, squeezes his eyes shut then he starts to shake.

I hate this, hate myself, but I'm so close. It's almost over. Tears run down his face and I practically run towards that finish line so I can hold him.

"You were alone and they took you! You were helpless and they hurt you, Dominic! There was no motorcycle, there's no hospital, you need to remember!"

"Stop! Stop, stop, stop!" he dry heaves, "I... I was... I was kidnapped? I was kidnapped."

When he opens his wet eyes I stop clicking the pen then lower my hand back to my side. The stabbing pain that starts in my stomach is the only thing that prevents me from pulling him into a hug. A terrible but good thing, because as much as I want to, if the past has taught me anything, he'll get violent, so I let him take a minute to comprehend what just happened.

I watch as he shakes his head, each time as if it's a reaction to someone hitting him, then, he closes his eyes again to relive the moment. It's what I planned, and I did the job well, but that only makes my guilt worse.

All his pain is because of me, and because of me, he'll never forget it again. I wouldn't blame him if he hated me after this—I'm barely not hating myself—but I'll have to shove that down until I find a better time to deal with it. Because it definitely isn't now.

Dominic snaps his eyes open. "Where am I!?" he screams frantically.

"Dominic, it's okay, I'm here."

But, like he doesn't hear me, he swings his head around and blinks rapidly while tears continue down his red cheeks. "Where is he? Where is he!?"

"Dominic," I gently grab his face, trying to calm him, "look at me. It's me, I'm here. You're safe now, okay?"

"Sis?" he asks, ever-so-slightly starting to relax in my touch.

It's my turn to cry, and god I wish I could, but I only let a weak smile cling to my face. "Yeah, it's me. Just breathe Hermano. Can you do that for me?"

I take a deep breath in and watch as he slowly does the same. Though when it's time to breathe out, he coughs and holds his side. I let go of his face and go to check his wound, but get sidelined when he pulls me into a hug and cries. He cries and cries as I hold him tight—not too tight—and I breathe in the lemon and coconut scent that somehow still lingers in his hair. I just let him take his time.

Moments like these are crucial when building a bond between the victim. Except in this particular scenario not only am I trying to build a new bond, I'm trying to rebuild an old one too.

After some time, after he gradually shakes less and less, I work up enough nerve to ask the question I need to, but definitely don't want to. The worst part is that I have to be careful not to mention any classified information about the agency, so I start with the light stuff. Slightly hating myself more and more.

"Dom, do you remember anything about what happened to you?"

"Where are we?" he questions, now sounding completely exhausted.

"I'll tell you everything I can, but right now I need you to tell me what you can remember."

He lets go of me as I lower myself on the edge of his bed, exhaustion beginning to hit me a little too. Between the upright way I slept and the small bit of alcohol that's still in my system, everything in me wants to curl up next to him and sleep, though I fight it.

Later. I can rest later, can let him rest, but not here. Not now. I position my body in the most uncomfortable way, to stay alert and focused, and when my attention completely zeros in on Dominic I watch the way he does a hard swallow. That alone tells me his answer won't be that helpful.

"Most of it is a blur. I tried to be aware of my surroundings like you taught me, count the turns, find any kind of weapon, but I... I don't know what happened," his voice shakes.

"All that comes to mind is bits and pieces of a man's voice repeating something. A name maybe? But it's escaping me. I'm sorry."

"No." A sharp pain digs into my heart. "No, you have nothing to be sorry about Dom. I'm sorry this happened at all. I never should've—"

The metal in my ears start to vibrate, interrupting my train of thought. I completely forgot that the world is still going on outside of this room. For good reason. But, as it all comes back, like waking up from the chloroform all over again, I stand. Maybe the ringing will stop, I tell myself. I wait and wait, my feet planted firmly on the ground. But, when it doesn't, I take a step back from Dominic.

"Give me a second," I say to him, then sigh and answer with a bit of haste.

"Yeah?"

"N, is everything alright?" Minnie asks, her voice a bit uneven.

"I don't know. You called me. Shouldn't I be asking you that question?"

"I'm talking about you finding your brother, or more like him finding you. Is he okay? Did he remember anything?"

"He's coming along, healing now, but he did say that—" my brows knit together as suspicion hits my chest. "How did you know I found him?"

"Oh, come on," she scoffs. "You haven't figured out that I programmed Bethany? The minute you called her I intercepted and listened in."

"Minnie!"

"What? I was very concerned after our last conversation. I would've called sooner, but I was on with Manager." She starts typing, the sound becomes something of white noise for me. "He's worried about you by the way. I mean, he sounded worried at least. But he's *definitely* afraid Foreman will try to enter the system again soon."

"Okay first of all, even though you spied on me, your concern is appreciated. And second, I'd prefer *not* to talk about Manager right now. But, as for Foreman, I do think—"

"Foreman," Dominic utters from behind.

From the ghostly way he said the name, like he's heard it before, my face begins to burn, and I start to taste the bitterness of the isopropyl all over again. *Please no.* I ominously turn back to him, and when getting the full view of his horrified expression I tell Minnie, "Give me a minute here M."

"Why, what's wrong?"

"I'm not sure yet," I take a slow step closer to Dominic, "but I think we might have a new connection, and if so, a bigger problem."

Dominic's eyes drop to the white sheet covering his legs and as he shoves a hand into his noir hair, his gaze shifts up to me. Full of fear. "Foreman," he repeats, "I... I know that word. That's the word the man kept saying! Like he was referring to someone. Like it was a name or a title."

Oh hell no.

I hate myself for asking, but—"are you sure that's what you heard Dom?"

"Foreman... Foreman, yes! That's it."

Every limb goes stiff—the memory of George Samberg mentioning that very alias instantly coming to mind, and I've found that a dying man never lies. All at once, each of my emotions from the last two days swirls into this tornado of hate, but I don't let it blind me.

I've never seen what I have to do more clearly. Yet, at the same time, I can almost literally feel the melting of my brain. None of it makes sense, and for some reason I can't piece it together. Why take my brother, and what does this 'Foreman' person want with me?

Obviously they want to pick a fight. Not one of my questions will get answered if I don't take action. So that's exactly what I'm going to do, because this person is fucking with the wrong woman.

"Minnie, did you get all that?"

She lets out a sharp breath. "Yes, but I'm still trying to piece this puzzle together."

"You and me both, but until either of us can, I need to get my brother out of here. Can you find a secure place to hide him from anymore of this? It needs to be restricted access in the system. Somewhere way off grid so Foreman doesn't look or find him."

"Do you want me to contact your grandfather and have him sent there too?"

I wince at the question. The thought of him sends a chill down my spine, but it would be the smart thing to do. Just until I figure out who this 'Foreman' person is and kill them. As much as I don't want him anywhere near Dominic—considering he couldn't protect him the first time—I swallow my disappointment remembering that I didn't protect him either.

"Fine, yes, have him brought over, but make sure the person bringing him in is warned. Abuelo isn't exactly a friendly person. He'll definitely fight dirty to get away."

Minnie roughly exhales. "Alright. And I'm right in assuming you won't be going too?"

Every fibre of my being wants to, however I have unfinished business. Before I answer her, I turn to Dom, to swear to him that I'll get revenge on those who hurt him. That vow gets sidetracked though when my phone rings, echoing throughout the space. As I go to pick up, I quickly answer Minnie.

"No, I'm not."

"Okay, so only hideaway tickets for brother and grandfather. I'm on it."

Taking the phone from my coat, I see Rebecca's picture light the screen. And over twenty messages from her. I tilt my head up. "Shit. I totally forgot," I grunt.

"What is it?"

"Nothing. I gotta go, but I'll call to get confirmation that my brother is safe, so wait by the phone," I let my voice shift into tenderness. "And Minnie, thank you."

"You're welcome, but don't get into any more trouble, alright? If you do, I will not hesitate to spy on you again. I'll hack into every electronic you own N. I'll find a way inside your goddamn toaster if I have to."

I genuinely snicker at her odd way of threatening to watch out for me. "I can't make any promises, but I'll try."

"Good."

When she hangs up, I pick up my phone—ready to apologize, but Rebecca talks first. Or more yells.

"Where the hell were you Elle? I waited for an hour and a half at The Bean! I texted over and over, because you clearly didn't wanna talk on the phone, but—"

"Yes, I know, I'm sorry Becca, time just got away from me. I'll be there in—"

"I'm not there anymore," she cuts me off, "I'm at your place, because I wanted to yell at you in person. But you're not even here!"

My surroundings slightly tip as I do a double take, remembering that my apartment isn't safe. "What... what no," I stutter as my hand reaches up to grab a fist full of hair. "Listen to me, Rebecca you need to leave my place, right now."

"Oh relax, I won't make a mess while I *continue* to wait. It's actually way cleaner than the last time I was here. Plus, I'm already comfortable."

The air goes thin as my eyes wander down to Dominic, who is falling in and out of sleep. She won't leave. She's too stubborn, especially when she's pissed off. *Fuck. I have to get over there, but I can't leave him. Can I bring him with me? No, not when I don't know why he was taken. It's too dangerous.*

Part of me wants to start hyperventilating until I pass out only to wake up to find all my problems solved. Unfortunately, I've never had the luxury of letting others solve my problems for me. Even if I did, I don't think I could sit back and watch. That isn't who I am. It hasn't been, and never will be.

This is my mess, all of it, and I'm not going to let anyone else get hurt because of me. I need to remember my training—need to calm down. Nothing will get done right if I have emotions influencing every decision.

I take in a sharp breath, hold it until I'm lightheaded, then speak with order. "Okay, listen to me Rebecca. Keep the door locked until I come, alright? Don't let anyone in, and don't leave. I'll be there as fast as I can, but I need you to do exactly what I said, understand?"

"Umm, sure, but I feel like you're grounding me," she laughs.

I don't join in with her amusement and only repeat myself. "Just make sure the door is locked and I'll be there soon, alright?"

"Fine. Just get here before I eat all your food!"

"Rebecca...?" I hear nothing but silence, yet I call her name again, louder. "Rebecca!?"

I roll my eyes while shoving the phone back into my pocket then sit down next to Dominic and lean closer to him, placing my hand on his cheek. His chest rises up and down uneasily, but I'm just glad he's breathing at all. *This sucks*, I think while removing my fingers from his face, getting ready to leave. I reach out to shake him awake, feeling terrible, but I can't leave without saying anything.

Not like last time.

"Dom. Dom." I shake harder. "Dominic!"

His eyelids slowly rise like the sun as he grunts. After a brief silence, I take it it's my turn to talk. "I know this is terrible timing, but I have to go. You're going to be taken to a safe location where Abuelo will meet you, okay?"

"What, why? What's going on? Why can't I just go with you?" The hint of desperation in his tone almost makes me bring him.

"No, you're not safe with me, and I have something else to handle. But—"

"You're leaving me behind, again?" his voice rattles with anger as he sits up on his elbows. "Sis, I'm not some helpless twelve-year-old anymore. And Abuelo is the last person I want to—"

"First of all, don't cut me off..." I narrow my eyes at him, "ever again. I taught you better manners than that. And second, Abuelo has taken care of you since Mamá and Papá died. He's probably been worried sick."

"No me importa!"

(I don't care!)

"Dominic Rogelio Castillo, *por favor* no discutas conmigo!" I yell, but then sigh and step closer.

(Dominic Rogelio Castillo, please don't argue with me!)

"Necesito saber que estarás a salvo, y ahora mismo eso significa estar lejos de mi."

(I need to know you'll be safe, and right now that means being away from me.)

"Pero—"

(But—)

"Vas a ir," I demand.

(You're going)

His eyes drop from mine as he frowns, and his face turns red. *Still a baby*. Part of me thinks I could stay with him, at least long enough to make sure he got to the safe house alright. All I'd have to do is call in a favor, ask an agent or two to surveil my building for any suspicious activity until I got there.

But what if something goes wrong? What if he does come back and kills them then gets to Rebecca? If he's willing to take me out he wouldn't hesitate to terminate other agents, or even civilians for that matter. I can't do it. I can't risk putting more people, innocent people, in danger because of this war between me and him.

The sudden threatening pressure of a migraine enters my skull. "Fuck," I utter viciously.

"Tell me why."

Whipping my head his way, I stare at Dominic, slightly losing my breath. "What?"

"You can at least tell me why you're leaving me this time. Right?" He still doesn't look at me.

"A friend, they're..." I trail, my heart skipping a beat. "They're in trouble, could be in serious trouble, and I need to get to them. To protect them."

Slowly, Dominic turns his head towards me again. "To protect them," he lets out an airy laugh. "Well look who's running towards someone who needs help instead of away from them."

That, those words, I feel in my chest, sharp and deep. I wish I could stay with him, but there's just too much that can happen if I don't go. I'm not going to gamble with Rebecca's life. She wouldn't be okay without me against the odds right now, he will, especially here.

"Dom, I... I'm—"

"I was kidding," he tells me, snickering low and bitter.

I see right through it. "No, you weren't."

"No, I wasn't, not entirely, but still, you should go."

"Go?" My brows knit together. "Are you sure?"

"You're clearly worried about your friend, and like you said, I'm safe here, right?" He turns his head up, looking at his surroundings with confusion and awe. "Wherever this place is?"

"Yes," I eagerly reassure him, "you're more than safe here, and you'll be moved to an even safer place soon."

He sighs, and a large part of me sighs right along with him. Guilty relief settles into my bones at his somewhat acceptance with why I have to go. It helps, more than he'll ever know. I lean over him and then plant a kiss on his bruised forehead.

"I'm coming back for you this time Dominic. No matter what. I promise, okay?"

"Go. I'll see you soon," he tells me with such enthusiasm it's hard to believe he wanted to tag along.

"Lo harás." I brush the hair from his face before walking away. "Te querio." (*You will. I love you*)

I look back at him for a split second and he gives me a weak smile, one that's half telling me to go and half asking me to stay. I have to force my legs to move. My stomach feels like it's caving in on itself as I go, even when he said to. And once I get outside it doesn't get better.

This time is different, I tell myself, *this time he really is safer without me.* I keep repeating that as I get into my car that's already waiting for me and start driving for the second time today. More than I have all year.

On the way back to my apartment, speeding through every yellow light, my mind—as if preparing me—goes over different scenarios that involve Rebecca hurt. And with each one, it brings the same outcome. There's no way I can handle it, especially not when I know it would be one hundred percent my fault. If 'he' does anything to hurt her it's because I was stupid enough not to trust my gut.

I should've killed him that night. It *definitely* would've avoided this situation now, but I was in no place to pull the trigger on him. Although it looks like that bad decision came to bite me back in the ass. So many people are, or were, in danger because of me. I got out to prevent that very problem.

Supervisor may have been right all those years ago, I don't know how to separate my place at the agency and my personal life, even after all this time. I've only proven to be reckless with the lives around me. *Ugh.* Hopefully that just solved the mystery of why he appeared in my nightmare at work. *God I hate him.* The memory alone is making me sick.

Focus on one thing at a time.

The tires skid on the road as I fly down the street, my pulse racing all the same. None of this should be happening. My worlds weren't supposed to collide like this, and the fact that there's even a chance that they might, shakes me to my core.

Rebecca is a normal person, who loves her normal job, her normal apartment, her normal life. But now, because of me, that could all change because I was stupid enough to believe I could live a life like hers. Normal. I don't want to admit I was wrong about that, not yet. I can still fix this, protect her from it.

My building comes into view. My back straightens with determination. Every part of me is itching with impatience and worry. My grip tightens on the steering wheel, but all I can do is breathe. It also helps that I don't waste time on pedestrians—well I try not to. My attention is solely on the person I have to save at the moment, Rebecca.

Protect her. Protect her from 'him', is the only thing I let run through my mind. When I reach the apartment, I park on the street, not taking the time to go to the parking garage. I force the glass door open and don't waste time on waiting for the elevator. I'm faster on foot, so I race up the stairs.

Each step I take is another closer to her, but it still doesn't ease the images of my best friend bleeding out, or tied up, or—no I can't do that, not right now. *Remember your training*, I think, *remember that emotions have no place on the battlefield, and this is now war. You're officially at war on both sides of your life.*

The realization forces me into a new kind of control. It's the only thing I set in my mind on as I reach my floor and run down the hall to my apartment.

Both hands go steady as I unlock the door and quickly breathe in and out. On the phone she was calm. I was the one who sounded freaked out for no reason. I can't do that again. If she sees that I'm not worrying, then she won't worry. I have to be Michelle. Cool, calm, and collected Michelle. One last time I take a deep breath then I swing the door open, and when it's wide enough, there Rebecca stands, completely unharmed. *Oh thank god,* I think, and then casually, but quickly, walk over to her.

"Are you okay?" I ask, more steadily than I feel.

"Well, look who's finally here," she says before crossing her arms.

I shake off her playfulness. "Did you hear anyone try to get inside?"

"No."

"And you're alright?"

Rebecca's eyes widen at me with slight annoyance. "Yes Elle, I'm fine. I should be asking you if you're okay. You're the one who's been acting weird." She looks me up and down and laughs lightly. "And what are you wearing?"

I completely forgot how I left the apartment. The place I didn't think I was coming back to. Khaki cargo pants and a black crew neck sweater, all of which cling tightly to my bodice. It's nothing I'd wear to The Steam Bean. I ignore her snarky comment about my out-of-place outfit, too busy focusing on the pounding in my chest as I drop my gaze and start to circle her. Just to be completely sure she's alright.

She's fine. She's totally fine. Maybe I can go back, to see Dominic off.

The thought causes me to let out a deep breath, but, when I come face-to-face with her again, my stomach drops. Something's not right. Her dark skin is drained of color, eyes wide. Slowly she starts to point her finger past me, fear covering her face. Turning to see what got her to change her expression in the blink of an eye, I don't like what I find. There, in the hallway, 'he' stands behind me. A mischievous smirk shines on his face yet it doesn't distract me from noticing the silenced pistol in his hand. Pointed right at me.

CHAPTER TWELVE

DO ME A FAVOR

As the world spins back into motion, my reflexes act just as fast. I slam the door shut, not a hundred percent sure why that was my first move. I don't dwell on it and instead grab Rebecca, pull her into the living room then down behind the couch just as he fires a bullet straight through the door. My fridge takes the hit, making a loud rippling sound of metal colliding with metal, and it echoes throughout the apartment.

Beside me Rebecca flinches. Shit, this isn't good, for so many reasons, but at least one of them I can control. Screw the fact that getting even just a *glimpse* of his face is slightly destroying me. I need to focus on Rebecca.

When he lets off another shot, then another, I almost roll my eyes. He's only using scare tactics, considering the door isn't locked. Pathetic really, but I'm the only one who is aware of that. My best friend isn't. I grab her hand and look her in the eye, to reassure her that I got her, but then I notice she's not breathing.

"Rebecca. Rebecca, breathe, please!" I shout at her.

Her shaky eyes quickly drift from the door to me, then, she exhales. The breath comes out ragged and uneven, and her body tremors, mimicking the rattling in her stare, but the important thing is that she's breathing. The wide-eyed pale expression donning her face though, tells me that getting her out of here fast is my next priority.

My room. My room is the safest option. We just have to move swiftly then—whoosh! I snap my head up towards the washroom and immediately my day goes from bad to worse.

"What's with all the banging?" Shane asks, strolling out without a care in the world.

Me on the other hand, I curse under my breath then snap my fingers to get his attention. "What the fuck are *you* doing here!?" My glare then darts from Shane to Rebecca. "What the fuck is he doing here?"

Shane lightly chuckles. "Jeez, what's your problem Elle?"

His amusement at my concern for his life comes to an immediate halt when three hauntingly slow knocks strike my bullet ridden door. I take Rebecca by the arm then rush over to Shane and grab a fist full of his shirt. Then, just as the door busts open, I jerk my head towards it.

"That!"

"What—?" he starts, but I let go of him and quickly place a finger on my lips then shake my head. He then immediately goes silent. I don't know if it's the lack of knowledge in what's going on that shuts him up, but I take advantage of his obedience and move us to the dining area. Each step as calculated and quiet as a ballerina.

When we reach, huddling by the table, I let them go and flip it on its side while grabbing for the gun that's supposed to be strapped underneath. But just my luck, it's gone. *Damn it!* He must've swept my place last night for all my obviously hidden weapons so his invasion today would go smoothly. I was so focused on getting out of here that I didn't check if anything was missing. *That bastard.* This *definitely* complicates things.

Again, he fires a shot, but this time, silence doesn't follow. "Hello?" he says in a sing-song tone. "Anyone home?"

My cheeks burn and my heart skips a beat. Up until this point I've more or less kept myself calm. Seeing his face took its toll, except looking through those pictures at the Winery earlier took away most of the sting. But hearing his voice, it does something to me. *He sounds exhausted.* The thought echoes in my mind, immediately falling back into the routine of caring. A sudden heaviness overwhelms my chest. I squeeze my eyes shut and listen to the thumping, trying to steady it.

No, this can't happen right now. It's been three years; I can't let it. I don't care. The words cycle through my head over and over again for the next five seconds. Some part of me deeply believes them, but then there's a part that… doesn't. In a desperate attempt to prove the very opposite to myself, I force out words. Any kind of words to fill the void where the sound of his voice lingers.

"Still a showboat?" I call out, as if nothing is wrong.

He laughs. "Still don't appreciate my flare for the dramatic?"

Something in my chest warms at the sound of his laugh but I force it to die as I answer coldly.

"When that "flare" leaves my door looking like Swiss cheese, no."

"Oh well," he sighs, but then—like he didn't hear me—his tone becomes cheerful. "So, *Michelle* now is it? Long time no see."

Slowly, I get to my feet. Shane follows, now crouching behind the overturned table, but Rebecca doesn't move. She remains frozen with fear, which I completely understand, though it isn't something I have time for.

"Bedroom, go," I whisper to Shane. "And take her with you."

His eyes are filled with questions. I can see it. But he does as he's told and gently takes Rebecca by the arm. While they're on the move, I pick up the metal chair next to me and throw it in the direction of his voice. After it crashes to the ground—not hitting him at all—I proceed to distract my intruder.

"We *both* know that's a lie." I tell him, anger seeping from my voice as the files from the Winery make a reappearance in my mind's eye. I grip onto another chair until my knuckles turn white.

"True," he answers nonchalantly. "But this more *close up* interaction lets me ask you how you've been."

"Oh, I'm *sure* you already know that answer."

"I do, but enlighten me for the sake of conversation. Or…" the silence that comes after his trail off doesn't last long. Another quick round of suppressed bullets pierce through my wooden shield, each closer to me than the last, then he stops to finish his threat. "I can just keep shooting. Your choice."

My stare wanders to where my weapon *would've* been, but then shifts to my room, where my other 'tools' await me. They're in there and I'm out here, which means getting Rebecca and Shane to safety might mean having to play his little game of catch-up. No matter how psychotic I think it is.

This is going to be irritating as hell, but I just need to buy myself some time to work up the nerve to execute my plan. *My half baked plan.*

"Okay, fine." I huff and clinch my jaw. "Work, home, the usual. But everything started to get real shitty when a crazy ex left roses all over my apartment, drugged me, then started shooting at me and my friends!"

He gasps dramatically. "That sounds awful sweetheart," he says, sounding concerned.

I brush off his false compassion. "Well…" I start and then sit back down, getting ready to use my body as a spring in order to thrust another chair as hard as I can. "You wouldn't happen to have firsthand knowledge as to why my life has taken such a turn for the worst, would you?"

"Maybe. But I've definitely been in a similar situation before."

"Yeah, well, I intend to fix things."

"Really?" he snickers. "How?"

"By fighting back!" All my weight goes into tossing the metal chair at his face, and then I sprint.

"Seriously? Again!?" he bellows.

He fires his retaliating faster than I anticipated, so when I make the mistake of looking back, I'm not entirely surprised when one bullet catches me in the arm. It pushes me backwards, thankfully into my room, but still pain pulses through me. I groan.

Damn it, it fucking burns! Now I *really* want my gun. The thought of putting a bullet in him to get even helps with the fiery agony traveling up and down my arm. I hold the wound, feeling the heat of my blood oozing out, but the sound of his hefty footsteps coming our way forces me to ignore the red liquid filling in my hand and activate my room safety protocol.

Shane frantically gasps. "Holy shit, are you okay!?"

I was shot, what do you think!? I scream in my head then take a breath. I need to concentrate. Using my foot, I shut the door then stand quickly and twist the lock in a left left right right pattern. The doorknob inverts, and a silver button takes its place. I slam my hand down on it then watch as thick metal triangle panels slide from each corner of the wooden frame until they connect like a giant puzzle.

"Whoa," Shane mumbles behind me, but in front there's a bang on the door.

"Honestly, it's been great seeing you these past few weeks, Kitten. I've missed you, more than I should have. But you know," he dryly laughs, "you have a funny way of showing you've missed me too."

So much is wrong with his sentence that I snort. "Oh please. I moved on Elias. Let things go." His name tastes like chalk in my mouth, a shiver down my back following, but I press on. "Why didn't you?"

He pounds on the door again, this time with more untamed violence. "You know exactly why!" he yells, then his voice takes on that dark tone I never thought he'd use on me. "This door won't protect you Nova, and you know that. I'm coming in there, and when I do, I'll make you *and* your friends wish I gave you the easy death of shooting your brains out!"

He's right, the door won't keep us safe for long, and that's all I choose to let sink in. The rest of his words—the ones I don't want to hear—I throw away. I have a new commitment to control I need to focus on, which includes ignoring Shane and his bombardment of questions.

"What the *hell* is going on?" He raises his voice. "Why are we being shot at!? Michelle, what's—?"

"We gotta move," I mutter and steal a glance at Rebecca to see how she's doing. Some of the color has returned to her complexion since this nightmare started, which is a pro. But con, her expression hasn't changed. Not good. I can't say I prefer her screaming, though her not talking at all just doesn't sit well with me. The extra quiet is kind of helpful, especially when Shane continues to speak enough for the both of them.

"In case I missed something while I was on the toilet, who is this guy? Why did he call you *Kitten*? And who's Nova? And why—?"

I finally face him and calmly ask with a new amount of speed, "Do me a favor? Can you go in my nightstand and grab the blue glasses case please?"

He swings his head from side to side then looks back at me, completely perplexed. "What!?"

On the other side of the door Elias viciously bangs again, making all of us jump, and doesn't stop. *Looks like he found another use for my chair.* I quickly gather myself and rip a long piece of fabric from my bed sheet to tie around my arm—my blood now dripping onto the floor. I wrap until the section slightly goes numb then lift my head and find Shane still standing in front of me, staring blankly. Needing to equip myself, and fast, just in case we don't make it *out* before he comes *in*, I slightly lose my temper.

"Come on Wendell, nightstand, glasses case, now!"

His eyes follow to where my finger shoots out and he swiftly rips open the drawer then tosses the case to me. "Michelle," he sternly calls.

"Thanks," is all I say while opening the leathery case and grabbing the bottle of eye drops inside.

I haven't used this particular device since it first got developed, and even then it had a zero point zero three percent chance of melting your eyeballs. Not ideal, but beggars can't be choosers, so I toss my head back and drop the liquid inside. When the nanobots in the solution start to form something of a contact lens in both eyes, my skin crawls.

It feels as if tiny insects are tickling my eyeballs, which isn't a feeling I like. Swallowing down a quick breath helps with the slight urge to claw out my eyes. Well, that, and repeating *I need to protect them. I need to protect them.* It does mean blowing my cover, but safety first consequences later... I guess.

Once the contacts are fully formed around my irises, I blink twice to activate the scanner, and a whole new augmented reality appears in front of me. Everything hovers in the air. The date, the time, my current location, and even the news plays in the corner of my eye. It also highlights a number that indicates my blood pressure on my wrist, something I *really* don't need to see right now.

I disregard the flashing number, slide under my bed, and wait for the digital keypad atop my beam to reveal itself. It's only a matter of seconds before I can insert the pin. But, just when I'm about to punch in the last digit, Shane pokes his head in next to me.

"What are you doing?" he asks.

I ignore him—for his own good really—then shove him out and roll my eyes. Between the pain in my arm, and the conflict in my heart, he really needs to back off. I can't blame him for being curious, but I can sure as hell dismiss it.

After successfully entering the code, the once blank box spring that held my bed turns into a full arsenal before me. A dim red light fills my eyes—the lenses relaying how much ammo is in each weapon, and which ones will best suit my fighting style. I can't help but take a brief moment to smile at the sight of all my pretty polished weapons.

Even with them there, my hand still stretches out towards the Bo staff first, but I stop. It has to be a gun, according to the now flashing lenses, and common sense. I'm not exactly a big fan of using them, too quick for my taste, however in this situation—I glance at my bleeding arm—it seems *more than* appropriate.

Just when I pick one—a silenced desert eagle fifty AE—the internal alarm in my room goes off. "`Door breech in two minutes,`" Zoey announces.

My heart pounds, from either fear or adrenaline. I don't know which, but I don't care. I use it. I come out from under my bed then stare from Rebecca to Shane. They both have their eyes locked on me, but it's Shane whose stare drifts down to the gun in my hand.

"Where did you..." he does a double take then looks up at me. "Why does that look so comfortable in your hand? Like it's second nature to you?"

I adjust the weight of it between my fingers. "Oh please. It's been a couple of days since I've had to use a gun." I say without fully thinking of what I'm admitting.

His eyes widened. "Did you just say *days*?"

"Door breech in one minute."

"We're leaving. Now," I demand and get to my feet, grabbing the remote to access my hidden room.

I hurry to the closet, promptly go through each security measure, then after putting in the last code, I swing my hair I really wish I tied up earlier over my shoulder.

"Come on, let's go!" I kindly yell at them, but they don't move. The only thing that does is their expressions, shifting from scared and confused to scared and amazed.

"Door breech in thirty seconds," Zoey says with a calm I really could use right about now. Forcing them in seems to be my only option. You'd think they'd be more than willing to move on their own, given that the banging coming from the only other exit isn't exactly translating as 'I totally won't kill you'. I'll have to slow him down to buy us more time, but that means I need to "*nudge them forward*" now.

"Guys?" They don't look over. "Guys, get inside!" I try again. This time their eyes land on me and the gun I point at them. I then darken my expression. "Get. In."

That definitely works, and just in the nick of time.

"Door breech in five. Four..." I watch the metal barrier dent inwards faster and faster as Zoey counts down. I step back until my heels are half way into the closet then ready myself for the recoil. One sharp breath later, he's in front of me, and without hesitation, I fire two shots. One near his left shoulder and the other straight in his calf. He grunts in pain as his body hits the ground.

Now's my chance.

I run into the room, every step feeling like cement, but I do reach the panel to shut him out. He manages to get to his feet and limp over to me. Before he can say or do anything else, the door slams in his face. As he bangs on it I work up the strength to ignore him and roughly sigh. That was too close for comfort. I can faintly smell his mixture of cedar wood and sweet mint. *God, how does he still smell the same after all this time?* I shake my head to stop any fond memories.

Moving towards my bug out bag, this one labelled 'BREAKAWAY PROTOCOL 3,' I catch Rebecca and Shane looking around the room, and I enjoy the silence that comes with their awe. It gives me a minute to hear myself think, and then, my eyes wander to the back door. Our escape.

"What is this place?" Shane marvels. I glance back at him and notice he's reaching for a grenade that's shaped like a travel-sized perfume bottle.

"Don't touch that," I tell him, and as his hand drops back to his side I sigh. "Look, things are going to be moving pretty fast from here on out, so bear with me."

"What does that mean? What things?"

I shove them towards the exit. To anyone who's not me it simply looks like a wall, but no. Not quite. The door blends in almost perfectly, except for the slight indent of a handprint. I press my hand against it and warmth quickly kisses my palm from the biometrics. As it scans me, I look around, just to make sure I haven't forgotten anything else important. This nagging voice in the back of my head tells me I am, but nothing comes to mind. So, when the door opens, I let my attention diverge from the room and everything in it. I'm more than ready to leave this place.

"Wait, what's down there?" Shane asks, staring into the absolute darkness.

"Brace yourselves," I reply with more nervous energy than I would've liked. But I push them through with the right amount of urgency I have.

CHAPTER THIRTEEN

Darkness, and the smell of damp wood and old carpet surround us as we fall—or rather slide—to our escape. Not a long trip, but Rebecca and Shane still find the need to scream the entire way down. I'm more concerned with bracing myself—the mixed smells jogging my memory of what's to come.

When I constructed my 'powder room', first priority was making sure there was a quick getaway. An escape hatch that led somewhere no one would expect. The roof was out. Too expensive. The sewer is actually on the list of top five places professionals look. So, a hard pass. That left me with the building's basement. The one no one either knows or cares is here.

We stumble into the filthy room, a pile of old newspapers and wall insulation breaking our fall. The air fills with a cloud of dust, so thick I can almost taste the nineteen hundreds. Gross, though it does choke up my frightened friends, giving me time to act fast without interruption. They cough violently, and after a few rough heaves myself, I get up and dust off, then clap twice to activate the lights.

As they flicker on, part of me prefers to go back to the dark. Leaving the space looking untouched was an immensely important detail in my plan, yet somehow it seems worse off than I left it. The appearance of a poor-man's bunker had always stuck. An attempt for any kind of shelter during some war—the relatively wide space having nothing to it but a single grimy window and a slim door with the white paint stripping off. But now, now it's like its being decomposed by darkness and silence.

Sad, but it has served its purpose. I disregard the ghostly presents, and focus on leaving this grey tomb. Despite the pain I'm in, I move swiftly in the dim light barely illuminating the weary stone basement. I grab at the doorknob rusted by age, and use the shoulder on my good arm to shove it open. When it pops out, I stiffen, the cold breeze hitting my throbbing wound. It's still bleeding, but not as much as before, which can mean two things. The bullet just grazed me, or the worse alternative, it's become infected already. I choose to believe the former, then take in a sharp breath while pushing down the ache.

Deal with it later.

We're spit out into the alleyway between my building and another, a dumpster covering us from view on each side. I quickly scan the area and only notice a few people walking by, just as I hear the faint sound of police sirens. No doubt they're heading our way, which does complicate some things. Getting to my car being one of them. It's not particularly this protocol's mode of transportation, but with the unexpected company, it would be useful. Unfortunately, with where I parked, I'd have to remotely drive it over to us, but there's no way someone in the forming crowd won't notice it suddenly moving on its own.

By now people will be calling security, more than worried about the gun shots, and leaving the car behind might be a good thing anyway. Elias is most likely watching it or had a GPS tracker placed on it. He may not be in commission right now, but he'd find a way. The thought of facing him again, especially after I shot him, sends some of last night's many drinks back up my throat.

He was never good with being shot, his pain quickly turning into a wild fire of rage and revenge. Around the second time a bullet pierced his skin, I was present for the hell fire being cast upon that poor sucker. I *still* can't look at fireworks the same without hearing silent screams.

Again, fear rocks my stomach, and just that small gesture gets me moving. Instead of finding another means to get away from the building—one that would be easier for my friends—I only think to do what I would if I were alone. I run.

As soon as my feet pick up off the ground, abandoning the alley to get to the back streets, I realize it's not only my boots crunching the fresh snow. Twisting around, without instruction, Rebecca and Shane follow behind me, trying to keep up.

In most cases, when coming face-to-face with danger, people become completely immobilized. But here, it's good to know that they're capable. It means I don't have to pace myself, and I don't. I continue running, channelling my pain and fury into energy to keep going strong, just until we get to what I deemed a safe enough distance in the protocol. We weave in and out of the back streets, slowing our pace in some areas to blend in, but for the most part we avoid people walking by, and anything that resembles a cop car.

It seems like forever, but eventually the portion of the city map I memorized for this protocol comes to an end, just behind an elementary school park. And only when we turn another corner into the safe zone, do I stop and look up at the night sky. It feels like I just woke up tied to my bed, but time flies when you're being hunted. Either way, now that we're far enough, I take a minute to collect my thoughts while moving towards the rendezvous.

Control. Control, is all I repeat as I gently bring my hand to my injury and breathe. It only takes a minute to return to a normal breathing pattern, but behind me, Rebecca and Shane wheeze. My gut tightens with guilt. However, despite the lack of air in his lungs, when Shane resumes his questions, it's more annoyance that twists my stomach.

We were doing so well.

"Michelle, *what* is happening? Who was that?"

"Classified," is all I say.

"What's classified?" he quickly retorts.

"Classified."

This couldn't have all happened at a worse time, especially with Dominic being in the open again. It's better that I know he's alive and will be safe, but that still doesn't stop fresh guilt from flooding into my heart. Guilt that stops me in my tracks. I draw a breath to calm my nerves, then go back to focusing on getting Shane and Rebecca out of the city until I can handle everything. When I spin around to face my friends, I realize they must've been staring at me, waiting for some kind of answer I can't give them, this entire time.

It's hard to have them look at me with such absence. Like they don't know who I am. Like they just met me. I never wanted them to look at me like that. Mostly because it's true. They don't know this whole other side of me. They were never supposed to. But, as much as I wish I could change that—thanks to my oversight—I can't. The only thing I *can* do is let my agent persona completely take over, so I can ignore their blank looks. If I don't, I'll cave and tell them everything.

We're just about to reach the exact spot for pick up, which means that according to the instructions engraved into my mind, it's time for phase two. It'll be too risky to use my phone, given everything that's gone down in the last few hours, and I can't contact Minnie to get us. Her sending transport is a last resort, plus, she's done too much for me today already. *Shit.* Calling this in is the *last* thing I want to do. Normally, I wouldn't. I'd just deal with Manager's scolding me later. But now that Rebecca and Shane, civilians, are involved, my options have been sliced thin.

I have to call. However, since my devices are useless at the moment, my gaze lands on the outline of Shane's phone in his pocket. "Did you call the police when we were at my place?"

He blinks then slightly flinches back, as if just realizing I'm talking to him. "No, but—"

"Good," I sigh, relieved that less work has to be done. "I need to borrow your phone, please," I more demand than ask.

He shifts his feet in the snow, his deep blue eyes looking me up and down with what I'm assuming is his rendition of taking charge. "No," he says sharply, though I hear a hint of unsure fear. "Not until you answer at least one of my many questions!"

I raise a brow, smirk, then dryly snicker. "Many? So you consciously *know* you're asking too much?"

"Despite all your strangely witty banter with that crazy guy, this isn't a fucking joke! This is our lives. So, until you see that, no, you can't use my phone."

My expression melts into frustration and impatience, one I've never used with him before. He slightly shivers and steps back but still doesn't give it up. At any other time, I would've respected his bravery. Now though, I don't. I lose hold on some of that control I'm desperately trying to grip, just a little.

"Wendell... I'm *not* in a good mood right now, as you can imagine. So, give me your phone before I really lose my temper with you." I grit my teeth. "*Please.*"

He sticks his hand into his pocket, and within seconds he has his phone extended out towards me. I gently take it from him, but as I do, from the corner of my eye, I see Rebecca tremble slightly. A crushing pain comes to my chest as I try and figure out if she's still shaking from being shot at, or because I was even just a little bit closer to her.

Either one it is, I can't help when more guilt starts to flare up exactly where that pain blooms in my chest. *Not her,* I think, but before the thought can turn ugly, I push it aside and dial. It rings once, twice, and then a man picks up, sounding bored as hell.

"Thank you for calling Bloody Hell Winery customer service. How may I assist you this evening?"

I know exactly who that voice belongs to. Addams. So much of me wants to laugh that he got phone duty, but I focus on the task at hand. Very clearly, I say the dreaded phrase.

"My shipment came early. All bitter. No sweet."

On the other end there's silence, which is quickly followed by typing. Then, shortly after he speaks with more attention.

"I'm so sorry to hear that ma'am. I'd be happy to assist you right away, but first I'll need some *unknown* information. And don't worry, this line is *secure*."

I breathe out slowly when hearing the code words to proceed, then, I say the three short and simple sentences I never thought would come from me. "Alpha 401 compromised. Send evac Tweedy to rendezvous point Bravo 727. Bring Medical assistance."

"Finally, something interesting—umm, I mean, roger that. Tweedy is five minutes out Alpha 401, over."

As I hang up, I go to hand Shane his phone back, but then stop and remember to take out his SIM card.

"Sorry," I swiftly tell him as I snap it in half.

"Hey, this isn't some movie, you didn't really need to do that did you!?"

"Classified. And keep your voice down," I mutter while proceeding to evac Tweedy. But I stop, this time almost tripping myself up when turning to look at Rebecca. I slowly approach her.

"Becca I... I need your phone too," I say delicately.

She reaches for it and hands it to me while shaking her head, not even trying to hide the fact that she doesn't want to make eye contact. I can't blame her, but I also can't waste time. I quickly snap her SIM, as well as the one in Michelle's phone too.

Dropping them to the ground, I stomp down on them before walking off again. This time though, Rebecca doesn't follow. The urge to roll my eyes disappears when I see the frustration and unease on her face.

All I can do is sigh.

"Look, I'll explain as much as I can, but I can only do that when I get you both to safety. So please, you need to come with me."

She doesn't move, much less lift her gaze to me. Shane is the only one to say something... of course.

"Why can't we just go back to our place? That guy can't follow us there, right?"

"Class—" I start to repeat my poorly work shopped answer, but that's when Rebecca finally locks eyes with me. The fury in them makes me rephrase. "That guy is a tremendously dangerous person that's seen your faces, and he knows you're important to me. He'll go after both of you, and I can't afford to deal with that more than I already have to."

"What do you mean *dangerous*?" Shane gulps, moving a bit closer to me now.

The wind picks up as the jet starts to come down from the sky, landing just up ahead on the field, causing me to slightly shout. "I'm sorry, but that's classified. Just take my word for it when I say both of you *need* to come with me!"

They don't move, even when I slowly start to walk backwards towards the jet, my eyes never leaving them. They think they have a choice. It's important they do, especially when I'm telling them to 'take my word for it.' In all truth though, they don't, and if I have to, I'll force them onto the jet to keep them safe.

It wouldn't look good on my part, but they need to get out of the city as much as I do right now. And seeing my face drop into a frown, Shane rolls his eyes and goes over to Rebecca. He attempts to whisper something in her ear, but with all the noise he practically yells.

"I know you don't trust her right now, but what other choice do we have? Just do this for me, please. And if it helps, you know you can trust me to keep you safe, okay? I'm not going anywhere."

She stomps off in the direction of the jet, and while Shane follows after her, he finds the need to quickly lean into me and proudly remark, “you owe me Hannigan. And I want answers.”

CHAPTER FOURTEEN

ROCKY SKIES AHEAD

I've been in a lot of tense situations, including the time I had to choose between jumping off a twenty-story building, or losing my favourite blue scarf. But in this jet, facing Rebecca's glare, I can easily say this is in the top ten. Shane on the other hand, has been staring at me with slight excitement and rage as the medical drone—that I'm informed is being operated by none other than Dr. Eric—works on patching up my wound.

Turns out, it *was* just a graze, thank god, but the relief is short lived—it quickly becoming replaced with restlessness as Rebecca and Shane continue to stare. Though when the automated flight attendant speaks, they both jump in their seats, not at all trying to hide their fascination and nervousness.

"Agent 401, you have a video call request from agent 500. Would you like to connect?" Bethany says, thankfully breaking through some of the tension.

Shane crosses his arms as his eyes fill with wonder. "Agent?"

I flick up my index finger at him, wave off the drone while thanking Dr. Eric, and then respond to the request. "Yes, but only if it's double encrypted. And I'll need a small quantity tray of acid."

"Of course. Please insert your personal identification key now."

Reaching into my bug out bag, I grasp for the compact mirror that holds my emergency identification chip for these kinds of situations. But my hand only grabs air. *Shit, I knew I was forgetting something,* I think, *and it just so happens to be the thing that'll stop us from being ejected from the plane.* I try not to panic, because if I panic, Rebecca and Shane will panic, and panicking while trying to strap on a parachute in mid-air is difficult.

For first timers anyway.

I squeeze my eyes shut, digging deep within my mind to find my override code. Back when I had first gotten it, I laughed. I never thought those situation drills would apply to me, but boy was I wrong. I was a cocky little shit, though being that way helped me program emergency protocols into my head just to show off. All it takes to draw it out is a key word. I would've picked something simple like—

My eyes snap open, and I almost smile as I recite my code. "Compromised protocol *override*. Personal identification key code U.N.K.N.O.W.N 143A401."

For a minute Bethany doesn't reply, and I hold my breath. But, when a light ding sounds, I sigh.

"One moment please," she finally answers.

A loud ringing takes over the silence between the three of us, and as the screen rises up from the table in front of me, so does a small tray of acid. I remove the contacts in my eyes and place it in, more than happy to see those nanobots die. The glass lid then shuts on its own just as they're destroyed—a small puff of smoke filling the inside of the tray. Then, as it sinks into the table, the TV locks into place and a blank screen greets me. That is until I grab the glasses provided in the side of my chair.

Putting them on, just like the contact lens, I'm shown something that really isn't there to the naked eye. But unlike the lens, these glasses are specifically designed to display encrypted images on this screen alone. And tonight, that image is my old friend.

The first thing I'm met with is strands of teal hair, which I'm assuming is her latest hue for the month—she hates the concept of normal colored hair—and a large picture of Inuyasha that stretches across her top. My chest slightly warms. *She hasn't changed a bit.* Though after a few seconds of continuous typing, when she speaks, I realize something's off. Frustration lines her words, replacing her usual ironic smartass tone, and her gaze still hasn't met mine.

"What the hell is going on N? After you left the winery, I waited for you to call so I could confirm that your brother made it to the hideout, but nothing. And when I finally traced your location, the police scanners in your area were going crazy, saying that multiple persons called in with shots fired."

"M, I need you to be a little—"

"Where are you? I can't ping your exact location anymore. Are you moving?"

"Minnie—?" I try to interject again.

"I—" she pauses when finally looking up at me, and her grey eyes widened as she squeals. "Oh my god, your hair is so cute! Brown suits you. I mean I'll miss the bangs—you're one of the few people who can pull them off—but this long hair thing is *so* adorable!"

"Minnie!" I yell, making Shane and Rebecca slightly flinch. I take a breath and tie up my blanket of hair, wincing at the pain it causes in my arm.

"Thank you. But as I was trying to say, I've been compromised, and I have civilians with me, so *please* be discreet."

"Oh, sorry. I didn't mean to—wait, is it Rebecca and that cute guy Shane?" she blushes and pushes up her glasses. The exact pair from years ago, black with a Hello Kitty bow on the frame.

I roll my eyes. "... yes."

Shane moves to the edge of his seat. "Who is that? How does she know our names?"

Sharply shifting my eyes down towards Minnie, I glower at her and raise a brow as she mouths 'sorry.' I shake my head disapprovingly as I lift my hand to the glasses, ready to fully immerse myself into my coming conversation with Minnie.

Shane's words briefly stop me. "You have to tell us *something*. You owe us that much, right?"

"Yes, fine. But after I'm done here, so just relax. It's a bit of a flight," I say, colder than I meant.

"To where exactly?" Rebecca asks. I don't answer.

Instead, I tap the side of the glasses frame, and flat padded cups swirl out to cover both my ears. The action only deepens her glare—one that makes her eyes look like they're on fire, and with the moonlight on her dark skin, her appearance only seems more intimidating. It's chilling, especially when it's coming from the girl who I stopped from falling on her face last night. I can't look away though. At least not on my own.

"Sorry," Minnie huffs out. I immediately use that as my out, then look down at her while she continues. "I had to check up on your life dealings for the last three years. First year was rough, but *very* interesting. When I hit that two-year mark though, things got a little… slow. But then that *Shane* entered the scene, and now I have a total crush."

"Choosing to ignore that, I'll skip to forgiving you, then get right to saying that I have to fill you in on the whole 'police scanner thing' later. I need you to repeat what you said about Dominic. Is he safe?"

I feel my voice threaten to break. Finding him lifted an unbelievable weight from my shoulders, but guilt is still tightening my chest. Something tells me it's not going to go away for a while, which means all I can do is try to manage it. Right now though, as I clear my throat and steal a glance at Shane and Rebecca—who are still staring—I don't think I have a choice. My eyes dart back down to Minnie.

"Right, sorry. There was a little bit of a delay with transport, and we're still trying to locate grandpa, but yes, little brother had safely and untraceably reached the secure location thirty minutes ago."

I lean forward, my face almost in the screen. "A delay? What delay?"

"Nothing serious. Just had to wait until after Supervisor left for headquarter Beta Z, so I could highjack one of the jets and get him out without superior authorization. Having two of the three bosses at the winery made things a little more challenging, but it was only a twenty-minute wait."

"And that's all?"

"Yes, but there is something else important I need to discuss with you."

With the way she stretches each word I slouch in my chair then rub my temples and sigh.

"Great. First Elias, and now more bad news. Like I need that right—"

Her head snaps up so fast strands of teal hair hit the screen. "Holy shit. Did you say Elias? As in Elias *Meyers*? Our Elias Meyers? Your ex-partner slash—"

"Yes!" I accidently shout, then lower my voice when Rebecca and Shane jump. "That Elias. Yes." *God, I've said his name more than I have in three years. It feels abnormal, yet liberating?*

"Jeez, sorry. I forgot that's a *touchy* subject. But how did he even find you? Last I heard he was on some disciplinary watch."

"Not sure. I didn't get much time to figure that out. The files I did manage to get a glimpse of using Manager's log in date back to him getting closer and closer about a month ago."

Minnie raises a brow. "Huh. Last month *definitely* seems to be our jumping off point, doesn't it?"

"Yeah…" I close my eyes and take in a slow uneven breath. When I let it out, I open my eyes and find Minnie with her head tilted. She looks up at me with sympathy I didn't know I wanted.

"Are you okay?"

"Yes. No. I don't know," I grunt. "All I wanna do right now is focus on finding *anything* else that'll help me with this ED case."

"Yeah, I totally—wait, speaking of the case, didn't your brother absolutely recognize that 'Foreman' alias?"

"Yeah, he did. Fearfully so. Why?"

"After we spoke, and while waiting for your call, I re-familiarized myself on the files that were cloned, and something didn't add up. So, I took some steps back to connect some dots, then looked at the bigger picture," she pauses, and only the sound of her typing fills the headphones.

I wait for a few seconds, but when I still don't hear words, I attempt to bring her out of her own head. "And what did you discover?"

"I think my information dot, connected to all your dots, might be something huge." Before I can ask what the hell she means, she whips her head up at me then rushes out, "I'm making sense, just keep listening."

"Your brother went missing last month, that's a dot. That led to you coming back to work. Dot. Then, you said that Elias got closer and closer around last month, another dot!"

I dig my fingernails into my temples and roughly sigh again. "Am I supposed to understand all that, or—?"

"N, tie all that with my findings—that Foreman's been in the system since last month—and add in him clearly having something to do with your brother, and what do you get...?" she trails.

"A timeline and incident pattern," I admit, my tone hollow as I start to see her point.

"Exactly! Your brother, you, even Elias finding you, it's been the mole from the very beginning. That's the starting point. That's what created this chain of chaos that's wrapped itself around your mundane life."

"Okay, but there's no solid reason why the mole went through all that trouble in the first place."

"I know," she sighs, "Foreman could be working under someone else's orders. They could be cleaning house to make way for something big they're planning, and they're merely using you as an example to keep the others that were involved with Echo Delta in line. Or, all of this could be some kind of set up."

Overwhelming annoyance rattles the inside of my head. I groan. "All of that could be true. But to bring Elias—" I do a hard swallow, "to bring *him* into this, the mole would've had to have known about our 'history' to be sure that luring me back into the agency by using Dominic as bait would cause us to try and kill each other."

"Yes, I know, and that's where things get even *more* blurry. Especially because your last mission was so classified it took me months to find it, decrypt all of my old encryptions to re-read it then lock it up again. So how they figured it out I—"

I know she knows what happened between us. Hell, she was inside my head for seven years. With me on every mission. But still my face heats and I jump forward, partially trying to reach through the screen to strangle her.

"You did what!?"

"Oh relax," she chuckles bitterly, "that's not important. What's important is that we know the *reaction* the action caused, but we don't know the actual *action* that started everything. Don't know why—after three years—the mole wants you guys dead now."

"So, until we figure that out, we don't know the endgame either?"

"No," she sighs.

We look at each other then go quiet, both completely lost. God, it feels like my head is about to pop off, and I'm going to let it at this point. This is too much. Everything is flying off the fucking tracks on this train I'm not even driving, and definitely don't want to be on. I've never needed a second or two more to think in my life. Yet when I'm about to ask for it, a blaring alarm fills my ears. I wince at the sound, and in the background I listen to Bethany's amplified voice.

"Alert, alert, agent 500 requested. Alias 143138401 has been illegally allocated with no distinct justification. Initiate immediate strict lockdown procedure."

"Oh shit, this isn't good. I have to go N. I have to confirm whose alias—"

"It's me," my heart skips a beat just saying it out loud.

Her voice goes low. "What?"

"That's my number M."

Again, despite the pounding of my heart in my ears, I hear Bethany makes another announcement. "Alert, alert, agent 500 requested. Alias 513102404, marked AWOL, has been illegally..."

I let the rest of the sentence fade into the background as I catch the last digits of the alias number. But, as if I need someone else to confirm it for me, to make sure this sinking feeling in my chest is real, my voice takes the shape of innocence when I ask,

"Whose number is that?"

Minnie's eyes fall when she reluctantly acknowledges me. "I really have to go N."

She knows. I know she knows. I just need her to say it, to tell me so I can prove it to the coming programmed paranoia creeping into my head. Prove that this situation is something to fear. So, I drop my arms to my sides and slowly sit up. "Whose number Minnie?"

She taps on her keyboard, and not even a minute later the glow of her screen lights the timorous expression now drawn on her face.

"It's him," she huffs out. "It's Elias."

Numbness sets into every part of my body when I notice more sympathy in her eyes than before, and I strain to find any words to reply. Really though, what am I going to say? I'm fucked in so many ways. That undeniable fact alone is what's keeping my jaw locked. And just when my speechlessness sets in, Minnie's chubby face fills the screen. Her silver eyes now sparkling with determination.

"I have to go, but I'll handle this."

"Video call ended."

The TV slowly disappears back into the table. When it's completely gone, I look up and am suddenly reminded that Shane and Rebecca are sitting across from me. Their eyes are wide, and I can see the tension in their shoulders from where I sit, but still only annoyance is the main emotion burning in me.

"Genial, ahora está esto," I say, finally getting my voice back. *(Great, now there's this.)*

They still have the same irritated and perplexed expressions, kind of like I paused them. Despite my slight amusement, I don't have the energy to explain anything. But, I *do* owe it to them. I take off the glasses, tighten my ponytail, like getting ready for another mission, then close my eyes and try my best to brush off the fact that I've been exposed *and* compromised in the same night. They both sound the same, but they're not. Which is worse though... I have no idea right now.

Deep breath in.

Deep breath out.

As soon as I open my eyes again, Rebecca crosses her arms over her chest and abruptly shrugs. "So?"

"Becca," Shane turns to her, "maybe we should give her a minute to—"

"No," I interrupt, "it's fine. I'd rather do this now anyway before we land."

"So?" Rebecca repeats, and I try to swallow down my frustration as I answer her.

"I'll fill you in with what I choose to tell you, and what I can actually tell you, alright? But, you may not ask me questions that involve the words who, when, why, how, or what. That's all—"

"Classified!?" she shouts.

Shane loudly whispers at her. "Rebecca!"

"What!? We were shot at, we're being taken to god knows where, and we don't even really know who she is!" She throws her arms in the air. "I mean, are we even really your friends, or just some cover for a secret spy mission!?"

"I'm not a spy. Well, not in this particular situation anyway..." I mumble before realizing I spoke out loud, and she doesn't take my comment well.

"Oh, I'm so sorry *agent 401*—or whatever your real name is—did I offend you!? Did you think I'd be calm and think you're *so* cool like this blue-eyed air head!?"

"Hey!" Shane angrily interjects, "I'm just as terrified as you. That means you don't get to use me as a punching bag. I want answers too!"

Both of them argue. For a minute I let them get it out of their system, hoping they'll be too tired to argue with me. When they don't show any signs of stopping though, heat travels up my face. My arm is still throbbing, I'm emotionally exhausted, and even when we land, and I do lay down, there's not a doubt in my mind that my waking nightmares will follow me into sleep.

I let myself lose it. Just enough to have them swallow their bitter words. I make a fist, then slam it on the table. As they go quiet, Rebecca's face sets back into its furious expression. I don't care about that right now though. I calmly shake out my fist.

"Both of you need to shut the hell up!" I point a finger to Shane. "Between your constant questions—" I then switch to Rebecca— "and your *bitchy* attitude, I'm not getting the fucking time to explain."

Fixing my tone and posture, I still have the anger in my throat as I finish speaking. Taking on the kind of scary mother approach my mamá would've been proud of.

"Just. Stay. Quiet. Before I don't tell you guys anything, take the shirts off your backs, then shove them in your mouths as gags so I can sit in sweet silence for the rest of the flight!"

They gradually sit straighter as they realize I'm not kidding, because I'm not. I make sure my glaring eyes show that. I've never raised my voice at either of them like that before now. I've wanted to plenty of times, but I didn't. I couldn't. It feels… wrong. Given everything on my mind, I ignore the slight shift of discomfort at my presents that glosses over their eyes, then take another breath, listening to my heartbeat in my ears.

I'm not particularly ready to die of a heart attack, so I conjure up the memory of my morning stretches and lean back to relax. Then, once I'm at the comfortable level of what I'm calling calm for now, my glare drops and I start to explain.

"Now, my name is, or was, Nova. I say *was,* because when I changed my lifestyle—mainly to create a more stable balance—my 'profession' caused me to alter things in a drastic way. But recently, I've had to insert myself back into that lifestyle because my brother went missing, and I needed specific resources to find him."

Shane slides back into the leather chair, his stare dripping with concern. "So, all those nights you left to 'go get your brother,' you were really searching for him?"

"Among other things, yes. But the situation has escalated a bit, and another part of my past has caught up to me, which is the reason we're on this jet, and the reason I need to get away for just a moment."

"That guy that was shooting at us, he's that other part of your past?"

"Yes, he is. He's..." a lump catches in my throat at the thought of his voice, but I clear it away. "He's not exactly the 'let's just talk about it first' kinda guy—as I'm sure you've noticed—which makes him sinister in situations like this. I've had a distressing feeling for a while. Turns out that feeling was a warning."

Shane's gaze somehow deepens. "What happened between you two that was so bad?"

A sour flavour tickles the back of my tongue. "Sorry, I... I can't say."

"So…" Rebecca chimes in, "we've just been your cover? *Michelle* was your cover, for the last couple of what... days? Months? Years?"

"I'm not going to lie to you alright, but I'm not going to apologize for the safe life I was trying to have either. My life—my new life—is going to work, going to The Steam Bean, and being with you guys. But for the last couple of weeks, yes, you've been a temporary cover," I admit.

She frowns. "So we're only your real friends when you're not off being a spy? Which also isn't true, because the rest of the time in between we've been a cover."

She's not getting it. Why isn't she getting it? Why can't she see that I didn't want this? That I never wanted to hurt anyone, never wanted to get them involved. Judging by the look on her face though, and the fact that it feels like a slap in mine, it's clear she doesn't *want* to understand.

I'm not going to keep explaining myself, no matter how much I want my best friend to look at me again without light disdain. I have a job to do, and unfortunately that job doesn't involve people liking me or my decisions. *But they're not just 'people.' Over the last two years they've been the family I chose when I couldn't be with the one I have.* I sigh at the thought, and try to reassure her one more time.

"Becca, you are my real friends. I got close because I thought it'd be safe, but then my brother went missing, and everything turned upside down. He's my family—the only good piece I have left from my old life—and that trumped everything else."

I sit up and stare, even when she's not staring back, then temporarily dismiss the hurt I'm not supposed to be feeling and finish with nothing but the truth. "I'm not going to apologize for what I had to do for him then, and I'm not going to apologize for what I have to do for you now."

She doesn't say a word, and surprisingly, neither does Shane. So much is up in the air, the tension like rising pressure with no one speaking. I've said everything I can and will say. Something is telling me to elaborate on certain points, maybe my brother, or who I really am, but... I won't. Being compromised is bad enough, but bringing along company makes everything much worse.

It's already a miracle they made it out without a scratch. I'm not going to screw up their minds even further with the horror movie slash romcom that was, and now is again, my life. If I did, nothing would go back to normal, but, then again, I don't know if it ever will.

Heat rises from my stomach to my head. I can't tell if it's left over adrenaline, anger, or fear. Whatever it is, I'll have to mask it. Our flight still has a couple more hours, and from what I've seen, Rebecca still isn't going to come to terms in that time. It's written all over her face.

Despite my inner dread, putting on a stone mask it is. I can relax a bit knowing Dominic is safe from all of this, but all I can do with my best friend, is hope she'll eventually understand what—

"Oh shit!" Shane shoots up, his eyes wide as he yells. "I completely forgot about Theora! What if she's trying to reach me?"

My nails claw at my chest at his sudden panic, like a scared cat clinging to the ceiling in a cartoon. I let out a rough breath. "Relax, okay? It's best that she stays out of contact for the time being. Trust me on that one. You'll be doing her a favour."

"But—"

"Do you really want to be responsible for her worrying about something, rather than have her think you're just sleeping? No. So, until I can fix the problem that's plaguing all of us at the moment, for the time being just breathe and try to feel relief in knowing she's not thinking the worst." I grab his arm and pull him back down as the thumping in my chest begins to smooth out.

No matter how much he bounces his foot up and down uncontrollably, he'll settle for my better version of Theora and her not being overly concerned for now. He'll have to. I've seen the strong love between them—one I knew all too well. He'll have an ache in his stomach for the rest of the time he can't contact her.

I on the other hand, don't think twice about it, and not because I don't care about his feelings or Theora. A voice in the back of my head just tells me she really *is* better off being out of the loop. According to Shane's now slightly green tinted face though, I'm pretty sure he thinks otherwise. I sigh. *Rocky skies ahead.*

PART TWO

CHAPTER FIFTEEN

TAG, YOU'RE IT

São Paulo, Brazil

God, I forgot how beautiful the city is from a hill top view. After climbing up from the field below where the jet dropped us off, I look out and slightly beat myself up for missing other days like this one. The last time I was in town was just to buy the place, strictly as a plan B, which I hoped I wouldn't have to use. That ship has clearly sailed given where I'm standing. At least the villa is still stunning.

It is a bit luxurious, which would've been stupid to buy, if not for the fact that it's almost completely hidden within tall bushy trees, and it came with a field large enough to land several planes.

The villa itself has a brown bamboo like exterior with a grey stone walk way, large opaque windows, and overhead the roof extends outwards into a pattern like inverted stairs. Now, one might think, given my moment of nostalgia, I'd remember the code to open the front door, but, as I step up to the keypad, I draw a complete blank.

"Damn it," I mumble. "Why does this keep happening?"

"What?" Shane saracastically questions beside me. "You forget the pass code on one of your secret houses?"

He huffs out a light laugh as his hand slides in his hair, looking up at the long trees with a half-smile. But, when my absent stare quickly shifts from the ground to meet the piercing blue of his eyes, his smile fades, and dramatically drops his hand to his side.

"Seriously, Elle? Don't you have like a super memory or something?"

"I'm not some kind of super soldier Shane. I don't..." I trail off, suddenly remembering the code. *The keyword: soldier.* When I bought this place, I kept telling myself, if this plan B were to ever go into effect, to soldier on.

I punch in the code, 'feet forward and heart will follow'. A bit wordy, I know. I shove aside the poetry of it though as the door pops open. But, before I take a step inside, I slightly jump at the sound of the polite automated male voice that greets me. *Completely forgot about that.*

"Bomdia, srta Vega. Por favor insira o código da chave de voz."

(Good morning, Ms. Vega. Please enter the voice key code.)

"Modo de acesso. Senha, EV0010."

(Access mode. Password, EV0010.)

"You can speak Portuguese? And did it just call you Ms. Vega?" Shane swings his face in front of mine, a brow raised amusingly.

"Irrelevant," I answer straight-faced while stepping inside, instinctively lifting my foot higher than I normally would when going through a door. For a moment, I don't remember why. My theme of remembering things at the last minute might not be for the best, for a number of reasons. One being safety, which springs to mind just as I recall why I lifted my foot two inches higher. My chest tightens.

"Wait!" I shout.

It's too late. By the time I spin around, Shane had already walked through the doorway, his foot stepping into the green laser light that lines the bottom of the door. It sets off the armed security measure, and as a red dot shines in between his eyes, the first thing I think is, *I was so paranoid back then.*

"Pessoal não autorizado. Iniciando o protocolo de morte em cinco, quarto, três—"

(Unauthorized personnel. Starting the death protocol in five, four, three—)

"Comando stop. Code Alpha 401 Whisky Tango Charlie Golf!"

(Stop command. Code Alpha 401 Whiskey Tango Charlie Golf!)

A sweet melody plays, then the voice speaks in the same melodic tone. "Comando aprovado. Tenha um otimo dia." *(Command approved. Have a great day.)*

I breathe a breath of relief, thankful his head didn't explode all over the place, though my calm manner doesn't do much to help Shane relax.

"What just happened?" he frantically quivers. "Can I move?"

"Yes. Sorry about that. You can go wash up on the right then take the first room on the left," I say, sliding off my coat.

Slowly dragging his feet across the floor, his eyes glancing from side to side, as if he had seen a spider but forgot where, he moves from the door and scurries inside. I'd say it's a bit excessive, but with everything that's happen in the last couple of hours, he has every right to be jumpy. Fuck, I'm just as jumpy as him, yet I don't have the luxury of showing it. And watching the way Rebecca hurries inside, she's jumpy too.

I wish I could just talk to her about how I'm really feeling, for probably the first time ever, but I can't. It would be selfish to ask her to ignore everything that's happened and just be my friend right now. Besides, I have to be strong for them, for everyone who's trying to cope with what I put them right in the middle of. My time to breathe will come, though something keeps telling me that that isn't going to be until this is all over, and that's just me forcing myself to be optimistic.

"I could seriously use a pick me up after that long ass flight. And, you know... everything else." Shane calls out, not doing anything to hide the tiredness and slight tremble still in his voice. "Do you remember if you have coffee anywhere around here?"

"No, not really," I shrug. Then immediately focusing on what to do next I absentmindedly blurt out, "I don't actually like coffee."

"What!?" Rebecca exclaims, and my head snaps up.

"You don't like coffee but you had it almost every day for two years?" Shane chimes in, not helping at all.

She strides towards me. "You let me waste money on something you *'don't actually like'* for two years!?"

I try to reassure her, but something of the 'Michelle' in me slightly shrinks back at her upset tone when I answer, my voice going soft.

"Well, yeah. But I always felt bad about that, so I had a jar I'd put money in every time you'd buy it for me."

Oh god, being Michelle has made me sloppy. What a terrible choice of words for rebuttal. Even *I* know I didn't sell that. It came out completely unsure and rushed. My voice even slipped a bit, and judging by her bulging eyes, it was *definitely* the wrong thing to say.

I've taken out foreign vice presidents, helped infiltrate at least four crime syndicates, and went undercover in a prison called 'Satan's Hell Rejects', but her being angry is twisting my stomach? She doesn't even respond. She merely stomps off in the wrong direction.

I raise a finger. "It's actually to the right."

"I got it!" she yells back while passing by again.

Breathing out roughly through his nose behind me, I hear Shane's disappointment before I see it. Turning to face him, I let out my suddenly too tight ponytail and swallow my sigh when I see the frown creasing his lips. I never thought I'd care about him ever looking at me like that, but in this situation, it kind of hurts. I don't let the pain show anywhere in my expression, and when he deeply sighs, I only stare at the floor. My hair pouring into my face. Odd how I can stare into the eyes of people I've tormented and eliminated, but I can't seem to look into the eyes of someone I hurt emotionally.

My other best friend.

His eyes are on me, I can feel them, but he doesn't say anything. He's probably not going to speak to me again for the rest of the day, which I should be fine with. Both of them can hate me, as long as they're safe. I can live with that. I don't lift my stare as I turn to walk away, but I'm stopped when Shane pulls me into a warm embrace. My cheeks grow hot as I slowly return his hug and tell myself, *you couldn't live with it.*

"Personally, I don't know why I'm not as pissed about everything as much as Rebecca is, but I do understand what wanting a fresh start is like." He squeezes me then let's go.

"Maybe it's the cool jet, the free trip to Brazil, or how this reminds me of almost every spy movie known to man."

"This is *not* a movie."

"Fine. Not a movie, and you may or may not be a spy," he takes a step back and crosses his arms. "But if you ever lie to me, hurt Rebecca, or nonchalantly downplay the importance of my relationship with the woman I love again, I won't be as forgiving as I'm choosing to be right now."

That coffee thing was really the final straw, huh?

A bitter laugh echoes in my head at the comment. This time I have the sense to keep it to myself, because of the clear hint of a threat I detect in his tone. Biting my tongue—trying not to mention that off the top of my head I could kill him at least five different ways with just the blue scarf I'm wearing—I only nod sincerely to reassure him that I understand his frustration. That loosens him up enough, and as he uncrosses his arms, he gives me a quick smirk, kisses me on the forehead, and then goes off towards the other room.

As weird as I find it, I let the warmth of his compassion hang in the air for another minute, and smile at the fact that he's still talking to me. Despite the threat, I know he's worried about me. I'm thankful to him for that. It's nice. But, while walking over to the couch, too tired to go to the other rooms upstairs, somehow my last thought of the night is a question.

W*hy didn't I shoot Elias in the face?*

I don't know how l[illegible]sleeping for, but when I feel someone watching [illegible]y sit up. My eyes take a second to adjust. When they do, I sigh. At the sight of Rebecca sitting on the floor in front of me, I let go of the gun that I've hidden in the couch cushion. There's something haunting about her just sitting there with her legs crossed, her twisted hair hanging off her shoulders. Although nothing is more bothersome than the unreadable expression on her face. I dismiss the subtle chill she gives off, lean back while tying my own pesky hair into a messy bun, and then get the ball that is our coming conversation rolling.

"Is everything okay," I ask delicately, but then drop my eyes to the floor. "I mean, despite what's already happened."

"That guy that was at your apartment earlier, shooting at you, did you love him?" she asks, surprisingly calm.

I'm caught off guard by her question at first, but then her look of blankness shifts into what I assume she was trying to hide earlier. A look that says she's been thinking of what to ask me first without getting angry. So, I decide to let that wall down ever-so-slightly for her. For the friend that's always been there for me.

I take in a deep breath, yet my palms still become sweaty. "Yes. Once upon a time, I thought I couldn't breathe without him."

"So your random comment in the car, when Theora told us about Shane proposing, that really *was* your answer based off of experience?"

I stare down at her, a little surprised she remembered what I had said. "Yes."

She tilts her head. "You were married to him, but then something happened? Something so bad that it caused you to leave?"

"Not married. No. But almost."

She stares, waiting for more. I then sigh and open that door a little wider.

"I've always felt so alone in the world, but that feeling was nothing compared to the loneliness I felt when I started out at the agency. I was young and scared but trying not to show it. But when I had first seen him, it... it was like I found a piece of myself I didn't know I was missing."

I smirk at the memory of seeing Elias for the first time. His rich brown eyes, messy hair, gentleman-yet-mysterious-like manner and that stupid smile that made my heart fall straight into my stomach.

"I hadn't even spoken to him yet, and I wasn't the type of person that felt those feelings, unless it was completely necessary to my survival. It was both confusing and new, like everything else, but, I don't know, with him, I immediately thought the feeling would make me weak."

Rebecca's eyes land on me, without rage in them for the first time since we left Brooklyn. She then leans in closer, wanting me to go on. I've never told anyone about how I felt in that moment—not even Minnie—but for some reason, the words just continue to pour from my mouth.

"That same day, just my luck, we got partnered up together. I was pissed, but honestly more nervous than anything. I figured that some god somewhere heard what I was thinking and decided to test my patience. That, or my willingness to trust anyone again. I say it was the latter, because when we first spoke, you know what the first thing he said to me was?"

Her orderly demeanour falls to intrigue. "What?"

"He looked me dead in the eyes and said, 'I think we were made for each other. Till death do us part.' Without completely meaning to, I laughed right in his face." A grin sets into my hot cheeks as I chuckle, but quickly I force myself to stop.

Dryly she snickers as her brows knit together. "How did he take that?"

"Great, actually. I immediately apologized, while using every ounce of strength to avoid looking him in the eye of course. When I finally did stare up at him, he was just... smiling at me. After that, we kind of just fit perfectly together. Hand in glove, you know? Despite the strict rules against our 'personal' relationship."

"Wow. That's the kind of love people don't let go of easily. So... what happened that made him want to kill you?"

My expression darkens at the thought of his face that night, at the thought of my heartache hours earlier that day. I can't tell her what I had done. It's classified, but mainly it's because she'd never speak to me again. In her world, I'd be the monster in that story, and I don't think I see all of the fault in what I did.

At least that's what I continue to tell myself.

Being the monster in the normal world is what I've always been good at. But at least in the world *I* live in, the one where Unknown exists, I get to be figuratively "seen" as the good guy. So, when I stare down at her, seeing the interest rising just as she breathes, I continue with what I can, trying to change the subject.

"In a lot of ways, I thought of him as a gift. The first good thing I earned after making it through my supremely shitty childhood and becoming my own woman. Especially when he always made me feel like... like I was worthy enough to be loved, and capable of loving, despite being scarred inside and out. Elias..." my voice breaks again as I say his name. My eyes start to water, but I finish.

"He knew me better than anyone ever would, because I let him, and at first, I thought that that would drive him away from me. But umm... whenever I'd start to pull from him, he'd always pull me back closer, and never let go."

Tears stream down my face and I violently wipe them away with my sleeve. I don't want to remember him that way, I can't. I need to remember him the way he was when he broke my heart, to remember him shooting at me only hours ago. Remind myself—like I have for the last three years—that I hate him. He doesn't love me, and I *don't* love him. I *can't still* love him.

I breathe, composing myself.

"I *am* sorry Becca, for bringing you into my mess. Truly." I drop my stare from her. "You should get some sleep. There should be more comfortable clothes that'll fit you in the closet."

She lets out a deep breath, filled with frustration, then speaks in a sharper tone. "When can I get back to my life? When can I go home Mich—Nova?"

I flinch at the sound of my real name coming out of her mouth with so much bitterness. "You don't have to call me that if you don't want to."

She crosses her arms. "That's your name, isn't it?"

"No. Yes. I don't know," I sigh. "The situation and circumstances have changed. Please, just try to get some sleep. We'll talk more in the morning."

Without another word, she heads towards the room. Before she completely disappears though, she stops and twists her head back around, not looking at me.

"I was supposed to start my new position today you know," she says with a sting that mimics the subtle pain in my arm. "With that promotion I got on Friday? The one I worked so hard for? It started today."

"I'm—"

"Sorry. I know," she walks off.

CHAPTER SIXTEEN

DISCONNECTED

It felt so good to get yesterday off me. Thank god the hot water still worked after all these years. Being clean and finally sleeping a solid four hours gave me a new kind of determination to deal with my problems. The positive energy helped guide me in my search to find all of my hidden weapons. A lot of the motivation came from wanting to look back on what I was into three years ago, but more of it was just in case Rebecca or Shane decided to off me. Can never be too careful.

What I did find did *not* disappoint, unlike my outfit choices did. I mean, short sundresses and heels? Who was I going to force myself to be with Elizabeth Vega? Though despite the very yellow dress and white heels, I start to feel much more like myself when I grab a retractable bo staff, and twirl it in my hand. It almost acts as my version of a stress ball. I keep twirling as I go through my bag of goodies again, and find one of the many burner phones I've had in my life. Though this one's still in the plastic. I rip it out, set it up, and call Minnie.

"Name," is all she answers with. Her voice not quite sounding like her own.

"M, it's me. Nova." That name—my name—feels weird coming out of my mouth.

"Oh," she yawns, "why didn't you call me on the studs?"

"They're dead, and I left the case to charge them back in Brooklyn. So it's burners from now on."

"Okay, well, I hope you're only calling because you and the civilians got to your fail-safe location alright. If it's for anything else, I'm sorry, but I can't spare the time."

"Yeah, we made it without further hiccups, but I'm also calling to see if you have any news about what's going on." My voice softens. "You sound awful by the way. Did you sleep at all?"

She yawns again. "Not a wink, but that's not as important as what I have to fill you in on."

"Your tone is already getting me worried."

"Good."

Shit.

"You heard the lockdown that went into effect after you and Elias's aliases were exposed. Since then, however, more drastic shit has hit the fan. I had a hunch that the triggered lockdown would slow the copying of information, and it has, but..." she trails off.

"Minnie?"

"Sorry. Brain blip," she roughly breathes out then continues.

"As I was saying, the lockdown means that if Foreman—or their skilled hacker—tries to enter another virus into the system it won't work, which is good. But that also means that all assets and agents are completely frozen, which leaves a lot of our protected 'clients' vulnerable. Who knew presidents and entire armies could be such babies without us."

"Believe me, after being on "security detail" for a couple of them, I did," I groan.

"Well, they're being babies again. Upset babies. And since that's *not* good, Commander is pissed. She's channelling all that anger towards two agents she believes to be working in cahoots as Foreman. A hunch she *claims* is her own, but it seems fishy to me."

Her beating around the bush is beginning to get on my nerves. It does force me to think in the silence, but when I finally "connect the dots"—as she'd say—I get a visual of the picture. I don't like what I see.

"Oh, fuck no," my mouth goes dry. "Minnie, *please* don't tell me that those two agents are—"

"Yeah. It's you and Elias."

I don't react. Not at first. I only pull in as much air as my lungs will allow through my nose, and just stand there. I hold it in as my entire face slowly turns hot with anger. It's just one terrible thing after another terrible thing, followed by yet another terrible thing. Snowballing and getting bigger and bigger, seeing how far I can be pushed until—I take a throwing knife from my bag then thrust it at the wall in front of me, desperately needing to harm *anything* right now.

"Seriously!?" I shout, but then lower my voice, remembering that Shane and Rebecca are still asleep. "How would we even do that? From what I heard, he's been AWOL, and I'm in a completely different department."

"Well—"

"It was *our* aliases that were exposed!"

"Nova—"

"You of all people know that she's wrong. You figured most of this out! Connected the dots, saw things even Manager didn't. What would give her reason to think it was us?" I choke back the rest of my rage and take a breath so she can get a word in.

"You done?" she asks, her tone filled with tiredness.

"No. But talk anyway before I do."

"She investigated both of you after your names were leaked, factored in your involvement with Echo Delta in the past, and tied that with your connections to the mole both now and three years ago. All of which included your brother's kidnapping."

"You gave her the information I distinctly told you to only give to Manager!?"

"Oh, yeah, about that..." Minnie trails off, sounding anxious and guilty.

I freeze mid throw. "What. Did. You. Do?"

"Okay, yes. I kinda already updated her with everything after the alias alerts and lock down procedure went into effect."

"What!?" I yell.

"She wants to speak with you," her voice shrinks.

"Minnie, what the fuck!?"

A shiver runs through me as I grab every knife from my bag. One by one I throw them into the wall. Each make a satisfying thud, yet not satisfying enough that it calms me down. Not when this much fury is bubbling in my gut.

My head starts to pound with all the words I want to say swarming around inside it, but deep down I know nothing will stop the throbbing. Nothing but the feel of a knife leaving my hand in a swift motion. I reach the last one, my headache already beginning to subside, but then Minnie fires back.

"I'm sorry! She called me *right* after the exposure and insisted I tell her everything. I couldn't say no, okay? She's scary as shit."

I throw my final knife at the innocent wall, and sharply inhale. I'm not happy with the way she found out. From her angle it does make me look guilty. Especially my running-away-to-Brazil part. Completely losing my temper with Minnie wouldn't be fair though, not when I'm fully aware of how scary Commander is. I slowly exhale, letting some of the anger melt away to speak calmly.

"It's fine, alright. I just... I just need to buy myself more time so I can figure everything out. Deal with Elias so Rebecca and Shane can go home safely, form anything that resembles a plan to clear my name, then I can talk to her."

"Look, I know this is bad, but I also know that you're not Foreman. Honestly, Commander thinking it's the both of you sounds like a reach, especially for her standards. She has eyes everywhere and works off hard facts, not hunches. I think someone might be steering her your way on purpose. But I just don't know who or why." Her once worried tone becomes stern.

"Frankly, you'll never know either if you don't talk to her, Nova. That's the only way to clear things up."

"Oh, because she's the 'let's sit down and talk about it' type of person Minnie? She'll hunt me down, skin me alive, and then use me as a rug in her office bathroom to send a message!"

"That's grossly graphic and specific," she says, not hiding the cringe in her voice.

"I can't talk to her yet, okay? Not until I find out who would go through the trouble of sending Elias after me, but then turn around and decide to screw up my life even more by framing *both* of us."

"Umm... N, she's waiting to speak with you on the other line."

Within that same unsteady heartbeat, I hang up the phone, toss it at the wall, and smile as it shatters and falls to the ground. How could she just set me up like that? There's *no* way I'm talking to Commander about my mess. I'll eventually have to, so she doesn't go on believing that I'm the mole, but right now, no fucking way. It's crazy, and what's even crazier is that it's me *and* Elias in the same boat with this bullshit.

The *one* person I don't want to be in the same anything with. The *one* person who is hunting me at the moment—over something I did three years ago. I get that we're the only agents from the operation to suddenly resurface, just when the mole did, but we were also the only ones closest to figuring out who the real mole was. How is it that doing our jobs back then is coming back to bite us in the ass now?

So unfair.

I shouldn't even be thinking of "*us*" as an "*us*" in the first place. We're not, and never will be an *us* again. This is just *my* ass on the line. I can't even say for sure that he isn't the mole, but it wouldn't make sense. He's been too busy hunting me and has been AWOL while doing so.

No. No. I don't need to care about him anymore, especially since he's trying to kill me. For one last moment though, before completely blocking out all scenarios with him in it, I do allow myself to think. Not as his ex-fiancé Nova, but as his ex-partner, agent 401.

From the beginning it was Elias and I who stood out from the rest of the recruits with our combined skills. And once we came to have a greater... understanding of each other, we always delivered results. The higher-ups saw that, so when approached with the opportunity to join our first in-house covert op, we jumped at the chance. It was an honour. But, if I knew then that we'd be blamed for its downfall now, "honour" isn't the word I would've used.

I say it again... so unfair.

Supervisor *was* the one who led the whole damn operation. Yet apparently, his failure to produce the real mole isn't as easy as blaming the two agents who suddenly have a connection to the most recent situation. Hell, at this point, I'd bet that he's the one feeding lies to Commander that Elias and I have been in cahoots this entire time.

I've always hated that fucker.

Wishful thinking hopes that that's true, just so I can pack all this shit up and end it, though my sense of logic pushes me back into the reality where all the facts are stacked against me. Which reminds me of Commander's coming wrath. An uncomfortable knot forms in my stomach just at the thought, and so much of me wants to scream from both fear and irritation.

I'm going to die young at this point, and I swear I'm *so* close to just going off to do so like a wounded cat. My heart is already pounding in my chest like a ticking bomb. All I'd have to do is wait for it to explode. Unfortunately, I'm too busy to die right now. So instead, I breathe.

Deep breath in.

Deep breath out.

I stroll over to the wall, to pull out each knife, but stop in my tracks when Shane comes out of the room and glances from me to my homemade target board. I completely forgot he was behind there, and judging by the tired and irritated look in his eyes, he noticed. Another thing to apologize for, I guess.

Before I open my mouth, he smoothly yanks a knife from the wooden panel and turns to me. He stares, his ocean eyes trying to see into my soul, but when that doesn't seem to pan out for him, he takes a deep breath.

"I think you need some fresh air," he says, handing me the knife, his eyes softening. "Rebecca is probably still asleep. Let's go for a walk."

Grabbing the hilt, I nod and look away. "Yeah, sure," I huff out. "Let's go."

CHAPTER SEVENTEEN

HIDE AND SEEK

We walk silently in the overflow of nature throughout the grounds of my secluded house for a while—the mild late afternoon air mimicking the awkward uneasy heat between us. Only when we continue further do I notice how big the property really is, and at the same time I realize how stupid I was for buying the place. I had gotten it on a scared whim, after figuring out I'd probably have to run from Elias eventually, but that eventually came *much* sooner, and with *much* more baggage than I thought.

As naive as I was back then, I found comfort in knowing that, at the very least, I'd get over him and the fear of him finding me in the future. Sadly however, that comfort was a lie. The thought of that fear alone brings up the same memory of his face from that night on the pathway. His lips pressed together, and the slight crease in his brow, even though his eyes were soft, like he had come to some understanding in his mind. Before the entirety of that repetitive nightmare starts to overtake my vision, Shane's surprisingly tranquil voice breaks into my thoughts.

"So, after having some time to think, I've come to realize something."

I raise a brow, forcing down the rest of the lingering memory. "Oh yeah, and what's that?"

"From the beginning you've had this whole other life. You've probably done things I can't even imagine. You lied to me."

"I know," I sigh. "But—"

"You lied. But you know what the most upsetting thing is? You lied about being a brown belt," he dryly snickers.

Stopping in my tracks, I turn and stare up at him. Although, instead of finding anger on his face, I find a teasing expression, and I can't help but laugh with him. It comes out slow in the beginning, but as I continue, it turns into something of a villainous cackle; letting some of my past and present stress escape me.

Once I start, I can't seem to stop. I laugh and laugh until I'm holding my sides from the pain. And at some point, during this display of donning insanity, my problems start to cloud whatever I found funny. Next thing I know, I'm crying as my body shakes violently.

I attempt to stop. Attempt to regain some of the control I've tried so desperately to grab onto, except the hot tears only continue to stream down my cheeks. I close my eyes to support the tightness in my ribs, and one by one the memories of my life leading up to this point—the very ones I tried to ignore—come bursting out of that dark corner I threw them in.

The guilt of leaving my brother behind twice.

The gut-wrenching ache of Elias drifting away from me, and then breaking my heart.

Then, worst of all, the remorse I forced myself not to feel after I did what I did.

Without even realizing it, I let myself become this empty person by eradicating all these feelings from my life. I didn't allow myself to open the wounds so that they could heal properly. Instead, I just numbed the pain, covered them up, and moved on. How can I handle anything if I'm not strong enough to process my emotions? I choke back the sudden question and slowly start to calm down as it bounces around my head.

I search for an answer, running through all my traumas, and grasp that every single one would've taught me a lesson I probably could've really used right about now. The realization does take me a few steps back in the process of settling down. Though what finally does the trick, is remembering that Shane is in front of me.

My cheeks heat even further when I look up at him and notice through blurry vision that he's taking a step towards me. I quickly move back and shake my head while wiping my face.

"I'm okay, Shane, really. I didn't..." I catch my breath and sigh. "I didn't mean to burst into tears like that. I'm sorry."

His voice is soft. "You don't have to apologize, it's okay."

Compassionate Shane isn't one I'm used to, but I'm starting to like him. His sweet attitude warms my chest, and I stop shaking. My shoulders loosen for the first time in a while, and I give him a weak smile for a minute before roughly wiping away the rest of my tears.

"Thank you. Thank you for being you in a moment when I really need it. And, before you ask, I'm alright. I only needed a minute to regroup."

"I just realized I've never seen you cry like that before. Actually, I've never seen you cry. Ever," he awkwardly comments.

"Only about three people have, and two of them are dead," I say, a new awareness in my tone.

"That doesn't seem healthy."

"Yeah. I have a lot of shit to work out apparently."

His hand travels around to the back of his neck, and as he begins to rub it, he lets out a harsh breath. "Well, in that case, are you *sure* you're okay? I may not know the exact amount of pressure you're under, what with not being a... government assassin of some kind?"

I only give him a slight smirk and shake my head at his sentence turned question. He stares at me with wide eyes, waiting for a yes. When my expression doesn't change from mere impassiveness, he shrugs off the unanswered question then glances away.

"Worth a shot. But what I'm trying to say, is that I may not know all that rest on your shoulders, but I do know what the feeling of pressure is like, *and* the feeling of not being able to control what comes next."

"Don't go completely soft on me, Wendell," I joke, but his serious demeanour stays the same.

"Just be careful not to let the could've's and should've's of the past cloud any future decisions. Because if you do, you'll regret it. Okay?"

A weak smile plays on my lips. "Okay."

"Good," he sharply nods, and then turns on his heels to start walking back towards the house. "Now we can go back and enjoy your air conditioning. It's hot as a mother out here. Gun to my head, and I mean that ironically, I never thought I'd miss the Brooklyn cold—"

I walk up beside him and lightly punch him in the arm. "Is that the only reason you wanted to come out here?" I ask, laughing slightly.

"First of all, ouch, and I can say that out loud now without my masculinity taking a dive, because you're an... expensive contract killer?"

I snort. "Come on, really?"

He sighs. "Okay, not a contract killer, but clearly, given the knives in the wall, you needed to talk. And I thought, since your emotional support Rebecca isn't available at the moment, I'd step in. I may not be as 'forthcoming' as she can be most of the time, but I'm here. And despite everything, I don't see you differently. Minus the guns, high tech gadgets, obvious extensive training, and random private jets of course. I love you, Elle. You're still one of my favourite people, and I want to know how you're doing. Plus..." he twists his neck to glance back at the city, "I've never been to Brazil before. Thought I'd take in some sights."

"It is beautiful, isn't it?" I say, completely captivated by the scene in front of us. But my mellow tone shifts into slight astonishment. He really is worried about me, isn't he? "Thank you, Shane."

He brushes a hand through his chestnut hair before snickering bitterly. "You sound surprised that I care for your well-being."

It almost sounds like he's trying to hide his hurt.

"I'm just not used to Shane Wendell showing his sweet side. Or is that the real you that you've been hiding from me?"

"*You're* talking to *me* about hiding who I really am... Nova?"

A dry laugh escapes me. "Touché."

"Seriously though, can I ask you something?" his tone dips into unease.

"Don't think I didn't notice the redirect, but sure."

"Theora and I have been going in circles, having the same argument about why she didn't... why she didn't say yes when I asked her to marry me. But the second I realized that I couldn't contact her, all of that didn't matter anymore. I guess... I guess I'm asking, do you think she'll be pissed that I haven't called? Something kept telling me she's worrying."

"With everything that's going on between you two, no, I don't think she'll be mad. She'll understand, and if not, when this is over, I'll explain what I can to her. And besides, if it helps, I don't think she'll be pissed with you more than with me," I tell him, my voice coming out as softly as I can make it, hoping to sooth his nerves.

He doesn't answer. Instead, he only nods while letting out a deep breath. Sounds like he's been holding it in since the flight here. I feel horrible, having to put him through that, but it's better Theora not be added into the mix. It may just be me who thinks that though, considering our walk back is silent.

Getting back to the house I find the front door cracked open. Shane and I had gone through the back, and I closed the front door last night. Something is very wrong with this scene. Without hesitation, I grab the knife that's tucked into the thigh holster under my dress and stop Shane in his tracks.

"What's going on?"

I don't say anything. I only glance back at him with a finger to my lips. The second my stare meets his, out of the corner of my eye I catch sight of something. Footprints. One pair, women's size seven. No signs of dragging or skipped steps in the gravel. Nothing out of ordinary except the open door, but even his "flare for the dramatic" wouldn't be so obvious.

I tuck my knife away to pull the door open, then call out to Rebecca. There's no answer so I race to her room. She's not here. Just scattered clothes, messy sheets, and a quickly scribbled note. And with each word I read the angrier and angrier I get.

Nova, I have a life, a good one, so I'm going back to that. I don't need any of this. On some level I get that you were trying to protect me, but I don't want the kind of life you have. A life where I can't trust the people around me, not even my "best friend." I'm sorry it had to be this way. Please don't try to find me. Now that I'm away from you, I'll be fine. He's after you, not me. Good luck, and goodbye. —Becca.

P.s- I love you, Shane, but I'm sorry. ☹

Shane comes running into the room. "Where's Becca?"

Looking over the note again, my eyes scan for any form of false speech, tear stains, or places where the pen was pressed harder than others, but there isn't any of that. It's all her.

"¡Esta maldita chica me está volviendo loco!" I shout viciously.

(This damn girl is driving me crazy!)

Something like fear slowly rises in my gut, among other justifiable emotions. Outrage, irritation, frustration—my fingers wrap themselves around the paper as I continue down the list, so tightly my nails rip through it and dig into my palm. I don't flinch at the pain. I'm too busy forcing emotions down before they come up and out in a much more *violent* way.

I turn and lock eyes with Shane to answer him. Maybe I should've taken a minute to cool off, but Rebecca's stupidity gets the better of me, and my frustration unintentionally becomes more present in my tone.

"She's gone." I shove the note against his chest then stomp out the door. "She left."

He follows me out of the room. "What do you mean she left?"

"She's a smart and resourceful woman, Shane. She probably went through my closet, found some hidden cash, and took off as soon as I fell asleep again to god-knows-where."

This is one of those incidences where I know I'm right, and it's *not* a good thing. It hasn't been for about four days now. Panic starts to settle into my bones. That same panic I felt when she told me she was in my apartment yesterday, and now I have to repeat the same cycle of having to get her?

She's such a stubborn little— no, not now. The best thing to do is breathe, though even that's hard to do. Especially when civilians—stubborn civilians like her—always think they can handle shit like this on their own. As if they even have the *slightest* clue how.

They have no idea what's really going on under the surface, or they just choose not to care. The worst part is, I can't even think about that right now. That would be wasting time, and I need to get to her... again. I pace back and forth, thinking of where she might go. She wouldn't go back to Brooklyn, not when what happened there still has her shaken.

That only leaves two other places. Her parents in Jamaica, but she hates it there, or her aunt's place in—I cut my own thinking short, figuring it out, then go into my bug out bag for another burner phone. I grip it until my knuckles turn white while making the call.

"Minnie, it's N. Sorry to be so pushy, but I have an emergency. I need you to send me a jet going to Toronto."

"Good afternoon, agent," she answers, almost as robotically as our old system Zoey.

"Yes, I get that I sound more and more like a spoiled brat who only calls when they need something, but this is an emergency," I repeat.

This time, when I get a reply, it's not Minnie who speaks. A knot tightens in my stomach at the cold voice I hear instead.

"Hello, agent 401. What is this emergency you're speaking of?" Commander, a.k.a Athena Harrington's tone is calm and collected on the other end of the phone, but I've worked for her long enough to know she's biting down her fury.

This woman is the scariest I've ever met, and that's including my mamá. I haven't seen her in person in years, yet that doesn't stop me from straightening my back before answering, as if she's standing in front of me.

"Good afternoon, Commander. I'm honored that you took time from your busy schedule to contact me. Though please excuse my bluntness when I say that this emergency is a personal matter; therefore, it does not concern you nor the agency."

"Oh, good. For a minute there I thought I'd have to remind you—though it should be common knowledge at this point—that the use of agency resources for personal dilemmas are strictly prohibited while a lockdown is in effect. But it sounds to me that you completely understand that, and the punishments that come if that rule is grossly disregarded. I'm *sure* you have things under control on your side, agent?"

"Yes ma'am," I lie.

"Great. Now that that's cleared up, let me ask you something," she says, her voice starting to dip into that fury.

"Yes ma'am?" I rush out, desperately trying to hide it.

"Am I taking up your time, agent?"

Well, that didn't work.

"No ma'am," I lie again, a bitterness coating my tongue this time.

"Okay, good. So, back to my inquiry. Do you think that it's smart to hang up on your superior, especially after being informed that you're a suspect involving espionage?"

"No ma'am, not smart at all. But you must understand that I—"

She cuts in calmly, yet somehow it terrifies me. "I couldn't care less about your civilian friends, agent, or about whatever "personal predicament" that's happening between you and agent 404. I want your ass here, at Beta Z headquarters, *now*."

Old lessons of obedience almost make me say that I'll be on the next flight out. But when Shane steps into my eyeline, I shove down the urge as I watch his eyes widen with a simple question in them. 'What are we doing?'

I remove the phone from my ear and whisper, "we're leaving."

He nods and heads towards the door. As I do the same, I bring the burner back to my face, grab my bag, then address Commander on the move.

"Ma'am, I understand, but with all due respect, I cannot do that right now. I started something that needs to be finished. I'm not leaving until it's done. And frankly, I find it insulting that I've even been considered to be the mole."

At my last words, my voice threatens to break, but I hold it steady. A very powerful woman like Commander having even the *slightest* notion that I'm one half of Foreman doesn't exactly help with that steadiness. In the back of my mind though, I cheer myself on for even talking back to her. It helps diminish a bit of my self-doubt.

What really extinguishes it is seeing the old agency issued black Lamborghini when I open the hidden garage. I quickly knock twice on the windshield then wait for the car to come to life and scan me over. Then, as the doors fly upwards, I catch sight of Shane's expression, and it's priceless.

Despite the jaw dropping amazement plastered across his face, and the fact that I know he *really* wants to say something, I get in the car, and use the biometric scanner to activate my plan C. But, as the sensation ends, that sweet confidence high I'm riding turns sour when Commander answers me.

This time using my name.

I swear for a second, she sounds like my mamá the day she found out *I* was the one who skimmed some "nose candy" off the top of every brick that came in or out. For three months I replaced it with talcum powder, selling the brush off to pay for my first phone.

I'm in so much trouble.

"Nova, let me make something clear to you. What you're doing is irrelevant to me, and your opinion of whether or not you're guilty doesn't matter. *Especially* when you're denying me the extra assurance of looking into your eyes to determine if you're telling the truth. We are under attack here, and if you do not come in to brief me on *everything* you know in person, I will have no choice but to send out for you."

"Ma'am, please," I beg, "I promise you I only know as much as you do at this point. I'll explain everything again when I can. I just need some time. I can't come in right now. Not until I deal with my business first."

"Alright, if that's the way you want it, agent." She fidgets with something on the other end, then that calm and collectiveness tone dives straight into cold fury. "The next time I see you, it'll be in chains"

Before I think, the terror of having to deal with more causes me to speak before I mean too. "Wait. Don't make the call, not yet! I can—I will come in, but after I fix this, and I can make it worth something to you."

"I'm listening."

"If you let me do this, I'll..." I look to Shane then take a deep breath, "I'll turn myself in for questioning, and bring agent 404 with me. Giving you the two most wanted agents on a silver platter. No strings."

"What are you doing?" he whispers angrily.

I open my mouth. Nothing comes out. I know what I'm doing, I'm buying time, but beyond that, I have no idea. I'm afraid that he'll be able to see that lingering in my stare. My chest and shoulders become heavy as I attempt to lock myself up. To be the way I was with him before our talk. But, finding it harder to do than I thought, I turn away then focus on the car zooming through the streets. Lonely streets that no tourist should travel on alone, unless they have a heavily armed smart car. Or me. Well, me on one of my *better* days.

Pull it together.

We come upon the abandoned warehouse where my plan C is to take place, which can only happen if Minnie heard my request. Solitary silence echoes in my ear as Commander thinks over my offer, but I know she'll take it. Elias and I were her best recruits in years, and if worst comes to worst, I'll kill Elias, or he'll kill me first before we get there. Not the best state of mind, though it's also not the worst either. As we reach the lifeless location, Commander finally replies.

"I'll take you up on your offer, given that you seem to be agent 404's only focal point lately. But I'll only give you twenty-four hours to deliver the both of you. And know this, I will *not* play another round of hide and seek with you, understand?"

"Yes ma'am."

"And if I even get the *slightest* bad feeling from you, or hear anything else from Supervisor *or* Manager on that front, I'm sending out for you. Priority one, Nova."

Those last three words force me to recall the memory of the last poor sucker I was sent to bring in. Once that shiver somewhat clears, I stiffly respond. "Understood, Commander. Thank you ma'am."

"Twenty-four hours agent," she sternly repeats. "Twenty. Four. Hours."

She then hangs up.

CHAPTER EIGHTEEN

KNIVES OUT

There's no jet.

We reach the extraction point... and there's no jet.

I hear the echo of Minnie's voice. "Hello...?"

What have I done? How stupid could one person be in the span of two hours?

I'm losing control, in every sense of the word. Being hunted by my ex, chasing after Rebecca, and now having to make good on that deal with Commander? It's all turning into a disaster. A swirl of shit about to hit the fan. There's no way I can deliver on that deal, not without dowsing some of the flames burning around me. My life is in between a death wish and a hard place, which doesn't give me much wiggle room to handle my business.

"Nova, can you hear me? Are you still there!?" she shouts now. I slowly bring the phone to my ear.

"I'm here..." I answer as my jaw clenches, "standing in an empty warehouse parking lot with no patience, no time, and no *fucking* clue Minnie!"

"Hey! Don't get upset at me for being ambushed by our boss, okay? I told you earlier that she was on the line and wanted to talk to you, but you didn't want to hear it. So, I strongly suggest that you project all your anger towards someone who—I don't know—is trying to kill you instead of help you!"

I rub my eyes until they hurt and take a deep breath, to make it easier to return my attention on getting to Rebecca. And to ensure I don't lose Minnie because of my own stupid decisions. I shouldn't have yelled, especially not when I know how things work with Commander. Within the first ten seconds of meeting her, she'll determine if she likes you or not. She's an all-round scary lady. If I were in Minnie's shoes, I would've done what she did too, which leaves me feeling guilty for the unnecessary attitude.

"I'm sorry. I didn't mean to lose it," I let a bitter laugh escape me. "Well, not towards you anyway."

"Seriously N, what kind of shitty apology was that?" she sighs, then starts typing away, like it calms her. "Look, I get that you're under an excruciating amount of pressure, but I'm here to help."

My second apology becomes an abandoned sentence on the tip of my tongue when Shane yells in the short distance between us. "Elle, is that it!?"

Turning around, my gaze follows to where his finger shoots out in the air towards an approaching plane. I hadn't even noticed it at first. Most of my focus was on the fury and anxiety bubbling in my stomach. But, when my eyes catch sight of our way out, I move my coming panic attack aside. With new excitement, I twist my body away from the noise, sticking a finger in my ear.

"You got a plane?" I ask, sounding more shocked than I actually am.

"Yes. While you were being scolded by Commander, I located one of ours on the radar that made it out under the wire after the lockdown went into effect. It's a pre-authorized flight that's dropping off a shipment from the Winery to

Canada, so I sent them to pick you up," she answers with clear offense at my surprise.

"You really are amazing, aren't you?"

"Yeah, I know. You're welcome." She hangs up.

I slide the phone into the pocket of my dress, my chest tight. She has every right to be angry, but that doesn't stop the fact that I'm proud of her. I've always been. Having her back in my life is overwhelming, but the good kind. She was my voice of reason when nothing made sense in the new world around me. The first person I was able to call a friend, a real friend. I have to fix things with her.

Later though.

As the jet gets closer, Shane stomps over to me, lips pressed thin, brows tight, and irritation lingering in his stare. Everything about him screams impatience. I place a gentle hand on his tense shoulder when he stops in front of me, remembering the comfort he offered on our walk. I attempt to return the favour.

"Nothing is going to happen to her. She's still in the air. Just try to relax," I tell him kindly.

"How can I do that when my so-called best friend of five years left me to face all of this madness alone, didn't say goodbye, my girlfriend is probably pissed because I haven't called her, and you..." he trails, taking my hand off him.

"You're planning to turn yourself in with the maniac who wants to *kill* you. Which means *you* have to go to *him*, and that doesn't sound like a good idea at all!"

"I can handle that maniac when worst comes to worst. And turning myself in doesn't mean I'm going to die," I reply boldly, trying to convince myself as well.

Leaning down, giving me no choice but to look him in the eye, I see the concern swimming in all that blue.

"How do you know that Elle? Honestly, how do you know? It could just be a trap to kill the both of you. That bastard can go to hell for all I care, but you?"

"Shane..." I begin to reassure him—for a brief second seeing my brother the day I left—but my words come to a halt when the jet smoothly lands in the empty lot. The door pops open and a man steps out grinning.

He has a generic male face. Everything symmetrical. Brown eyes, straight nose, thin lips, and a sharp chin with light stubble. Maybe he could pass as slightly handsome in the grey dress pants and shirt with rolled up sleeves he wears with ease. But aside from his perfectly laid midnight hair and perfectly white teeth, I'd mistake him for a familiar face, knowing full well I've never met him before.

It's unsettling.

"Did someone order a lift!?" the man snickers, as if he just told a joke.

Without a beat, Shane goes to the plane and hurries up the descended stairs. I follow right behind him, while trying to think of what to say to make him feel a little better. But nothing comes to mind as I begin to climb. It sends a jolt of worry through my body, because I now realize, *I* don't even know what will come of this whole affair. It can't get any worse than it already is. Yet, when I reach the top of the stairs, something tells me that I spoke too soon.

"Good afternoon, Ms. Hannigan. My name is Wes Black and I'll be assisting you during your trip today." He smiles broadly at the end of his greeting, but there's something threatening behind it.

I don't know his face, but I *swear* I've heard the name before. I just can't place it. My sudden state of incertitude sends a warning ping to my brain, causing the question of 'why is he calling me Ms. Hannigan?' to run through my head. There's a five second patch of silence while I try to figure out who this man is. It's like it's right there in front of me yet I can't see it. But, when Shane speaks, it becomes clear, and my heart almost stops.

"Wes Black? Where have I heard that name before?"

"Shane..." I trail, my eyes drifting to him with a hint of worry in them. "Get out. Now."

"What, why? What about Rebecca?"

"Please," Wes Black says as he moves forward, forcing me down a step, "I don't think that'll be necessary. I'm sure we can handle this like *adults*."

I receive every ounce of his force as he pushes me down the stairs, and I brace myself for each pain to come. Loosening my body, the first step pushes into my hip, agony coming in fast, but I focus on using my arms to protect my head. Then, just as fast as I was shoved, I reach the ground and try my best to get to my feet. I wobble as a horrible throb spreads through my body.

My vision blurs, and I taste blood. Swallowing it down, I heavily breathe out through clenched teeth, eyes forward. I manage to make out Shane at the door as Wes Black slowly makes his way down the stairs, rolling up the sleeves on his shirt.

"Elle, are you okay!?" Shane shouts.

I dig my fingernails into my knees and lift my head in his direction, then use every muscle to speak. "Go," I demand.

"I'm not leaving without—"

"Tell the pilot to go, double time. Now Shane!" I cut him off, breathing rapidly as my stare focuses on Wes Black.

He smirks as he approaches. "You really should listen to her, Mr. Wendell. You're not going to want to see this."

All my senses are scrambled from the fall. Down feels like up, and up is spinning profusely, which I'm sure is supposed to be still. The only plus side is that my body doesn't hurt as much as it would've if I didn't act fast, but I can feel the ache coming on against my hip. Adrenaline starts to pump into my system, so fast I can almost taste its addictive thrill. It dilute most of the agony, but with every step Wes Black takes closer to me, I step back, and that pain starts to travel down my leg.

I have more drastic problems to deal with now, which I can't do until Shane does as I said. But the plane still hasn't left. I need to know he'll be safe from what's about to happen, and that means he has to get away as soon as possible. Everything is screwed up enough. I don't want to make it worse by him seeing me kill this guy.

He stands at the door, a foot on the step coming over to me, but I soften my glare and plead with him.

"Please Shane... you need to go."

He stares at me for what feels like forever, but once a look of understanding flashes across his face, he takes a step back. As the door closes, he says, "Fuck him up."

A slight grin forms on my lips as I watch the door to my escape shut and listen to its engines start. I stare at Shane through the window and let myself feel the relief that he'll be safe.

A bad idea.

As soon as the plane lifts off, a deep punch enters my gut. I fall to the ground, quickly gasping for air, then glance up to find Wes Black's smiling façade melt into a hateful glare.

"Let me re-introduce myself, Nova, now that it's just us amigos," he laughs dryly. "I wouldn't want us to get off on the wrong foot."

"I think..." I cough and try to take in another breath. "I think we're way past that. I already hate you. Very, *very* much"

Towering over me, he tilts his head sideways then plasters a sly smirk on his lips. "Well, that's your right I guess, but I find you captivating. Given everything he's told me about you, I feel like we're family. I bet you'd feel that way too if you just got to know me," he sticks out his hand. "Agent 504."

504? I search my mind to find out why that sounds familiar, and then, I remember. Agent 504; that was the agent listed who replaced me as Elias's partner. At the time I didn't think to look into him—clearly a mistake—but I did catch his name. My brain feels like mashed potatoes right now, but I think it was—

"Andre Low," I croak out.

"Ding ding ding!"

As it dons on me that this man has been following me for almost as long as Elias has, the churning in my stomach gets worse when I come to further recognize his alias. Wes Black: Theora's so-called travel agent. I knew I couldn't trust that bitch. She's been talking to him for the last two years. The guy who's associated with my crazy ex. What the fuck has been happening right under my nose?

I don't get the time to stew in my confusion and rage. When I look up at him again—Andre—his once friendly outstretched fingers begin to curl into a fist. Before it comes down, I act fast. Quickly sweeping his feet to get time to jump up onto mine, I hurry towards the bag that's full of my old weapons. My senses are still too shaky to fight him off without some kind of help, even though I'd much rather shut him down with my bare hands.

As I run, pushing down my pain becomes an afterthought when I don't hear him running after me. Only light footsteps follow behind me, which for some reason, makes me uneasy. There's not much I know about this guy, as an agent or a partner to Elias, but I've already gathered he's slow.

Except, while grabbing the first thing in my bag, still not hearing a thing from behind, I realize I'm wrong. He wanted me to trip him, wanted me to get to the weapons. Weapons he could've easily taken when he walked past them. Immediately, that tells me more. He likes to be challenged, even when that means giving his prey tools to fight him off.

Not the ideal person to be fighting right now, but I don't let that faze me. I don't let my ready expression falter either, as I watch him reach his hands behind his back then swings out two silver-grey karambits.

He holds them in his hands so delicately, almost as if they've become an extension of his hands. It slightly makes nervous energy travel up my spine. I grip my rainbow spectrum brass knuckle a little tighter as Andre fixes his stance. He then raises his stone eyes to mine.

"Now, I must admit, I'm a man that enjoys a good knife fight. Especially since I've never lost one," he boasts, like having a regular conversation with an old friend. "But don't worry, I won't enjoy this win any less because of my perfect streak."

Pushing aside the urge to swallow away the sudden dryness in my throat, I mask my worry by whipping out a retractable Bo staff. I spin it skillfully while stretching a mischievous smirk across my lips.

"Let's put an end to that streak, shall we?"

He shrugs and laughs dryly. "Knives out."

Just as he takes the first step forward, the memory that comes to my mind before proceeding with the slaughter warms an old part of me. *Oh yeah, I was really into my weapons being rainbow spectrum back then. I liked the way blood shimmered on it.*

A spark like lightning flashes, his karambits clashing with my steel staff, both of us putting as much force as we can into our attack. He's very light on his feet, but I see it as an advantage on my part. My fighting technique includes the skill of reacting on my opponents last minute decisions, which means that I'm just as fast as him, if not faster.

When he drops one arm and slices through the air—trying to catch me in the side—I quickly tilt my staff downwards. It blocks the blade within seconds of it becoming embedded into my ribs.

My foot then advances, my Bo following as I force Andre back. While he tries to correct his stance, that's when I swing, aiming for his head like it's a piñata. He recedes promptly, but I launch forward, thrusting my staff in a stabbing motion near his gut. A knife extends out at the end, yet it just misses. He ducks, then presses his lean body against the ground, as he somersaults around to my six. Swiftly turning, I hold my Bo at the ready while he jumps up. Something of an animalistic growl comes from him and then he starts talking.

They always start talking.

"I've been waiting so long to tell you off, though to be honest, I thought I'd be able to control my temper. But now that I'm standing in front of you, in the flesh..." he twists his mouth into a murderous grin, "I'd rather just slice you open for all the pain you caused him."

Ignoring his ignorance, I lunge, meeting him half way, and jab the knife near his neck. He sidesteps, cutting my attack short. I briskly have to fall back when he lets a karambit lose from his grip, it dangling from his thumb as he grabs at my wrist. I move, kicking him in the gut to gain some ground, but soon I'm shown why that was a mistake. Andre grasps my bare ankle with his meaty hand, then tosses me aside. I violently collide with the rough ground and roll, pain shooting up my hip.

Again, my senses become unsteady. Things teeter, though I get up, using my staff for support. I take a breath so things clear, and as my surroundings go upright, I notice Low has stumbled too. My heel pushing into his gut had to hurt.

Good.

The sight of his pain quickens my second wind. And while another round of fury and adrenaline complete their course within my blood stream, almost every part of me goes numb as I rush him again.

My calm response surprises him. And me. "You don't know anything about who I am."

With my staff rotating in both hands, like I'm rowing a boat with one long oar, my feet dart forward. Andre dodges each strike, his karambits taking the full force of my attacks, that is, until I advance with a stab. Blood drips from the clean slice across his shoulder, but, like it didn't happen, he keeps coming. He lifts his foot, getting ready to deliver a crushing blow, though he doesn't get the chance. I raise my staff to shield me, but he only uses the block to his advantage.

He forces all his weight onto me as he flips in the air, causing my Bo to collide with my chest. It's a light pressure, though not so light that it doesn't force me to catch my breath. I only get a second as he lands uneasily on his feet.

For a moment he stops, staring at me while drawing his lower lip between his teeth, and then smirks. He doesn't even glance at the new cut I graced him with. That right away is a warning as he strides towards me, forcing me back like we're dancing. His skills are there, but they weren't before.

Someone trained him, recently. With the way he somersaulted and flipped, my moneys on it being Elias. Those moves are ones I'd do, if I wasn't so discombobulated. Start low then go high. He taught him my technique. Well, tried. Given his sloppy foot work, it looks like he hasn't been learning long. It should worry me more than it is, but I don't let it. My main focus is controlling my breathing, as I catch myself slightly hyperventilating.

We come together again and he manages to slash my forearm. If I hadn't seen it happen, the cut would've gone unnoticed. But, since the sight of my flesh being ripped apart is something I witness, a fiery sting shoots up my arm. Adrenaline slows most of the pain. It becomes more present when I lift my head and see his cocky grin quickly turn into a frown.

"On the contrary, *Kitten*. I know a lot. Like I know you mattered enough to him. That you were so important that he just *had* to track you down for all these years," he hisses.

Him calling me Kitten makes me wince. I drawback as he comes closer.

"Lucky me, is that what you're trying to say?" I ask, smirking, though find nothing remotely funny.

I balance back on my heels, getting ready to meet my foot with his face, but he stops dead in his tracks. His expression suddenly becomes a stone-cold reflection of vengeance as his eyes lock with mine. Then, without even blinking, he slices the Bo staff right from my grip.

Holding my hand, watching the blood drip down my knuckles, I only notice him moving closer when he stomps on the ground. With every stomp he takes forward, I move back. In those seconds between each step, he loses it.

"*Day* was all about you. *Night* was all about you." He angrily slices near my face but when he misses, his voice only rises. "And in those rare moments, when he wasn't brutally beating himself up about you and what you'd done, he slowly unravelled and became a true monster!"

The feel of my heart skipping a beat brings me back to where I am, what I'm facing, and I seize my opportunity. Stopping in my tracks, I take advantage of his closeness, and smash my brass knuckles into his face then hear the crack of his nose.

His eyes water and become blurry. All he has left to do is swing his knives in literal blind rage. While he does, and continues to miss, I slide my thumb down the smooth side of the shiny knuckles causing a hidden knife to pop out.

I attack in a zigzag pattern, slitting his cheek, returning the favour and cutting his forearm, then I slice the knife down the side of his leg. *I'm getting pretty good with my knife handling.* The chop down takes mere seconds. And just because I find extra time to be a menace, I punch him in the nose again. He grabs his face, roaring in pain. I take a slight step back to give myself some room then intertwine my legs with his and drop him to the ground.

"He was already a true monster to me," I rapidly breathe out, then press the knuckles up against his neck and activate the third and final surprise. The taser.

His body shakes on the cold pavement. I don't let up until the karambits drop from his hands. When they clang to the ground I move back and quickly pound my fist into his jaw, rendering him utterly unconscious. The thought to kill him crosses my mind—multiple times within five seconds—but my instincts tell me to keep him alive.

For now.

Just in case I can get more information about Elias, or *any* about Theora from him, which seems unlikely.

Although, with the way Theora had mentioned "Wes" always complaining about his partner, something tells me that Andre isn't just his loyal friend gone rogue. The way he spoke about what Elias went through, despite his clear resentment for me, there was the slightest detection of doubt. He was trying to convince himself of something. Or trying to get some specific information from me.

This has gone way too far. And the fact that I had another moment of guilt is making me feel sick.

I let out a shaky breath, trying to calm myself, but the adrenaline in my body takes care of that for me by gradually dissipating. The strong throbbing in my hand only becomes a slight distraction, stopping me from taking in the rest of the ache in my body.

I roll onto the ground. A faint feeling of being burned alive slowly enters all my limbs, just as the day goes in and out of my vision. *I may not have protected my head from the fall that well.* Though, before I allow myself to black out or give up, realization hits me almost as hard as Andre had.

Rebecca and Shane.

I need to get to them. Make sure they're safe. Looking around now though, there's no way for me to do that. I can't call for another plane. Not when I don't understand how

Elias's lackey found me. Even if I did, I'd have to deal with Commander thinking I had already failed. Which leaves me back to square one. And to add insult to injury, I can't think of anyone I trust enough to come and get me without ratting me out.

I'm completely stranded here... or so I thought. My eyes are starting to become dangerously blurry, but I swear on my parent's graves I see a plane landing in front of me. It could be a mirage, wishful thinking getting the better of me since I can't hear the roar of the engine. If that were the case though, why does a sudden strong gust of wind whip up my already messy hair?

Again, my eyes cross that line between day and darkness as I slowly rise onto my elbow to stare at the could-be-hallucination in front of me. Everything hurts. Breathing hurts. I can taste blood and dirt and salty sweat. I'm too tired to have my mind play games with me. But, as I watch a very unlikely individual emerge from the plane, reality hits me like a ton of bricks and I believe every aspect of what I'm seeing.

She runs out in my direction. I see her mouth move, but no words register with my ears. Only my eyes—in their last good moments—take in what I can perceive. And that is, within those last seconds, Theora Salano. After that, I let my heavy eyelids fall, completely pulling me under into the gloom of unconsciousness.

CHAPTER NINETEEN

YOU'RE WELCOME

Coming to, the first thing I see makes me smirk, despite the pain. Before me, Theora sits on her knees, towering over a still unconscious Andre. She adds what looks like a third layer of duct tape over his mouth. In my head, I chuckle with delight at the strangeness of this all. But, without fully meaning to, a quiet laugh escapes me.

I quickly regret my amusement when the gesture rattles my chest. The pain may have been worth it though, because as I watch Theora's stare land on me, a certain sense of clarity soothes my insides. She's an agent. I knew there was something eerily unbecoming about her. Although, when her serious expression doesn't let up, I let my smile fade, realizing I have no clue who she *really* is. She could very well have been sent by Elias, or Foreman.

"Who are you?" I rudely demand.

She gets up and sighs. "Are you okay?"

The question confuses me. Not because I don't understand it, but because it comes out of a woman with Theora's face, but not her voice. This woman's voice is much lower and much more mellow than Theora's usual high-pitched tone, and a slight French accent is attached. For a minute I let that trip me up, though when my reply is ready, I recite the answer I'd tell a woman I never clicked with, which I now know why.

"I'm fine. Who are you?"

There's a moment of silence, me glaring at her, her glaring right back at me. But soon she breaks our scold-off by rolling her eyes and letting out a loud frustrated sigh. As if to declare that she has some sort of upper hand by not answering my one question.

"You weren't out long, but we still have a couple of hours before we land. So, during that time, you can bring me up to speed with everything that has been going on," she then looks away from me and mumbles, "and I'll probably have to bail you out, like I usually do."

"Who. Are. You?" I repeat, the words now carrying more bite.

"You're welcome by the way."

"Excuse me?" I mutter sharply, narrowing my eyes. I thought the action would make her shrink back, but I greatly miscalculated that.

It only sets her off.

"No! You *do not* speak to me like that. Not after I had to come down here to get your ass. What the fuck is the matter with you anyway? You just *had* to get mixed up in some kind of shit, right when I was starting to enjoy a normal life!? But now all that's gone out the window, because of you and your stupid past. And to think..." she rubs the bridge of her nose then sighs heavily, "my assignment was to simply make sure things ran smoothly. But that didn't last as long as it should've."

Me being calm seems to upset her, so I continue to push that button to see where it gets me. Also, it's funny to see

"Theora's" face yell in that accent. "Yeah, well, I figured something was up. And who 'assigned' you to me?"

"First of all, you are not allowed to—and don't deserve to—ask me any questions. And second, I seriously doubt you suspected anything. I've seen your file, *Nova*, and it's not that impressive," she snorts.

Finishing the bitchy know-it-all routine, I take a second to register her caginess towards my question but put that on the back burner for now. Just until I address her attitude. I slowly sit up to support my coming fury at her shitty insolence, and then roll my eyes before enlightening her with that same calm tone I now know she hates.

"Any agent—even a 'not that impressive' one—would've seen Shane was your give away. You were the exact same when he wasn't around, like you didn't know how to portray a normal person when he was gone. As if your whole identity was built just for him and no one else. Now, you were either an agent who was rusty with undercover work, or you're just *stupidly* in love with him."

At the sound of Shane's name, the hostile look on her face melts away, and all that's left is an endearing smile. A smile I know all too well. It lasts a while, and I watch as she stares off into space. It's the obvious 'I'm in love' behaviour, but her smitten gaze slowly begins to fade, as if she just realized she was grinning from ear to ear. "Theora" then swiftly wipes the look off, then retreats into the same bitchy mannerisms from before.

"I'm not," she replies sharply.

"You're not what? Rusty, or in love with him?"

"Why would it matter if I was in love with him?"

Shane's pale face on the plane, his threat, and the fear and concern that overtook his demeanour on our walk spring to mind. A knot tightens in my stomach answering her, sounding almost as protective as he had. "Because he's in love with you. Look, if it's a no, it's a no. If it's a yes, then it's a—"

"Yes okay, yes! Merde, tu parles beaucoup plus que je ne le suis habitué," she angrily huffs out.

(Shit, you talk a lot more than I'm used to.)

"Commentaire inutile mis à part, it's not a bad thing, like you're pretending it is."

(Unnecessary comment aside,)

"I'm not. Stop acting like you're better than me just because he made me drop the ball ever-so-slightly."

"I'm not acting like I'm better than you. Given my situation, I don't think that's even possible." I sigh, holding my stomach from the pain. "But at least my instincts were right."

From there, we resort to silence. I draw my attention to her surprisingly good duct taping work. A tight strip covers his mouth, from slim cheek to slim cheek. Men with his bone structure can be tricky to get a nice tight seal that'll shut them up. Usually, it's easier to wrap the tape once around their head. She didn't find the need.

Though I realize, as my eyes slightly drift back towards her, her handy work isn't nearly as jaw-dropping as her appearance, something I only now let myself take in. I scan this new female from head to toe and come to the annoying conclusion that she's even more stunning out in her true element.

Her auburn hair flows down to her mid back in a cascade of loose curls, and instead of her usual baggy clothes, she now wears an Unknown uniform. Skin-tight. General tasks; Class A-elite judging by the colors she wears. A maroon half zip sweater, black shoulder holster, and noir cargos with matching double leg thigh holster, all of which hug her just right. Revealing a figure I didn't know was there. And her facial features—much sharper somehow—only highlight what is only cold authority in her bright jade eyes.

She realizes my stare has wandered back to her, and despite my shock and aw, I shift the expression to show my enjoyment at her frustration. What I said did the job of sweeping away any high ground she thought she had on me. Her face twitches with equal parts being pissed and confused, but, when that frown turns upside down into a sly grin, she starts to laugh maniacally. It makes me slide away from her a little.

I might've liked the girly Theora better, because this version is kind of freaking me out. And since I'm still in the dark as to who she *really* is, who assigned her to me, or how the hell she found me, I stay alert. But, just as the thought rolls around, her grin widens as she stares back at me.

"Camille Maxwell," she blurts out, as if trying to one up me, and it works.

Holy shit.

Unintentionally, a bright smile takes over my face. Though fully in control of my movements, I scoot back a bit more, knowing what that name means. My level of respect climbs as I lock eyes with her, and I don't try to hide my surprise anymore.

Taking in my excitement, she nonchalantly boasts. "Yeah."

"You're Camille Maxwell? *Thee* Camille Maxwell? As in the legendary agent who did that thing with the shelf? Or the blanket? The pencil!?"

"I *really* try not to mention the pencil, but yes. I guess I was kind of an improviser back then," she shrugs then crosses a leg over the other.

"Kind of? You alone *still* have the highest kill count in five countries, eight capital cities, and all of Australia. Yet—up until this point—class B agents are still in the dark about your general appearance."

"Yes, well, I've had a... colourful past."

The mention of her 'extensive experience' brings to mind everything else I've ever read about her. It sends warmth throughout my stomach. A completely different one than the warmth of excitement I had earlier. She's one of the most notorious agents in the history of the agency, and she's sitting right in front of me. It's not exactly reassurance that I'm safer now than when I was alone with Low. The uncertainty slightly moistens my palms.

"Oh god, what did I do to deserve Camille Maxwell as my Watcher? And for two years?" I shakingly utter.

"Ah, so you don't have it all figured out then?" she taunts me.

I cross my arms while trying to sharpen my voice. "I never said I did. But I would appreciate it if you did fill me in."

"Oh, you'd appreciate it?" she chuckles. "I bet Rebecca and Shane would've *appreciated* if you told them who you are and what you've been doing, prior to them being caught up in your mess. But you didn't, did you?"

"That's completely different, and you know it," I fire back. "They're civilians. I had no reason to tell them anything before everything went to shit."

"With you and them, or with you and agent 404? Or with the agency and the mole?" she leans back and smirks the kind of smirk that makes my insides burn. "It seems like no matter what, you always have more than one problem going on at once, *Nova.* You can't seem to catch a break, can you?"

I swallow down the fury that she seems to be drawing out from me and feeding off. "Why are you here, to prove something about me?" My shoulders tighten. "You think I'm the mole, don't you?"

"Oh, no. No, I don't think you're... capable enough to be the mole. Neither you, nor agent 404. Take that as you will." She then goes quiet while staring at me. Her eyes empty.

Not one bone in my sore body can read her after that. It's like she completely shut off every kind of emotion and general facial expressions. Part of me envies that she's capable of that.

I'm not that lucky. Not at this very moment anyway.

Knowing who "Theora Salano" really is, is shaking me up. This is a woman who's been in the game for a long time. So long that I've heard that Commander owes *her* a favour. It could just be a rumour, but if it isn't, let's just say I'm glad she doesn't think I'm the mole. Insult on my skills as an agent or not. Honestly, her disclosure on the matter gives me enough courage to speak up, to get the answers I need.

"Look," I huff out, "you already told me your name, and gave me a baseline as to why you were assigned to me. You might as well tell me everything else."

Camille smirks. "Is that so?"

"The less information I have, the less I can help."

"And what makes you think I need any kind of help from you?"

She's right. There's not much I have to offer in exchange for her information. But I just need it to *seem* like I do, to keep her interested in the conversation so I can get to my point.

"Do *you* know why Low insisted that Shane be on that plane? Or why he came after me without Elias tagging along?"

"Do you?" she snickers.

I sigh. "Not entirely, no. But if we want the truth from this bastard, I have to know how we got here, and to know that, I need to know who he *really* is."

"You're proposing a united front," Camille infers while loosely crossing her arms over her chest.

"Yes, I am."

She rolls her eyes, looks from me to Andre, then lets out a heavy sigh. "Fine. Long story short, a year after I retired, I got bored and became an assassin for some shadow site that killed snitches."

My brows come together. "An eye for an eye.kill you.com?"

"Yes, that's exactly it." Her eyes narrow. "How'd you know that?"

"I did some freelance work for them a couple of weeks after I left. For some extra cash."

"That wasn't in the file," she mumbles and starts to loosen up ever-so-slightly. "Huh. Small world."

"Yeah..." I trail off in an awkward huff.

"Anyway, by the time I decided to come back, they had already been surveilling you for a year after the whole 'mole situation' happened. But, when you hit that second year, seemed to be settling, Commander decided to lighten surveillance and insert someone to keep a closer eye on you. So, I was sent to make sure your transition into real retirement went smoothly, as I mentioned." She leans back in the chair next to me.

"You could have your freedom, but your involvement with Echo Delta meant that that freedom came with strings attached. Especially when one of the agents from the op was thought to have helped the so-called mole. So—"

"No matter what, Commander stationed a Watcher on all agents involved in the operation. Retired or not," I groan, finishing her sentence. *Manager said as much, back when I confronted him.*

Camille nods. "Exactly. Hence this piece of shit here. Now, since we're doing full disclosure, this, is Andre Low. Real "lone wolf" type idiot, originally stationed in Civilian Safety. He's agent 404's Watcher. Commander brought in agents from different departments to become Watchers for those involved with Echo Delta, so it'd be impossible for any of you to trace. Since you and 404 have a... history, Low and I have had to converse—unfortunately—for a while, as I'm sure you gathered. However, after our check in last week, when Low also got assigned to be agent 404's P.E, he didn't show for our scheduled monthly brief."

He's his W*atcher? But why—* "Why would his watcher also be assigned to be his prospective exterminator?"

"Agent 504 was supposed to fill me in on that. But, after your aliases were exposed, neither I, nor the agency has been able to contact him, which classifies him as AWOL as well. So, I have no idea."

As soon as the words leave her mouth, like what she said had flipped a switch, Andre slowly starts to come to. Noticing from the corner of her eye, Camille turns towards him and plasters a haunting smile on her lips.

"But I'm about to find out."

Andre's head sways from side to side as his eyes flutter open. I cross my arms over my sore chest, getting ready to appease the overwhelming feeling in my gut to either kick him or yell. Either one would make me happier about how today went.

The first thing his eyes land on is me, and as they focus, under the layers of tape, his cheeks move. Only a muffled sound comes from him, making Camille and I both look at each other with amusement. I watch her smile grow to the furthest reaches of her face, which I have to admit frightens me a bit. Not as nearly as much as it does Andre when he finally turns and notices Camille.

His eyes widen as they land on her, almost popping out of his face like a cartoon. He swiftly wiggles away and as his frantic behaviour continues, so does our humour. But my merriment gets cut short when pain spreads throughout my torso. The agony reminds me of our little dance earlier, which conjures up more anger. I lift my foot to his face, but Camille holds out her hand to stop me.

"Wait. This jackass might have something to say that could fill in some blanks. And if he doesn't, we can skip right to the fun part." She violently rips the layers of tape from his mouth.

"Bonjour, Andre. You know, I don't appreciate you manhandling my op. Don't you remember when I said I'd kill you if you ever came in contact with her?"

A chill passes through our general area as her voice sweetens. Her eyes narrow and she starts to grin, it only making her more intimidating somehow. Then, suddenly, all the stories I've heard about her pale in comparison to the real thing, and the once perky Theora completely dies.

I guess it's true what they say about her. Bitch at best, angel at worst.

I've never seen a man swallow so hard in my life. After the desperate gulp, he does answer, his eyes never leaving hers as if showing respect. Yet his tone doesn't come out that way at all.

"Nice to see you again, Maxi," he challenges.

She sharply slaps him across his face, so hard even I flinch. "Try again," she says, stern.

Andre, head twisted away from her, spits out blood next to him. When he straightens his neck, he gives up his focus on Camille and instead chooses to agitate me.

"You're in deep shit, you know that right? Instead of questioning me, you should be worrying about either A—being wanted by a black-ops agency for espionage, or B—the fact that you don't know how far Elias is willing to go with all this."

"Yeah, yeah. I'm wanted and Elias hates me. Old news. What I'm curious about though is why—right after you were assigned to be his P.E—you decided to risk your career to help him illegally track down and try to kill an agent that has nothing to do with you."

"Nothing to do with—you actually think you know what you're talking about, don't you?" he laughs. "Well, sorry to say this and pull the rug out from under you, but you're asking the wrong questions."

"Oh, then what questions should I be asking, Low?"

"Sounds to me like he wants to get something off his chest, agent 401," Camille chimes in.

"That's exactly what I was thinking too, agent 420."

He rolls his eyes and huffs out with fake compassion, "awe, isn't that cute. You guys are friends. I didn't think I'd ever see the day where a Watcher and their op could have such a great coordinated rapport."

"Well, that's clearly a lie. You and Elias obviously have a close relationship," I remark, my head tilting slightly with innocence lining my words.

"You don't know what you're talking about," he snipes.

"Maybe not, but just let me run my theory by you real quick, "lone wolf". You left your post because you found a friend in him. And that friendship is what made you think, 'there's no way he could be the mole,' right? I have to protect him?"

Andre's golden face goes cold. "You're wrong."

"Wait, let me finish. When you were told that our aliases were exposed, you figured that your next orders would probably be to bring him in. So, you bailed, for him. Disregarded your new P.E status, for him. That way you could help him fully execute his plan to take me out, in the hopes that when you told him the truth, you handing me over to him just might take some of the sting out of you lying to him for years."

With the grace of a ballerina, Camille re-crosses her legs and snickers. "That sounds right to me."

"Me too," I agree. "But what I don't get is why he didn't just take me out the night he broke into my place? Why involve civilians only to let them go? He clearly knows that they matter to me, given the bullet showboating back in Brooklyn. So why'd you let Shane get away?"

"He's on that plane because I'm a good agent."

Sharp laughter echoes throughout the plane, so fast that it takes me a moment to realize that it's Camille who's laughing. It's so different from Theora's that I do a double take.

"Oh," she wipes away a tear, "oh please. What world do you think you're in that has you believing that bullshit?"

Andre's serious expression doesn't change. "Laugh all you want, but your civilians are still alive because of me. I was the good agent with the voice of reason that convinced him not to kill them during the grand plan he has laid out for you. One that would've had NYPD carrying out Rebecca's body from your apartment by now. And I guess Shane's too."

"Watch it," Camille growls, and I briefly see Theora's love in her eyes.

In some crazy way, I guess she really did fall in love with him. Though given my situation, her falling for a normal guy makes more sense than me ever loving a killer. She has every right to get worked up. I'm just as worried about both of them. Her worry though, makes me tense up a bit, waiting to see if she'll blame me for everything. But she merely leans back, her brow furrowing as fury re-enters every inch of her face. I take over questioning Andre. She needs to cool off, and I need my anger present as well.

"So, what? You want me to thank you for letting him go? For slicing me up like fucking fruit ninja?"

"If he hadn't have gotten on that plane, if I hadn't suggested to 'help out', your civilian would've been a casualty. I may have been transferred to Interrogations for Watcher purposes, but Civilian Safety will always be my priority. And don't be a baby. It was only a few cuts. They'll barely leave a scar."

I bite down the urge to break his fingers. "Fuck you."

"Look," Andre uninterestedly sighs, "his plan isn't exactly solid anymore. Finding you was somewhat simple, thanks to the twenty-four-hour tracker solution he injected. But, when he found out the girl wasn't with you, things changed. He saw it as an opportunity. A way to make you suffer even more. So instead of facing you here, he dropped me off as a mere distraction."

"He was on the plane!?" I shout, the realization that I practically gave Shane to him elevating my voice and pain.

"More like flying it," he tells me. "We may have 'borrowed' it from Unknown while everything was in chaos."

Camille gut punches him then turns hauntingly calm. "Where's he going Low?"

Andre coughs, and after taking in a deep breath he turns to me and slightly chuckles. "That friend of yours, Rebecca, is a hot little number, isn't she?"

Andre glances at Camille again. "I have a thing for black women," he happily admits.

This time, I don't restrain myself. I punch him in the mouth, grab a fist full of his strawberry blond hair, and then rip it back until he has no choice but to look up at me. He knew that comment would make me upset, but judging by his widened stare, he didn't think I'd do anything about it. Too bad for him. I've been patience enough. I wipe the blood from his mouth off my knuckle onto his sleeve, then, as if my mind goes on auto pilot, I portray dominance.

"He's going to find her, isn't he? To bring her back into this shit?"

"I have no doubt about it," he answers smugly.

Camille cross-examines me. "But how's he going to do that? There's no way he'd know exactly where she's going, right?"

I search my brain for answers, my eyes shifting from side to side. The possibility that he looked into both Shane and Rebecca is high, which means he probably knows about her possible getaways. But Camille's right. There's no way he'd know exactly where she'd go unless—I gasp.

Fuck. Minnie! She sent the plane to me without knowing it was Elias, which means she told him the drop off point.

Camille throws her arms up. "Wrong," she groans. "Great. More errands."

Glancing to Andre, a cunning smirk curls onto his busted lip. For the first time, I have to look away from him. A shiver goes up and down my back as I turn to Camille, slight panic lining my words.

"We need to hurry."

CHAPTER TWENTY
HAUNTED PAST

After a series of tiny meltdowns, I finally calm myself enough to contact Minnie for any updates. I need to confirm Andre isn't lying about Elias flying the plane I let my other best friend escape on.

Calling won't be easy, considering how we left things, but not doing the easy thing has always been a part of my life. Whether I'm being Michelle and dealing with Nova's haunted past, or Nova handling Michelle's messy present.

Each have their own problems, which are now, no matter how I look at it, in the same boat. And one of those problems is that I'm starting to become short on friends. The realization pushes me to call. Wasting no more time—a luxury I don't have—I glance from a dozing off Andre to Camille, before turning my back to them.

A number of familiar pains shoot down my spine and up my ribs. The long plush couch I designated as my power napping area helps with the soreness though. It reminds me of my mattress back in Brooklyn, with its softness that just wraps around you. Perfect, since my right hip definitely has a bruise or two.

A jolt of anger rises up my gut. For lack of a better way to deal with Andre, for nearly breaking my entire body, I clench my fists and force myself to ignore the hot rage in my belly. I slide the burner from my pocket, praying it didn't get completely damaged during my fall.

Four or five shards of glass fall in front of me as soon as I flip it open, and a few of the numbers are dented so far into the phone they'll never come out. The grey is terribly scratched, but the screen still works, so it's in good enough shape. I sigh with relief, then redial Minnie.

It only takes a second, but with everything Andre said about Elias circling my head—about him not having a full plan but that it *does* include Rebecca and Shane—it feels like an hour before she answers. And in all that imaginary time, about ten bloody scenarios run through my mind at once. I hate that my brain is wired this way. Ready to expect the worst. Though when I hear Minnie's voice it pulls me from the violent thoughts.

"Nova," she answers coldly, and before I could get a word out, she continues in the same tone, "I was ordered not to speak to you unless it was to inform you that your time is up."

"But you answered," I whisper with hope.

She sighs. "I was worried."

A slight smile forms on my lips at of her sincerity. "I'm sorry, M. I shouldn't have lashed out at you. Especially not when all you've done is help me, even when I don't deserve it after the way I left. I just—"

"Oh stop," she faintly giggles. "Of course I forgive your bitchy temper tantrum. I know how tense a position you're in. And besides, I can tell how badly you want to ask for my help, which in its own way is a better apology."

"You have no idea how happy I am to hear you say that. After the last couple of hours I've had, there's no one I trust more than you and your skills. I have a few things to go over, but only if you're a hundred percent sure we're good."

She lets out a breath then lightly chuckles. "Well, considering this call just so happens to not be on the monitors, yes, we're good, and uninterrupted. Go ahead."

I quickly look over my shoulder to see if Andre or Camille's positions have changed. They're in the same tableau so I turn back around, then proceed to brief her on everything that's happened since our last conversation. I tell her about the plane and who was on it—something she does confirm and apologizes for.

I quickly forgive and forget then move to the part where Theora turned out to be Camille Maxwell. Her reaction was much tamer than I thought it'd be. I may have even heard a hint of nonchalance in her tone. I couldn't tell. But, after mentioning Andre and all he said, and what he's claiming, I definitely heard the slight growl on the end of each of her words.

"And you believe that asshole?"

"Well, not entirely, no. Especially not the part about Elias flying the damn thing, but that's where you come in. I need all the info you can get right now regarding Andre and the particulars he's spitting out," my voice grows louder but the change in volume rattles the ache in my body, reminding me to keep quiet.

For about two minutes I hear Minnie typing away without so much as a pause. Though when one comes, it's her concerned voice that fills the silence.

"Umm... N, did Low tell you why he was assigned to be Elias's P.E.?"

"No." I emphasize my wonder. "Why? What did you find?"

"Under reason on the P.E. file, it says that it was issued because a surveillance team—your surveillance team at the time—caught him lurking. They reported it, naturally, but there's something more you should know, and it's... troublesome."

My stomach turns as the question leaves my mouth. "What is it?"

She sighs. *Uh oh.* "Three years ago, agent 504 was moved from the Civilian Safety Department to Creative Interrogations—Elias's unit—to get closer to him, as per Commander's 'Watcher' initiative. But, unlike the others, Low was the first agent to be assigned an 'Up Close and Personal' relationship. An order that came a year sooner than Maxwell's U.C.A.P. for you."

"Well, that makes sense. Elias and I were the two agents closest to finding out who the mole was. The only difference is that he stayed with the agency."

"Yes, but by that logic, it seemed less likely that he was in cahoots with the so-called mole at the time. If anything, you looked guiltier by leaving as soon as you did. No offense," she adds swiftly.

"None taken. But if that's the case, then why was Low given a U.C.A.P. order before Maxwell?"

"*Yeah*, that's what I was worried about, because it has nothing to do with Echo Delta. Under reason, it says that Elias started to become inattentive the day after you left. Says that he began to show questionable obsessive psycho behaviour within that same week, which was believed by his superior to be caused by mission—"

"Over and out. My last mission at the agency before I left," I finish her sentence, my voice turning hollow.

A slight pounding enters my head, and the flash of images pass over my tightly shut eyes, like someone turned on a strobe light. All of Minnie's words start to sound like a faraway echo to me after that.

"That's the exact one..."

'I can still feel the slick stickiness of his blood coating my skin...'

"And according to Low's reports, about six months after that, he finally thought he was making progress; helping him move on. So much so that he stopped obsessing..."

'...that look he gave me. The one that tells me everything he's feeling. Everything I'm supposed to be feeling too...'

"But then Supervisor came to them with an assignment. A breach in one of our New Orleans safe houses. And that's when he started spiralling again..."

'... a grossly familiar face forces its way into my eye line.'

I don't realize I'm crying until I feel the tickle of water on my nose. I wipe the tear from my face and sigh. Everything, every word, is just a reminder of all the pain I caused. To myself... and him. But what really hurts, is knowing that the one time I slipped up back then just *had* to be when he was finally getting over what I'd done. Finally getting better.

I don't believe in coincidences, but somehow they keep following me around like a shadow. Beyond the surface though, there's something bigger than all of us. Something that's connecting all this in some way I'm not seeing yet, but right now Minnie's information explains why Low became so protective.

It doesn't put my mind at ease at all. It just means that Rebecca and Shane are in worse danger than I thought. Then it hits me, hard, what Andre meant when he said Elias 'slowly unravelled and became a true monster.'

"Okay," my voice booms as I slowly sit up. Then, just like I predicted, my sudden speech immediately gets Camille's attention. "As unfortunate as all that information is, it doesn't change anything. Getting to Rebecca before Elias does and retrieving Shane is still priority. We just have to take much more precaution, that's all."

"Who are you talking to?" Camille asks, stern.

"Someone I can trust."

"But can I trust them? Remember agent, only one of us here is not wanted by Unknown."

"Let me talk to her." Minnie snaps.

"Are you sure you wanna do that?" I groan out, finally sitting upright.

Repeating herself with almost the same amount of demand as Camille, I sigh and give her the phone. To my surprise, almost as soon as the phone touches Camille's ear, she starts smiling, which really isn't reassuring. But my unease quickly dissipates when she lets out a light chuckle.

"What an honor. It was nice to finally talk to the woman behind Haystack, Darling. I've admired your excellent consulting work within my department for years."

What the hell?

Not even looking me in the eye, Camille hands the phone back to me. Before I can ask Minnie what she said, she turns to Andre, almost purring with excitement. "Now, what to do with this asshole."

She holds the knife above Andre's jugular and gently taps it to wake him. It takes him a minute to realize what's happening, and when he does, Camille quickly freezes him up by pressing the knife to his throat and brushing his hair back. Like petting a dog.

"Minnie, give me a minute," I hastily mutter then turn to Camille. "You of all people know you can't kill him, so for now, just leave him the way he is. Maybe we can trade him for the others."

"That's not going to work," he comments.

"Oh, shut up," Camille tells him. She takes the knife from his throat then adds a fresh strip of tape to his mouth.

The deeply disappointed look on her face almost makes me want to let her cut him, at least just a little bit. My unexpected sympathy swiftly vanishes when she speaks again.

"If Meyers even touches a hair on Shane's or Rebecca's head, his "loyal" partner's blood will be all over me, and this jet," she straightens up, bringing all her focus to him and only him as she finishes with a haunting whisper.

"Et ce ne sera pas à cause d'un couteau, croyez-moi."

(And it won't be because of a knife, believe me.)

Jesus, this girl is a nightmare to be trapped on a jet with. I'm just glad it's not me she's mad at. Well, at least not yet. The real reason I reminded her that she has to keep Andre alive, is so she can direct all her anger towards him. If I let her incapacitate him in any way, her taste for revenge will only continue, and all the danger I've put Shane in for the last couple of days will be all she sees. So, without remorse, I'll use Andre as the perfect distraction. It lets me give my attention back to Minnie while fixing myself in the seat, pain radiating with every movement.

I hold my side as a slow and shaky exhale parts my lips. "M?"

"Yeah, I'm still here. But I'll have to get back to work soon or Commander will start to assume something is up."

"I have no doubt," I say, but not being able to help myself, "but I have to ask, you and Maxwell?"

She chuckles, it sounding mostly to herself. "Oh, that? Well, long story short, I merely cited Operation Haystack and my involvement in the matter."

"Operation Haystack?" I question, trying to remember why it sounds familiar. Didn't I read about that somewhere? "Wasn't that the—"

"The op where every electronic within the city of Dubai was hacked to pinpoint one sniper drone," she says with so much pride I can almost hear her blushing. "Yeah."

Realization blooms in my chest and my eyes widen. "That was you?"

"Maxwell was in the city, unofficially, to take out a terrorist threat, though she couldn't do so until the sniper trained on her was found. But in a city that technologically advanced finding it was like trying to find a needle in a—"

"Haystack," I snicker.

"Exactly. And to find that needle, I became the haystack."

"Wow," is all I manage to get out. That was the event that shored up Unknown's ties with the United Arab Emirates, furthering our own technologically advancements.

"Surprised?"

I can't help but shrug. "Not really."

"Aw," she says, a grin in her voice. "Thank you."

"Hey, from getting to work with you firsthand, I should've guessed. Anyway, I don't want to keep you any longer. But before you go, did you find anything else on Foreman?"

"No. Commander has just been counting down the minutes till you deliver, and since the lockdown it's been quiet," she dryly laughs, yet I note her weariness.

"You should see it. It's like a ghost town with all the real agents ordered to stay where they were positioned before things went to shit. Pretty much just all analysts left here."

A new strand of guilt seeps into my skin at her mention of the lockdown. I'm literally stopping the world from being protected from Specter, or whatever other threats there may be. I can't take all of this on my shoulders. I shouldn't, but I am.

In my mind, I'm only blaming myself. Not Andre, not Commander, and not even Elias. All of this is fucked up, no matter which angle I look at it at from. It's giving me a migraine. I push all that aside and put on a comforting voice for my friend... and for me.

"Minnie, you *are* a real agent. A badass one at that. You'll be alright. I'll contact you again and check in as soon as we retrieve Shane and Rebecca."

Her reply is the question I was trying not to ask myself. "Do you really think he's going to hurt them?"

All of me wants to say no, but I don't know what to believe when it comes to him anymore. The Elias I knew would never hurt civilians if he could help it, but now... now I have a bad feeling that almost imitates the pain in my stomach. No answer comes out of my mouth, despite all the words swirling inside my head. I only sigh.

"I'll be in touch, okay? And I'm going to be holding onto this phone, so contact me again by this number if anything changes over there."

"Will do, agent," Minnie says, putting on her best 'good soldier' impression.

CHAPTER TWENTY-ONE

ACQUAINTED

Stone pathway stained in warm red.

The photo hanging loosely between my fingers.

Feet shifting in the rain.

His face.

The bullet.

A rapid breath pulls me from the dream. I snap my eyes open to stop the flood of images from invading my mind. I hadn't noticed I fell asleep again, but I guess injury is a good enough incentive to drift off. At least that's what I've told myself during my years at the agency. And as it turns out, a sundress is much more comfortable to sleep in than Kevlar. Still though, it doesn't feel like my slumber lasted long enough, especially since my brain is working itself into overdrive.

I was so used to being calm and composed right up until Dom went missing, that I forgot what the real feeling of being overwhelmed is like. It's been over a month and I'm still adjusting. It gets harder when things keep piling up. People are in danger. My friends, my last piece of family, and right on top of that list is my sanity.

I barely have enough of it left to figure out the truth behind all this. I'm just hoping that that truth isn't heart stopping, because I've had my fair share of surprises over the last couple of days. One of the biggest is walking over to me right now.

Camille Maxwell. Wow. No matter how much I repeat that, it's still unbelievable.

She has a hand on the roof, sliding it along with each powerful step she takes. The action reminds me of when elders hold onto a car's grab handle. The same way my driving instructor Mrs. Markel would when I'd jump curbs and speed.

Is she scared of flying?

The thought gets dismissed as my attention shifts towards her peculiar walk. It's not a long trip from her seat to mine, but it's enough of a distance that I notice the extra weight she adds on her left leg. It seems like a weight she's used to. Though factoring in that it's the first time I'm witnessing Camille Maxwell's strut instead of Theora Salano's usual happy skip, I let my eyes fall as she sits next to me.

It's not a big deal. I only notice because I trust her even less than I did a couple of days ago. That lack of trust has my body slightly tense when she reaches for something under the seat next to me.

"Relax, Castillo," she snickers then hands me a tied-up grocery bag. "It's just a change of clothes. I didn't know we'd be making a detour, but it'll protect you from the cold of Canada just the same as it would've at headquarters. Much better than that dress will."

"Thanks."

"Now I finally get my thanks?" she laughs again, this time sounding exactly like Theora, when she'd giggle with Shane.

A smirk curls my lips as the sound brings up a treasured memory of all four of us at The Steam Bean. The good times. So much love was between them. Between all of us. I may never get that back, but her laugh jogging the memory makes me think. I could've asked so many other questions, but, before I can catch the words from falling out of my mouth, I ask,

"You wanted to say yes, didn't you?"

Her demeanour suddenly becomes defensive. "What?"

"Shane's proposal. Did you want to say yes? In the car that morning it seemed like you wanted to when he first asked, but—"

She narrows her eyes and I stop talking. I do my best not to flinch back, not to display any emotion. Especially not the one I'm holding back. The one that'll give away that I almost *need* her answer. It might have something to do with my love life not going so great at the moment, which is a complete understatement. Or maybe it's because I swear she can smell fear. Either way, when I don't react further, her standoff-ish expression slightly starts to ease away from 'I'll kill you' and dips into a bit of compassion.

Clearly the question wasn't only circling my head.

"Like I said, I do—I *did* fall in love with him, but marriage is obviously complicated. Honestly, at first, I thought he was the most obnoxious asshole on this earth. One I was stuck with. But then..." she trails off.

My mouth goes dry and my voice sounds empty inside my head when I elaborate for her. "You let yourself try. It may have been for just a minute, or a second, but then everything changed."

"One night, when we were arguing about something petty, out of nowhere he just stopped. He stared at me, and his whole attitude changed. He completely crumbled, apologized while telling me why he acted the way he did. Told me that he was once the nice guy, but it always backed fired no matter how hard he tried. I read his file, I knew it inside and out, but that was the first thing I learned that wasn't in a prep report."

She tucks back a strand of hair then drops her eyes from mine.

"It was refreshing. But at the same time, I began to feel bad for him, and me feeling bad for anyone doesn't happen often. I was just going to ignore it, but since I figured I'd be with him for a while, I thought I *should* try. So, I told him about my fucked up abusive family. Leaving out the whole 'having a momentary psychotic break and murdering them' thing. Obviously."

"Obviously," I repeat as bitter laugh escapes me. I shift uncomfortably in my seat.

"I didn't do it for sympathy points. I thought he'd try to comfort me with a hug or some shit. But to my surprise he... got angry. I'm used to presenting calm when it comes to family matters. I have for decades. I had to condition myself to. Though in that moment, it felt as if he was letting out everything for me. All the rage I wished I could've unleashed. No one had ever done that before."

I raise a brow at her. "And that's what made you fall in love with him?"

"It worked for me. Helped me move on. Plus, I thought it was hot." She shrugs.

"Really, I was glad to have found a reason. Unlike you and Meyers, we are completely different people from completely different walks of life. He was a privileged garçon de la ville, and I was an unstable girl from la Campagne Française. But, after that night, we kind of just became the way we did. Theora's love became real."

The blank stare on my face is all I can answer her with. Yes, Elias and I have similar pasts—a child trying to survive becoming an adult too soon because of the world our parents surrounded us with—but damn.

And here I thought I was screwed up.

"Hey, you asked, Castillo," Camille chuckles.

Still, there isn't anything I can think to say, but with the silence I leave in the air the pilot comes from the cockpit. Unknown's newest prototype. It resembles a female, though clearly, it's made of very expensive high-quality tech all wrapped up in a curvy silicon package. With flawless mocha colored skin, glowing blue eyes and short black hair.

I stare in wonder for a minute, but when its eyes go straight to Camille, I let the coming view of the lit-up CN Tower grab my attention.

"We'll be landing now, agent 420, and I did as you requested with that other jet we were tracking."

"And?" she demands.

"It landed approximately an hour ago, but as soon as it did, its location became unknown. We tried to radio the pilot again but got nothing. They've torn out the agency mandated GPS."

"Alright, thank you," she waves the android off then turns to me, her tone shifting from orderly to cold. "We need to hurry up and find *your* psycho."

"Why is he *my* psycho when he kidnaps?" I joke, knowing I shouldn't have.

She forcefully gets up, stomps over to Andre, and then violently shakes him awake. The second he opens his eyes Camille starts interrogating him about Elias again. I listen for a bit, but tune out when nervous energy creeps into my stomach at the thought of seeing him again, and what he might have done to my friends.

In all this chaos, the notion of actually coming face to face for a second time didn't cross my mind. My main focus to get Shane and Rebecca out of harm's way again blocked any other kind of apprehension. And then there's the fact that I still have to find a way to bring Elias in with me for questioning. Another stupid thing I did, but I can't back out of that, or any of this, now.

"Castillo!" Camille yells, indicating that it's not the first time she tried to draw me from my thoughts.

I snap out of it. "What?"

The feel of the plane gently landing down from the night sky intensifies my realization of what's about to happen. I get changed, then string my hair up into another high ponytail to give my neck a break. The motion tightens the skin around my graze wound, mimicking the tightness in my chest. I breathe slowly, deeply, before glancing back up at Camille, waiting for her to repeat herself.

She huffs out a breath. "Like I said, I'll go in with you, but when your time comes with Meyers can you handle your business?"

"Of course I can," I tell her with a bitter taste of uncertainty coating my tongue.

"You better be dead serious, agent. I'll have to keep an eye on Low, which means I can't pick up your slack. So, if anything starts happening, which I suspect it will, it's going to happen fast. And if you freeze, he becomes fair game, and I won't hesitate—"

"I said I got it, alright!?" My cheeks run hot, but the rest of me is cold as I lower my voice. "I'm good."

Camille sharply looks me up and down. "Good."

The look in her eye makes it clear she doesn't think I can handle this. I can. At least I think I can. That has to be good enough right now.

Relying on 'good enough' shouldn't be my only tactic. Not when other people's lives are at stake. To recoup, for a brief moment, I retreat into my mind and allow the words from my training years ago, Manager's words about emotion, to ring in my ears. *'As powerful as they can be, emotions aren't superior. You can contain them—control them. But that requires strength. And it's up to you to have that strength.'*

He may not be my favourite person right now, but his voice in my head does help me grasp some of that control I'm supposed to have. The same control I should've had when Elias was on the ground in front of me the first time, but I can fix that now.

I can fix all of this.

CHAPTER TWENTY-TWO

Toronto, Canada

When the plane finally landed, Camille and I didn't wait for it to be put into the hanger. Instead, we focused on getting transportation. It took us no time at all to "acquire" a vehicle. The only thing that took a while, was putting Andre in the trunk, which did break of sweat. It quickly vanished when the familiar icy Brooklyn weather bit at my nose. Yet this cold has a sharper Canadian sting.

I had a bad feeling about bringing Andre for the ride, but according to Camille, leaving him on the plane was riskier, plus we needed something to trade with, so I left it alone. She seemed used to people caving, because in no time she dismissed my concern, and then we were off to Rebecca's aunt's apartment. Traveling in complete silence.

Thanks to her crazy driving, we get there almost at light speed. I say almost, because, despite the chilled weather and late night, the city is still buzzing with life. It's nice, but it's also a bad factor. All I see each person as, is a pair of eyes, and more eyes means a stew of witnesses, or casualties, who could possibly get involved.

Unknown already has a number of problems to worry about. Hell, *I* have a number of problems to worry about. 'Cleaning up witnesses' shouldn't be one of them. We'll have to be flawless in our approach to the situation. One we're walking blindly into. Not the best scenario, but this needs to get done without fault. I have no intention of recreating the scene from Brooklyn.

When we get as close as we see fit, despite the throbbing that travels throughout my limbs, Camille insists I be the one to get out of the car to survey the neighbourhood. Saying I have a 'friendlier face.' Utter bullshit, but I do need to walk off some of my nerves. I get out and stroll down the street, my eyes slyly darting back and forth, like a tourist who's desperately trying not to look like a tourist.

I'm anything but, though, for this mission, I keep my shoulders tight and walk swiftly in the night while shyly examining my surroundings. It's charming. The area has a middle-class feel to it, and judging by the amount of Canada Goose and Wuxly jackets, I'd say it is.

The building itself though, as it comes into view, immediately says 'I have money but I'm humble about it.' With the lights on, a couple from each apartment, I count ten stories. It's matte grey with pristine windows, even though it's snow season, and the front is as clean as a whistle.

Stopping about two buildings down, I look around, as if lost, then pull out a device that would seem like a normal phone to anyone walking past me. In actuality, The Peeker is a rather handy tool. The gadget—at the right range—can scan any building then tap into their live surveillance feed, inside *and* out, by shooting a micro magnet onto any one of their security cameras.

In this case, Rebecca's aunt's apartment is the target. I tilt the device upwards, so its muzzle is facing the building, then double tap. The screen comes to life, imitating Google Maps, and in seconds it locates all the apartment's cameras. Once it locks onto the closest one, I press the home button and a small jolt forces me to flinch.

I step back, steadying myself, then keep moving, the cold now biting me. My stare doesn't stray from the video feed I'm getting, which helps me blend with the rest of those glued to their screens. Everything seems normal in and out of the building, yet that doesn't sooth any of my unease about the situation. Elias—to say the least—is an expert.

Like me.

We were both trained by the best, which means I know exactly how he'd get in and out without being seen, and, by extension, how he'd get others out unseen too. It terrifies me. I'm not sure if that terror is because I know what we're capable of, or because I can think like him.

A shiver, and The Peeker's light beeping pulls me from gut-wrenching indecision. I welcome the distraction, and glance down at the device, it showing me something I wouldn't have noticed otherwise. Just on the left, next to our targeted high-rise is what looks like the entrance to a slim alleyway.

It directs me towards it and I follow swiftly. But, as I'm about to slip into its shadow, I see a woman buzz into the building. Using a key fob. *Of course this has to get harder.* I can't just button mash and hope someone just lets me in now. *Shit.* The more complex way in *does* put a damper on my confidence, but it's very useful information. Information I table for now while proceeding into the alley.

It stinks. Not as bad as a Brooklyn alley, but the stench is a close second. Other than the foul odour, it looks like the perfect spot. I put The Peeker away, cover my nose with my scarf, then do a complete analysis. No security cameras with a clear view point in or out, it'll just fit the Mini Cooper we "borrowed", and the apartment across the way has its sight obstructed by a building being put up behind it. Honestly, it's kind of alarming, and there's no doubt in my mind that someone was maimed here.

The thought that it was Rebecca quickly follows. I violently shake the images from my disturbingly vivid imagination then get back to my objective.

I walk back the way I came, this time staring up at the dark sky until I reach the car. I slide in and inform Camille about where to park. She asks a million questions first—as if finding a place to hide a stolen car with someone in the trunk is difficult. After another minute, I seem to appease her enough, and then, and only *then* do we move out. As we get into position, I ready myself for the cold again, then turn to Camille to run through how we should play this.

But of course, she beats me to it.

"Okay, we should be fine here for about twenty minutes or so. I'll come up from the back, and you can take the front," she twists her lips into a smirk and proceeds to patronize me. "I'm sure you'll find some creative way to get inside."

So bossy and arrogant.

As much as I want to disagree with her—and I mean *really* disagree—I keep my mouth shut and nod. Taking orders during personal missions has never been anything I was good at. In this case though, it's probably best to stay quiet so I don't get murdered with a sidewalk pebble or anything else she might find. We split up, but this time, when I casually join the crowd, my demeanour shifts. I walk with purpose, despite the sting in my hip.

My steps are wide and calculated. My shoulders loose. And looking towards the apartment, I let all worry subside and present a pure lackadaisical attitude. Making it seem like I've lived here for years is the easy part. But, getting inside, that does cause me to almost break my relaxed facade. The door doesn't have an ordinary lock, which means I can't pick it, something I'd ordinarily do. There is something from my bag of goodies that can help me out here.

Pulling out my other means of entry from the inside pocket of my coat, I unwrap it, pop it into my mouth, then chew. Immediately, the slight taste of mint and metal coats my tongue and throat. A terrible combination. Everything in me tries not to gag as I chew faster and faster to set off the heat sensors that'll activate my special "gum."

I took it three years back when it was still a prototype, with a zero-point zero three percent chance it won't over heat and start a bonfire on your tongue. Lately, the odds have been stacked against me, which doesn't exactly ease my mind when it comes to having this potential torch in my mouth.

But, coming upon the building's front door, a slight vibration tickles my tongue and rattles my eardrums, meaning I'll be safe from catching on fire today. The rapid pounding in my chest slowly begins to return to its normal rhythm, then I go forward with the plan.

My eyes never leave the key fob access control panel as I casually remove my glove and stick my thumb in my mouth to cover it in the gum. Then, reaching the door, I place the gum on the panel and soon, after a hot pinch nips my thumb, the door clicks open.

I'm in.

The second I slide inside, warmth seeps into my frozen face. A slight burning sensation follows, but I'm more focused on getting rid of my throat's dryness, and the awful after taste of the gum. I remove the grey substance from my thumb, place it back into its wrapper, then go straight to the stairs.

Her aunt's apartment is on the third floor, so the journey isn't long. The door, however, is already cracked open when I reach. I push my back up against the wall, then grab the Glock nineteen from my waistband. Heaviness starts to travel up my chest and heat sticks itself to my forehead as my hands go clammy. *You can do this,* I tell myself. *Pull it together, agent.* I force my feet forward.

Choosing to focus on the silence coming from inside, my mind ponders whether its gut-sinking effects are a good sign or a bad one. Either way, I have to know. I breathe in, the breath shaky in my throat, then slowly push the door open.

First impressions of the place are exactly what I was expecting. Rebecca had told me that her aunt liked things classy, everything in its place, and her apartment was no expectation. The entire space has a neat black and white aesthetic going on, with pops of color throughout.

Nothing seems out of place. No blood, no overturned furniture. The only thing that doesn't seem to belong is the brown leather duffle bag that looks to have been lazily thrown beside the couch. I recognize it. It once housed five thousand dollars cash at my place in Brazil. Quickly going through it now though, it seems about two thousand short.

Rebecca made it here, and she had the place all to herself with her aunt on vacation. Everyone in her family hates the cold, she told me once. Everyone but her. This would've been the perfect place for her to hide, if I hadn't unknowingly given up the location to a psycho. I keep moving, letting an apology echo in my head, to distract from the guilty knot tightening in my stomach. The sensation turns into something else entirely as the sudden sound of footsteps catch my attention.

I raise my gun, ready to fire as the steps continue, coming from the bedroom on my left. I swiftly swing my arms in the direction, my heart racing as I move closer. I try to relax—god knows kickback is hard enough to handle when you're not stressed out—yet something in me can't seem to get a grip. The demand '*control, Nova, have control*' rings in my ears, but the taste of metal and salt fill my mouth. Damn it.

Just when I start to realize that saying I have control definitely wasn't good enough, Camille casually strolls out from the room, her expression empty.

"They aren't here," she tells me.

I let out the breath that was caught in my throat. "Por el amor de Dios, no hagas eso!" I whisper shout.
(For God's sake, don't do that!)

She only rolls her eyes, not saying anything more. In the silence I steady my breath, and lower the gun. Camille watches me with a stare that says 'I knew you couldn't handle it.' Even though she doesn't say the actual words, my blood heats with fury. The look alone is enough for me to want to protest, but she puts up a hand, like she knew. Then, without so much as a blink, she removes the vain look in her eyes then simply points to the kitchen.

"Happy valentine's day," she remarks with false joy, in Theora's false voice.

I huff, annoyed at her not reacting, or annoyed because she had seen me flinch. No matter the reason, I tuck the Glock back into my waistband and turn. I'm met with a wide marble island, decorated with a simple crystal bowl filled with green apples. I barely glanced it on my way in, though now that I take a minute to really look, I see it. A light brown envelope sitting next to a bouquet of roses. *Red* roses.

How unoriginal.

Each of my steps feel as if I have cement for feet. Like I'm walking down an endless tunnel towards darkness instead of light. I'm not sure what to expect, but it doesn't matter. This all needs to end.

Eventually I reach the island then grab the envelope. I open it, carefully, then rip the red seal on a valentine's card inside decorated with a kitten holding heart shaped balloons. I flip it open and then read the two words neatly scribbled inside.

'Trade you.'

Frustration overtakes me as I rotate the card back and forth in my hand. I don't get it. There's no location to meet him, just more infuriating roses and this crappy card. This man's plan is to slowly drive me crazy, forcing me to try and figure out what he's playing at. A fact that's all too true. I know he knows I *hate* puzzles. For the last couple of days—hell, this last month—it's like all I've been doing is trying to piece together puzzles.

The eerily connected 'my brother being kidnapped' and 'Foreman' puzzle, then the 'why am I being framed' puzzle, and now him again? Now I *really* want to kill him, which can't happen until I know where he is, *or* where he has Rebecca and Shane. More frustration comes in waves, filling my head. I thrust the card like a throwing star across the room then violently rub my throbbing temples.

"How are we supposed to find them?" I question out loud, tired of hearing my own unanswered questions in my head.

"Castillo," Camille calls out, her voice faraway even when she's standing beside me.

"They could be anywhere, and if they could be anywhere, how am I going to take him in in time?"

"Castillo," she tries again, but I continue to spiral.

"Time is running out. Rebecca and Shane might be dead because of me, and I still don't know who Foreman is, our why they tried to frame me! No puedo—"

"Nova!" Camille quietly screams in my face as she grabs my shoulders and shakes me straight.

Some bit of composure regenerates itself in me. I close my tired eyes, then inhale sharply. The silence left hanging in the air calms me; reminds me that nothing gets done when spiralling. Soon though, the quiet collapses when a faint buzzing echoes off the walls. My brows knit themselves together as I lift my eyelids to locate the sound. The first thing I'm met with is Camille staring at me with both pity and concern. I quickly twist my head away from her, not completely sure if the concern is genuine, or that I want it right now. I cut to the chase.

"Where's that coming from?"

"I have a hunch."

Hearing her slight condescension, I face her again, but she's not looking my way. I follow her stare and my eyes find their way back to the kitchen island. For a second, I hear nothing again, but keeping my eyes trained on the roses, when another buzz goes off, I notice them move with the vibration. I take Camille's hands off me and move towards the bouquet.

"Ten dollars says it's a bomb," Camille laughs, like there's sandpaper in her throat.

Whipping my head around to her, I shoot her a sharp glare before retraining my attention on the flowers. The thought that it might be a bomb did cross my mind, especially given his last chloroform stunt. Considering he didn't kill me in Brooklyn, the possibility of it being an explosive is very low.

It seems as if he's hesitating, like me. Some kind of feeling of comfort comes with that revelation. Yet so does a wave of vomit. I've never been scared of him before, even when knowing his skills, but now, the whisper of a cold voice in my ear is telling me to think differently.

'You did this on purpose, didn't you?'

It's one I recognize. His. A bad sign unto itself, but one I ignore to wrap this up. That method, pushing the problem away, *may* have been proven not to be the best one for me. The memory of my meltdown in Brazil supports that. Except in this case, I don't have the choice to do anything otherwise. I have to face this head on.

Lifting one heavy leg after another, I take in a deep breath and hold it while swiping the roses aside. They fall off the counter, with something of a nostalgic grace, and for just a second, I swear I can smell that same mixture of blood and rain from that night.

Turns out though, as I stand over the island, only one of those scents is truly present. What's left in the rose's place, is a more modern burner phone with a blood smear across the cracked screen. I shudder at the accuracy, but soon the burning in my lungs propels me forward. Even with the fiery discomfort I still don't breathe. That is, until it buzzes again, then I finally exhale in pain. But, when I tap on the screen, what follows only knocks the wind out of me all over again.

CHAPTER TWENTY-THREE

WELL, THIS IS AWKWARD

Picture after picture is of Elias taking selfies. As each slide across my eyes, I take notice of every background. It transitions from him being in the city around mid-day, to night, to him inside the apartment. I swipe and swipe through all his fucking around, until I finally come across our second clue.

It's hard to make out where he is exactly, but as I continue to move my finger across the screen, I realize that each picture after the last is him backing up. When I reach the end of his little frame by frame movie, I freeze.

I stare at the photo, him standing in front of the jet Shane got on, with a pilot's hat on. My heart begins to beat like a drum in my ears. In the background, is the exact airport we had landed at. The only difference is that the hanger doors are now open, and inside is a red tipped jet, identical to the one Camille and I had come in on.

They were right behind us the entire time, but of course we weren't focused on what was behind us. If we had just waited, we would've—the phone buzzes in my hand, derailing my train of thought. This time, a photo of him, Rebecca and Shane fill the broken screen.

My friends are tied up. Arms and legs, along with the extra assurance of them being tied together. They sit on the smooth ground in front of our jet, fear in their eyes. It causes my stare to drift up to Elias. I stare at the smirk on his face, the expression stabbing me in the gut as my cheeks run hot. Of course he's treating all this like some kind of game. The phone shakes out of my hand. On instinct, I catch it before it hits the ground with a furious grip, so tight I hear and feel the glass crack further in my fist.

Camille steps in beside me and then pries the phone from my hand.

"We need to go back," she utters.

Rushing out of the apartment, all I hear is my rough breathing in my ears. Not one part of me cares if Camille is following me out the same way or not. I keep going until I reach the back alley. *Why can't I feel the cold anymore?* is the first thought to come to mind when I make it outside.

The question gets answered quickly, as my heart sings a murderous tune in my ears, forcing me to realize that my anger is warming me. I use it. I stomp around to the driver's seat and rip open the door, ignoring the sting rolling up my wounded hand.

Camille comes over to the same side, but the evil look shadowing my face makes her take the passenger seat instead. It's the first time I've ever seen her appear afraid of me, yet I ignore the accomplishment I feel and drive. While I manoeuvre through traffic to get back to where we started, the ear-piercing ring from my burner fills the car.

I think to answer it, but reconsider. Instead I reach into my pocket and shove the phone into Camille's hand. I'm driving way over the speed limit, to an airport that's only twenty minutes away. I'm *not* getting pulled over because of a phone during all of this. Without argument, Camille opens the flip and puts it on speaker. Then, Minnie's voice booms through it, anxiously.

"Nova. Nova, we have multiple problems. Everything is going crazy here! Our system is detecting multiple phantom viruses trying to break through our firewalls, almost all signals are down, and somehow Commander is missing."

"What?" Camille angrily interjects. "How does the leader of a global black-ops agency just disappear?"

I can practically hear Minnie's eyes roll over the phone before she answers her. "She doesn't exist to the world. She only really exists to us. So, when she's no longer in contact, she's either dead, or someone with access and an insane amount of luck, and balls, took her."

Coming up to the gate, the once hidden jet in view, I briefly look to Camille to find her expression matching my consternation. I turn away, pulling my focus back towards the hangar as it comes closer. At the same time, I answer Minnie, my heart heavy in my chest as I spew out the unhelpful truth.

"This is the last thing you're going to want to hear, and trust me, it's the last thing I want to say, but there isn't much I can do. Not from here anyway. But I'm about to end this game with Elias, so until then just locate her tracking chip and—"

"I tried that. Both of them!" she shouts at me. "Come on N, don't talk to me like I'm an intern. And even if they were both still implanted, the whole system is shutting down! The only reason I'm able to contact you is because your burner hasn't been updated in years."

"What about the winery? Did you try to contact them through customer service?" I blurt out, running over every other option.

"Not working. And I can't reach Supervisor or Manager to find out if they know what's happening."

"Shit," Camille sharply lets out.

As I burst through the gate and drift onto the tarmac, I echo her reaction as my stare lands directly on Elias, Rebecca and Shane in front of us. "Yeah, shit is right."

From the corner of my eye, I see Camille turn her head away from me to glare at Elias. The dim lighting from the headlights brightens things enough for us to see him, to see them, but something in me would've preferred the dark.

In the slight shine, about ten security guards—who are hopefully just unconscious—litter the smooth pavement before us, each face more broken than the last. Unfortunate, yes, but why I'd prefer a thicker blanket of darkness, is so I don't have to see the undeniable fear embedded in Rebecca's and Shane's faces.

It wrenches something in my gut, yet their terror doesn't hold my attention for long. I know I'm here for them, to save them, yet for some reason I still can't seem to explain, my eyes drift up from them to meet Elias. At the exact moment his stare locks onto mine, February's cold finally returns. He offers up a shy smile in my direction, then raises his free hand and waves 'hi'.

Taking a deep breath to shake off the shiver trailing up and down my spine, I wait until it's entirely gone before grabbing the car handle. I pop the door open, but the sound of Minnie's anxious typing forces me to stop in my tracks. The system shutting down, a system designed to never shut down, is bad, but Commander missing is even worse. A monumental deal. If our system shuts down completely, at least she'd know how to work the lines. Old school morse-code style. That option though, won't be one if we lose our digital eyes and ears.

I can't do anything about either though. Not when the original problem that started years ago is right in front of me. I'm going to sound like a complete tool here, but this needs to end. One hole in this sinking ship that is my life needs to get plugged.

I grab the phone from Camille, whose eyes are still dead locked on Elias, then take Minnie off speaker.

"Okay Minnie look, as soon as this is over, my next trip is to you."

Camille clenches her teeth. "The sooner we get out of the car, the sooner we can make that trip. Let's go, now."

I glance to her and nod while we both open the doors. Before I'm completely out, my attention briefly returns to Minnie as I put her back on speaker. "Stay on the line," I whisper while shoving the phone in my pocket.

"Alright," she says with the faint sound of typing accompanying her.

Camille and I stand on the sleek tarmac, both of us aiming our guns at Elias. Just as I expected, the grin on his face never leaves. As I watch him, a knot forms in my stomach when I realize he isn't staring at me. From where I stand, it's clear he's looking behind the car. But why? Shifting my eyes slightly, I glance into the rear-view mirror and immediately regret it.

Lurking there with a smile, and one of his karambits, is Andre. Without thinking, I spin around to him, but he's already moving just as fast as when I fought him earlier. He quickly comes up behind Camille with the knife to her throat. I aim the gun at him anyway, despite knowing he'd slit her open before I can shoot.

"We both know you're not going to do that, agent," Andre snickers and lightly begins to slice.

"Alright!" I shout and gently place my gun on the ground. Straightening, I stare at Camille, then slowly shake my head in disappointment.

"I told you to leave him on the plane, didn't I?"

"Fine!" she exclaims. "I'm a little rusty, okay? You happy?"

"Well, the knife against your throat *is* taking away some of my joy, but—"

"I hate you so much," she grunts.

"Enough side chatter ladies," Andre demands. "Move. Let's go."

Camille's expression doesn't revert from stone cold as her glare finds its way back to Elias. While we walk, Andre slaps the gun from her hand, and as it drops, I hear Camille say something, but the words don't quite register. Considering I'm walking *towards* and not running *away* from my crazy ex.

Shit.

We were so close to ending this. I guess it's my fault. I let her steal a car without making sure it didn't have such an easy trunk you can unlock from the inside.

Rookie mistake agent 401.

I get lost in the thought for a minute, and then get lost in thinking of all the things I should've done. Shane letting out a sharp 'what the fuck' brings me back to the present though, and retreating from my mind, I realize as we get closer, that his mouth is hanging wide open. Oh right. This is the first time he's seeing Camille since all this started. Or Theora, as he still knows her.

He has every right to be pissed, and clearly, he is. I watch him for a minute until Elias's sudden melodramatic movements has my stare transferring to him. He turns his head from a struggling Shane to a serious Camille. His divided attention gives me an idea of how to get out of this. Except when he opens his mouth, his voice momentarily distracts me from any escape plan, as he takes it upon himself to address the elephant on the tarmac.

"I'm sorry," he says innocently, "I don't mean to be intrusive, but..."

Yes, you do, you prick.

He swings his gun back and forth between Shane and Camille. "Do you two know each other?"

This asshole. Of course he wants to turn every stable thing around him into rubble. Okay, maybe 'stable' isn't the word now, considering Shane's glare. Catching on to that, Elias feeds off it, him looking almost giddy. Like I said... asshole. I shake my head at him. He only winks at me then goes on, his face lighting up with obvious forced surprise.

"Oh, are *you* her boyfriend?" He shifts his stare from Shane to Camille, who is fuming. "Well, this is awkward."

Jerking forward, Camille tightens her jaw, but Andre only pushes the knife closer. A bit of blood trickles down her neck. Shane is the one to flinch. A hateful expression twists his features, directed towards Andre, and doesn't let up when we reach a distance Andre seems comfortable with.

Mainly it's still anger that underlines Shane's usually tame features. An anger I've never seen on him before. It's unsettling, and I'm slightly left to wonder who it's mostly for now, as it bounces from Andre to Camille. I want to ask if they're alright—despite being tied up and held at gun point. Before I can say anything, we're forced to a halt, and standing as close as I am to Elias, all my words get caught in my throat. I force myself not to meet his eyes, but my will power falls flat.

Carajo.

(Fuck.)

Only three feet apart and I can see that there's something in his expression urging me to come closer. I don't know if it's the yearning in his eyes, or the slight blush that's come to his cheeks. But just when I tell myself not to move, it's him who takes a step towards me. My brain slightly goes numb as the smell of him seeps into the air around me like before.

Cedar wood and sweet mint.

Desperate to rid myself of the fond aroma, I step back then glance at Rebecca, checking for visible injury. She only scowls, then turns away. The familiar pain of that look fills my chest again. This time though I can't help but be angry too. If she had just stayed with me in Brazil, we wouldn't be having this problem. Or at the very least, it wouldn't have escalated to this.

The scent I was trying to avoid re-enters my personal space. Quickly I lift my eyes and see Elias. He's closer now, as close as he can seem to go, and then he smiles. It has an alluring effect on me that slowly starts to melt my insides.

Out of all the outcomes I've played over and over in my heavy head, I wasn't expecting this to happen. That I'd be so weak I wouldn't even try and do anything about the situation right away. Even with the faint specs of blood I see decorating his face.

An eternity passes as we stare at each other, his brown eyes trying to pierce through every wall I've put up since our last encounter. The hold he seems to have on me starts to tighten, but then I remember, it's a two-way street. No matter how much I don't want it to be. I force myself to see past his smile, to look into the cloud of thoughts that begin to form in his mind as we continue to gaze at each other.

Despite the time gap, between the day we broke to now, somehow we still know how to get under each other's skin. How to read each other. Except, when his smile flips into a frown, for the first time, I truly start to realize he's changed.

I give myself a moment to accept it, but within that second he moves fast. He tosses the gun between his hands before I can react, then raises it to me. I feel the agony before I feel my forehead split from the force of the hilt. Stars dance in my eyes as my vision sways in and out of darkness. Under me, my legs wobble, yet I don't fall. No. Elias reaches out and grabs me by the throat.

I hear the echo of someone calling my name. My mind can't place who it is exactly. I try to focus on the voice it could be, but that quickly becomes an impossible task when Elias slams me up against the jet. Air deflates from my lungs as I groan.

Violently I gasp as he lets go of me, and I fall to my knees. My eyes seep in and out of darkness again. Not a sound around me can be heard but my own deep breaths, and things only happen in blurry fragmented moments for me from then on.

Elias strolling over to Rebecca and Shane.

Slowly turning my head to see Camille and Andre staring at him.

Between the gaps I see an opportunity, so I take it, even though I'm moving like an old tortoise and my brain feels like mush. I reach into my pocket and hide my burner in my sleeve. A bit of my hearing starts to come back as the faint sound of Minnie shouting my name echoes. With how out of it I already am I can't be sure. Either way, I talk fast before my moment passes.

"L-listen M, please make sure m-my brother stays safe, and if you can, turn my burner into a tracker," my voice shakes as I push out each word.

"I'll try, N, but the service is getting—and I—just—Nova, can you hear me? Nova—?" she cuts out completely.

"Minnie?" I frantically whisper. "Minnie!?"

Only static on the line answers and my stomach sinks. I put the phone back in my pocket, hoping she'll be able to track me. The chances are slim by the sounds of it, but if anyone can do it, she can.

To shift my focus from the little bit of doubt I'm feeling, I look up again, my head throbbing. I find Elias still hovering over my friends. He has a knife with him now. Everything in me tries to get up, but gravity weighs me down, along with the reintroduced pain of breathing.

My sight continues to come in and out when I see him cut the ropes binding them. After that, nothing follows.

I feel myself sinking deeper into the coming cast of black, but I fight against it. My eyes flutter open again. Where I lay, I watch Andre lead Rebecca and Shane further away from me and Elias using Camille, who still has the knife at her throat.

She starts to fight against Andre, flipping him onto his back, but soon a loud shot rings out. That, I hear all too clearly, and next thing I know, Camille is on the ground. Shane runs to her side and Rebecca stops dead in her tracks, her hands over her mouth.

Again, my vision slips in and out. A firm grip on my arm brings me back to the nightmare unfolding around me. Camille, Rebecca, Shane and Andre have become smaller. It doesn't make sense at first, though when the rumbling sound of a jet engine starts to rattle my head, I realize why. Elias is boarding the plane, with me in tow.

I try to fight against him. God knows I'm fighting, but then nausea slams into my gut and I stop. As he throws me over his shoulder, my eyes find Rebecca frantic while crouching by the Mini Cooper. They then shift to Andre. He stares at Elias, as if speaking telepathically, then sharply nods and lets his eyes drift to the jet that Camille and I had taken to get here. To this failed rescue attempt.

An ache penetrates past the nausea in my gut as I figure out what they're planning. I use all my strength to flare out my arms and legs. I get in a few hits before Elias roughly shoves me into a chair. The force disorients me, but I keep fighting the coming dark. I crawl to the door as the other jet rolls out of the hanger and scream, to warn them to run, yet for some reason it seems like none of them can hear me.

Finally I reach the door, but at the exact moment my fist makes contact, the other jet explodes. I shake fiercely as tears pour from my eyes seconds after the loud bang.

Rebecca and Shane were still on the tarmac, alive. But now they're gone.

The only thing in my blurry vision is a ball of fire and while the tears continue to stream down my cheeks, the rush of takeoff only makes me feel worse. I swallow down my vomit and lift myself up onto my elbows, trying to balance the pain in my body with the pain of just watching my friends die.

Eyes wide, I freeze on the cushioned floor, looking out into the night as all the time I've shared with them slide across my mind. The memories hurt worse than anything my body is going through, but I don't dismiss it. I can't.

This is my fault.

A sort of guilty tranquility sets over me, except, when Elias touches my arm again, I lose it.

"Y-you killed them, you son of a bitch!" I scream. "You killed them!"

He slams me back into the seat. My eyes start to flutter shut but I use the anger in my heart to keep myself awake as long as I can. They're gone. All because of me, three great people lost their lives. How could things have gone so sideways so fast? How did I let it? I could've stopped him, but emotions blocked my judgement, like an idiot.

Idiot. Idiot. Idiot.

The word rings through my head; the only music playing at my pity party. Every part of me goes numb, and when Elias breaks out the rope, I don't even fight him.

Who do I have to fight for now anyway?

"I know it's been a very... eventful couple of days for us Kitten, trust me. But I swear things are about to settle down," he promises, so kindly it slightly confuses me. He then smiles, so caring it almost makes me sick to look at.

"Tell me if that's too tight, sweetheart."

My eyes are still dripping with tears, but my expression is all but literally on fire with fury as I glare at him.

"No? Okay, good. If it gets scratchy just let me know."

The charming grin never leaves his lips as he leans down, wipes away my tears, then pulls out a roll of duct tape. He snaps off a strip, and before putting it across my mouth he kisses me on the cheek.

"I'm sorry about your head, I'll patch you up in a minute, and after that we're going to fix even deeper wounds, Nova, I promise," he gently whispers. "And the only way to do that, is to go back to the beginning."

CHAPTER TWENTY-FOUR
MEMORY LANE

Utrecht, Amsterdam

The darkness overtaking my vision slowly recedes as a dim light shines in my eyes, replacing the empty void of nothingness I was in. A sudden rush of intense pain fills the left side of my head, though the throb doesn't stop me from trying to remember where I am and how I got here. And as my mind and sight start to clear up, the events over the last couple of days begin to flood my memory. My brother, my friends, Elias, Andre, Camille, Foreman—fuck.

Things just pretty much went to shit.

Overwhelming force rocks my vision again as my mind replays the last few days. The first instinct is to stay calm. Through my nose I softly take in a deep breath, despite the pain. Pain that comes in two different forms as I recall that my friends are dead, and realize where I am.

I let my surroundings grab my attention, and I lean into the slight fear I feel, to distract from the fact that I lost my other family. The long dark wood panels plastered on each wall. The polished stone floor now covered in a thick layer of dust. The high beam ceiling and lack of furniture of any kind, except for the chair I'm tied to. First time I was here, I thought this part of the house was an extension, but now fully inside, instead of looking in, it's more like a spruced-up garage or tool shed.

It's been a while. The season of summer is long gone—it smells like winter now—but I recognize the place all the same. Mission over and out, location: Amsterdam. My last assignment, where I took out [TARGET 41822]. The one person who would've set off this chain of events.

Daniel Meyers. Elias's older brother.

I stiffen in the chair as heavy footsteps coming down the pathway echo around me. Within seconds, Elias comes out from the shadows, as if on cue with my thoughts. A Smith and Wesson M&P in one hand and a chair in the other. While he sets it down in front of me, his eyes never meet mine, but my glare never strays from him.

The gun, I know, is just for show, and knowing that, is what has me tense. It's a prop. A tool. Something to look at. Something to distract my brain with while he uses the real weapon. His words.

Once we became comfortable enough with each other as partners, Elias would go on and on about joining the Creative Interrogations Unit. I thought it was cute, the way he'd try to get me to confess to stealing his Dragon Ball hoodie during early stakeouts. At the time I was working on my interrogation resistance training. I had the longest hold-out time among my fellow recruits, which came in handy, because sometimes he'd get really intense with the questioning. He could never get me to admit it though.

Of course, I knew he was going easy on me. I'd tell him that one day I'd actually like to see him give it his all. But, when that one day came along, I wasn't ready for it.

Eventually, whispers of Elias's interest to join the CIU in the future went up the chain, and they let him take a real crack at it, to see what he was made of. As his partner, I got to observe.

He was a good talker, and listener. Always had a way of making you feel safe and seen, which I knew. But in an interrogation, those wholesome qualities became different. Almost sinister. He twisted his compassion and used it fully to his advantage.

The worst part—something I found out as I watched behind that two-way mirror—was that with his smile, charm, and gentlemen-like nature, you wouldn't even know if you were a friend or an enemy. Not until you lied to him. If you did, then you'd definitely figure out which you were, and spill your guts. Figuratively and literally.

Every. Single. Time.

So yes, despite my rage, my body still goes taut with fear.

Before anything, he rips the tape from my lips. With the swift motion, I flinch, my body rattling in agony. Hard breaths force my chest to rapidly rise and fall as sweat has my tossed hair sticking to my forehead, despite the cold. After a few huffs, Elias slowly plants himself in the chair.

He slumps his shoulders over, resting his elbows on his thighs with the gun dangling in his hand between them. The curls of his onyx hair spill over his forehead, casting a shadow on his almond skin. A thin gold chain swings from his neck, with the weight from whatever's hanging on the end slightly leaving an indent inside his grey golf shirt. For a second, I wonder, but as the silence around us thickens, his flair for the dramatic more than present, his eyes finding mine takes away any curiosity.

He doesn't look away.

A lump begins to form in my throat as I glare into his beguiling eyes. His expression then softens in light of me not looking away, and the sudden facial cue of his brows slightly jerking upwards tells me. He's searching for a way to start our inevitable conversation. I open my mouth first—rage boiling up my throat. But, before I can explode, he speaks, so softly it hurts.

"Well, here we are."

I stay quiet and swallow, controlling my temper.

"Would you like some water?" he asks, his words sounding too sincere.

I narrow my eyes at him, only hate in them.

He shrugs. "No? Okay."

I give him nothing but anger. I keep my eyes tight, furrow my brow, and wrinkle my nose. Unexpectedly, the gesture makes him chuckle with a warm smile. He then sits up straighter and speaks fondly.

"You know what that look reminds me of?"

I answer with silence once more.

"Do you remember that mission we were assigned the same day we finally kissed? After our long will-they-won't-they?" His calm voice warms an old part of me. Maybe that's why I decide to answer, even as it burns.

"You mean the mission we completely butchered, because we weren't talking? *Because* we kissed?" I growl.

"Yeah, but I meant after that. After we got scolded by Supervisor for the whole 'accidental explosion' thing."

I remember the moment like it was yesterday, but I don't say it. I don't want to remember the tingling exhilaration he made run through me that day. Though despite my silence, he goes on for me, smirking.

"You were so angry. And the fact that *I* wasn't, only made you even more pissed," he snickers. "Something I found extremely adorable; the way your face would always scrunch up, like an angry kitten—"

"I didn't like that we messed up," I say defensively, like he's teasing me all over again. "And acting like you didn't care, didn't help."

"I didn't. And you know why, right?"

"No," I roll my eyes and find myself asking, "why?"

"Because, during that entire mission, even during Supervisor's rant on responsibility, I could only think of you. Your lips on mine." A sweet smile tugs at the corners of his mouth. "So no, I didn't care. Not about that. The only thing *I* cared about, was looking into those precious sea green eyes and asking you out."

I laugh bitterly as my face turns hot, getting caught up in the moment. "And you did. Right after the mission, and our lecture, you came up with that lame line."

He playfully scoffs. "It was *not* lame, it was the truth. And I didn't lie, did I?"

"That if I just went out with you instead of over thinking about it, that we'd always be able to focus on missions? Because of the certainty that you were mine? Rules be damned in light of our forbidden love?"

"Yes," he says, his playful attitude shifting to surprise at my ability to recite his exact words. "Precisely. And okay, maybe it was *a little* lame, but did I lie?"

"No, you didn't. Not at first."

"Oh, come on. Even you have to admit that every mission following you saying yes made us an unstoppable team, sure of every move we made."

The denial of his own blindness on the subject almost makes me pity him, but I'm not going to allow myself to feel anything more for him. Not even pity. I know what he's doing, trying to goad me into being on his level, but I refuse to go that deep in the dirt again. His little trip down memory lane may be making him feel something that's not there anymore, but I'm not having it. Whatever fairy-tale he's spinning in that psycho head of his isn't going to bring back those happy memories. They're only ones I have left and he's not taking from me, so I burst his bubble.

"Yeah. Until we weren't a team anymore Elias," I spit out, force behind every word.

"Ah. So that's the excuse you're using to justify killing Daniel here? That we weren't a team anymore, so I brought his death upon myself?"

"That's not fair."

He leans back in his chair and slides a hand through his hair, laughing dryly. "Really? *That's* what's not fair to you?"

"It was just a job, Elias," I slightly raise my voice, trying to hide the dread filling my chest.

"I know you, N. So I know that that's utter bullshit."

My entire body shivers with anger. "Don't sit there and pretend to know me. You don't know me, just like I don't know you. Not anymore."

"So, after all this time, you'd still rather have me go on thinking that you're a monster for killing my brother? Because you hated me that much?" he scoffs. "I never *once* laid a finger on Dominic after what you did, *or* while I was looking for you."

"And what, you want a thank you for that? Fine, thank you, but let's get one thing straight here. I'm not the monster, because correct me if I'm wrong, it was just you who blew up my friends and your own partner, right?"

His voice and expression go cold as he drops his hand. "That wasn't personal."

"That wasn't—do you hear yourself?" I ask, completely baffled. "You're so far gone that you don't even know where the line between personal and business is anymore! All of this, you hunting me down, you going after my friends, was never *not* personal, Elias, and you know that. Me terminating Daniel, that..."

I trail off but then force myself to tell him the truth, even if it doesn't change anything. I lower my head at the sour memory, but still try to portray dignity as I continue.

"That wasn't personal, because—"

"Fuck, Nova, you're so full of *shit*. Of course it was personal!" He shoots out of his chair and starts pacing.

"Are you sure? Because from where I'm sitting, you don't sound like you truly believe that. Especially not when you just accused me that what I was saying was utter bullshit." I look him up and down.

"You haven't killed me yet. You took your sweet time tracking me. You clearly suspected foul play."

"Yeah, at first, I did. But when you vanished, Nova, you only left me with two very different conclusions. And the more time that passed, the more the one conclusion where you killed Daniel on purpose became the only logical and real one."

"That isn't true. It—"

He stops pacing and glares down at me with impatience in his narrowed eyes. "If you say that it wasn't personal one more time, I swear—"

"It *wasn't*!" I shout, but then steady myself. "Not at first at least, because I... I didn't know it was him."

"Just another excuse."

"Oh yeah? And what's your excuse for breaking off our engagement? For cutting me out of your life before we even got a chance to have one together." My words threaten to break a part in my throat, but I catch them.

"I let you in. I broke down my walls for you, and what did you do? You broke my heart with no real reason, Elias. So please, enlighten me."

"You tell me your truth, and I'll tell you mine."

Heat rises in my cheeks. "Fine, you want the truth!? I did what I thought I needed to do because I lost you. That meant making the decision to take the early retirement offer Supervisor was *constantly* on my back about. 'An out to protect the only family I had left' he'd say."

"He did what—?"

"But when I found out who he was on my own—something he neglected to tell me—it was too late," my voice goes thin, like it's been grated down from killer to timid victim.

"You claim to know me, but you clearly don't now, and didn't back then. Because if you did, you'd know I *never* would've killed him just to spite you. Even if it meant a way to protect Dominic. That's the truth. *My truth.* So what's yours?"

"Why didn't you tell me he was pushing you to leave?" he asks, sounding like air had just returned to his lungs.

I let a bitter laugh come from me as I raise a brow. "And when was I supposed to do that? You were either too busy requesting solo missions behind my back, avoiding me, or ripping my heart out of my chest."

"It was because of the plan, Nova. I had a plan. You weren't supposed to—if you had just gotten there a minute later," he mumbles and again drags a hand through his messy hair. I ignore his stalling.

"We had a deal, so tell me why you—" I stop my voice from breaking completely— "tell me why you broke us."

"I was..." he pauses his ghostly response as his eyes drop to the dusted ground, then they shift back and forth, as if trying to figure something out. But, when he finally retreats from whatever maze that he was running in his head, he finishes his abandoned sentence, barely a whisper.

"Blackmailed," he then says it louder. Surer. "I was blackmailed."

A cynical snicker forces its way out of my mouth. "Seriously? That's the best you can—?"

He snaps his head up, then stares at me with a serious glint in his eyes. "I was blackmailed by that asshole Supervisor."

"What? Why would he...?"

The rest of the words get stuck on my dry tongue, and only silence sits between us as my brain tries to process his words. Why would Supervisor, the man that said we were a great asset to the operation he was running, blackmail Elias and guilt me into thinking—the thought comes to a full stop as every cell in my brain starts to run in overdrive. Then, I finally see it. Finally see that all the strings lead back to him. To Supervisor.

Oh my god I've got it. I've got it!

A chuckle travels up my throat at my new exciting and horrifying revelation. And I'm not completely sure why this keeps happening, but when Elias looks at me like I'm crazy, my gut laughter turns into crying. Hollow, soul cringing crying, but I blink away the tears when I see his stare shift into the pity I didn't allow myself to feel for him earlier. I get control, desperately shaking off my short moment of insanity, then talk, fast and stern.

"Elias, listen to me."

"I'm missing something here, aren't I?"

"Elias," I repeat.

"Be quiet, please, I'm trying to think." He uses his gun to point to himself. "I was blackmailed—" he then uses it to point at me— "and you were guilt tripped. The answer is right there but—"

"*Por el amor de Dios.* Elias, I'm trying to tell you that it's Supervisor. The mole back then, and 'Foreman' now, has always been Supervisor! Just think about it for a second. Not as someone who was in love at the time. Think about it as an agent."

I mumble the last of my sentence to myself, slightly laughing for not seeing all this sooner. "We were the only ones."

"What are you talking about?"

"I'm not just talking to talk. I'm asking you to listen. Listen and think about what we both got assigned when all our problems started happening. Think about what you said earlier about us being an unstoppable team, sure of every move we made."

He slowly plants himself back into the chair. "He knew how much of an asset we were to the agency, especially on operation E.D."

"Exactly. He knew we were good together," I lock eyes with him and then lean forward, "but I bet he didn't expect two agents, who only spent a year in the field to be *that* good."

"So, what? You're saying he picked us to be on the operation to fail?"

"Yes! But when we actually came close to finding out who the mole was, right before we had them cornered, I bet that's when Supervisor blackmailed you. Then when he saw that you went through with it, he assigned me mission over and out conveniently after we split."

"He did have a suspicion about us. One I guess I confirmed when I got defensive that time he said he's thought about removing you as my partner, like a rookie. He could've—no, he *did* use that to his advantage."

"Yes. He did."

We stew in cumbrous silence while I wait for him to decide whether to see the facts or let his hate for me cloud his judgement and dismiss the truth anyway. I don't even mention the part about what's happening at headquarters, which only makes me think about Minnie and how in the dark they really are over there.

Straight from the beginning the perfect map to solve this has been laid out. I was so blinded by the mess around me—the mess he caused—that I missed all the signs.

Supervisor, the one who started the operation.

Supervisor, who insisted Elias and I be as hands on as possible, so we'd be liable and stand out. And Supervisor, who was "helping" with the investigation into my brother's whereabouts, which was no doubt to control the information I was getting and to cover up the fact that he took him in the first place.

Fury travels up my spine like a shiver, making me desperate for Elias to see the clear facts. I hate him for killing my friends—an anger I'll take out on him later—but right now, the agency is in danger. I need to take down Supervisor and I can't do it alone. I need to get him to abandon his plans for execution.

This can go either way for me though. Whatever way it does, I need to be prepared. Shifting my eyes from him to the gun in his hand, I roughly shake my wrists. The movement slightly loosens the knot a bit, but given the fact that I'm very familiar with his tying skills, untying the rest behind my back shouldn't be too hard. Really, the only challenge is keeping my arms motionless.

Luckily, he's still thinking things over, and his eyes are nowhere near focused on me. *He always has to close them to really think. Still his biggest flaw.* I use the opportunity though, and violently shake my arm while tucking my thumb into my palm. Then, right when I get the last knot undone, his eyes snap open.

Just before the rope falls, I swiftly grab it, making sure it doesn't hit the ground to alert him. His choice to believe me has to come from him trusting he still has all the power here, and that won't happen if he figures out I'm not tied to this chair.

It's a risk, but it's one I have to take, because the sensation in my gut is telling me I'm right. With his information about the past, and mine, it creates the foundation. Or 'it's what connects all the dots' as Minnie would say. Everything that's been unravelling one after another is enough to support the accusation, so hopefully it's good enough, because it's all I got.

Finally breaking through the quiet, Elias slowly sucks in a breath then sighs. "Throughout all of this, I've tried so hard to hate you, Nova, but I guess I finally figured out why I couldn't. Can't."

"So?" I ask, almost too excited.

"So..." he sighs again and puts a hand on his forehead, "if what you're saying is true, then Supervisor ruined us. And that was the one thing I cared most about."

"You're agreeing to take him out? To calling a truce?"

He doesn't answer, though seeing him tuck his gun away does cause relief to spread throughout my body. The type I haven't felt in a while. Then, after letting out a heavy breath and glancing me up and down, he walks over to untie me.

I simply drop one side of the rope to the ground, wrapping the other around my knuckle while standing, and oh, the look on his face... priceless. He quickly reaches for his gun. I jokingly raise my empty hand in surrender and roll my eyes, then drop a hip and let a devious smirk brighten my bruised face.

Despite my slight amusement, and the thought to just take the gun from him and shoot, I fight against it. There's too much I have to fill him in on. So, ignoring his defensive stance, and my dizziness, I don't waste any more time and brief him. I start with what I learned from Samberg, and how I found out about Foreman and my brother. Then I ease into what Minnie has helped with, and Commander's disappearance—reframing from mentioning Camille or Andre's part.

Where they stand in all of this is still unclear, and with the way he hesitantly takes his hand from his gun, I'd rather not risk agitating him even more with half-truths. Which is why my deal with Commander also doesn't make the cut. No use in telling him when she's not available to collect at the moment anyway. So, once I'm sure I've covered everything he *absolutely* needs to know, I leave the dusty space open for questions.

He doesn't have any. Like he just flipped a switch and decided to trust everything I say, like when we were partners. It unsettles something in me, but I can't tell if that's a good thing or a bad thing. It only takes him less than a second to process everything I've told him and then nods. Classic.

"Alright, truce. But there's a condition."

Without waiting to hear what it is, I sigh and start walking backwards with a weak smile. "Oh come on. I'm not going to pick a fight with you now. Not after our *phenomenal* break through."

"I don't believe you." His eyes narrow as he starts strolling beside me.

"Good," I find myself saying darkly.

I wasn't going to do anything. Honestly, I'm too weak, too drained emotionally and physically for a full out brawl. But now that I do have some freedom, for Rebecca, Shane and even Camille, I find a small sliver of strength. Just enough to cause him *some* kind of physical pain.

I stop in my tracks and turn towards him, using the rope to whip his chest, then quickly swing the other fist in his face. He moves back fast, rips the thick string from me, then takes both my wrists in his hands. He twists them up against my back, presses his body against mine, and mumbles in my ear with a slight chuckle,

"Liar."

Swiftly locking my leg in with his, I trip him up, and we fall to the ground. I get onto my knees first, but he promptly takes hold of my arms, spins me like a fucking alligator, and then climbs on top of me.

"I've missed seeing you from this angle, Kitten," he purrs, smirking while taking a deep breath. Though his smug look quickly disappears when I plaster a grin across my face.

I thrust my hips into the air, wincing at the sharp sting that goes down my right side, but the pain is almost worth it when he goes flying. In those seconds—the ones between his face aligning perfectly with mine, and him shooting out his arms to protect himself—the smell of his honey lemon shampoo distracts me. Though not enough. I lift my arms into the air, level my hips back onto the icy floor, then wrap my arms around his. My whole body is screaming for me to stop, but I don't. Instead, I flip him onto his back while grabbing his gun.

As he raises his hands in the air, the small moment of triumph washes away the ache in my bones and heart. I sit on his stomach and steadily point the gun in between his eyes, my breath heavy in my throat.

"Are we done?" he roughly breathes out.

The first thought that comes to mind is my friends. But then, the memories of us overshadow their faces. After all this, I *still* can't pull the trigger to end him... or at least not yet. A voice in my head tells me to hold off until we deal with Supervisor and fix the agency's mess. *Fuck!* I lower the gun, drop down mere inches from his face, and then reply with the kind of sweetness that would frighten any grown man.

"Yes, for now. The enemy of my enemy *is* my friend."

My glare softens as I let an evil grin spread across my face. A heavy pulse in my heart almost pushes me to press the gun right into the side of his skull, as a clear image of my friends faces flash across my mind. Instead of giving into that urge, with all the threat I can muster in my sore body, I let my voice go dark with revenge.

"But as soon as we set things right with that fucker, you had better run, Puppy."

As I get off him, trying not to look at his lips, or focus on his smell or warmth, he replies almost as cold.

"Same goes for you Kitten."

CHAPTER TWENTY-FIVE

ENEMY OF MY ENEMY

Having Elias as an ally was definitely not where I had seen my situation going. I thought I'd have to bring him in tied up and gagged with a head injury. In a way that would've made more sense than how we are now, walking at an arm's length while undeniable tension wraps itself around us as we occasionally glance at each other. It's just plain weird. Oddly enough it's not the whole 'he had a gun and was ready to take me out' thing. Yes, admittedly that's a big part of it, but if I'm being completely honest, it's just his presents. Him being near me again without it being because of a heart shattering breakup, or a violent death.

As much as I want to stab, shoot, strangle, cut or just plain burn him, for some reason, that same resistance from my place in Brooklyn returns. A few hours ago, I had only wanted to hurt him in a number of ways, but now... my heart throbs. Maybe it's all *his* crazy and *my* conflicted energy in the air, or maybe it's that the silence between us is kind of reminding me of our old stakeouts. Either way, it's only screwing with my head. I need to keep my distance from him, and I can do that, but it doesn't stop me from thinking as we approach the jet,

'What did that bastard blackmail him with specifically that made him actually follow through and break up with me?'

Exposing our relationship to Commander would've been enough to have us stationed in different countries. And with the way we were back then, it would've hurt, would've nearly broke us, but we'd survive.

No, it must've been something worse. A combination of our separation and what else? Part of me knows I shouldn't be thinking about any of that, but the yearning in my heart is telling me otherwise. A feeling that grows when I sense Elias's eyes on me, watching and trying to read my thoughts through the expressions on my face.

I quickly shift into a stone-cold facade. No way I'm letting him in again, not after what he's done to the only family I've had for the last two years. And especially not when I know I'll have to return the favour and kill him later. But right now, as my unlikely ally continues to stare down at me, I finally get tired of the numbing silence and his eyes drilling a hole in my head. I stop in my tracks then turn to him.

"Do we have another problem?" I snipe.

"No," he says, smiling but just when the word comes from his mouth, his stare drifts from me to behind me and his smile suddenly melts away.

"I think there's about to be one though."

Whipping around to see what made him go so rigid, when my eyes land on them, my heart skips a beat. My knees slightly buckle, and from the corner of my eye, I notice Elias reach out to catch me, but I quickly gather myself and let out a small gasp. Each wobbly step I take comes with doubt, but I continue forward anyway, towards Rebecca, Shane, and Camille. For the life of me my brain can't seem to process how, but I don't care.

Before my voice rips from my throat to call out to them, the furious glare from a grit covered Camille stops me. It may be directed through me, but I still feel its chill as I swing my head back around to Elias. I look from him to her, and notice what looks like a jumper cable wrapped around her hand as she starts sprinting towards him. When I step out of the way, looking to Elias again, his mouth opens in shock.

"Seriously!?"

"What? After all the shit you pulled you thought I'd shove it all down and forgive you?"

"I mean, as an agent, yes," he gulps.

"As an agent, sure. But as a woman scorned, no. I'll have a little fun with this first, and besides," I pause and watch as Camille draws closer, "you *did* shoot her."

Seconds later, unfolding before my very eyes is something I thought I'd never see. *Thee* Camille Maxwell about to torment someone I know. She moves like a panther. I step a bit to the left as she jumps on Elias. He quickly manages to create a little distance between them. But soon after, Camille uses his bent knee as a stepping stool to then enclose her thighs around his neck, pin him down, and then wrap the cable around his throat. Almost in record time to. Though as excited as I am witnessing this kind of 'unicorn grazing' event, I force myself to speak up.

"Alright, that's enough."

"I was assigned to protect you, and killing *him* would be doing that." She pulls the cable tighter on his throat as he gasps for air.

"As flattering as I find that, you weren't assigned to protect me. You were assigned to survey me, agent," I raise my voice. "So let him go. Now."

"I knew you wouldn't be able to handle him."

The soft layer of disappointment in her voice tightens my chest as I fight the urge to stare at Elias. That was a low blow. It travels, getting under my skin, but I brush it off. She's pissed, probably injured—or at least her ego is—and she looks exhausted. I want to be the bigger person and say that's why I let her words roll off my back, except it's not. Well, not entirely anyway. It's more because I know something she doesn't, and that's enough to take most of the sting out of what she said. Enough to ignore how the thought of "handling him" cuts some part of me deep.

I try to get her attention. "420!"

She completely ignores me. "Tell Rebecca and Shane to look away," she orders.

This can't happen right now. Time isn't our friend, *and* we have no idea what's happening at headquarters. Hours have been wasted by Elias already. And seeing how—in some strange turn of events—I got him to work with me, she needs to get along with him whether she likes it or not.

I'm not particularly excited to tell 'Camille Maxwell' to cool it, but we have to go. I conjure up as much courage as I can in my too-tender body, then speak with a sliver of confidence.

"We have bigger problems than him at the moment Maxwell. And despite your obvious hate, we need him for this. So at least just hold off on killing him for now, okay?"

Camille lets up just a bit, to the point where Elias can take in a breath, though she does keep the cable tight enough that each breath he takes comes in and out strained. I probably should help him, but the thought gets shoved aside when she brings her attention back to me.

"What are you talking about?" she asks, interestedly confused.

"I don't mean to interrupt," Elias coughs out, "but can you please get off me!?"

He really isn't making this easier on himself. All he needs to do is lay there and be quiet. My eyes shift to the frozen over patch of dirt his twisted body is currently occupying, a glare already queued to shut him up, but Camille beats me to it. She slightly tightens the cable around his throat, and he coughs as she stares down at him again.

"You shut the fuck up—" she then looks over to me— "and you; did you find out more about Commander or what's happening at headquarters?"

"In a way, yes," I quickly answer.

The lack of oxygen getting to Elias means I have to hurry and explain what I've figured out in the last hour. If not, she'll kill him. Or at the very least, cause some serious brain damage, and seeing him on the ground trying to wiggle free doesn't give me as much satisfaction as I thought it would. Instead, when I see him gasp again, I tell her everything as fast as humanly possible.

I explain who Foreman is, how I put the pieces together, and, once I get through all of it, Elias's eyelids slowly start to fall. Just before his chest doesn't rise again though, Camille unwraps the cable and forcefully kicks him away. She then gets up and dusts herself off.

"Okay," she shrugs. But when she tries to sneak a swift side glance to the ground, I figure that there's something she's not telling me.

"What did you do?"

"Nothing," she tells me with false innocence. "Based on the timeline and incidents, your assumptions are solid. Plus, not that it's relevant, but I never really liked that prick anyway. I just wish I was briefed sooner."

My question 'why' gets muffled by the sound of bursting metal and shattering glass. I quickly hit the dirt. During the first explosion, my head wasn't in any kind of state to fully take in the sound—maybe an unintended mercy—but now... now I shake. Not just because the ground is rattling underneath me. No, I feel it again. That feeling where my heart drops into my stomach, and no words can come out. My hands go clammy, my eyes wide, but I remember to breathe.

Deep breath in.

Deep breath out.

I swallow hard. No time for fear, especially not the kind I used to let consume me. I'm better than that now. I have to be. A rush of heat warms the cool air above, then, when it's over, and when I trust myself enough to stand, I rise to see *exactly* what exploded. My mouth hangs open.

What are the chances of two agency jets exploding within a day?

In front of me, the very transportation we were going to use to save the agency from damnation, is on fire, and doesn't look like it'll be stopping any time soon.

"Well, shit," Elias unhelpfully comments in deep breaths as he staggers to his feet, lightly stroking his neck. "Copycat."

My eyes do a double take from the fire ball to Camille. "What the *fuck,* Maxwell!?" I shout.

"Yeah, at the time, it seemed like a good idea, though I may have let my anger win. Ma faute."

"Oh, this is great. Just great!" I throw my hands up in the air. "I guess we'll be taking the long way to headquarters then!?"

Camille slightly lowers her head. "J'ai dit ma faute." *(I said my fault.)*

Everything seems to be getting harder and harder, and only now do I want to take out my aggression. Personally, that's progress. It can be also interpreted as my so-called "control" slipping away, but whatever. I've come this far, which is way too far to give up and just turn around to find a new life. *As tempting as that sounds.*

Any kind of bliss I'd find with that life wouldn't last long though. Not if Unknown—the world's only *real* safety net against whatever Specter is planning—crumbles to dust. Things need to be fixed. The thought starts to take up the rest of the space in my head, but I focus on what's in front of me and glare at Camille with raw annoyance in my eyes.

"How did you survive both a gunshot to the chest *and* the other plane explosion?" I ask as calmly as I can, my shaking hands now going steady.

"Well—"

"And how did you find us?" I stomp towards her.

She rolls her eyes then loosely crosses her arms over her chest. "Are you finished?"

Beside me, Elias lifts his finger and takes a step forward. "Actually, I have a question too, if I can just interject here for a second."

Camille turns to him and hisses. "Okay, first of all, my demand for you to shut the fuck up still stands—" she then spins back around to me— "and you, the answer to your first question should be obvious." She unzips her jacket just enough for me to see the bulletproof vest strapped to her.

My brows knit together. "Okay, but how did you know that he'd shoot you after he got me?"

"Normally, I wouldn't be at liberty to discuss that with two wanted agents. But, seeing how we're in a crisis that involves us being in the same boat, I'll reframe from protocol. For now. Though you won't like the answer."

I cross my arms. "You're stalling."

"Low," she tells me, nonchalant.

"The original plan was to bring the two of you in the minute we got word of what happened in Brooklyn. But like usual, shit went sideways, and I guess we both decided to handle things our own way. Me doing the right thing, and him doing the... stupid thing. And that stupid thing caused my mission objective to change. Find and retrieve agent 504."

"And now you've circled around to my question," Elias chimes in. "Where is—?"

Cutting him off, Camille reaches into her boot, pulls out a small spear point knife and throws it directly at his face. He ducks just in time, then lifts himself up and looks at her with razor thin eyes and a frown, which soon finds me.

"Get your Watcher under control!"

She lightly holds her side but briskly stomps forward. "I'll show you under control, you son of a—"

"Both of you stop, alright!?" I rub the bridge of my nose and sigh. "¡Dios! Es como tratar con jodidos bebés fuertemente armados. Just shut it down and lock it up, now!"

(God! It's like dealing with heavily armed fucking babies.)

Both of them glare at each other, but they do keep their mouths shut. And after a deep breath, I swing my body towards Camille, going over her explanations. The bulletproof vest I can understand, but Andre's part in this is causing me to draw a blank. I've gathered that she didn't tell me the whole truth during our first conversation on the jet, but him helping her in any capacity seems unlikely.

Before I can ask her to elaborate on the part he played, my stare drifts to Rebecca and Shane coming towards us, their every step hesitant. All words dry up in my throat, along with most of my confidence when both of their eyes lock onto me like a target. I'm more than glad to see them alive, but that doesn't seem like a two-way street. In front of me though, Camille doesn't notice them, and proceeds to explain the connection to Andre. Flinching while taking in a breath.

"Like I was saying, when Andre decided to go AWOL, my mission objective did change. But even though I hate the guy, turns out he's a *useful* agent after all. He proved it when, while you were passed out, he told me Meyer's new plan, where he was planning to end all of this, and how it'd 'end with a bang' for the civilians back on the jet."

I'm running through what she said when realization strikes me. "When we questioned him, he said he didn't know what Elias was going to do next."

"He lied. I told him to. The less you knew about our plan, the more likely it was to succeed."

My attitude becomes sharp. "Why would he cooperate with you in the first place?"

"Because his morals are correct. He didn't want the civilians to get hurt, and I agreed. So, we devised a plan that would get Shane and Rebecca out safely. One, I admit, that did include causing a scene and giving you to Meyers as a temporary distraction. We just had to make sure you thought I was in danger, so back in Toronto I deliberately brought Low along so he could escape later, making it look like he got the drop on us."

"And the explosion? How'd you—?"

"When I tossed Low, it triggered Meyers, just like he said it would, and naturally, him shooting me made Shane come my way and Rebecca follow. That made us close enough to the car that it sufficed as cover from the blast. After that, the hard part was finding a way to get to you before he decided to end things."

"She was going to kill us," Rebecca furiously comments as she cautiously steps in beside me.

"No, I wasn't," she laughs bitterly. "We just didn't think we'd have time to drop them back in Brooklyn, so I had to *persuade* them into coming with us until I could put them back where they belong."

I know she would never hurt them, but to a civilian, it might have very well felt like she would've. Bluffing is a dangerous game when no one knows the angle you're going for, and in this case, both Rebecca and Shane didn't have a choice in playing scared victims.

I ready myself to ease their fears of her, but hearing Elias's foot slightly shift behind me stalls any words from coming out. I don't even have to turn to know that his expression has gone dark from the news about his so-called friend. Especially not when I notice Rebecca and Shane scurry back.

The shear amount of fear on their faces does make me turn towards him, and even I freeze up a little. With the fire in front of us burning bright, its glow causes the hair that's fallen into his face to cast a shadow onto his sharp features. Making him seem like a skeleton. And with his height, muscly body, and the red marks around his throat, he looks like he could be an angel of death.

"Where is Andre now?"

"Mad that your watcher *and* P.E. betrayed you?" Camille goads him, unshaken by his appearance.

"Where. Is. He?" Elias growls, forcefully breathing out each word.

He stomps forward, and without thinking, I place my hand on his chest to stop him from going any further. The old instinct resurfacing, because I know what that voice means. He stares down at my hand, and with the simple touch, I notice a slight wave of relief push through him. He loosens up.

In the moment it seems like it's only us here as my eyes meet his, and I feel his heartbeat at the same speed as mine. This is the first time I've voluntarily touched him in three years, but all the emotions that would've rushed from my heart to my head gets interrupted when Camille's voice cuts off my stream of emotion.

"He's alive, if that's what you're asking."

Taking my hand from him, my cheeks heat when I avert my gaze and let my attention bounce from Rebecca to Shane, then finally Camille. Without completely understanding why, something of demand comes over me. Maybe it's to distract from what just happened. Either way, I run with it. We can't waste any more time standing here going back and forth with our individual anger. It isn't going to help us get to headquarters faster.

I start walking, even though I have no idea to where. "How did you guys get here?"

"With Unknown resources on lock, I had to improvise, with a small plane I "borrowed." Landed it in a field nearest to your location, which unfortunately took a bad toll on the left wing. We walked to the nearest vehicle from there. A van that's up the street and should get us to an airport."

"No," I spin around to her, "a plane would be all over the radar. He's probably had us all flagged. The car will take too long, and there's not a bus on earth that'll be fast enough." I rub the back of my thumb on my lips and think. "We could..."

"We could," Camille interjects, "take the van to the train station a couple miles from here. It's faster than any of our other options, less on the radar, and we'll be better able to anticipate an attack. Plus, we can take the tunnels to headquarters from there. Back swamp route."

"Risks on train transportation tracking is very low. I don't like the time it'll take, but it does gives us a minute to come up with some kind of retaliation." I nod. "Okay. Let's do it."

Camille agrees and then tells everyone to get to the van. I go to move again, but Elias catches my eye, frustration instead of murder lining his expression.

"I'm not going anywhere until I see Andre in front of me, alive," he says through clenched teeth.

Twisting back to Camille, I place a hand on my hip and tilt my head. I have no idea what she might've done to him, even if he helped them get here. But, for the sake of this mission moving forward, I glare at her. And when I don't let up, she only rolls her eyes at me.

"Fine," she huffs out then stomps off, I'm guessing towards the van. "But he's still technically my haul, meaning..."

She leaves her sentence open ended. A bad sign. When she starts to take wide steps, I quickly surpass everyone else and follow closely behind her. Once we reach a rust bucket looking cargo van, Camille opens the back doors and a certain amount of pleasure comes when I see what I see.

A handcuffed and gagged Andre squints up and scans over all of us. But, when his eyes shift to Elias, that's when he tries to speak. His words only come out in mumbles. I bring my stare to a fuming Elias and some of my pleasure washes away when I see the glimpse of hurt in his eyes.

It's something no one else here will see. It only lasts for a second before drifting into something else, but whatever rage or other emotional turmoil that's going through his head we don't have time for. He can kill him later for all I care. Right now though is not the time. And to my surprise, he only lets out a heavy sigh while shaking his head and slamming the doors shut.

"I call shot gun," he announces with a hint of pain in his voice.

"Oh hell no!" Camille calls after him.

Bringing myself back to the present—the one where I don't care about his feelings—I push down my brief moment of sympathy. I also ignore that it felt as if I had just been bombarded with exactly what he felt towards Andre. I don't miss that. Our annoyingly accurate connection. I try to remove the sensation from my system.

Deep breath in.

I don't love him.

Deep breath out.

I don't care.

After my moment of emotional realignment my eyes flutter open, and suddenly I'm left alone with Rebecca and Shane. I stare blankly at them and with utter control ask,

"You know you can go home, right?"

CHAPTER TWENTY-SIX

THICK OR THIN

It's not that I forgot about them. It's just... having them stare so hard at me jogs my memory that they're here, with me, in Amsterdam. Despite the unbelievable nature of all of this I reach out and hug them, over the moon that they're not charred corpses.

When I draw back, my happiness quickly switches to bewilderment. Figuring everything out and getting Elias to work with me instead of against, means I can send them home. Foreman never involved them. That was Elias. They'll be safe back in Brooklyn. By the looks on their faces however, it doesn't seem like they know that.

I call out to both Elias and Camille with new order lining my words. "Give me a minute here."

"We're waiting on you, Kitten," Elias replies.

I roll my eyes at his decision to call me that right now. *Prick.* I cross my arms to draw attention away from me blushing ever-so-slightly. Great. He's already getting under my skin. Not the best sign, but also not the biggest issues. That, is the two very angry people—people whose lives I've fucked with enough—standing in front of me. I brush off

Elias's voice, then, as if nothing happened, I speak to my friends as gently as handling grenades.

"You two should go home. The problem that was threatening your lives has been stabilized, so—"

"Oh my god, seriously!?" Rebecca shouts, like I offended her somehow, then throws her hands into the air. "Don't. Don't you *dare* talk to us like we're just some helpless... helpless..."

"Kittens?" Shane offers up with a silent laugh so bitter it reminds me of that terrible coffee taste. He doesn't sound like himself, and it twists my gut.

Stepping closer to me, Rebecca ignores his interjection. "I'm not leaving. I tried that and look where it got me! So don't you dare say it's 'safe for us to go home now,' cause I've been through enough for the last couple of days to know that if there's still a problem with you in any capacity, then there's still a problem with me and mine!"

I have no idea how to answer that. Well, I do, just not with an answer she'll like. Part of me is glad that she's talking to me again, even if she's yelling. Her tone causes my eyes to drift from her to Shane, looking for some backup, but I don't get any.

He's the quiet one now, like they decided to switch roles on the way here. I know that that's not it though. Not with the way his gloomy ocean eyes lift to stare at the body beside me. I don't have to glance over to know that it's Camille who's walked into the conversation.

I catch every expression on his face as they shift from one to the other, making me understand without words why he wants to stay.

Love.

Rage that she lied to him definitely lingers, and anger. No doubt because he was forced to watch her completely change in seconds, and only had that same amount of time to process it. But above all else, it's the relief that she doesn't have a hole in her chest that shines the brightest on his face.

Nonetheless, as much as I do understand, I don't let that stop me from pushing through the awkwardness between them and trying to find a way to continue with my 'go home' speech. But with her need to be in command, it's Camille who finds the words for me. Just maybe not the *exact* words I'd chose.

"I know you're both beyond hurting and confused, especially given everything you've been through," she sighs. "But—and I don't mean to sound harsh here—you need to be all of that at home, where you *will* be safe and—"

Shane lets out a forced laugh.

"Here we go again," Rebecca mumbles under her breath.

Shifting my eyes to him, I watch Shane pull a hand through his dirty hair, and exhale. "Sorry. I can't help but express my amusement, because safe? Really? Is that only referring to the potential danger, or is that also referring to being safe from your lies? You?"

Camille steps forward, and I don't know if it's on purpose, but she lets her accent slightly fall away.

"Shane, I—"

"It just... it doesn't sound like you're including that. You and your lies. The fact that you played me," he laughs again, this time much darker. "Did the last two years of you fucking with me not require you to care about keeping my feelings *safe,* until now?"

"Shane—" she tries again.

"I still can't figure out how I let myself be so stupid. Why I let my guard down with you so fast. Yes, you were beautiful, and kind, and you made it so easy, but I guess that was the point. Right? To have me wrapped around your finger?"

"Things are more... complicated than that now. It's different—"

"I don't care," Shane softly whispers, and in front of me I see something in Camille break just a little. And for the first time since I've met her, the real her, she flinches.

"I'm coming. Not for you, but for my friend. Because at least after I found out she wasn't who she said she was, she explained why she lied. I still don't even know your real name... *Theora.*"

Her name—her alias—comes out with such venom and sadness. As if she murdered the bubbly girl he fell in love with right in front of him. I can almost see all the anger he's holding back when he gives her the cold shoulder as he walks by. She doesn't follow. Not at first. But, after a few intense silent seconds, she turns to go after him.

I grab her arm. "Just give him a minute here, Maxwell. He still thinks that your love for him *was* just a cover," I say gently.

She rips her arm from my grip and goes off in the opposite direction, leaving me alone with Rebecca.

Her focus is on the way Camille went. "Jeez," she says.

"Yeah," I sigh. "She's *a lot.*"

"I never thought I'd be utterly terrified of *Theora.* A woman I saw once trip on nothing and almost poke her eye out with a pencil."

I slightly shudder. *The pencil. Irony?*

When I turn my gaze onto Rebecca, trying to rid myself of those graphic case photos, it's like our entire conversation never happened. She stares at me like I'm the bad guy. I don't want to be the bad guy any more than I already am to her. She needs to go. She made it clear she doesn't want to have anything to do with me multiple times, and despite what he said, the main reason Shane is still here, is because of Camille. I can respect that. Rebecca on the other hand, doesn't need to be around this anymore. She should leave like she did in Brazil, but, before I repeat myself on that front, she speaks first.

"I'm not going until your mess is sorted, and that's final."

Frustration starts to travel up my chest, and I let it out in a heavy breath, then frown, recalling the feeling when I thought she was in danger the first time in Brooklyn.

"Becca, I've already put you in a terrible position more than once, and one of those times I thought you died. I couldn't deal with that, and I wouldn't be able to live with myself if something else happens to you because of me." I take a step closer.

"There's no quick escape plan this time."

When I finish, not one ounce of care is present anywhere in her expression, and that doesn't change as she walks towards the van and says coldly, "I'm staying, Nova."

I know that stubborn look. Nothing I say will make her leave. Or at least that's what I'm telling myself. If I'm honest, some part of me is being selfish, letting them stay. I could make them leave.

It would just take the right words, or the right 'hands-on' approach. The thought to drug them and send them home does come and go. But, given the state I'm in, both emotionally and physically, the only thing I can seem to do right now is shrug it off.

In doing so, it leaves more room to think about travelling in a metal tube with my slightly unstable ex. Maybe not the best idea from the looks of things, but it's all I have to work with. Another mind-bending dilemma to dismiss for now.

I start towards the van to get a move on with the mission, yet just as I step forward, my legs stop short when seeing Elias rush over to me.

"Here." He tosses me my burner phone. "I doubt the call is for me."

Ignoring the fact that he took it but didn't destroy it, I quickly answer. An unpleasant muffling sound is all I hear as soon as I place it against my ear, bringing back the faint memory of when I first heard the similar static back in Toronto. Minnie had said that the signals were going down, but it seems like she may have found a way to get it back up. I'm about to call to her, but soon her frantic whispering fills my ear.

"Nova. Nova, you have to get to Beta Z headquarters, now. I figured it out. It's—Supervisor! There's some—else, but I didn't have time to—"

She cuts out completely.

"Minnie?" My pulse begins to race as I call her again. "M, what's happening over there? Can you hear me?"

Only the sound of static answers, and it's not reassuring. I know everything was beginning to go to shit over there, that she was scared, but I didn't know how bad it actually was. Still, the distortion is all that occupies my eardrum.

I try to zero in on any other sounds I may hear, but it's no use. The continuous static overtakes the phone, despite my focus, and the only thing I can think to do is give up on the call and go.

I'm about to, but then, as clear as day, I hear Minnie's voice full of panic, yet it also carries some kind of peace. I know that tone. I've heard it over a hundred times. It's a tone I've never wanted to hear from her. Tears begin to well up in my eyes before I even allow my crying to start as I hear her.

"I'm sending everything I found to one of my personal hard drives. Something they'll never get to. I don't know if it'll upload in time, but if it does, the code to access all the information will be sent to your burner. That'll create a signal so my hard drive can locate you."

"Minnie, Minnie please. Tell me what's going on!" I shout unevenly.

"I'm sorry about how things turned out, but it wasn't your fault, and I know you can handle it. Please be safe out there, Nova. Take care of yourself."

"Minnie..."

'Alpha user purge sequence activated. Locking onto nearest encrypted hard drive for file transfer now,' Bethany declares in the background.

"Thank you for letting me live a life of action through you, N," she whimpers. "Thanks for... thanks for the ride."

She says nothing more. All I can do is listen to the sound of a door being kicked in. I flinch as the gunshots ring throughout the room, and then the heart-breaking sound of a body dropping to the floor follows. Everything in me freezes to the ground. The only thing I can seem to remember how to do is blink. My tongue goes dry, feeling as if it's been glued to the roof of my mouth, but in some miracle, I manage to mumble softly.

"Minnie? Minnie, are you still there?"

Her wet cough hollows out my heart, and then she stammers out, "finish this."

Her sudden silence plagues me. All I can make out is the faint sound of gunshots going off throughout the building. I release the breath I didn't realize I was holding in and feel the slight tickle of a single tear rolling down my cheek. Still, my feet are stuck to the ground, and my eyes follow suit as I let the phone dangle at my side. A heat begins to stir in my in.

I just heard my oldest friend get murdered over the phone.

The world around me goes blurry as tears cloud my vision, and my face soon settles into an expression of hate and vengeance. I curl my hand into a fist so tight the sting of my nails penetrating my skin is the only thing to slightly bring the world back into alignment. That, and the sound of footsteps coming in my direction. I raise my head up slowly and blink to clear the tears. When they fall away, it's Elias who's standing in front of me, a genuine look of concern lining his features.

I don't want it.

If it wasn't for him. I would've been there. Would've been able to save her. I breathe and force myself to let the thought melt away. I can't change that now. Screaming at him might make me feel better, but it won't bring her back, and definitely won't help the others. So, before I let another tear fall for him to see, I close my eyes and breathe in the cold air around me.

"What do you need?" he asks.

I know he knows me, or at least he did. But right now, one thing's for sure; he's seen the expression I'm wearing before. The deep creased brow, tightly shut eyes and pursed lips are all familiar to him. Meaning his somewhat rehearsed question doesn't surprise me in the slightest. Whenever I've made this 'nothing better fuck with me right now' face, he's always asked the same question. It brings a moment of comfort to my heart, but when I open my eyes to answer him, I have no words.

All I can do is allow myself to let him see my hurt, even if it's just for a second. Though once I harden my expression again, replaying Minnie's last words in my mind, movement comes back to me. I quickly stroll past him, and in the process, I catch myself from completely breaking down. Then, only order pulses through my voice as I finally reply.

"We need to move. Now."

CHAPTER TWENTY-SEVEN

OLD HABITS DIE HARD

The gentle cruising of the train rocks me as I stare out the window, taking in the landscape as it passes by. Something about the barren trees calm me. After Minnie's death and everyone's icy facades—on the *entire* drive to the train station, *and* all while we snuck onto the train—I needed to be calmed.

It also numbs the pain of loss. Just enough.

Being left alone with my thoughts wasn't ideal, but the idea of sharing a roomette with anyone other than myself didn't sit well at the time of making the arrangements. With everything that happened with Minnie, images of my brother beaten and bloody started to come to mind and I... I couldn't deal with anyone else or their problems.

The train is nice. Red with a retro look but with a white streak modern finish. My roomette has the same kind of retro-modern feel. A decent size and cozy, with the smell of freshly cleaned carpet and a long-finished dinner service. It has the look of a three-star hotel room. White walls, black curtains, and two neatly made single bunks.

As soon as we got on, after slipping in just before it departed, everyone branched off, as if on instinct, with who they could tolerate the most.

Rebecca went with Shane, leaving Camille to go with Andre. The saddened look on her face even hurt *my* feelings, though something told me that she wouldn't give him the space he needs. And considering I had seen her walk past my roomette to theirs an hour ago, I was right. Of course that leaves Andre alone, which means there's a ninety percent chance that Elias abandoned his car to have a "conversation" with him. That *probably* won't be good for either of them. Or the rest of the train for that matter. But what can I do about it?

Seeing that hurt look in his eyes, an old part of me—a part that seems to be resurfacing—wanted to do something. But, right now, I couldn't care less. I'm glad I'm on my own. Or at least I was.

I slowly spin around when I hear a light knock on the door. Through the slight crack in the curtain, I see Elias and sigh before turning to face the landscape again. My heart aches for the first true friend I just lost, because I couldn't be two places at once. I need to be alone, to mourn her, and it's not like we have nothing to talk about. But still, for some reason, my mouth disobeys.

"Come in," I tell him, my voice hollow with sorrow.

He gently slides open the door and closes it with the same amount of care. The tenderness has me turn towards him, and taking in his appearance makes me want to both laugh and hug him. His clothes are rumpled, face lightly flushed, and just a little bit further up—

"You two kiss and make up?" I humorlessly tease.

"Pardon?" he answers, confused.

I tap lazily at the corner of my forehead, where the slightest bit of blood peeks out from behind his tossed glossy hair. Shifting his eyes up, he mimics my movement, fingers coming away with the blood.

"Oh," he stares down at it for a second then wipes it away, laughing dryly. "Not exactly. More like we... had a conversation."

I snort softly. "With your fists?"

"Maybe conversations end more productively that way."

"Yeah," I run a finger over the patched up cut on my own head. "Maybe." With annoyance now brimming inside me, I ask, "is there a reason you're here?"

Elias meets my stare and hesitates for only a second before answering, words coming out fast.

"Sorry. I know you wanted to be alone." His voice sounds rehearsed. Like he practised what he was going to say on the way here, either for my benefit, or to hide something.

Is he grieving too?

Minnie was a friend to us both. Partners share an operations analyst, to make sure everything went smoothly on missions. After a very short time though, she noticed our chemistry and quickly established herself as a friend and our 'first fan' she'd always say. She rooted for us and basically pushed us to be together from the beginning. Always creating intense romantic scenarios she *thought* we didn't know about.

The tight pain of loss returns to my chest, but I breathe it out. If I hadn't had to deal with his bullshit, I could've saved her. He's the reason I wasn't able to save her. To be the friend I was supposed to be. *No*, I tell myself. *It's his. Supervisor's.* Yet thinking it doesn't keep the base out of my voice.

"And yet here you are, Elias," I mutter, harsher than I meant, but he doesn't react.

"I just came to let you know that everyone turned in. Or at least, it looks like they have. It could be that they just turned off the lights to avoid me."

"Because of the whole 'you almost killing them' thing maybe?" I patronize him.

"Yeah, that's the reason that makes the most sense. Either way, they're all in quiet mode," a light chuckle escapes him. "Well, everyone except Maxwell and your friend..." he trails off.

"Shane."

His stare falls to the ground. "Right. Shane. Sorry."

"He's still arguing with her?" I ask, mostly talking to myself.

I slip a hand into my unbound hair and cover my face. From the second I was filled in that Theora is actually Camille Maxwell—after the shock and awe set in of course—I figured Shane was going to be pissed. Especially since he pretty much used all his understanding and forgiveness with me. I didn't think he would be able to hold his own with her though.

I guess he's tougher than I thought. Or maybe his anger towards her right now is. Either way, I can't help but laugh dryly as a memory of my own comes up. And before I notice I'm thinking out loud, that memory comes out in words, directed towards Elias.

"I can't blame him. Not when I can understand how he feels."

"What do you mean?" he asks, his voice sounding like a faint sound in the background.

"When I realized how I felt about you, it was right around the time I discovered the rules against partnered agent fornication, or romantic relationships of any kind. There was nothing I could do, so I tried to force myself to stop loving you, but I couldn't. I couldn't just flip a switch to make that overwhelming frustration and anger go away."

Elias's light chuckle pulls me from the scene in my head—me letting out my feelings for him during our defence training sessions. My stare wanders back his way. He slowly shakes his head. Immediately I read the smirk on his face as cocky, like he's mocking that I've ever felt that way about him. But it's his actual words that shock me. No sly remark, no calling me 'Kitten', he just simply... conversates.

"That's probably the only reason they're still fighting. Because they really do love each other, despite everything they went through. Everything they're *going* through."

I huff out a laugh. "Old habits die hard I guess."

The smile on his face begins to fade as he stares at me and so does mine as I stare back. We both know he just went there. The place we haven't gone since we broke. The mood in the room changes around us. An uncomfortable lump starts to form in my throat.

That undeniable tension from before creeps back in between us, but I realize it's because I'm right. We both are. Throughout this whole "adventure" we've been having, that one feeling in my heart has never gone away no matter how many times I've wanted to kill him.

Countless times he had opportunities to take me out too, but I bet the longing ache in my heart that stopped me, is the same feeling that stopped him. And finding out I only terminated Daniel because I was manipulated into playing some game, amplifies the sudden wave of guilt I feel. Although it's quickly pushed aside by the memory of what Elias had tried to say, right after I finally told him the truth. I quickly shift my eyes from soulful gazing to skeptical confusion.

"What plan did you have, E?"

His eyes narrow, bewilderment in them as if he doesn't remember, and then he tilts his head. "Pardon?"

"In Amsterdam, you said that you had a plan. Said 'if you had only gotten there a minute later.' What did you mean by all that?"

His expression becomes stern but flushed, then the atmosphere completely shifts again as he speaks sharply, like I offended him by asking. "It was nothing."

"Oh, now you *have* to tell me after that little performance," I smirk, even though I probably shouldn't.

"It was nothing," he repeats, "and besides, it was three years ago."

Those same three years didn't stop you from hunting me down.

I sigh and get up to stand in front of him.

"Look Elias, you may never believe me, but in light of figuring out that everything had been a play at us back then, I'm so sorry about what I did." I drop my stare. "If I'm being honest with myself, I've always been."

Once the words come out, I finally let all the guilt I told myself not to feel run through my mind and become a real feeling. I am sorry for taking his brother away from him. Sorry for hurting him in that way, and most of all, sorry for leaving the way I did. For leaving so many holes in our story.

A weight gets lifted from my shoulders. A small one, but it's liberating all the same. Though now, without worrying about the weight, it gives me room to explore what's always lingered in the back of my mind. Quickly it becomes a new weight, though this time on my chest. I bring my eyes back to his as the question of '*why* he was there that night in the first place' surfaces.

I've never gotten that answer. I've never asked the question. Except now, seeing his expression smooth out a bit, I think I might receive it. Some of the tension in his shoulders loosens as he crosses his arms, but his tone is still a tad hostile.

"Thank you. But as much as I want to, Nova, especially since I've finally found out the truth, I don't think I can accept that apology right now. It's just... the blame is still being tossed around in my head."

My heart skips a beat as my mind for a second thinks of what I'd feel if I were in his shoes. If it had been Dominic. "I understand."

"But I due owe you an apology too. For letting that bastard fuck with us, and for things escalating the way they did for the last few days. And years," he says, his voice soft. "I'm sorry."

It's been a while since I've heard him sound sorry and mean it. But despite all the time we've spent a part, I know what he's doing. He's done it so many times before that it feels like nothing's changed between us, and I pretend it hasn't when I shift my sorry look into a glare. My arms mimic his defensive posture and I lean on my hip as I raise a brow at him.

"I appreciate that, thank you, but you're avoiding my original question, E."

He drops his arms and lets them dangle at his sides. "I thought I answered your question."

"No. You didn't."

"Yes," he steps closer, "I did."

About ten inches away from me now, I can see the blue flex around his brown iris. All we do is stare. After about thirty seconds go by, slight warmth goes down my back and into... other parts of my body. Him being here is bad, I know that, but damn. I forgot how dangerously handsome he is, and that he knows how to use it.

Though since we started down this road, I ignore his looks and the warmth he seems to be radiating throughout the room. I want to know what he was doing there that night. I need to. It's the only thing I have to cling to pull me back from that familiar heat, and the *very bad* decision I want to make.

In my mind, I take deep uneven breaths and grab onto my concept of control harder than ever before while standing my ground. And well aware I'm poking the bear in the room, I take my eyes from his and glance at the grey carpet beneath us.

"Come on, Elias. Just tell me why you were there that night. I doubt it'll make a difference, but—"

"Exactly, Nova, it *won't* make a difference, so just drop it, okay?" his voice raises slightly.

I continue to pry anyway. "You said you had a plan, and I know for a fact that when you have a plan you rarely don't follow through."

"Nova," his jaw tightens, "please stop."

"You of all people know how stubborn I can be." I take a step forward, nearly in his face.

"Yes. And you of all people know that when I say stop, I mean it."

I shouldn't keep asking, especially when I notice him move closer too. Yet now I'm starting to think that his answer actually *might* make a difference. He's not going to tell me straight to my face like this. Too much pride. But maybe if I guess it right, he'll cave. I run through the facts in my head, completely ignoring the stern look on his face, and think.

He didn't know I was leaving after Mission Over and Out, or that I had even been assigned anything. And given the recent information that he was blackmailed to end our relationship, Supervisor clearly orchestrated it so he would've thought that's why I took Daniel out. A clever domino effect.

The entire situation is like one of those jigsaw puzzles, and I hate puzzles. My head is starting to hurt, and with Elias staring down at me like I'm about to pop, I force myself to stab a few eyes and slit a few tees. What I come up with is... oh my god.

That night, he wasn't tracking my location. He was going to his brother, not knowing I was already there. He wasn't trying to get to Amsterdam before me, to stop me. So, he must've had a plan to fix things by—

"Tipping him off." I look up at him again and move forward as the words come out. "You were going to defy the agency's rules and risk exposing Unknown by letting him go... weren't you?"

The accusation leaves me and seeps into the silence, but it's the way his eyes soften and whole body seems to sigh that confirms it before he opens his mouth. The sound of his voice, the slight quiver in it, almost makes me cry.

"I... I know how bad it sounds. It sounded just as bad back then, but—"

"Elias, they would've sent out for you. They would've killed you!"

"I know!" He softly clears his throat and sighs. "I know, but I thought it was worth it. *You* were worth it, Nova. With the constant competition our parents put us through, my brother and I were never close. Ever. But he was still my brother. So, when that prick threatened to send out for him, because of his involvement with Aqua+, that company that manufactured a dietary virus to cause a pandemic, I thought moving him somewhere off the radar was the least I could do."

He loosely crosses his arms as his brow furrows. "I could never get close enough though. Not without Supervisor noticing. He was watching my every move, waiting for me to respond. So, I requested solo missions and kept my distance to keep up appearances while I came up with a plan. Yes, one that meant possibly destroying the agency, but I swear it was only supposed to be temporary. Me... ending things."

"Elias..." my suddenly dry throat grips the words I had planned to get out, and in my silence, he looks away.

"But seeing you there that night, the other half of my heart I had just snapped off mere hours ago, I just froze and watched you kill him. I... I couldn't face you after what I had done, after what I had *said* to you. The shattered look on your face was all I could see, and when you turned and noticed me, I saw it again. That's when I knew it was too late to take it all back, so I put that bullet on the ground to show you I understood."

Nothing. I have nothing. Nothing to say, nothing to do, just... nothing. The only thing I seem to have is this heat inside my heart. A feeling that only makes my eyes sting with angry tears. He should've told me. He could've just told me. We would've figured it out together. But instead, he let Supervisor—we both let him—divide us, which gave him room to manipulate.

All of this is so much more fucked up then I thought, and now, standing right in front of me is the man I told myself to hate. Day in and day out. It turns out though, that all the energy I wasted doing that, I should've been using to find out why he did what he did. I feel so stupid, so used, and when Elias brings his eyes back to me, I feel fury come up my throat. That's when the words come fumbling out.

"You should've told me!" is all I yell at him, completely dismissing the fact that knowing me, I wouldn't have listened. Especially when I believed I wanted something. And that something was out.

"We should've told each other a lot of things," he calmly replies, drawing closer.

"Yeah," I sigh. "I guess communication really *is* key."

A sad smirk appears on his lips, but it quickly turns back into a frown as he stares at me, raking a hand through his hair. The gold chain around his neck is gone, which he only seems to remember when he rubs his neck. He glances down, as if looking for it, but then returns his stare to me and takes a step back.

"I should go and let you get some sleep. I'm... I'm sorry things didn't work out differently between us, Kitten. I wish I was strong enough to face you back then."

He starts to slide the door open, and my brain finally seems to function again. I shoot my hand out to catch his wrist. I may not have the right words right now, and this might be a *terrible* idea, but I don't let go.

His skin is so soft.

My entire body pulses as everything around me begins to fade. The gentle sway of the train, all my problems, and all the problems I have with him. The only thing that remains as he turns back around and looks into my eyes, is the pushed down bottled-up fact that I missed him.

The feel of his skin turning hot in my palm melts me, and the silence almost turns sweet as I catch his stare shifting from my eyes to my quivering lips. My heart beats loudly in my burning ears, and within the next few heavy thumps, Elias comes closer. I don't move away. Instead, I let my eyes fall to his mouth before stepping into the small space that's between us, and the feel of his lips gently touching mine confirms it.

I still love him.

In my mind I'm trying to stop, trying to pull myself away, but as our kiss goes on, I get lost in him. After all these years, after all the hurt and hunting, the rhythm of us isn't lost.

Memories of how we used to be start to flood my senses. The savoury taste of him, the sweet smell, and his strong touch. All of it intensifies as his hand slowly slides down my lower back.

It makes me greedy for more.

I press my body against his and he pushes me back until I'm against the cool window. As my arms find their way around his neck, the thought to stop while I can comes to mind again.

When his kiss becomes deeper though—craving almost—all common sense subsides, and I appease his wants as well as my own. By allowing myself to have him again, and by allowing him to have me, it releases another weight from my shoulders.

We end up falling onto the made bed with his lips on my hot neck and my hands in his hair, a rush of adrenaline pulsing into my blood at his touch. Whatever control I thought I had completely goes out the window now.

Even while his tongue and hands re-familiarize themselves with my body, his resentment for what I'd done still manages to show itself as we go on. So does mine, as I rip off his clothes. Like we haven't really forgiven each other but are about to. It may just mean we're both beyond repair, given that we're about to give in to the person who has caused us the worst kinds of pain.

But all of that doesn't seem to matter as we become tangled between the sheets, every kiss, bite, and moan only calling up our history together. Good and bad. It starts out rough, like we're still fighting, though soon we become encased in the passion we once shared. Reading one another like a book. And as our ardent grapple comes to an end, using our bodies to forgive and move on, in the sweet voice that somehow still makes me weak in the knees, Elias tenderly whispers,

"I still love you."

CHAPTER TWENTY-EIGHT

MIXED EMOTIONS

Lyon, France

The fog of awkward sets in between all of us. So unbelievably thick the feeling I'm drowning invades my lungs. It gets worse when I notice Rebecca from the corner of my eye, watching with a judgemental stare that briefly shifts to Elias then back to me.

Is our rendezvous written all over my face?

After a couple more sideways glances, and scolding looks, I shove down the question then go on to voice my undeveloped plan.

"Alright, here's what I've come up with so far," I relay confidently, lightly placing my palm on a table in the empty dining car. Courtesy of our not-very-merry band of agents and stubborn civilians.

"Shouldn't we wait for—?" Andre, who is now featuring a bruised cheek, begins to say, but then Camille walks in, her eyes puffy and slightly red.

"I'm here," she reluctantly announces to me. "Talk."

I draw a blank as my stare bounces over to Shane, to see if he's taken note too. His hard stare is only aimed out of a window, so I take that as a no. It's none of my business anyway; the sudden cold breeze and the look of suppressed betrayal that covers Shane's face. Or that's what I tell myself in order to focus.

"Now, I'm sure we all know what it's like to be on a 'most wanted' list," I sigh and give everyone in the room a once over. Well... almost everyone.

"Argentina," Andre mumbles.

"Greenland," Elias counters, like it's a competition. It's not, but if it were, Camille would've won.

"Russia," she chimes, like she's bored.

We all whip our heads around to her, including Rebecca and Shane. The looks on their faces is a cross between 'you're lying' and 'I need to know more'. Her expression, however, matches her voice. Bored. Like she didn't walk in here a minute ago with tears still in the corners of her eyes.

They're long gone now though, replaced by a nonchalant demeanour and suddenly shiny hair. Inspiring, and as much as I want to hear her Russia story myself, I bite my tongue and recenter the conversation. Especially before either of the civilians can ask for any kind of elaboration.

"Like I said, we all know what it's like, but being an enemy to our kind of agency puts a different, more lethal and glowing target on our backs. Especially in the top headquarters' territory, which we're about to be in. And I'm sure that I don't have to tell any you that this'll be extremely dangerous. There'll be eyes everywhere looking for us. Rouge agents or Specter lackeys that work for Foreman crawling around."

"And since this stop is closest to our shortcut, they'll most likely have a perimeter block on the platform and parking lot," Camille adds.

"Yes, it's likely, but taking over the agency would've taken a lot of bodies, which means only so many would be spared. So, I'm guessing our welcome parade will only consist of about six men, if Foreman thinks Elias and I killed each other already—" I stop myself from looking at him— "ten if he doesn't."

The bit of resentment in Elias's tone slightly catches me off guard. "How do we avoid early detection in order to eliminate interruptions while getting to our access point to?"

I glance his way, but it's Andre he's glaring at. A hateful look that, despite their "conversation", doesn't seem to be going away any time soon. Something like relief washes over me, but I don't bathe in it. I get a grip and whisper in the back of my mind, *'pull it together. Stop caring'.*

I shake my head, then go on. "Early detection is what we want so we have the most control over the situation. That's why you, one of the most wanted agents, and Camille, the most decorated, will be our first distraction on the platform. Andre will—"

"So that's your name..." Shane trails, so softly I barely hear him. His eyes are back to being glued to the window, but something of a sad smile slightly curls his lips. His face though, remains dark.

Everything in me wants to stop talking and pull him into a hug. To tell him it's easier to hate her now than to admit that he's ever loved her. To lie to him. But I don't. I only bite back the urge to protect him, the urge to glance at Camille, and continue.

"Andre will be in the parking lot as bate in order to lead Foreman's men to the tunnels. There, he'll use their retinas to access the gates for us. And while you three are playing your parts, civilian one: Rebecca, and I will travel to our transport from the back of the parking lot as civilian two: Shane, follows from the front. Then, after you and Camille lead Foreman's men away from the platform and deal with them, you'll meet us at transport, embedded with Bethany."

"Bethany?" Camille steps forward, lightly holding her side. "How can we trust Bethany right now?"

"Who's Bethany?" Rebecca cuts in, but I dismiss her.

"Before Minnie died, she sent me a code to access her personal hard drive, which she uploaded all of the Foreman info to, proving that all of this has been Supervisor."

Elias looks to me now and softens his voicce. "How do you know that she'd use Bethany as her personal hard drive?"

Minnie's words resurface in my head as I clutch the burner in my pocket. *'Thanks for the ride.'* She had told me she programmed Bethany a few days ago, but it wasn't until she said those exact words, the same words Bethany had said after our first trip, that I knew she was giving me a clue. Her swan song.

"I just do," I tell him, desperate to avoid the thought of her gasping for air.

The train comes to a full stop before anyone can protest my knowledge on the Bethany subject. Then, just like that it's go time. We get off on platform seven using separate exits, and just as I suspected, four men—who are doing a terrible job trying not to look like their talking into their sleeves—stand like statues on the busy platform. The other two, and I'm praying it's just two, should be close by.

The main goal is for Shane, Rebecca, Andre and I to sneak away to our positions. That becomes much easier once Camille positions herself in between a metal beam on the platform. Snug enough to look like she's been waiting there the entire time with her arms crossed, nose scrunched up, and her foot tapping roughly on the ground.

Elias gets off the train, carefree with a wide grin on his face, as if he's gotten away with something. He strolls down the platform, whistling to his heart's content. When he "unexpectedly" bumps into Camille, the happy tune dies on the wind, and his smile flips into a horrified frown as all hell breaks loose.

That's our cue.

Andre speed walks over to the parking lot first while the rest of us branch off, slowly though, just enough to blend in with the crowd that stops to watch Camille and Elias. She raises her hand swiftly then a loud slap echoes throughout the long stone station covered by a weathered steel canopy. Some part of me feels bad for sticking Camille on him, especially with everything that's happening between her and Shane.

The logical decision would've been that I be the one paired with him to cause the distraction, but logic got tossed out the window by need. Shane needed a break from Camille, and I needed to keep my distance from Elias.

Besides, after our little "reunion", I don't think I could've kept a straight face anyway. Especially not if I had chosen the same topic Camille had chosen to yell at him about. Juicy enough to keep people interested, with words most will understand and be drawn too. Smart. And her hate for him *does* up her performance.

"Vous bâtard! Vous êtes retournée voir l'une de vos maîtressess, n'est-ce pas? Alors, qui était-ce cette fois? L'Oréal? Caroline!?"

(You bastard! You went back to see one of your mistresses, didn't you? So, who was it this time? L'Oreal? Caroline!?)

The three of us don't stay for his reply. Especially not when the four men slowly start approaching Elias and Camille. We turn on our heels, heading towards the parking lot, the first to look away from the scene. I take advantage and search for Andre. Quickly, I scan over the parking lot but don't see him. Not until the sound of feet stomping on the pavement catches my attention.

Casually I glance over my shoulder and see Andre running in the direction of the entry way, two men following behind. So far, we're on track. I just need to get us to the car. I roughly breathe out, focus, and turn back to the lot. It's filled with slanted parked cars as far as the eye can see, all unique in their own way.

Amongst them one stands out to me more than the rest. In the distance of this dull parking lot, sits the same BMW that picked me up at the start of all this, only a few cars down. Now is the time that it being a nice car comes in handy.

Sudden crippling sadness almost stops me, but the fact that I was right about Minnie's hard drive relieves some of the pressure on my chest. More than I realized, I hoped that she'd be standing there waiting for me with her colorful hair and a smirk. Except, wishful thinking didn't make it true. I shake off my sorrow but leave the rage in my stomach.

Rebecca and I casually walk to the car, my focus starting on Shane, watching him from over my shoulder to make sure he doesn't look too conspicuous while following on the other side. Surprisingly enough he doesn't show any trace of fear, or any kind of emotion for that matter. As helpful as it is for this situation, I'm worried that his *issues* with Camille may have completely broken him.

To see him like this hurts, and so much of me wants to double Camille's pain. But I can't, and I won't, because no matter how bad it sounds, I see nothing wrong with what she did. Okay, maybe just the 'actually falling in love with him' part, but despite that, I know what it means to be an agent. To have to pretend and block people out. To have to tell yourself that being alone is better, safer, so you don't get too close. So it doesn't become real.

But I also know that slip ups can happen during assignments. No matter if one is the great 'Camille Maxwell' or not. Given her puffy eyes from earlier, and Shane's face now, it's clear that she hasn't come to grips that she *did* slip up and truly hurt him. Or she just doesn't want too.

Things don't always work out the way people think. I learned that even before joining the agency, yet somehow it feels like I'm going through the lesson all over again. And I re-live that lesson as I swiftly glance back to where Elias stood on the platform, thinking of what he whispered in my ear mere hours ago. The words echo in my head, and, despite my best efforts, warmth begins to spread throughout my chest. It immediately goes cold when my gaze catches Rebecca's critical stare.

It's identical to the one from the dining car. But unlike then, we're much more alone, and heat radiates through my cheeks. I'm not one to get all hot and bothered when people try reading me. Except in this case, Rebecca isn't just *people,* she's one of the few I let past my walls. Maybe that's why her looks are starting to get on my nerves.

I put on an unbothered façade in the hopes of at least fooling myself that I'm fine, and on some level, it starts to work. My nerves relax enough for me to ignore her, and, with my façade intact, I glance away to check on Shane again. A single movement, that apparently, was a big mistake. Somehow my turning away is what triggers something in her brain, telling her that me removing my stare from her's is a reason to open her mouth, and next thing I know, she's jumping down my throat.

"Did you sleep with him?"

I only sigh.

"Oh my god you did, didn't you?" She stops mere inches from the car. "What's the matter with you?"

"Rebecca," I say as calmly as possible.

She ignores me. "He was trying to *kill* you. He abducted me *inside* my aunt's apartment. He held Shane and I at gun point."

"Rebecca."

"He's been playing with our lives like a dog with a bone!"

Grabbing her arm, I pull her behind the car. "This is *not* the time or place, Rebecca, seriously."

"Don't do that. Don't make me feel like *I'm* the unreasonable one here. He's fucking crazy!"

"Keep your voice down," I viciously whisper.

She rips her arm from me and crosses both over her chest. I mirror the movement with a serious expression. It almost falters when Rebecca shifts her jaw and narrows her eyes while looking me up and down, the exact same way my papá had when a "guy friend" was over. I swear it's almost uncanny. A chuckle comes up my throat, but I swallow it down to keep my commanding demeanour, which turns out to be the right move, considering all the attitude she throws at me.

"I feel like I shouldn't have to say this, and I'm sorry I'm stopping you from handling your business here, but *come on*. You—"

"What?" I cut in. "No, seriously, I want to know what could possibly be going through your head right now for you to think you have some sort of sway over me." My foot stomps forward, forcing her a step back. She almost hits the car, but I dismiss the fact that that would've set off the alarm as I glare at her.

"Actually, before you answer, let me make it clear. You don't. And if you believe that this little scene has helped in anyway, you're sorely mistaken, Taylor."

Shane's voice is stern behind me. "Michelle."

He's telling me to stop, to back away from her, but I only stare down at her now timid body and don't move. I know what Elias did was wrong. He stepped over countless lines and I'm not going to forgive him for all the unnecessary trauma he's caused. It's just her tone, the underlining hate I detect, the same hate I've felt towards myself the minute I put them in danger, that makes something inside me snap.

Before my very eyes she morphs into someone I don't love, and becomes something that's in my way, which is a dangerous place to be. I told her to go, said I didn't want her to get more involved, but she's the one who insisted on staying, and I let her. Fine. That's my fault, but I'm done tolerating her attitude. That needs to get through her thick head, now, before she can jeopardize the plan any further.

I roughly plant my feet on the ground as my eyes shift into a scowl. I hear Shane again, stepping closer, but the damning words are already on my tongue.

"You made it very clear that you're only here to make sure that my life doesn't boil over into yours again. So why don't you just sit back and shut up so I can do my job. Then, once we're finished here, you can get back to having a perfect life without me."

"You really don't get it, do you? How fucked up this is? How you—my best friend—becoming someone so different so fast is a hard pill to swallow?" A mixture of obviousness and misery drenches her tone.

Shane again tries to intervene. "Rebecca, stop,"

I force down more rage in the hopes of ending the conversation. So I don't completely lose control and hurt her. Though holding back starts to become a very distant thought when I fully assimilate her question. She's asking as if I'm blind to the fact that she left. As if she also didn't change from being someone I can always talk to, someone I can rely on, to being someone who gave up on me and started to resent me so fast.

I know her finding out that there's way more to me was hard, but she doesn't seem to realize that I found out there's more to her too.

My own voice rings in my head, telling me to end this with her while I can. To shove down all the frustration, devastation, and confusion I feel to finish the mission. For a moment, the logic of that triumphs in the battle between my head and heart, but for only a moment. Because what Rebecca says rocks my head and fractures my heart.

"I'm trying to understand how someone goes from being Michelle, my dependable, quiet yet funny friend—a good person—to being someone like... you."

Someone... like me?

My expression switches from slightly annoyed to calmly pissed as I curl my fingers into fists. A million thoughts rush to my head. A million emotions that I can't seem to push down. Not anymore. Instead, they all become one. Hot wrath. I open my mouth, to destroy whatever good image she seems to be clinging to of me but become engulfed in another voice.

"Nova," Elias gently calls as he steps in front of me.

Not one sense detected that he and Camille made it to us. But hearing him say my name, the way he used to when he'd notice me starting to only see red, draws me from what would've been bloody violence.

I'm left staring at the fear in Rebecca's eyes. I back away, as if just realizing what I was about to say, or do, then quiet the sound of blood rushing in my ears. From where I'm standing, it looks bad. No matter what she said, I know better.

I don't apologize, like I should. I only walk around to the driver's seat and wait for Bethany's system to recognize me. I contemplate whether to risk a glance at everyone on the other side, but by the time my head does turn upwards, the car comes alive.

The doors pop open and I'm the first one in. Everyone else quickly follows, not giving me a second to breathe un-hostile air. It's probably for the best that I don't get the time though. If I stop, I might not be able to function the way I'll need to. The way agent 401 needs to, and besides, we need every second we can spare to get to headquarters. As soon as the doors close, Bethany addresses me while taking control of the wheel.

"Good evening, agent 401. Please enter programmer personal hard drive key code to access confidential materials."

A stinging light shines from above the dark car, projecting a keyboard in front of me in mid-air. I blink away the brightness, then without hesitation, my fingers whiz over the keys, as if I'm playing an imaginary piano while typing in the code. It's the last piece Minnie died to get me. I made sure to burn it into my brain. Every last instruction.

'The code is o16<ll39 >$=Φōpμav, but don't be fooled by the order of it. Type numbers first, then letters, then symbols. And just when you reach the end say the phrase—'

"プログラマーの母国語に30秒間切り替えます。"

(Switch to the programmer's native language for thirty seconds.)

As soon as I get the words out, one by one the letters on the floating keyboard flip into Japanese, and a digital stopwatch appears in the rear-view mirror. It starts to count down from thirty, but really it only takes me ten to input the last of Minnie's code. Just like her to make it backwards and diagonal with an extra twist. Though, despite the maze, I smile, then as I press enter I whisper to myself,

"Goodbye, old friend."

A slight pain in my chest causes my heart to skip a beat, and a breath catches in my throat. For a minute my entire body goes numb as I replay her death again. I hear the gunshot in my ear and jump back, like a jolt of lightening had pierced through my skin. Beside me, before I get lost in the memory of her last breath, Elias's voice replaces the ringing inside my head as he gingerly whispers my name.

Time slows when I spin towards him, and all at once, the moment of us on the train seeps in. His hands weaved into mine, whispering in the same way. I shouldn't let it, but a familiar comfort sets itself into my skin.

I live in it. For just that second. But my grip on the real and tragic reality I'm in twists back into play. My attention quickly shifts when the overhead light disappears, and the steering wheel gets swallowed into the car, replaced by a large tablet.

Numbers and letters swirl across the screen in a theatrical display that resembles a hurricane. When the digital dust clears, only a large red file labelled 'Finish This' is left behind. Slowly my grief resurfaces, seeing its title. Her last words. Without taking another beat, I force it down, then click the file.

The first obstacle, as it splits into four, is the lengthy read ahead of me. According to the GPS, I'll have approximately twenty minutes before we reach the drop-off point, which isn't enough time to explain the rest of the plan. *Shit*, I think as I let out a long sigh through my nose. I don't want to do this, but he was the only one in the room when I brainstormed this part of the plan.

Again, I sigh, then turn to Elias—as hard as it is—and defer to him with slight hesitation. "I need you to walk them through part two of execution. And keep it civil."

Swiftly, he glances back at Rebecca, at an angle only I notice, with a silent threat only I can hear. Quietly I clear my throat. He has no right to be protective over me, especially not in this situation.

"Elias? Part two of execution," I repeat, and just to make sure he behaves, I softly add, "please."

The word relaxes some of the irritation in his face, then he sharply nods and gets right down to it. "Alright, part two of the plan will have to move much faster and smoother than the first part did, so listen carefully. Approximately—"

"I'm curious," Rebecca interrupts, with no hint of her earlier fear. "Did you two work all this out *before* or after—?"

"Don't." I stop scrolling but keep my attention on the queue of words filling the screen as I cut her off, my tone with no patience.

"What?" she shrugs, asking innocently, clearly trying to get back at me. "I just wanna know if—"

"Stop it," I demand, with as much fed-up dominance as I can muster. I briefly look up into the rear-view mirror and glare at her until she slightly shrinks back into the seat.

When she seems to completely swallow the rest of her words, I go back to the tablet. Before my eyes leave the mirror, Shane leans forward, a disapproving look on his face. Not sure if it's towards me, or the entire situation, I don't let concern manifest and simply glance away, addressing Elias as I begin to read again.

"Continue."

He softly clears his throat. "As I was saying, approximately ten minutes from now, Nova: code name Tigress, and I: code name Dragon will—"

I arch a brow. "Really?"

"What?" he shrugs. "Tigress is cool."

"But Dragon?"

There's a slight playful pout in his voice. "I like it."

"Fine," I sigh. "Proceed."

"We'll continue on foot to the tunnel entry way, where Weasel is waiting."

I guess that's Andre.

"While that's happening, both civilians and... Jaguar will be taken a few blocks down from headquarters, where—"

"Excuse me?" Camille protests. Beside me, Elias sighs as she goes on. "What do you mean both civilians and *Jaguar*?

"Do you not like Jaguar?"

"You're not leaving me behind on civilian watch. Out of all the agents in and outside of this car, I'm the most experienced."

"Yeah," I interject again, "but you're also the most injured one, Maxwell. Don't think I haven't noticed the way you've been trying to hide the fact that any sort of breathing or simple movement is making you flinch. Your ribs are most likely cracked from the shot to your chest, and you know it."

"And whose fault is that!?"

Elias apologizes with gruff sincerity. "Sorry."

She lightly leans forward from behind my seat and answers with kind hostility. "Oh, you apologize? Well, that'll *definitely* fix the cracks in my ribs now, won't it?"

"No," he says, and then mumbles, "but maybe it'll put a band-aid over your bruised ego."

"You piece of—"

"Hey! I'm not dealing with another argument between you two. Elias, knock it off, and Camille, you need to stay on the sidelines for now. So, civilian watch will have to fall unto you." My lips then curl into a smirk as I give her a quick taunting side eye. "Considérez cela comme une expérience de liasion pour vous trois, Jaguar."

(Think of it as a bonding experience for the three of you, Jaguar.)

"Ir al infierno, Castillo."

(Go to hell, Castillo.)

"Flatter me all you want, but it isn't going to change the fact that you're not coming with us."

"The only way I'm not coming, is if you can guarantee that we'll not only stay in contact the entire time, but also *guarantee* that *when* I find it necessary to step in, I get to. Free authorization."

"You're a really stubborn person, you know that?"

She sits back while lightly crossing her arms over her chest, grinning. "I know. And look how far it's gotten me."

"Fine, you can have free authorization, *if* an opportunity presents itself."

"*When* it presents itself. And communication."

"Yes, and communication," I sigh. "Bethany, we'll be needing ear comms please."

"Of course, agent."

My focus returns to the screen, scanning through the rest of Minnie's notes. The last of it is merely an image link, </(¬_¬)224 Scout Drive./>.jpg. The only picture in the entire file. I go to click on it, but I'm briefly distracted when the glove compartment flips open. Four earpieces, one matching each agent's skin tone, slide out, comfortably fitted into a foam board.

Elias gives Camille hers before turning to give me mine, our fingers grazing as he does. I should've brushed off the simple interaction, the soft touch, but I don't. The words he said, 'I still love you'; I haven't had the time to, or wanted to, unpack them yet and just rest in the back of my mind. Close enough to the surface that the sudden heat in my cheeks isn't a surprise. *Did I always act like this when he was around?*

It's funny really. Not caring and being able to turn off emotions is literally a part of my job description, yet here I can't seem to switch that portion of my brain on.

After everything, I shouldn't care this much in the first place, but then again, after everything... how can I not? The thinking process is making me feel nauseous. Things really do change without you noticing.

I shuttered at the thought of Elias even in the same country as me before, but I didn't know then what I know now. Didn't know that my resentment towards him and my guilt that turned into misguided anger, was time and energy I wasted.

But the second his lips touched mine, after three years, it felt like no time had passed. Made me feel at home again. And apparently, that feeling still lingers between *both* of us, and can be sparked with a simple touch. It's not something that should be explored, especially not when needing to get even with Supervisor remains at the top of my list.

It was a mistake anyway. On the train. A moment of confusion, I tell myself.

I quickly thank him, retreat my hand, then place the device in my ear as I return my attention to the last piece of the file. The picture.

I loved Minnie, but damn that girl really didn't know how to write a report that got to the point. I did enjoy all of her *'holy shit'* and *'well that's not good'* side notes though. Like she was sitting next to me reading it herself. I take a deep breath as the thought passes, and then finally click on the link.

Immediately the large red circle scribbled around the words 'FINAL DOT' typed in bold catch my eye, and it definitely does justice to what the picture uncovers.

My mouth slowly hangs open as I scan over the photo of Supervisor and Vice—Specter's second in command—very cozy on a couch. Given the direction, it was taken by a security camera from the house across the street, I'm guessing 224 Scout Drive. The date at the bottom is four years ago. Only a *week* before operation Echo Delta was formed.

I'm not completely sure if I should laugh or swear. Punch something or sit quietly in disbelief. With the sentence that slips out of my mouth though, I guess my mind chooses to go into default mode. Which surprisingly enough is 'no nonsense agent'.

"Bethany, speed up. Our problem is *much* more real, and *much* worse than we thought."

CHAPTER TWENTY-NINE

PROJECT CLOAK AND DAGGER

From the drop off point I can smell the sewage near the tunnel's entryway coming up ahead. With Elias walking beside me, the familiar scent of him masks the stench. Only some, as we walk at a distance.

I make sure of it.

Honestly, the fact that his body is shielding my nose is the only reason I know he's still there. With the number of overwhelming thoughts racing through my head, he might as well be halfway across the world.

I wish I could be focusing on one situation, like how awkward this is, or that despite that, it still feels kind of nice, but I can't. What's taking up most of the space in my mind is the information from Minnie I crammed in there. Along with Rebecca and Shane, and the last looks I had seen on their faces. Disappointment and fear, which were not expressions I ever wanted to see from them.

Leaving them with Bethany and Camille, to make sure they stayed safe, it forced me to wonder if I really am just a monster who doesn't fit into the world of coffee shops and business casual clothing. I mean, I tried hard to be that person. To be the friendly Michelle Hannigan.

Looking back now, all I'm stuck seeing is a person tricked into being someone they aren't, and never will be. Maybe I never really did consider them as friends. Maybe I just thought of them as side characters in an undisturbed two-year filler episode in the shit show that's my life. But, if that's the case, then why do I have this ache in the pit of my stomach? This *need* to say 'I'm sorry.'

"Tigress," Elias says, like it's not the first time.

"Yeah?" I answer, my voice distant.

He lightly places his hand on my arm as he taps the comm in his ear to mute it. "I asked if you're okay."

When did he get so close?

"Oh, yeah, I'm fine."

"Are you sure? Because if you're not ready to do this—"

I stop, close my eyes, then sigh and tap my own comm, taking his hand off me with as little force as possible. "I really don't have a choice here, do I? So I'm fine, Dragon. I have to be."

I open my eyes as a small, frustrated laugh brims at the edge of my words, a mocking smile spreading itself across my face as I tease him. "But if *you* want to talk about your feelings…"

"Can I?" he leans closer to me, hair falling into his face. "Because if you're serious, I would like to talk about that new trick you did with your—"

"Okay, you know what, we're officially done with talking." The words come out much more girly than I meant, with a slight giggle.

Damn it. Pull it together, agent. You're not some lovesick teen.

At the sight of his eyes lighting up, I quickly clear my throat, then fix my joyous demeanour into an emotionless stare while moving away from his sudden gravitating body heat. I can literally feel the weakness creep its way back into my bones. As if it's our first encounter all over again. That fuzzy sensation only grows as he continues to watch me.

The only way this mission is going to be completed, is if we both keep it as our main priority. Though, based on the hole he's drilling in the back of my head, he doesn't seem to be very attentive to that fact.

In an attempt, to snap him out of his mooning, just as I come near the eight-foot wall we'll have to scale, I spin around to face him. He slightly flinches back at my sudden movement—proving my point—and I fight the urge to roll my eyes.

"It was a mistake, you know. Us."

The light in his eyes go dark as his jaw tightens. "What?"

"Us. On the train. It was a mistake."

"Oh," he exhales, something of relief in the word, like he thought I meant something else. His entire body relaxes a bit, yet quickly it tenses back up.

"Why?"

I can't help but choke on a laugh; on all the reasons that come to mind so fast. Not one comes out though. Only a slight snicker does as I start walking away from him, but I don't get far. He grabs my wrist, spins me around, then forces me back until I'm up against a crumbling brick wall standing alone amongst rubble.

It happened swiftly, with such a gentle push, that it throws me. My eyes travel up, taking in his body over mine, pressing me into the faded red bricks. His palm is flat against the wall while his other hand firmly grips mine as he rests his bent knee on the weathered stone. He's blocking me in, close enough that his smell starts to invade my senses. I even taste it. And when I finally bring my eyes to his, the desperate wonder in them almost makes me shiver.

"Why? Why was it a mistake?"

I could take him off me. Move on with the mission, but the yearning gleam in his eyes says he won't be useful if I don't answer now. It should be obvious. Very, but apparently, I have to re-cap. I sigh, then wipe any trace of emotion from my voice, sticking to basic answers.

"You drugged me."

"Only slightly," he rebuttals nonchalant, then shrugs.

"You shot at me. Multiple times."

"Like we haven't shot at each other before?"

I roughly huff out a breath and roll my eyes, knowing exactly what situation he's referring to, and it's not Brooklyn. "Jesus, that was five years ago. I was undercover and I only grazed you. Let it go."

He chuckles. "Still hurt."

"I know the feeling," I tell him, suddenly becoming very aware of the graze on my arm. But then, out of nowhere, I glance away from him and smirk, getting caught up in the memory of the first time I shot at him.

Next thing I know, the words are falling out of my mouth. "Though, if I remember correctly, I kissed yours better."

My cheeks burn. *Where did that even come from!? I didn't mean to think that, let alone say it out loud!* Without meaning to, my eyes shoot up to his, heart racing with embarrassment.

He smiles down at me with all teeth; something wicked and hungry. "And if *I* remember correctly myself," he says, his voice husky, "I just did the same."

To ignore the tingling, *everywhere*, I rip my hand out of his and punch him in the gut.

"You were going to kill me."

He holds his stomach and laughs. "I mean... was I?"

My heart skips a beat. At the time, I truly believed he was, but now? I scan his face for a lie, a bluff, but there isn't one. Not knowing how to deal with that, I fume instead.

"What about kidnapping and trying to kill my friends? Got a smartass answer for that?"

Dragging a hand through his hair, he sighs heavily then lets out a dry laugh, looking off to the side. "Sorry."

I narrow my eyes at him as my jaw tightens.

"Look," I say, my voice sharp, then start walking again. "We can't be having this conversation. Especially not right now. We need to focus, Dragon. So, if there's something pertaining to the mission you need to get off your chest, in order to complete it, I suggest that it be said now."

"Full agent mode, huh?"

I stop and snap my neck back to glare at him. He playfully puts his hands up in surrender and tilts his head, a shy smile on his lips.

"Uncalled for, sorry. But I do want to say…" he rakes over his hair again, "that despite our obvious problems, I hope we still work well together."

I brush my ponytail off my shoulder, a slight smirk in my expression. "Yeah. We should be fine. As long as we don't think about it too—"

My sentence comes to a halt as I glance up, just catching sight of a man whose attention seems too drawn to where we're standing.

The wall just covering our entrance is out in the open, though with the plainness of it, it shouldn't appeal to anyone's interest or curiosity. Even if it did, all it would be seen as is a dead end. This area was bought by Unknown years ago then blocked off, claiming it was for "construction purposes". In reality it was used to test their silent micro-bombs for a few weeks.

Now only old broken-down buildings were around here. No people, unless they're the shady kind. And due to this man's terrible efforts on trying to hide his approach on us, he's clearly the shady kind.

I mean, at a point, it's just sad to see such sloppy spook work, but my moment of disappointment is short lived. Primarily since I don't know what kind of situation we're in. Yet.

Shifting my foot in the dirt to prepare for any kind of attack, Elias realizes my distress. He slowly twists his head around to follow my line of sight but stops just before locking eyes with our stocker.

"What do you see?" he asks, almost protectively.

"A man on your six leaning against the grey stone building we passed two minutes ago. Medium build, black hair, civilian attire with no visible lethal weapons, but he has a whiskey bottle." I narrow my eyes. "He's been watching us."

I don't let my glare drop from the bummy looking man, who's now choosing to pretend he didn't just make a threatening amount of eye contact with me.

"Let me see," Elias speaks up.

With a swift nod, I go for the first tactic that comes to mind. The classic public display of affection. Unfortunate timing, yes, but I proceed. I convert into young lovers' mode. A smile spreads across my lips as I wrap my arms around Elias's neck.

He doesn't skip a beat. He places his hands on my hips while I adjust my footing. By the time I'm done we've completely switched positions. I'm the one facing the wall now, giving Elias the perfect view of the man. His grip on me slightly tightens. I don't know how I was expecting him to react when seeing this guy, but the instant tension in his shoulders wasn't something I was anticipating.

A heavy sigh comes from him as he leans down to my ear, his voice dark. "You've got to be fucking kidding me."

"You know him?"

"I honestly wish I could say no, but sadly I can't."

"I meant is he a threat, Dragon."

He lifts his face to mine. "Yes."

A serious demeanour overtakes every inch of him. With the sight, I quickly un-mute my comm and whisper. "Agent—I mean Jaguar?"

Camille's sudden impatient voice fills my ear. "Yeah, I'm here. A good distance from headquarters, but not completely out of range. And the civilians are safely tucked away under strict digital lock and key. Is everyone in position?"

"We were about to be, but now we might have a slight problem."

"What do you mean? What's going on?"

Elias retreats his stare from mine, then goes back to glaring at the man he apparently knows. He may not have his eyes on me, though he directs his words my way.

"Is she asking about the situation?"

I tilt my head down until my face is buried in his shoulder. "Yeah."

He smells so good.

"Can you turn on my comm please?"

Quickly burying the thought, without hesitation, I slide my fingers down from his hair, then cradle his cheeks in my hands. Their warmth against my palms is so familiar that something in me lightly strokes my thumb down his face. My heart skips a beat when he does a hard swallow.

He stares down at me, eyes shining, full of desire, just like on the train. I ignore my body heating up and continue to smile as I pull him down to me. When he's close enough to my lips, I fight the urge to look at his and turn on the comm with my index finger. After the slight click, Elias's uneven breathing straightens out and he relays what he knows about the lurking man.

"Okay, so this guy is bad news."

I fix my own breathing before I speak. "Who is he?"

"Tristan Clifford. A.k.a Choker. He's one of Specter's. I first went toe to toe with him on one of my solo ops a couple years ago, and it wasn't pretty. Does look like his mouth healed just fine though," he replies, shifting his eyes to go back to watching the guy like a hawk.

Camille's accent becomes more present. "What did you do to him?"

"Let's just say he got on my nerves a little, and long story short, I stapled his mouth shut."

A chuckle jumps out of me at the thought of him trying to talk. "Seriously?"

"Yeah. You should've seen his face. When he came too and realized, I swear I almost wet myself," he laughs too, joining me. "By far one of my favourite—"

"We don't have time for this! You need to defuse the situation so you can get to "Weasel", find Commander, *and* take out Foreman. You two can flirt all you want when this is over."

I bite down the urge to argue and let my stare fall from Elias, desperate to get rid of the sudden thought to make out with him. *God, even from a distance she finds a way to get under my skin.* Dwelling on her annoying need to undermine me won't get me anywhere. I center my attention on the fact that she *is* thinking logically. So I swallow down my protest and agree.

"She's right. We don't want any extra eyes drawn to us while we're on the move, so this Clifford guy needs to go."

"Do you have a discreet plan to make that happen?" Camille condescendingly questions.

"We could—" I turn my head towards the comm in my ear, fully grasping her question. "Wait, did you say discreet?"

Elias clears his throat. "I have an approach, but it needs to happen now, because he's coming this way."

Before I can ask what his plan is, or look back to see our threat descending on us, Elias lets go of me and takes a step forward, forcing me to move back. Surprisingly, there's an emptiness that begins to form from the absence of his touch. One that I never thought I'd feel again. For a moment it freezes me up, and it doesn't get better when he gets down on his knee.

My heart pounds, ears turn hot, and the memory of his proposal—oddly in a situation similar to this—tears into my mind. That's *definitely* not what's happening here. When he meshes his fingers together, I breathe a breath of relief and force the memory to fizzle away. Then, understanding what he's getting at, I shake off the tsunami of emotions that had just water boarded my brain.

I place my foot in his hand, then he boosts me up. Being in the air reminds me of when I became a cheerleader, to intercept a coach giving his players steroids laced with fentanyl. Fun, until I land on the wall, my butt *just* catching the edge. The darting pain in my hip resurfaces. Not as bad as before, but I do flinch the slightest bit. I try to hide it, but Elias notices.

"Are you alright? Was that not high enough?"

"No, you're good," I call down in a whisper, but when another voice sounds in the distance, I glance forward.

"Hey!" Clifford shouts, already halfway to us. "You bitch. You killed my partner!"

Not even taking a beat, Elias draws back a few wide steps in order to get some running room for his coming climb. As he does, he steals a glance at Clifford but yells up at me.

"What's he talking about?"

"Why do you think he's talking to me?" I twist on my good side and lower myself down while shouting from the other side of the wall. "You could just as easily be the 'bitch' he's referring to."

"Wow," he says, then, after hearing a grunt from hoisting himself up, he stares down at me with a playfully offended grin. "Really?"

"Yeah," I smirk. But watching his eyebrow rise ever-so-slightly as he hops over, I roll my eyes then press my lips thin, nodding a 'you're probably right' nod.

It *is* more likely Clifford is talking about me, but I don't even know the guy. He doesn't look the least bit familiar, and I have equally no idea who he's yelling about. It's not as if I keep a personal log of all the people I've—a long realizing 'oh' comes from me.

Elias chimes in after my epiphany, charmingly arrogant. "So he *is* talking to you?"

"Actually, yes."

"You killed him!"

"You guys need to move," Camille orders.

We begin to run over to our entry point, Andre waiting in the distance with blood decorating his clothes. Judging by the beaten in faces of the men we pass who he led here, I say he wasn't only thinking of the mission.

Behind us, Clifford again yells, repeating 'you killed him', as if I didn't hear him the first time. I ignore his useless screams and focus on how I'm going to shut him up. But the second we reach the open wire gate, the tip of my foot just touching the stone archway of the tunnel, Clifford rips me from my violent thoughts.

"You killed him, and I know why!"

"Oh really?" I yell back, fed up at the sound of his coarse voice. "And who told you that? Declan?"

Ominously spinning around to face him, I notice him freeze in place, yet his expression drops into complete evil. Supervisor's name didn't even faze him. Now I'm the one who's taking a cautionate step back.

"Kind of. But really..." he trails, his voice lined with a devilish tone, "project cloak and dagger did."

We stand in a tableau of hate as my body slightly goes tense at his words. The last words I thought I'd hear from a Specter agent. But given the last few days, up is left and down is up, so of course this is possible. I may not know how exactly, but I know if I react, it'll please this prick. The only thing I want him to remember in his last moments of life is my stone-cold expression. Yet when Elias steps out from behind me, his voice, and Andre's, slightly breaks my concentration.

"What's project cloak and dagger?"

I shift my foot on the uneven stone floor towards the both of them, ready to answer with rehearsed cluelessness. They'll most likely see right through it, but now isn't the time or place to explain. Especially not in front of the enemy. Before the word 'classified' can come off my tongue though, it's Camille's voice that echoes out first.

"Don't answer that, agent," she says sternly.

I twist my head away from Clifford to the comm in my ear and mumble with untamed curiosity. "You know about the project?"

"I was updated the minute you were reinstated."

I think back to all the times she's covered for me whenever Shane or Rebecca would ask questions I was too tired to answer. She'd always change the subject, making herself the center of attention, and point out when I wasn't acting like "myself". Damn. She isn't as rusty as I thought she was. Something I will *never* say to her face.

"Okay, but how does this prick in front of me—" I steal a glance at Clifford— "know about it?"

"Clearly the breach runs deeper than we anticipated. If Specter has been informed, and has been receiving information about it, a lot of other agents won't be safe from exposure."

"So, the project is...?" Elias trails, his head tilted.

And like covering for me all over again, Camille answers. "Classified, "Dragon", so I suggest you move on with the task at hand."

I look back and find Elias and Andre staring at me, like I'm going to whisper it to them. They may have their problems right now, but you'd never be able to tell with the way they share the same waiting stare.

"Hello!?" Clifford yells, then smashes his bottle against the wall. "Man seeking revenge here!?"

The expression of childlike wonder fades from Elias and Andre's face as they look up at him, and soon murder glows in their eyes. I turn and catch Clifford's stare, and in the corner of his cloudy blue eyes a hint of panic blossoms, as if he just realized it's three against one. We have the numbers, but in the back of my mind I can't help but wonder if he's just stupid enough to be surrounded, or he's that confident in his fighting skills, even intoxicated.

Either way, he's got to go. An idea on how to do that starts to formulate, my eyes surfing over his lean body as I think of where would hurt the most and be lethal. A couple of arteries come to mind and I step closer, shifting my weight to get ready to end him.

With my injuries it'll have to be quick, sadly. Although I do take pride in my work, so I can put in a little more effort. But, when I begin to reach for my gun, Elias moves into the space beside me and chuckles darkly before speaking to Clifford, like they're old friends.

"Hey Tristan. Looks like your mouth made a speedy recovery. But how's the knee? And ankle? And that finger that just... *fell* off?"

I have to look up at him when I hear that one. "Fell off?"

He leans over and mumbles, "I got impatient."

"Interesting," I laugh, remembering Samberg's finger I put on ice.

"Enough! I'll kill you, after I'm done with her," Clifford snickers. "I wouldn't want you to miss her bleeding out."

Elias lets out a quiet growl as he steps forward.

"No, I got this." I hold out my arm to stop him, using the other to grab my gun. "It'll be quick and *painful.*"

"Yes, it will," Clifford says through clenched teeth. "I wish I could slice you up like you did to him, but you're not even worth the time."

How did he know exactly what I—my thought gets interrupted when he charges at me. Whether its fury or alcohol he's drunk off of, Clifford uses it. Heated blood rushes through my limbs as my sore body gets ready to fight. I relax and grip my gun as he reaches behind his back. Running up, I kick his arm away just before he retrieves whatever he was grabbing for. A berretta, I realize as I spin on his left and see it tucked in the back of his pants.

My hand wraps around the hilt, sliding it away from him, and then I move back, just dodging his fist. From that, I get a clear picture as to who I'm dealing with. He thinks fast but moves slow.

This makes things more interesting.

I toss his gun over his head to Elias, and as he watches it, I swing my foot into his face. He flies backwards, grunting in pain, but manages to stay on his feet. Impressive, except, at the end of the day, *I* still have my gun.

I fire at him twice. One shot for each leg.

His body awkwardly drops to the ground, like every one of his limbs give up on him all at once as they fold in onto themselves. With the gunfire rattling the pale copper stone tunnel around us, and the sound of his agony filled screams, it's the perfect symphony of defeat. The sound slightly shakes my ear drums, but I don't shrink back from the ringing. I only stare down at Clifford as he struggles to get onto his feet.

"So, let me guess, you're a drinker like your friend is?" I let a smile stretch my lips. "Or, I'm sorry, was?"

His brows furrow as hate overtakes his demeanour. He reaches for his ankle, which I'm assuming another gun is, in an act of desperation. I stomp my foot on his hand, grab the weapon myself, and slide it away while tsking.

"Well, even if you aren't, you're clearly on something. Or maybe you're just a terrible agent," I snicker. "Why did they even let you out to play when you're like this, Tristan?"

"Wrap it up, Tigress, you have to move," Camille demands in my ear. I do pick up the pace, but not without scarring this man a little more.

"You know, George died thinking that you had betrayed him. I made sure he did. But with you…" a dark cloud sets over me as I trail off and reach for his other gun. Then, as I stick it into his face, I finish my taunting.

"With you, I'm going to let you die knowing what he thought of you in his last moments. His only friend."

"You're going to die a painful death, then rot in hell, you evil *bitch*!"

I lean over his wiggling body and utter sweetly, "Well, only time will tell, won't it? But at least I'm not going to die in this tunnel beside filthy sewage like you. Just like the other *rats*."

Clifford opens his mouth to get the last word in, but my attention span was very limited on this pile of shit to start. I don't give him another thought and pull the trigger. The same echo rings in my ears, but this time it's a bit more muffled, as if the furious rush of blood is shielding my eardrums.

I've experienced close kills like this before—the hot blood spraying on my clothes and face always feeling the same—but this time, instead of waiting for the adrenaline to hit me, I close my eyes to see my next target… Foreman.

Throughout this entire journey I've more or less kept my cool and have loosely maintained control. But, with what happened between Rebecca, and now Clifford, I notice a new weight lifting off me. There was no intention of it happening. Really, I'm not completely sure why it does. No matter the reason, I use it. I slowly stand and turn towards Elias and

Andre to see their faces the portrait of unease. But I don't care. I walk past them with a new speed in my step, going back to the mission.

"Let's go," I tell them, my voice low and void of emotion.

CHAPTER THIRTY

DEALER'S CHOICE

As we come up through the tiled floor hatch that connects our secret entrance to a maintenance room in headquarters, Elias, Andre and I get ready for whatever may be waiting on the other side of the door. The chances of us being gunned down as soon as we leave the room are very high, but somehow that outcome isn't what I'm most worried about. No. It's the fact that it's way too quiet for what I'm assuming is—or *was*—a hostile takeover. It's a kind of haunting silence that doesn't warrant anything positive to come from it.

The hairs on the back of my neck slightly begin to stand as my hand touches the door's icy knob. Twisting it, I take in a deep breath to calm the sudden loud beats of my heart. I've made it this far. Dealt with some pretty big reveals and revelations. It's impossible for me to turn away from all of it now. Not when we're so close to ending what started years ago. This door is the only thing standing in the way.

I'm done running.

Done hiding and pretending.

I'm finishing this today. Even if it kills me.

I slowly pull the door towards me, though, in just the slight crack it creates my hand drops from the knob. I swallow, hard, and without my guidance, the door continues to swing open on its own. I don't want to move, but knowing that that isn't an option anymore, I pull myself together as much as I can and turn back to make sure Elias and Andre are alert. They both look to me and sharply nod. But, as we cautiously step into the French-style courtyard, guns at the ready, the sight laid out causes us to steadily lower our weapons.

The scene is nothing short of fucked.

From end to end, bodies litter the smooth stone ground, some riddled with bullets across them, and others with just a straight one to the skull. The sea of khaki pants and navy sweaters tell me these agents were only operations analysts and technicians, but I guess none of that matters when a fucking psychopath decides to come in with a few men with guns.

We stroll past all the innocent blood staining the eerie courtyard, and it only causes mine to boil at the thought of Minnie being among the fallen.

Nothing in her files predicted this, but I know Supervisor did it. We trained with him for years. No other person has this much knowledge in frightening massacre tactics. No other person who knows how to cause such mass violence. As angering as it is—that his past lessons have just been a huge red flag all along—that's not what causes me to instinctively raise my weapon in the air again. *That's* courtesy of the sudden spray of bullets that just miss my feet. They would've made their way through my torso if Elias hadn't pulled me back.

A small gasp escapes me from the force of his tug. It takes me a moment to collect myself as he pushes me up against the wall in a swift motion, my back hitting the marble with minimal pain. A bit of a sting travels up my leg, but a cool and steady breath gets my head back into the rhythm of what's going on. Even with Elias's warm body covering mine.

"You alright?" he asks casually, though for a second, I see him shake.

My eyes wander up to him, yet his focus is only on the gun in his hand.

"I'm good," I tell him, my heart still racing.

"Good." He rips the hammer back then drops his stare to me. "So how do you wanna handle this?"

I hear the sudden stomp of boots on the ground, and with each step that gets closer to surrounding us, the more I wish I had brought Camille. Too late to turn back now though, and I'm *not* giving her the satisfaction of her knowing that I know she's an asset. From what I've already learned about her over the last few days, her ego is big enough. I turn from Elias to a pipe with a blue sticker in the corner and let the details of my plan B surface.

God, I hope this place is insured for water damage. And electrical damage.

"Well, given the cluster fuck of the situation, I'd say we're on our own. I do have an idea, but it might be a little… much."

`"Try not to make a scene,"` Camille interjects. Really it goes in one ear and out the other as Elias answers me.

"Okay, let's go. Let's do it."

`"What did I just say?"` she tries again. `"Are you guys even listening to me!?"`

I catch his arm before he steps away and tilt my head as bewilderment takes over my tone. "Really?"

"Yeah," he smirks, "you got shot at first, so dealer's choice."

`"You're all going to die."`

A warm sensation travels down my back at the sincerity lining his words, and for a second, I could've sworn we went back five years into the past. Our long glances, intense solicitous feelings, and blind support. It's almost nostalgic. Minus Camille's pompous tone of course, and Andre's bitter presents. He loudly clears his throat beside us, ending our corny staring montage. Some part of me thanks him for interrupting, another wonders what we'd do if—I shove down the thought. We swiftly glance away from each other, like we hadn't been staring in the first place. Sentiment sits in the pit of my stomach, but I don't let it stay for long.

Revenge now, I think, *reminisce later.*

Once my attention completely switches to Andre, only then do I notice the alarmingly irritated look glazed over his face. For a second it seems as if that look is solely directed at me. I'm not sure if it's entirely because I'm near Elias again, or because he's not used to being a third wheel. No matter what the reason for his glare is, I don't cower in light of it.

He wasn't around to see me slightly lose it with Rebecca, who I actually like. Him though, I'd be more than happy to let this knife loving brooding douche bag have a piece of my mind. We may not have the time, though trust me, I'd make some. I was kind of looking forward to it too, but eventually that second ends. He blinks away most of the protectiveness in his stare, then backs up against the doorframe. He raises his gun to the sky, then speaks in a tolerating kind of way.

"As interested as I am to hear your plan, I don't think that it's going to be necessary." His eyes quickly shift upwards, and he nods to the balcony festering with our potential doom. Instructing us to— "Look."

I follow his gesture, and from where I stare out, just beyond the hoard of ominous men waiting to give us that *lovely* agency welcome, is a hand peeking out from behind the pale red pillar. It's not one I can say I recognize by merely a glance, but what I do notice in the unfamiliar hand is a full-on military stun grenade.

"Aw, shit," I grumble.

"What is it?" Camille's voice fills my head.

Elias sighs and remarks dryly, "I thought this was a little too easy."

"What's going on?"

"We need to take cover," Andre readily announces.

"If someone doesn't speak up right now, I swear I'll come over there and—"

I roll my eyes and answer her in an irritated whisper. "We're in the middle of a situation that's either just gotten a lot better, or a lot worse."

"You're terrible at explaining things! I need at least some detail about what's going on."

Tightness enters my chest with every deep breath I try to take, like I'm somehow drowning in the air inside my lungs. Faintly my body shakes as I reluctantly acknowledge her again.

"Yeah, well, explaining anything to you right now isn't exactly my main priority, sorry."

Her only response is an angry huff, but after that, she ultimately shuts up.

Gracias a Dios.

(Thank God.)

Dealing with the profoundly irksome effects of a grenade will always piss me off. And the fact that I don't know who's holding it, or which side they're on here, aggravates me even more. Camille pestering me definitely wasn't helping at all. But despite the angry rash starting to form on the back of my neck, I agree with Andre, and brace myself for the flashbang to come.

It's kind of funny to think that only a few weeks ago I was helping Rebecca with her presentation, and now here I am about to hit the deck in the hopes of avoiding the eardrum melting, head knocking, eye rattling ramifications of a flashbang. Given my track record so far though, I'm pretty sure that this won't be the last grenade thrown at me.

I swear some things never change.

Even when they *desperately* should.

Overwhelming unease immediately sets into my bones as I hear the sound of the can being dropped to the ground. Thus beginning my pre-hellish torture from past grenade related events. My body quivers, and the only noise to penetrate that sudden soundless moment—where your target finally realizes the threat—is the roll of the sound bomb. It causes a pounding in my chest as I crouch behind the wall, and the anxious throbbing lightly rocks me back and forth.

"Just breathe," Elias whispers beside me. "You'll get through this."

I snap my head up at him, and as soon as my eyes lock onto his, I watch as he takes a slow deep breath in and out. In the past, to help get me through an episode, he'd always do that. Always keep me calm enough with that voice. One it took him a while to master. And that was *after* he finally noticed that my falling out of a helicopter with grenades exploding around me *may* have given me just a touch of PTSD.

Why or how it still works on me, I have no clue, but right now I'm just glad it does. I relax just enough to remember what I have to do. After a few slow breaths of my own, I waste no time and hastily assume position.

It only takes one point five seconds for the grenade to go off, yet it feels like a lifetime of anxiety hits. Every mistake I wish I could fix, every person I thought I could trust. Everything. But when it's over, when the only thing left to hear is the repetitive sound of an assault rifle, I take a second to breathe. And *only* a second, because my next move, even with my heart still racing, is to either help or hurt whoever threw that grenade.

Breaking formation, I remove my fingers from my ears and open my eyes then spin towards the continuous bullets popping off, quickly placing the comm device back in my ear. Though with what's happening in front of me, it doesn't seem like I need to rush. With the way bodies are dropping like flies left and right off the balcony, it's not exactly giving off an 'I need help' vibe. My first thought, besides being glad that I'm not up there, is *I swear I've seen that technique before.* The speed of the gun to each person before they can fire their weapon, the precision, it all reminds me of a special someone.

This would be his cup of tea—or more like his glass of scotch—but there's no way it could be him. He's not a young man anymore. Still a strict bastard, yes, but not the same man with a loose back who trained me all those years ago. Yet as I continue to watch, with that thought in the back of my mind and the familiar momentum, I can't help but think it's him, and it won't shake. Call it intuition.

I turn to Elias—someone who'd definitely know if I'm right about this—and find a puzzled look sprawled across his face that matches the one I'm sure I have on mine.

"Is that one of us!?" he shouts.

"I have no idea, but I hope so!" I yell back through the shooting, praying it is.

Finally the shots come to a halt, and all three of us poke our heads out from behind the wall, looking at the fresh blood dripping to the floor as silence spreads throughout the space. But as long as it took for the grenade to go off, that's how long it takes for our "white knight" to call out to us.

Actually, it's *my* name he calls. A smirk gradually lights my face as I bask in my accuracy as to who was shooting the rifle with such grace.

"Are you coming or what!? I'm an old man. I don't want to do *all* the work myself," the distant voice says to me.

My smirk turns into a full-blown grin and I step out from behind the wall, completely ignoring Elias reaching for me. I'm not wrong about this, I know that, but as I leave Elias and Andre behind, I do leave my gun out. Trust seems to be a funny word around here, especially given our last encounter. So, when I do lift my head up to the iron balcony I also ever-so-slightly raise my gun.

Turns out to be a good thing too, because before locking eyes with Manager, the first things I'm met with is the business end of his rifle. It doesn't exactly match the tone of all that 'I trust you' crap he spewed out to me the other day. Although, in his defence, I do have my gun trained on him to.

"It's okay," I say to make the first good faith gesture, even though my gun doesn't move an inch. "We're okay. Right?"

With a smile appearing on his sweaty face, Manager lets his rifle hang loose in his arms. He nods slowly. "We're okay."

The words create a neutral bridge, and a wave of relief washes over me as I lower my gun with leisure. In all the chaos it's nice to know that someone you believed to be a good person actually is. Though when Manager's expression goes sour, I start to rethink that.

I follow his eyes and find him staring at Elias beside me. I make sure he's holding fire, which was the right move, because with the way his brows pull together, it looks like he's about to kill him. Well, that, and the way he has his gun pointing dead center at Manager's head.

"What are you doing?" I frustratingly mutter.

He ignores me and only speaks to Manager with sharpness as he calls him by name. "Colton."

"Agent," Manager replies just as coldly while raising his rifle again.

I twist my head between the two of them and start to get a whiff of the animosity in the air. There's a story here, and a large part of me wants to stop everything to hear it, especially since I wasn't around to see what became of their relationship after I left.

In the past they've had their little differences and disputes, but right now there's more of a protective father figure energy coming from Manager than anything else. As sweet as I find it, time isn't our friend here. Being flattered by the homicidal glint in both their eyes will have to wait. I put an end to their bitching before it can begin.

"Look, I don't know what problems you have with each other, but whatever they are, or were, it doesn't matter. Right now we have a situation we need to solve together." I switch my stare from Manager to Elias. "So can we agree to stop pointing our guns at our allies and be adults here, for the sake of the agency gentlemen?"

"Sure," Elias concurs with a bitter laugh. "As long as he doesn't threaten to kill me, or have me killed. Again."

I spin back around to Manager, holding back my intrigue. "Manager?"

"You needed to get some air, in France? With him?"

"That's a long story. One I'm sure you're dying to hear, and I *swear* I'll tell you, but for now the only thing I can say is... trust me. Please."

"Fine. But only because my threats seem null and void now," his stare shifts to me for a brief moment and then it goes back to Elias. "Though if he threatens to kill me, again, I won't hesitate to put him in his place."

"404?"

He looks to me. "Dragon."

"I'm pretty sure we can stop with the code names now."

"Fine. And I'll be a good little agent."

"Good," I nod. "Now's the part where you both lower your—"

"You had 420 sent out for me!?" Andre's aggrieved voice shouts.

So close.

I wait for Manager to react, and he does so by lowering his weapon while sighing with what sounds like disappointment. Elias follows, and after relief settles in, I find the strength to turn and face Andre. It's not so much worry that travels through me than it is annoyance at the fact that he's bringing that up now. But still, the murderous look that's staining his face does make me cautionate.

Thankfully he doesn't have his gun in the air, but the seconds between someone pulling the trigger and someone blinking isn't that much of a difference. So I watch him, just in case he decides to make that decision—

"Are you fucking serious!? You're bringing that up *now,* 504? How pathetic can a person be in one day?"

We flinch at the sound of Camille practically screaming into the comm, but its Andre who shrinks back the most. And at that exact moment, I figure me dealing with his deflated pride won't be a problem anymore. She has a certain *way* with words, and it's that *way* that allows us to make our approach up to Manager. Andre slowly following behind us while he argues with Camille. Their bickering becomes somewhat of white noise as I talk to Manager to find out how everything got so apocalyptic.

"Who was talking to you in the first place?"

"What happened here?"

"It doesn't matter! Stop being a little bitch because you got caught."

"Strange bed fellows', agent?" he counters with, glancing back at Andre when he raises his voice.

"I didn't get caught! I could've escaped or done some last-minute Batman shit if I wanted too. You're lucky I helped you at all!"

"Tell me about it. Honestly, you have my permission to shoot him if you want. But, if it's any consolation, he *did* help us along the way."

"I heard that," Andre says, though I tune him—and the rest of his conversation with Camille—out as Manager answers harshly.

"Tempting. Especially considering how incompetent and reckless I think he's been. But I don't think his partner would be too happy about that. We have a bit of a truce now."

My ponytail falls into my face as I steal a glance at Elias. He sluggishly strolls behind us, his head facing the ground, like he's patiently waiting for me to finish talking with Manager. The longer I watch him though, the more I start to feel this circulating ache in my gut for him. He has to walk around with the fact that the partner he's trusted for years, confided in, has been nothing but an agent handling his assignment. It's not like I set the bar high, but it still has to hurt.

Camille and I were never close, which she made sure of now that I think about it. Yet with Andre, from back when I spoke to him on the jet, it was obvious he had become a real friend to Elias. And, from where I stand, apparently that feeling was mutual. But as he continues to walk with a disillusioned behaviour, I can see that that feeling is fading.

It's baffling really, because the thing I find most upsetting right now is that Elias isn't even that hard to please. Despite him being one of the most meticulous killers I know, and in spite of his bloody start in life—his parents being mercenaries—he's genuinely a nice guy. It's one of the reasons I fell in love with him in the first place. Yes, he's changed in ways that have shown monster like qualities, but there's also been the same old Elias who would always step in front of anything to protect me.

I pull my gaze from him. The only place I can seem to look at next is the ground while continuing my conversation with Manager.

"Something tells me you wouldn't hear any objections from him," I mumble.

"Sounds like you've had quite the difficult trip, agent," Manager comments with a light chuckle.

Total understatement there, pal.

I stop in my tracks—mostly for dramatic effect—and let my eyes shift to him, then wander up and down to get a better look at his appearance. He looks like a butcher's dish towel, and I mean after they've finished cutting the meat. Blood is smeared all over his dress shirt, that I'm assuming was white at one point. Something of a unique splatter decorates his loose tie, and I don't even want to know what the chunks are in his hair.

"Not as difficult as you it would seem."

He drops his head down to see what I'm seeing. Once he seems to be finished going over how he got all the different stains in his head, he only sighs and continues walking. "Yes, well, I may have you beat I'm afraid."

"And that brings me back to my question."

"What happened here?" Manager repeats.

"Yes."

"Jesus," he takes a hand from his rifle and uses it to roughly rub his eyes, "that's a bit of a long story."

"Well, if I minus having to deal with Foreman's men, dodging grenades, and going through the emotional baggage that's piled up these last few days, I think I can spare time to hear your tale of woe."

"In that case, where would you like me to start?"

I twist back to Elias again, and this time, as he looks up at me, I mutter with a teasing smirk on my lips. "Dealer's choice."

CHAPTER THIRTY-ONE

Things have been spiralling so much in my life that I didn't think it could possibly be as shitty for someone else. According to Manager though, I was very wrong. As we go through headquarters, either looking for survivors or dealing with Foreman's hired help, Manager tells us everything, starting from what he's been doing since my last mission. And all I can say is that it really has been one hell of a ride for this old man. Even at one point Elias, Andre, Camille and I simultaneously asked, 'how are you still alive?'

He proceeded to tell us about Minnie informing him about the month-long theft of our confidential information. How he tried to help her follow the digital breadcrumbs as best he could, but his tech skills were subpar at best, so he didn't get that far. He then moved on to what happened after my visit, after I never came back following our discussion. Apparently, that warranted a call for my detainment, but before he could make it, he received one from Minnie telling him about my brother and his connection to Foreman.

The mention of Dominic slightly diverged my attention, as I got lost in the hope that he's still safe. Wherever he is. But almost as quickly as my focus shifted, I shook off my worry, the ache in my heart, then tuned back into the rest of Manager's elaborate journey. A journey that consisted of his admission that he went up to check on Dominic and me, yet by the time he got there we were both gone.

It was a nice gesture, really. Or at least it would've been if not for the fact that he was going to send out for me in one of my weakest moments. Any appreciation that I felt disappeared, especially when he moves on to talk about when our aliases were exposed.

A bitter taste enters my mouth at the memory of hearing my number in the jet, followed by the words that might've ended my career and life. It shouldn't bother me now though, especially not since I ended up exactly where I was supposed to be. *But goddamn if the road I took wasn't as difficult as hell.*

Manager then finishes with him trying to contact both Andre and Camille. He doesn't go into further detail on that subject, which is him probably doing his best to avoid another argument between the two. And us. Instead, he explains that Commander summoned him to Beta Z headquarters after the alert, to fill her in on everything he knew about me and my involvement. But apparently, by the time he had gotten here, she was nowhere to be found, and he was only met with a blood-soaked carpet and tossed furniture.

Right from the beginning he was here. When the system shut down. When Foreman's men in black jumpers took advantage of that and busted through the doors. And when they overpowered and slaughtered the innocent agents inside. All at Foreman's orders. Supervisor's orders. The confirmed theory I now share with him, but his shock never comes for some reason.

The features on his face only darken, like he knows something I don't. Something he's deliberately left out. Cold seeps into my bones, and just as we enter the main hall, where *he's* been leading us, my sudden grim skepticism only grows.

I stop dead in my tracks and then turn around to face him. But, before the acquisition makes its way up my throat, the words get caught when my stare focuses, not on his stony expression, but on the glowing red dot on his forehead.

Within the seconds of me realizing what's happening, his face quickly transitions from concealed to concerned. He's looking past me into the hall, and it's impossible for him to be seeing his own forehead right now, so whatever's behind me can only be worse.

"401," Elias says, his cool tone pulling my gaze towards him, but instead of looking him in the eye, it's the red dots sprinkled across his body that grab my attention.

This can't be good.

Slowly, I spin around on my heels, and I regret it. I'm met with a handful of mahogany masked goons doused in black, and their very high-grade arsenal. Despite the extra palpitations in my chest, my eyes scan the room, counting how many there are and calculating our options. Four exits. Two goons blocking each one and two per person for our little band of heroes. That's sixteen armed guards, not counting the perimeter probably set up outside.

We're in a bit of a box here, given the terrible design choice, though if we can fight our way to the stairs, we may have a chance to—my eyes shift up and land on the wooden balcony that overlooks the entire hall, and a sharp pain stabs me in the gut.

Commander sits in front of us, and the image of her isn't pretty at all. Her golden face is half beaten into her skull, blood drips down from her busted lips, and both eyes are nearly swollen shut. Zip ties bind her arms and feet behind her. I can't even tell if she's breathing. Yet despite all that—the mildly disturbing visual of the woman who was once my mentor—it's not what makes me shiver. No. What makes my blood run cold is Supervisor standing over her with a devilish smirk on his own bleeding face.

His arm hanging down at his side. Commander must've been able to hold her own during his take over. But judging by the needle I see sticking out from the side of her thigh, Supervisor clearly wussed out and went for the drugs.

"Oh good, we're finally all here. We've been waiting," he remarks with a poisonous amount of sarcastic enthusiasm.

I stomp forward with my weapon at the ready, completely forgetting about the other numerous guns aimed at me. I get an immediate reminder when the sound of them being cocked echoes all around us and Supervisor speaks up. His voice even more smug than our last encounter.

"Uh uh agent. I don't even think you're that stupid, so drop them. All of you."

"You *son* of a *bitch*," Manager spits out through clenched teeth.

Supervisor rolls his good eye that's filled with blood. "Now, old man."

`"Sounds like you need me,"` Camille says in my head, almost cheerful. `"Free authorization?"`

"Do some damage. But make sure the civilians stay out of reach," I reply, so low only she can hear me.

`"Copy."`

We drop our weapons and kick them to the side, all with transpicuous frustration. The sight of them skidding on the ground makes my skin heat with fury.

"All. Of. Them. Or I can have these fine men do it for you."

Each of us grunt as we travel down our bodies, reaching for knives, other guns, and gadgets. When we finish, Supervisor chuckles.

"Good. Now the fun part can begin."

With a swift nod, the faceless men circle around us and push, forcing us forward. I'm not seeing a lot of wiggle room here, but I have to stall until Camille is ready with whatever she's planning to do. An effective way to do that isn't an option I'm particularly fond of. But desperate times, I guess.

The closer I get to the psychopath, the more I prepare myself for the mind-numbing question I'll have to force out of my mouth. A question I know will have an equally exasperating answer. Nonetheless, I find my opening, and just as we're strong-armed to a halt, a small part of me already dies of boredom when I yell out,

"Why!?"

"Oh Jesus," Andre utters, "just shoot me now."

"Shut it," Elias whispers viciously.

Supervisor stays silent. Though the way his expression twists into a combination of slight disappointment and cunning amusement, he might as well be shouting. The goal here is to unsettle me. That's textbook in situations like this. But I can't help but sense something else. There can't possibly be any more surprises at this point, and yet, with the look on his beaten face, my gut tells me I need to stay alert.

So, I do.

I fix my stance, square my shoulders, and keep my eye on the target. I stay vigilant while waiting for an answer to my question, my distraction, except, when it comes, it's not Supervisor's doomy voice that echoes throughout the hall.

"I think that questions meant for me," they say.

This is someone else entirely, their voice young, but covered in a thick layer of maturity, sounding like they're trying to mask becoming broken by the world. It's familiar, though not enough that I can place it. All I can do is wait in confounded suspension for their dramatic entrance.

Finally, when they emerge from the shadows, donning a commanding demeanour from head to toe with every step, my heart plummets into my stomach at the sight of their face.

I gasp so hard it nearly knocks me off my feet, but the question that leaves Andre's mouth—so fast I barely think he knows he asked it out loud—keeps me standing.

"Who the fuck are you?"

They don't pay attention to anyone but me, and soon it becomes just us in the room. No one else. Everything around us fades into a blurry backdrop of indisputable chaos. The only thing that remains is the light tremble of my body, waiting for the emotional impact to crush me. I stand under them, stuck in a wide-eyed tableau, feeling a physical weight on my chest as their malcontent stare continues to snatch every ounce of my attention.

The only thing my brain can seem to do, besides begin to pound inside my skull, is try and nurture me. Trick me into not believing what's right in front of my eyes, and for a minute I allow the denial to pump through my veins. And as the words echo in my head, it feels like an eternity, our eyes still locked on each other.

This isn't happening Nova. This isn't happening. This—

A deviously satisfied grin plasters itself across their face, ripping me from the self-soothing mantra bouncing around my mind. The dank air in the room goes thin, and for a moment I forget how to breathe. As if I just watched the person they were only days ago die in front of me. As if smoke had invaded my already strained lungs, making them weaker than before.

It's then I realize there's no way I'm getting out of here alive. Not in one piece that is. At this rate, I'm running out of pieces to give. But this—as their voice breaks into the silence again—is going to be the worst and the most colossal chunk torn from me yet.

"Hey sis, guess what? I made it out of that hell hole we called home. Just like you." Dominic grins, pausing to adjust an 'F' shaped cufflink on his sleeve, and then manically continues. "But from where I'm standing… it looks like I've done better."

CHAPTER THIRTY-TWO

IF YOU CAN'T STAND THE HEAT

Every conversation, every gesture, every little detail runs through my mind as I try to find any sort of logical explanation.

He was brainwashed.

He was threatened.

He's just a doppelganger.

Something. Anything!

Because if none of that is true, and it's actually him, actually my little brother who's been Foreman this entire time, then it's my fault. He became this way, this ruthless killer… because of me. The impact of guilt hits me much faster than I thought my conscience would allow. I have to talk though, right? I have to say something, but the only thing I manage to choke out to my secret villain of a brother is,

"What the fuck?"

A smirk attaches to his already twisted demeanour at the sound of my bewilderment, and it's as if I'm formally being introduced to the man he's become. The monster that has been lying dormant in him for who knows how long. It's enough for a shiver to travel down my spine, and as he begins to speak, the once blurred background we shared falls away and the world starts to spin again.

"Oh come on, don't look so surprised. You, the 'great agent 401, Nova Castillo', really thought he could've done this all by *himself*?" He points to Supervisor and slightly snickers, "no offense, Riche."

His face goes sour. "Watch yourself kid," Supervisor grunts.

Dominic completely ignores him, which only instils more fear in me that he really is the one who's been in charge this whole time.

"I mean obviously you didn't think it was going to be *me* stepping out," he laughs, "but you must've had someone else in mind for a puppet master, right? Your other friend certainly did."

"I'm still missing something. Who is this kid exactly?" Andre mumbles on my left.

Manager pushes out a frustrated breath beside me. "Oh my god."

"He's Foreman, idiot. The kid up there, standing right above us, is Foreman. And considering he's the same one that said, 'hey sis,' he's obviously also 401's brother," Elias mutters. "Do you get it now?"

"Was the 'idiot' part really necessary?" he grumbles.

I'm surrounded by ignorant and arrogant boys in the middle of one of the worst moments of my life.

I roll my eyes, apparently the only motion I can do without feeling the urge to vomit at the turn of events. Just when I thought it couldn't get worse, I'm slapped in the face with the ugly reality that things can *always* get worse. This though, this is a new type of egregious circumstance I'm not sure how to approach.

From the moment he sauntered into the light, two voices began to fight in my head. One yelling: "*he's not Foreman*," and the other screaming the words I know are true: "*It's him. He played the victim to be discredited as a suspect. He played you.*"

The evidence is right there, standing over me like a King shamelessly looking down on his enemies, but I still don't want to believe it. All I see—even through the blood covering the decor around us—is the little brother I left in the monsters den we called home. The one I stole for to buy his first bike. The one I'd let sleep in my room because he was afraid of the dark. Now though, from down here, it doesn't look like he's afraid of anything anymore.

A sudden desire burns in me to know what happened to him. What I could've or should've done to save him. To bring him with me. But as soon as the thought—the regret—seeps into my throbbing head, surprisingly it's Shane's advice from Brazil that sooths me.

'Just be careful not to let the could've's and should've's of the past cloud any future decisions. Because if you do, you'll regret it.'

He's right. As much as I don't want him to be, he's right. I have to deal with this, one way or another. No matter who it is.

Dominic stridently clearing his throat brings me from gut-wrenching realization. As my attention whips back to him, his eyes narrow and shift towards Andre like throwing knives. Immediately it reads as displeasure at his lack of control of the room, but it doesn't last long. He regains his dominance as his stare quickly side swipes to the masked goon hovering over Andre. In a swift motion, the hilt of the man's M19 collides with his mouth.

"I'm kind of in the middle of something here, and I do have other plans for today. So we're finished with the side chatter gentlemen."

Andre lets out a low moan of pain while blood pours from his busted mouth. Elias angles his foot in the goon's direction, a murderous glint in his eye. His reaction surprises both me and Manager, but I quickly let out a brisk growl and he doesn't move another inch.

"Not yet," I breathe, barely moving my lips.

Camille is on the way, hopefully ready to advance sooner than later. I just need to keep talking, or at least keep *someone* talking. She can't be more than a few seconds out. So, I sluggishly elaborate on the original question I had asked Supervisor, when I believed he was temporarily the most evil person in the world. Not my baby brother.

"You still haven't answered me. Why? Why did you do all of this? For some kind of sadistic retribution?"

Not wanting to know his answer leaves a bad taste in my mouth, but I swallow down the extra saliva that fills my cheeks.

"You're thinking too small there, Sis," his voice plummets into an annoyed tone. "Sorry to burst that bubble you're in that has you believing everything is about you, but this isn't. Honestly, you've just been a minor inconvenience. Your emotional breakage however, has merely been a consolation prize in my path to success."

The condescension leaking from his voice makes my hand itch for the sensation of slapping some sense into him. To remind him of the 'little boy' he really is. To remind him that I'm still his older sister, despite his attitude forcing me to bite down an unanticipated titter at the situation he put us in. Put *me* in.

He's playing a very dangerous game that only ends with two choices for him. A, a body bag, or B, begging for death. Messing with the safety of the world doesn't have a light punishment like a slap on the wrist. I don't know what he's playing at, but clearly he doesn't realize, or doesn't care, about the consequences. Whichever one it is, it doesn't matter. Not anymore. Especially not when Manager rattles the inside of his throat. He's about to fill my arrogant little brother in on a few things.

"Someone ought to come up there and teach you some manners and respect, *boy.*" His lips press into a thin line as a slight crease forms between his brows. It's a look I've seen only once before. A look that led to one of the worst training days of my life. One I've worked so hard to never see again.

Dominic though, opens his mouth, not knowing what that look means at all. "And let me guess, that someone is going to be you?" he sneers.

"Oh trust me, you don't want that. The only reason I didn't shoot you on sight was because I recognized you, son, and I thought that shot should be taken by your sister."

"*Tú saber algo viejo hombre*, you and that other girl have given me a lot of trouble. Made me travel all the way to your prime headquarters and reveal myself." Dominic lazily swings two fingers in Manager's direction and within seconds almost every gun is aimed at him.

"I should put two bullets through your chest to match hers."

Is he talking about Minnie? Did he kill her?

"That's enough!" I yell, drawing myself from the thought. "You're not going to hurt anyone else."

"Is that so?" Dominic chuckles.

"Tick tock," Supervisor remarks, interrupting Dominic's detrimental train of thought. "We have to get moving, so decide what you're going to do, and do it fast."

Once again, Dominic completely disregards his accomplice and addresses me instead, grinning. "Fine, I'll give *you* the choice then. You either let me walk out of here unscathed, or watch your allies die one by one before you do. So, what's it gonna be?"

`"Coming in hot on your left,"` Camille hastily announces.

My eyes quickly dart to where the guns we kicked aside lay in wait. Then, as I bring my stare back to Dominic, just before we duck, I respond coldly to my brother's indifferent offer.

"Neither."

Elias and I drop to the floor, and before Andre follows, he promptly yanks Manager down with him. The cold marble pushes against my good hip as we slide on the ground, and soon the sound of shattering glass and the swift zoom of a sniper's bullets echo throughout the foyer. While they whiz through the air, we grab our weapons then flip the stone benches over for cover.

I'm not even going to ask where she got a sniper.

The guards that once stood over us begin to get shot down like ducks during hunting season, and I, as well as Elias, Andre and Manager join in. Not that Camille is leaving a lot of them for us.

By the time they raise their guns to where they think our secret gunwoman is sourced, they're too late. She's too fast for any of them. But for the ones that do manage to move in time, we get the privilege of taking out her leftovers. Given the child-like happiness in her voice, I don't think she cares.

"Everyone still alive?"

As much as I want to answer her, or at least comment on how my level of respect and fear for her has risen an equal amount, I force myself to hold back. Instead, I focus on the three most important facts as of now.

Not dying.

My tyrant brother.

And my *rage.*

I ignore Camille, and her joyful humming of 'La Vie En Rose', then go straight to biting Manager's head off. My rage momentarily coming out on top.

"You knew!?" I scream at him. "This whole time you knew, and you didn't think to fill me in!?"

"I figured you'd have to see him to believe it was true." He rips the magazine from his rifle, reloads, then starts shooting again. "And honestly, after you left, I wasn't completely sure if—"

"If what? If I was working with him!? Are you *fucking* serious?"

"Don't resort to being naive *again,* Nova. We don't live in a world where trust is an absolute. You were naive before, so blinded by love and guilt, that you let your guard down and brought him into the winery. Which, by the way, is how our system got hacked internally, and how your alias got exposed. You being sloppy got us here!"

"Fuck you, okay!" My grip tightens on the trigger as I shoot a Foreman lackey coming up on my left. "He's my brother. I practically raised him. You want me to fucking apologize for loving him and not suspecting he was a goddamn evil crime lord!?"

"Yes. I think that would help," he adds smugly.

"And *I* think we have bigger problems right now," Andre chimes in from across the way, his head bobbing up and down between shots.

Beside me, Elias also forces himself into the conversation. "I'd have to agree here."

"I don't give a flying—"

"Look!" he cuts me off.

Making an effort to push down my fury, I swing my attention from him to where his gun points upwards. And suddenly, as if he's been patiently waiting for my stare to wander over to him again, there Dominic stands, unwavered. His stare full of hate.

A piece of me crumbles away under his intense scorn, but I stay alert. I have to think fast, be the agent, even in this situation. As much as I don't want to believe that any of this is actually happening, or that Manager is right, I can't let my mind go back to seeing him as my fragile little brother. No matter how much I wish I could.

My time to be upsettingly astonished has run out, whether it's my choice or not. And given the way Dom—Foreman is madly rummaging through his jacket, I can say with ease that whatever he pulls out isn't going to be good for us. I continue to watch him with a disappointed gaze, even when I know I should do something. I just can't seem to move. The thought of raising my gun to him brings butterflies to my stomach. A sickness I'm sure won't pass anytime soon, despite my brains protest.

He knows this. He counted on it. Though as for Camille, I doubt he counted her.

"I have a clear shot to take him out," she declares, as if on my behalf.

"No!" I shout, "It has to be me."

"Nova, we need to do this, now!"

"Just give me a minute."

Manager spins in my direction. "We don't have a minute! You need to—"

"Wrong move!" Foreman yells, and the sound of mayhem becomes a dull roar in the wake of his loud screeching threat.

Our necks twist in his direction, bracing for whatever's to come from his pocket. But, instead of any kind of pistol, knife, or grenade, all that his fingers wrap around is a measly lighter. My stare doesn't stray from it, as its polish mirrors the ugly misshapen reflection of Foreman's monstruous face. Even when someone snorts behind me at the odd choice of his weapon, I only divide my attention between his malevolent expression and the lighter.

By the way he clutches onto the insignificant object, as if it were a life line, an insurance policy in his hand, the limited contents in my stomach tosses and turns. Within the seconds of a blink I dare not take, he flips the silver thing open, and while the flame dances freely in the air, its glow becomes a beacon of subtle danger to me. Especially when I have no idea what he's done.

Something as minuscule as that flame is useless alone. A completely inconsequential defence against our arsenal. But he's proven that he's much smarter than that. I break my gaze with the spark to glance around the ravaged room now quieted by death, checking to see if anyone understands the danger we're in.

I recognize no uneasiness. Their facial expressions, like mine, are dumbfounded. All except Supervisor's. The second my eyes land on him, I watch his irate demeanour quickly shift to panic and the hair on my arms stand up straight.

"What did you do?" he calls out while backing away.

Foreman menacingly cranks his head towards him, and before tossing the lighter onto the stairs, he shrugs and then says with a venomous smile, "If you can't stand the heat."

Heat? Why did he say—oh no.

The daunting scene unfolds with a speed like molasses, and my brain kicks into overdrive. I sniff the air once, then twice to make sure I'm right. Unfortunately, I am. *Shit,* I think, *gasoline.* The pit of my stomach drops almost as slowly as the lighter, and as the fire begins to swirl, its blaze engulfs the stairs. Only when I feel someone grab my wrist do I realize how close I've come to the erupting flames. My foot shifts on the ground, but the tight grip on my arm and Elias's serious tone reminds me of my vulnerability.

"Nova!" he shouts.

I back away from the inferno threatening to curdle my skin. That pain though, would only come in second to the betrayal harbouring in my chest. "We need to get up there," I divulge with clear outrage.

"Unless you plan on walking through fire, we're not getting to them that way."

Turning to him, I let the irritation overtaking my expression be my only response while forcibly yanking my arm from his grip. His words—a useless patronizing observation without any actual helpful solution—are correct, and it's the last thing I want to hear. *Especially* when it was my own brother who provided the spark that lit the fire, with a joyous grin spread across his face. He's trying to protect me physically to make up for the way he can't emotionally, but this is *not* the time to play the caring ex-fiancé. And with the room filling with choking fumes, it's not the place either.

"I have eyes on them heading up to the roof. There's a helicopter on standby," Camille relays, actually saying something I can work with.

"We need to get out of here before we're all cooked," Andre coughs out.

Across the way Manager elevates his voice. "No. Our objective should be to get to Athena before the flames do!"

"What about Supervisor and Foreman?" Elias cuts in, finally dropping his gaze from me. "We can't just let them get away."

Around my neck, the feeling of a noose made of smoke and overwhelming stress tightens, threatening to squeeze out the good air left in my lungs. Every one of them is right. We need to get to Commander, and we have to obtain Supervisor and Foreman before they get away, which is something we can't do if we're dead.

My eyes frantically bounce from one side of the smoky room to the other, as I think of our options. There isn't much we can do together, not with so many obstacles that need to be resolved.

No.

The only chance we have in finishing this is if we—

"Split up," I mumble to myself, but while I swiftly scan over the growing furnace again, I speak with louder demand. "We need to split up. Elias and I will take the east end fire escape to the roof and cut them off from there—" my stare then shifts to the right, drawing attention to the extinguisher, and then I lock eyes with Manager— "you and Andre take the extinguisher to clear a path to get to Commander. Then get out through the west end."

He opens his mouth to protest, but then quickly shuts it, knowing we don't have time to argue. And besides, I highly doubt he has a functioning plan of his own. So, without waiting for anymore irrelevant conversation, I firmly press a finger in my ear to muffle the burning in front of us.

"420, make sure they don't get to that chopper. Shoot it down if you have to," I add, giving restrained consent.

"Copy," she answers without hesitation.

"And what are you going to do when you come face to face with your brother again, agent?" Manager asks, suspicion coating his every word.

My voice is cold and stern as I turn away from him. "I'll handle it."

An ear-splitting bang from overhead captures my attention, and instantly I know: a gunshot. It sounded too close to be from Camille, which means it came from the roof. But who shot who is the question. The thought of going up there to find Foreman—Dominic spread out and bleeding sends an icy wave through me.

After everything, it shouldn't. Yet as we split up, Elias and I making our way to the roof, most of the speed in my step comes from the sisterly concern I've had for him for years. And up until mere minutes ago... days.

CHAPTER THIRTY-THREE

BITTERSWEET

With a swift kick, the metal door flies open, and right away Elias and I keel over, desperate to remove the smoke polluting our lungs. Each cough comes out heavier than the last, and with every new gasp of welcoming fresh air we take in, they only get worse.

Tears slightly blur my vision, my body tremors from the dryness coating my throat, and a dull yet excruciating pound eats at my skull. But despite all that, and my hand clinging to my chest eager to sooth the burning inside, I still manage to force my words out with intense anger.

"Fuck!"

"Nova," Elias coughs beside me.

I shout. "I fell for his entire sob story!"

"Nova!"

Again, his call falls unto deaf ears. I throw my head back and grab two fistfuls of hair that has completely fallen from its ponytail and let out a loud grunt through clenched teeth.

"I let this happen. I let him play me!"

This time Elias grabs my shoulders and shakes some sense into me. "Nova, you don't have the luxury of a meltdown right now, alright!?"

I swing my head back and forth. "Right. Right."

"Okay, then let's go."

Quickly taking my hand in his, Elias pulls me along. We run on the gravel roof until we come face to face with the ladder leading to our boss level. Its long narrowness is somewhat intimidating, reminding me that there's only more disarray waiting after the climb. But, when Elias let's go of me, I force myself up the iron staircase, yet I can't help but let that reminder grow into a nugget of indecision.

It sets off a chain reaction of thoughts, and that little voice inside my head becomes a blaring siren, telling me to go. Telling me to just turn around and let them escape. To just take the loss so I can begin to lick my physical and emotional wounds. Try to find a way to be happy and live out the rest of my life, without being in a position of knowing the in's and out's of this heart flattening situation. That doesn't sound so bad to me. And in some crazy way, I can even see Elias in that future, but as we reach, it's at that moment does the fantasy snap in half.

I smell the metallic scent before the long skid of blood across the concrete pathway greets us. Dark and fresh. For a moment, my eyes stay glued to the stain, like if I stare at it long enough, I'll be able to tell who it belongs to, but I quickly pull my stare away. Keeping my head clear is the only way I'll be able to finish this.

I glance back to Elias, and before we follow the red carpet left for us, we draw our weapons. Then, like every overly dramatic cop show I've ever seen, each step we take is slow, quiet, and calculated. *Left foot, right foot. Left foot, right foot* is the mantra I focus on while the booming thump of my heart beats against my chest, filling my ears.

The gut-wrenching feeling that I'll find Dominic lying in a pool of his blood almost causes me to bend in ill-defined pain. But surprisingly, with the thought of that outcome, a slight sensation of relief doesn't stray far behind. Instead though, it's Supervisor we find.

He holds the left side of his body for dear life, and it brings me a genuine moment of joy to see him sitting there. Even more so when I watch him cough and blood slowly trickles down his chin. My pleasure only lasts for two perfect seconds, because then of course he ruins my bliss by talking.

They always start talking.

"Well, look who survived the fire. The devil's older sister herself—" he wheezes, then lifts his head towards Elias—"and her mentally ill lover."

Elias grabs his collar without hesitation and practically lifts him off the ground, flexing almost every muscle in his body. "You manipulating, unstable, murderous bastard. Where's Foreman?" he says violently.

"Manipulating, yes. Murderous bastard, that's on my resume. But *unstable*?" Supervisor chuckles, "No. That title is reserved for you I'm afraid. A man who couldn't move on from one little bitch."

Simultaneously, Elias's jaw and grip on Supervisor's collar tightens, but he doesn't take the bait. "Where's. Foreman?"

"Oh, come now Meyers, I taught you better than that, didn't I?"

"Okay..." he trails while roughly dropping him onto the gravel, "let me try again then, you traitor piece of *shit*."

Supervisor laughs. "*I'm* the traitor here? Says the agent who hunted one of his own, because he couldn't leave his feelings out of the equation?"

"That's rich coming from you," Elias laughs, mocking Supervisor. "A man who betrayed an organization that devotes itself to protecting the world, all to be bossed around and dismissed by an in over his head little boy. But tell me, was it worth it? Abandoning a position where you were a highly respected?"

"Respected!? You actually think that this miserable place—this hell hole disguised as a sanctuary—respected me, or commended anything I've done in their so-called "good" name!? A name that represents an agency that's supposed to protect the world, but can't even protect their own people? After *everything* I've done, *everything* I risked working for them? Ha," he scoffs, "no."

"Day in and day out, all of the hours I spent here "protecting and defending" against mobsters, terrorists, or god knows whatever else was thrown at me, was time I wasted! There's no point continuing to do the same unsolvable puzzle. No results in running the same impossible maze over and over again. And yet, every day I—"

In two swift steps I reach him and slam a fist in his face, then gently rub my red knuckles. "You're pathetic."

A sharp sting pulsates through my mouth as I bite down on my tongue, trying to stop myself from firing off my rage, but it doesn't work. It comes out sharp and hot as I'm disgusted at his excuse for doing all this.

"You betrayed Unknown because they didn't put your name up under the word 'hero' in big shiny letters? Because you got tired of not being able to take credit? Of not getting the praise you *think* you deserve? What? Is that all you needed to give Specter what they wanted? A pat on the back and a pair of pretty legs? Did Vice tell you you were special, that Unknown was taking advantage of you?"

Now it's me who laughs. "Don't blame the agency for the cliché you turned out to be. That's on you that you gave up on doing the right thing just because it's the right thing, without glory."

He spits blood and scowls. "I more than earned my glory."

"No, what you *earned,* is the bullet lodged in your gut," Elias chuckles then leans down and pokes Supervisor in the stomach. "Congratulations. There's your metal of honor."

Again, I bite down on the inside of my mouth. This time it's to stop a laugh, and the urge to strangle Supervisor. With the grin on Elias's face, evil with a hint of mischief, it seems he has the questioning portion covered. So, with a new kind of speed, I force myself to step back to clear my head. I tuck away the feelings I don't need right now and focus on what I do need.

To find Foreman.

I twist to scan over the roof, my eyes immediately going to the chopper. It's still sitting on the pad, simply slicing through the air. No pilot and Foreman is nowhere to be seen, yet a chill runs through me. An all too familiar one that tells me eyes are on the back of my neck. I quickly remember whose.

"420, any sign of him?"

"No. I lost visual. You're in a clearing, but from this angle most of the air ducts are obstructing my line of sight."

I look out at the massive metal maze of ducts that spreads throughout the entire roof. *Well, that's not good.* She was supposed to be our advantage point up here, but it's too congested. Did he count on that? The question makes the hairs on the back of my neck stand up in the cold. Whether he's got something planned or not, it's just another situation to re-evaluate and recalculate.

But who has time for that?

I sigh roughly while spinning around on my heels, making sure to cover as much bases as I can before going over to Supervisor in a frustrated stomp. Despite his background in interrogations, Elias moves back with a bloody fist, and allows me to take over.

I step into where he stood, replacing him in holding the menacing position of casting a shadow on the man who ruined us. Then, as if all that matters is seeing him in even more pain, I firmly plant my foot on his stomach and slightly press. The small gesture alone is enough to make him yelp in agony.

"Where. Is. He?" I hiss.

"Why? Because your last family reunion was so great you want to see him again so soon? The fucking brat..." he snickers, but his humour quickly diminishes when more blood pours from his mouth.

"What reason do you have to cover for him?" Elias chimes in behind me, not hiding his amusement at all. "Given that he shot you, by your principles I'd say he's lost all rights to any protection from you."

I press harder. "I'll make sure you die much more painfully than you thought you would if you don't tell me where that 'fucking brat' is... *Declan.*"

"Aw yes, the threats," he coughs, "right on time."

"That wasn't a threat. That was a guarantee. They may sound alike, but there's a huge difference. The first one is just words, but the other, is a promise. A promise that I'm going to *fucking* kill you." I lean in a bit more so he can see the fury lighting my eyes.

"Tell me where he is."

Just like when I stood over Tristan Clifford, staring at the worthlessness in his eyes as the yearning to end his life slammed into me, the same feeling hits again. Though executing Supervisor, would be all the more satisfying. After all he's done to the agency, to Commander, to Elias, and to me?

I almost deserve to.

I'm so wrapped up in that greed, that when I hear the brisk steps coming from behind, it's too late.

"Look out!" Elias and Camille shout.

By the time I whip my head around, Elias is already pushing me out of the way. As I hit the ground, the boom of another two gunshots and the burst of immense pain from falling onto my bad side disorients me. I let out a low moan of agony as I furrow my brows. Slowly I twist until my forehead is gently pressed against the cool gravel, hair falling all around me

Everything is a blur, and my senses scramble to refocus, each coming back to me as faint as a whisper. The taste of blood coating my tongue, the sharp feel of small rocks digging underneath my fingernails, the smell of dirt, and my eyes trying to become steady. But hearing the traumatizing gurgle of someone choking on their own blood quickly has everything realigning.

I get to my knees and shake my head back and forth, eagerly trying to straighten my sight to make sure it isn't Elias dying beside me. When my vision finally clears, Declan is the one clawing at his throat for air.

"Goddamn it. Killing that man is like killing a fucking cockroach," Foreman comments nonchalant behind us, as if ending his life was nothing more than an inconvenience for him.

"Anyway, my rides waiting so... see you never, *Sis.*"

All I do is watch Declan die. He may have been a human shit stain, but he didn't deserve to go like this. *Way too easily.* To pull my focus away from his useless death, Camille's voice fills my ear, reminding me of the task I asked for.

"This is your fight, Nova. So end it, now. Before I do!"

I snap out of the trance and turn to Elias. With his swift reassuring nod that he's okay I get to my feet and grip my gun. Shoving back whatever love is left for him, I point it at Foreman. He simply struts away without a care in the world.

"Hey!" I yell before shooting into the air.

"Oh, come on Nova," he stops dead in his tracks and drops his head back, "you're not going to shoot me, and we both know you're not going to let anyone else do it. So why don't we skip the games and you just let me go."

"You're not going anywhere."

He spins around to face me, smiling with a wicked grin. "Fine. I'll play. Let's do one of my favourites. The ultimatum."

Before I can think or act, he raises his gun and fires at Elias.

"No!" I scream and run over to him then drop to my knees.

"There, now pick. You can either save the love of your life you lost precious time with because of an arrogant and angry man—a man that's never coming back, which you're welcome by the way—or you can risk trying to get to me."

Even with my attention on Elias, watching the blood come from him as he groans in torment, I can hear the smirk in Foreman's voice. His blood starts to coat my fingers as I press on the wound, yet even in its warmth my entire body remains cold.

Worry and anguish seep into my bones. Though as I shift my stare, only a murderous and heavyhearted feelings starts to bubble up in my chest as I look up towards Foreman. A barrel between my eyes is the greeting I receive, but with the rage growing in me every second, it becomes an obscure image. And all I'm left staring at is my brother with an entertained smirk on his face.

"Bittersweet, but it's your choice," he tells me.

My chest rises and falls as I rapidly heave out in fury, "what happened to you?"

"What happened to me?" his expression darkens, "you left me, that's what happened! We were supposed to be a team Nova, that's what you said, but you lied! You have no idea the things I was forced to see—to do when you went away. Things that changed me."

The wind from the chopper whips his hair up, casting a slight shadow across his eyes. In them I see the scared little boy I left behind. And despite the fact that I'm currently pressing on a gunshot wound that he put into the man I still love, my stomach sinks.

So much of me wants to reach out and hug him. To apologize on repeat until it fixes him. I fought so hard to save him, to redeem myself from the past, except now, I don't think I can. All of this has gone too far. He has gone too far and there are no other options I'm seeing, as much as I wish I could.

I have to take him out.

"I'm sorry Dom. If I could go back and fix all of it I would," I say with absolute sincerity, though it completely falls away as I slip into a condescending tone.

"But let's face it, if I did, you wouldn't be where you are. You wouldn't be important. Wouldn't have become

Foreman." I snicker and continue to taunt. "You keep saying all of this isn't because of me, but we both know you're lying, *baby* brother."

His moment of silent brooding ends almost as fast as it began, and like it never happened, his face returns to a wicked sheen.

"Shut up," he growls.

"Why? Because you refuse to accept it? Because you know I'm right?"

"What are you doing?" Elias tightly whispers, but I slightly press harder on his wound to shut him up.

Foreman scoffs then sighs, and nothing but rage fills my chest as he smirks down at me again. "You almost had me there for a second. Almost had me believing you actually *want* credit for who I am. But too bad you showed your hand earlier, the second I walked out and revealed who Foreman *really* is. I saw the same look you wore when you "found me". Pure horrified dread. You blame yourself."

"Pointless really, but don't get me wrong, your expression made my day. Your "apology" though, not so much, because—and I can't make this crystal clear enough—I don't want nor need your pity, *sis*. We both made our choices, picked our sides and in the process said goodbye to the moral standards of life."

I shouldn't be hearing this. I don't want to be hearing this, and yet... my plan to do something changes. *Everything has.*

"I do have to admit, when I found out that it was you who was tagging my shipments, making things harder for me to expand the family business, I was impressed. My big sister ran away and joined a black-ops agency. But then I thought, too bad she joined the wrong one," he chuckles.

My stomach drops. "Specter recruited you."

"Technically, I recruited them. Abuelo introduced me to Casper—or Overseer as you formally know him—when I first started out. A lot of people had opinions about an eighteen-year-old cleaning or supplying their extensive funds, so I needed some bodies to scare them straight. Hence Overseer."

He shrugs. "I provided the funds and Specter provided the fear. The order. And later on, when things cooled off after the first failed information grab, for an extra allowance, they threw in Declan. The high-ranking Unknown agent *desperate* to betray his agency, by any means. As long as he had some "honorable" mentions, and another scapegoat. Or two."

Foreman begins to back away, his gun still trained on Elias and I. "Kidnapping myself was his idea, to draw you out, his first goat, which inevitably led to Meyers following. His second. And you know, I was willing to let you live after fucking up your new life a bit. But you'll never stop coming for me, will you?"

"401, whatever you were planning, the time has passed. He's winding up to shoot," Camille chimes in.

I ignore her and slowly take one hand from Elias, my stare never leaving Foreman.

"I can't have that. Can I?" he asks.

"Castillo. Either you shoot him, or I do."

He stops and holds the gun steadily between his hands. "You've interfered enough. So maybe it *would* be best to just get rid of you now."

"Three..." she starts counting down.

I glance at Elias.

"Please know that this isn't personal, agent."

"Two..."

I stop my finger from shaking on the trigger as I slowly drag the gun from my side.

"Because other than us being blood, you mean *nothing* to me. Not anymore."

"One..."

I look Foreman dead in the eyes, then shoot.

Only when I feel the slight tickle on my cheek do I realize I'm crying. Gently, I wipe the tear from my face, and next thing I know I'm by Dominic's side. I don't know when I got up and walked over to him, but here I am, watching as his eyes widen, trying to comprehend what just happened.

Honestly, I'm trying to do that myself, especially when seeing the blood pool at his waist. It's not the image an older sister ever wants to see, but he brought this upon himself.

"Good work, agent," Camille says proudly. "Andre just confirmed they got Commander to safety. It's done. I'll be there shortly to take care of things from here. Over."

Tapping the comm to finally put her on mute, I soak in the silence for a minute before leaning down by my brother's side, tears still coming.

"I promised I was coming back for you, and I meant it. I still do. Even if that meaning changed from giving you love and shelter to putting you in handcuffs and a deep cell."

The loud thump of my aching heart reminds me that it's all over, that he can't hurt anyone anymore. *You did your job*, I think as I force myself to turn away from him and go to Elias.

This time I'm choosing him.

CHAPTER THIRTY-FOUR

SEE YOU LATER ALLIGATOR

I've had to deal with death all my life, and it's always been an easy thing. But right now, watching Elias's blinks become slower, I realize that I've never actually dealt with death.

Not like this.

I conditioned myself not to care for so long, but since I let him in again, every emotion hits ten times harder. He was a part of me for so long that it took me years to even dismiss the thought of him that crept into my mind every day. But now... now I find myself wishing for the time that was stolen from us to be replaced with sweet memories, and not useless hate and vengeance.

"Hi, Puppy," I say softly.

A slight smile lights his face as he looks up at me, like he just realized I came back to him. Like the first time we met. "Hey, Kitten," he mutters.

I have to keep him talking.

"I wanted to thank you for not killing me when you had the chance. I really appreciate that."

"Full honesty, I don't think I could've, but no problem," Elias laughs with a cough. "And ditto."

Another tear rolls down my cheek. "We had something amazing, didn't we?"

"I told you we were made for each other. Till death do we part," he grabs my hand, "but I guess I've got that section covered don't I?"

Without meaning to, a bitter laugh escapes me, and I tighten my grip.

"I have one final wish, Kitten."

Elias drops his hand from mine then reaches for the chain around his neck. He pulls it out of his shirt, and the glimmer of a diamond ring lights my eyes. I've seen it before. It graced my ring finger once for what feels like decades ago. *So that's what he was hiding in his shirt this whole time. He never got rid of it.* I shift my gaze from him to the ring as he gently drops the necklace in my hand.

"Once more for old times' sake?"

"Of course."

"Good." He does a hard swallow. "Also, I need you to know that I can forgive you for Daniel now. Truly. And I meant it earlier when I said that I... that I still love you."

"Thank you. Really," I say as the last of that burden lifts from my shoulders. Then, with a throbbing heart I roll my eyes, shrug, and smile. "And I kinda still love you too."

He takes my hand in his again, pulls me in closer and wipes a tear from my face. "After everything?"

"Yeah."

"Drugging you?"

"Yes."

Elias turns his head up at me. "Even almost killing your friends?"

I laugh bitterly at that one. "What can I say? I'm as crazy as you. So yeah, water under the bridge."

Going silent, he only looks me in the eyes, and when he seems to find what he's looking for—my forgiveness—he suddenly has a bit more pep.

"Okay. I believe you. Thank you"

I glance from side to side then draw back from him with a small smirk and a raised brow.

"You know you're not going to die right? I mean it's bad, but it's a through and through. You'll survive."

"Yeah, I know. Foreman has bad close-range aim," he grunts out a light laugh. "But I needed to create an opportunity to give that back to you, and to hear you say you forgive me. You saying you still love me though, that's the cherry on top."

Forcefully ripping my hand from his, I wipe the last of my tears while punching him in his good arm. "I hate you so much right now!"

"Temporary hate was a risk," he grins, "but it was totally worth it."

We laugh at his dramatic scene for a while, which was both charming and disturbing. Only he would use his pain as a way to propose to me again. I'm not sure if I'm saying yes. Hell, I doubt even he knows what giving the ring back to me means. After everything I just went through though, I'm too tired to over think about it.

"How are you doing?" Elias asks softly, giving me the perfect chance to go from one perplexing subject to another.

I lie down next to him and sigh, forcing tears back. "Honestly, I don't know. But what I do know is that I need a fucking vacation."

CHAPTER THIRTY-FIVE

OLD LIFE INCLUDED

Oahu, Hawai'i

A warm breeze picks up the sweet scent of my pineapple daiquiri as I swirl it in my hand, mixing it with the smell of the sea in front of me. And as I stare out at the white sand and calm water, I wait for complete tranquility to wash over me.

But it never does.

Not today. Again.

I'm in the middle of a picture perfect spot, a private beach barely on the map, and all I can do is sigh. Even pretending to relax hasn't worked for me thus far. But I started this vacation, so I might as well try to enjoy what's left. After last night though, I don't think 'enjoy' is the right word.

The old nightmares haven't come back, but a new one has taken its place. It took a while to put at least *some* of the broken pieces of my life back together again. Though still, after all this time, whenever I close my eyes, I see the startled expression that smeared itself across 'his' face.

Some days are better than others. Except the stain of Foreman's blood hasn't completely washed off. I don't think it ever fully will. A part of me knew that the minute I made the decision to raise that gun and shoot, that I'd be doing the right thing. But my guilt has been clouding that logic. Especially with his hateful words echoing in my head from time to time.

'Because other than us being blood, you mean nothing to me. Not anymore.'

The ache in my heart returns every time his voice resurfaces. I've been teaching myself to silence it, but it's not as easy when there isn't much to distract me from its sad echo. And even then, all that replaces it is the sound of Minnie's last breath. Again, the beach sitting in front of me tries its best to be soothing, its beautiful crystal waves slowly rolling in and out like a dance routine.

I close my eyes and breathe deeply, trying to get something out of the salty air and the balmy sun resting on my skin. For a moment, pure bliss finds its way into my bones, and all that plagues the world doesn't plague me. But, just like before, pure bliss slips away, and I'm only left with Foreman's bulging eyes staring back at me.

Before I get lost in its traumatic effect, the now familiar voice of my personal butler Finley draws me back from the edge of darkness before I fall over.

"Ma'am, you have a visitor."

I sigh. "Their name?"

"They won't say. But they're being *very* insistent," he tells me with a bit of a frightened stutter. From that alone, I know who it is.

A grin stretches across my face, and I slightly laugh. "Send her back."

"Yes ma'am. Right away."

He moves swiftly with such purpose, which is clearly driven by the urge to get my agitating visitor off his hands, the poor thing. While waiting, I take a long sip from my rum smoothie, then remove the cocktail skewer and slide the pineapple garnish into my mouth. As I flick the toothpick away, my smile remains, even while chewing the juicy fruit.

A minute later, the sound of assertive footsteps heading my way is all I focus on. And just as I shrink my grin into a smirk, the sun disappears behind her shadow as she stands over me.

"You didn't have to scare the living shit out of him you know," I tell her, slightly amused.

"He was being rude."

Pulling my shades down onto the tip of my nose, I glance her over, then raise a brow. "By asking for your name?"

"Yes," she answers sternly.

I slide the sunglasses onto my head, but the laugh I would've let out gets swallowed down when I notice the file she's holding—or more like hiding—behind her. It's blue. Blue means sensitive material, and in my experience, that can either mean bad news, or slightly less bad news.

Really, I'd prefer neither, but I have a feeling that she didn't make the trip just to say hello. Whatever the reason though, which I'm sure is going to be a topic of conversation *very* soon, I'm in no rush to hear it.

I take another sip of my drink, then force out a bitter laugh. "You're being ridiculous. And you're blocking my sunlight. Sit down."

She glares for a moment, but eventually she softens her fiery eyes and unbuttons her jacket, still making an effort not to display the file she's brought with her.

"You look exhausted for someone who's sitting by the beach drinking a daiquiri in a bikini." She plants herself in the lounge chair next to me. "What? Vacation not going great?"

I shrug. "You've been to one beach you've been to all." My eyes wander down to the hand remaining behind her, but they quickly find their way back up.

"So, what brings you to Hawaii, Maxwell?"

"Actually," Camille smoothes down the collar on her elegant burgundy blazer, "its Supervisor now."

"Ah. My congratulations." I sit up and place my drink aside. Then as I twist back around to face her my smile fades. "What do you want?"

She finally reveals the folder.

"What is this?" I ask, suspicious.

Camille leans forward and hands the file over to me. "Your new reinstatement papers, along with most of the information in Foreman's case file."

"And *why* is this?"

"Right now, Specter is running scared with their tail between their legs, because they backed the wrong horse. We've had the upper hand for the last couple of weeks—oddly enough thanks to that bastard Declan—and we want to keep the hot streak going. We've had sources tell us that Foreman and his operation was cut. So that means Specter is scrambling to salvage what they can while looking for a new investor to help them move on to their next evil scheme."

"So Foreman's operation is left vulnerable, which means we have free rein to shut it down. Completely uninterrupted."

"Exactly."

"So what do you want with me then?"

"I want you to take lead of the entire task force," Camille proudly replies.

I freeze just as I'm about to open the file. "Because I'm a good agent? Or because of my... family history?"

"Both."

"I'm so flattered. But isn't that a huge conflict of interest?"

My mobility returns, and I flip through the pages, each with a seemingly endless wall of redactions. But when I come across a clear profile of an elderly man, Camille's response sounds so far away.

"Yes, and it gets even bigger when you read who Foreman had shipped to Jersey. The former leader of his organization. A mister Hugo Castillo, a.k.a your—"

"Abuelo," the word travels up my throat and I roughly sigh, staring at his picture. "I noticed."

Shit. And here I thought him taking Dominic in all those years ago was a good thing.

I let go of the folder, and violently rub my temples, trying to rid myself of what I just learned. I didn't want to believe that Abuelo had anything to do with helping grow the "family business," but then again, what do I know? I guess hoping that someone is safe to calm your nerves, doesn't mean they actually are. A complete understatement in this situation, but it is what it is. My family was never normal, apparently not even those who were far away, and those "unconventional" traits rubbed off on both of us.

'We both made our choices, picked our sides and in the process said goodbye to the moral standards of life.'

His voice worms its way back into my head and I groan. Yes, the whole dilemma helped me realize how much I think of the agency as home, a place that I can be my best self, and yet... my mistake caused everyone to lose something. I've always loved the good with the bad in that life, except this time, all I'm seeing is the bad. How am I supposed to go back after having firsthand knowledge of all the lives I've ruined? The ones I cared most about.

Noticing my unease about being on the subject of my nefarious side of the family, Camille softly clears her throat and brings me back to the present. She scoots forward, and then gently places a hand on my shoulder.

"Look, I know this has really been hard for you. And judging by the bags under your eyes, I'd guess the situation has been following you around like a ghost. Is haunting you. But what's past is past Castillo, and that's where you should leave it. All you can do now is help fix the present."

"As oddly compassionate as I found that, honestly I... I don't think I have the right intuition skills for the job anymore. I'm just—"

"Don't have the right—what are you talking about? Nova, I was with you for most of last month's complex journey, and the way you handled everything was astonishing. Being compromised, dealing with the civilians, Commander's disappearance, getting Elias on your side, Minnie's passing, Foreman revealing who he really was *and* taking him down despite it?"

She moves closer, her tone taking on a much more friendly shape. "What I had seen, was an agent—a leader—who was forced into hiding before she got a real chance to shine. And one I'd like to work with, officially."

"You actually trust me to do this, don't you?" I narrow my eyes at her and smirk.

"Like I said, what's past is past. When it counted most, you did what you had to do, and that's all that matters to me. Most wouldn't have taken that shot, but the fact that you did, proves then and now that you share and understand the agency's goals."

I scoff lightly. "Yeah. That, and the countless hours of interrogation, right?"

She rolls her eyes. "Yes, that helped too."

As we both laugh dryly, I can't help but reminisce. It had been a rough couple of days in that dull room, staring at myself in the two-way mirror, but I managed to prove that my dismay at the situation was real. After I did, Camille and I realized we actually had a lot in common. Our shitty childhoods, our violent pasts, and even our reason for joining the agency. To prove that we can be good monsters. It made us become good friends. *Real* friends.

A few days after acting Commander ordered her to interrogate me of course.

But now, while we continue to sit in the silence of my indecision, she removes her hand, and instead of the sweet friend, I get the tough but constructively arrogant Camille I first met on the jet to Toronto.

"Let me ask you this. How did you really feel when you were back in the field, despite some slightly shitty end results? And with knowing everything you know now, about why you opted for early retirement all those years ago, how can you create a new life that includes the lie of you wanting it to be normal? A lie Declan made you swaddle yourself in."

Part of me just wants her to leave and let me wallow in the aftermath of the mess I helped make. Though a wave of coming regret causes me to blurt out,

"If I came back—not saying I am—but if I did, how would that look? And who else would be a part of this task force?"

"You'll be in charge of rounding up the rest of Foreman's members, as well as shutting down his side businesses that are still being operated by some greedy goons. The gunrunning, drug trafficking, and cleaning money. After that's all over and done, you'll have the option of staying within project cloak and dagger, or you'll have your pick of any department with mine, as well as Colton's and Athena's glowing recommendation." She slides herself off the lounge chair and sighs.

"And as for who you'll be working with, you'll meet them at Athena's welcome back meeting in two weeks."

That's the only amount of detail I'm getting out of her until I actually agree to do the job, which makes sense. In fact, all of this, me dedicating my time to shutting down the very "family" operation I've always hated, also makes more than enough sense. She's right. I can't fix the past but I can try to fix the present.

"So, are you in?"

With another quick glance at the file, making sure I want to do this, I find my answer. And as I look up from the pages, for the first time in weeks, Foreman's voice starts to become a dull roar. A grin spreads across my lips.

"Sure, what the hell. Vacation is overrated anyway."

CHAPTER THIRTY-SIX

THE BEGINNING

, Spain

How is it I'm still finding sand in places sand should *not* be? New apartment, new wardrobe, a new location far from any beach, and yet somehow it still ends up in my heels. I swear, if I find anymore, I'll burn this entire—

"You have an incoming video call," my virtual assistant announces, cutting my thought of arson short.

I violently shake the rest of the sand from my heel over the sink. "Answer."

"Hey. Does this jacket look okay, or should I go with the black instead of the navy?"

"You're spiralling already?" I snicker as I tip my head over the counter to see the TV, "and stick with the navy."

"Of course I'm spiralling! This is the first time I'm seeing her in person since our *strongly suggested* stay in France. And you I haven't seen since you left for vacation."

"You haven't, have you? Huh..." I trail off while finally putting on my shoe, then plop onto the couch, "it hasn't felt that long."

It's amazing how quickly things can get wrapped up. Like they never happened at all. But I guess that's kind of what comes with the whole *secret agency* package. Apparently, Unknown had a protocol for the *France situation*, which didn't surprise me in the slightest.

After getting off that rooftop, everything moved with such pre-planned precision it would've been weird if I hadn't noticed. Reinforcements arrived, those who made it to the panic room before the chaos hit were escorted elsewhere, and the location was already being scrubbed.

Of course when the cleaners showed up they were ready to swoop in and gladly take all the glory, though Manager was there to shut them down before they could. Though in his moment of leadership, that's when he decided to use his rank as acting Commander to have Elias, Andre, Foreman and I taken into custody.

Camille was off the hook, since she was technically working under his orders and completed her task. I was too tired to resist. And whatever strength I had left was used to convince Rebecca and Shane—who Manager also took into custody—that *they* weren't being arrested. That was only within a couple of hours.

When I was in and out of interrogation, I could only imagine how things were going as the days passed. Only on the plane ride back from Hawaii was when I finally got filled in on what happened, before and after I left. Courtesy of my new boss, Supervisor, a.k.a Camille.

It's still odd to think she'll get final say in my actions, but I could've gotten a worse boss. Like, I don't know, one that blackmails my fiancé, manipulates me into quitting, and is a mole sleeping with the enemy. But I'm about ninety percent sure that can't happen twice.

She told me about the cleanup with the more digital mess Declan and Foreman left behind, which apparently was a whole other story. Thankfully it wasn't a very long one. The system went back online—with a whole new security upgrade, courtesy of what Minnie left in her files—and all the files Declan had illegally copied were formally validated.

Instead of replacing it with new directives on current ops, hidden locations and aliases, acting Commander made the decision to create traps using the very information Specter had been relying on. A clever idea that led to my reinstatement.

"How was your vacation by the way?" Shane asks, concern slightly entering his voice. "I heard you were having a hard time relaxing."

I tilt my head, narrow my eyes, and darken my voice, mainly for my amusement. "Who told you that?"

He physically backs up, even when six hours and an ocean stands between us. "D-don't do that!"

"Oh god, your face was perfect," I giggle.

"I hate you," he deeply sighs. "And a certain someone told me. She was worried."

Him being all secretive stumps me at first, but then again, knowing Camille, I wouldn't snitch on her either. No doubt she'd find out it was you eventually. Though aside from her blabbing, I'm still glad they worked things out. According to Shane—who she also had to interrogate—their session went much smoother than mine. So much so that they've kept in touch for the last month, long distance, which was probably better for them. It's sweet, given everything they've been through. I'm more than happy that something good made it out of the other side of that shit storm.

"It was beautiful. Just like stepping into a postcard. And don't even get me started on the daiquiris, I mean—"

"N, that all sounds great. But you don't have to do that you know."

"Do what?"

"Tell me what you think *I* want to hear." He leans into the screen with a smirk. "And don't say you're not doing it, because I know you. Now."

I laugh dryly. *Sometimes he catches me before I do.* "Fine. Tell me what you want to know and I'll try my best to answer honestly."

"Are you alright? And somewhat more importantly, did you find any sort of peace with everything that happened?"

"On a certain level, yes," I sigh. "But there are a few things that I'm still learning to accept."

Shane steps back and crosses his arms. "Is Becca one of those things?"

At the mention of Rebecca a pulse of sadness goes through me. I glance away from him, letting my hair fall into my face. I've come to like the length now. Especially in moments like these.

"Sorry. Sorry, I didn't mean to—"

"No. It's okay. I just..."

I've tried not to think of her, of that entire situation, but I'd be lying if I said she doesn't pop into mind from time to time. She shouldn't though. Not when she made it clear that I was dead to her by requesting a strictly *confidential* life.

Strictly confidential from me.

No part of me blamed her for wanting nothing to do with me after everything I put her through. Now anyway. Back before I was cleared to go on vacation, that was an entirely different story. When I heard she decided to go, I made it my business to know her whereabouts, just to see her again and apologize. It was one of the last things I did before I left for Hawaii, and I had every intention of letting her go on with her life without me forever.

When I did find her though, I could only watch from a distance, because the way she looked at me last, with such resentment and fear, was all I could see. It stained my memory even from afar, and I couldn't get close enough to simply say 'I'm sorry.' In that moment, I knew exactly how Elias felt all those years ago.

She was my best friend, the other person I let come closest to knowing me, and I couldn't even apologize for fucking up her life. But, as I left, leaving behind all the hurt we caused each other, I decided that that—me walking away—was the least I could do to thank her for being one of the foundations that held me together when I needed it most. I loved her, so much that it was impossible to go back to that Michelle version of me, but I still reminisce about those times now and again.

"How is she?" I blurt out.

He and Rebecca still keep in touch, despite our fall out. And in exchange for knowing that information I was not to go looking for her again. I've kept my word, because just knowing she's okay is enough.

As for Shane, I was surprised he wanted anything to do with me. After all, I'm the reason his best friend moved to a completely different country. Yet even after all that, he explained that he understood Rebecca's reasons for going, but he couldn't ghost me, and especially not Camille. Wholeheartedly saying that his life was better with her in it. That despite all the lies, he never stopped loving her.

Shane's expression turns both stand-offish and concerned. "Nova—"

"I just want to know if she got the jar." I look back at him and put my hands in the air, protecting myself from his slightly defensive tone.

He uncrosses his arms and sighs. "She's doing good. She's happy with where she is. And yes, she got your jar full of pity coffee cash."

The relief in knowing that she's alright is much greater than I thought it'd be, and I take it in. With his genuine report on her well-being, I can relax a bit. That is until I notice the time.

I shoot up from the couch. "Shit, I'm going to be late!"

"Your car is waiting outside Ms.Castillo," my assistant announces.

"Ugh! Okay Shane, I gotta go," I tell him while heading to the door.

"Wait! I need you to see it one more time," he shouts after me.

My head drops and I groan before quickly walking back to the screen. "I've seen it four times already Wendell."

"I know, but I promise this is the last time."

The nervousness in his voice slightly makes me go all mushy for him, so I stay back for one more minute. Camille is going to notice. But, given that this is for her, if she goes off on me I'll have something to hold against her when she realizes why I was late. That makes it *all* worth it.

Standing in front of the TV, I come face to face with a beautiful jade ring, and something of pride rises in my chest. It's still perfect.

I smile. "She's gonna love it."

Seeing Shane with that ring I... I don't know. I'm more than excited for them, but it got me thinking. I fiddle with the chain around my neck, feeling the weight of the gold diamond ring while tuning out the meeting going on around me.

Elias.

It's been a while since I've seen his stupid cute face. The last time I had, was when I was granted access to visit him during his recovery on the days I wasn't being questioned. After he healed enough though, acting Commander put him back in the field and kept him on a leash, to make up for his *many* indiscretions against the agency.

Not being allowed to see me was a part of that punishment, which felt more like a slap in *my* face, but what could I do? Not even Camille gave me any hints on where he could've been assigned.

"Castillo, are you listening?"

"What?" I bring myself back to the present. "Sorry, what did you say?"

Camille grunts. "Things are wrapping up here. Are you ready to meet your new partner?"

Looking around the room full of high-ranking agents, Manager, and Commander, I say much more nervously than I mean,

"They're here?"

"Cool it," she chuckles. "They're not physically in this room no, but they're on the premises."

She gestures a hand towards the door, but before I can take an anxious step, I'm stopped by Commander. A noticeable wobble accents her walk now, and I try not to stare at the scars woven into her umber face. They've healed very well considering the damage. But soon, like she caught sight of me glancing at her wounds, Commander faintly clears her throat and acknowledges us. Both Camille and I stand straighter.

"Supervisor," she nods towards Camille then looks my way, and her tone softens. "Agent 401."

"How are you doing ma'am?"

"Much better, now that I'm back to work. Though my transition back into power wouldn't be complete without thanking you."

I raise a brow. "Ma'am?"

"I've already thanked Colton, Camille, agent 504 and 404 for saving my life. I've even renamed our new system after agent Darling, to honour her and her outstanding service and sacrifice. But, by the time I was well enough to thank *you*, I was made aware you were on vacation. So I'd like to say it now. Thank you, Nova. You've done great work for Unknown and made me proud."

"You're welcome, ma'am. Thank you for your kind words."

She takes a step closer. "I know it was not an easy thing to do, especially given your closeness in the circumstances. And even though I would've preferred to have Mr. Riche alive, I'm pleased you left me someone with enough knowledge of how deep the situation went. Someone who knows how Specter's inner workings have been laid out."

In all my years working for her, I've never seen the emotion of gratitude. Frustration and anger yes, but this is new. It's kind of alarming, yet it also has a nice chest warming feel to it. Commander then sticks out her hand, and as I take it, she smiles at me before swinging her attention to Camille.

"Where were you two off to?"

"I was just about to introduce 401 to her new partner, ma'am."

Commander's grip on my hand tightens. Next thing I know, she's pulling me in closer. *I guess her strength is back to one hundred percent.* I furrow my brows at her, though the response I get isn't what I was expecting at all. She only smirks at my confusion caused by the shift in her attitude.

"Say no more."

She lets go of me and I watch her make her way to Manager, as if our conversation never happened, power radiating off her. I turn to Camille and look at her with a raised brow, but she simply laughs and lightly begins to push me out of the room.

An odd encounter, but I brush it off my shoulders. There's a more pressing matter to think about, and we're walking towards it right now. In the silence, a number of potential people my new partner could be runs through my head, but I can't land on anyone specific.

I know who I want it to be, though not one fibre in my being is stupid enough to let my mind go there. All I focus on is that whoever it is, other than the basic need-to-knows, I'm planning on keeping to myself. If the past has taught me anything, it's that letting people in doesn't always lead to the best results. Closeness can lead to not thinking clearly, which can lead to being manipulated, and going through that again isn't something I want to do to myself, or to anyone else for that matter.

In front, Camille halts, and I barely stop from stepping on her heels. I move back just as she turns to me, slowly shaking her head and snickering.

"You're worrying *way* too much about this. I wouldn't pair you with someone I didn't think you'd work well with. And it'll help you to know that we *all* approved of this, if you catch my drift, so relax."

She takes in a deep breath, and I mimic her motion, hoping it'll calm me. While breathing out, I start to feel a little less anxious about the situation. Camille then nods towards the door, and I slowly reach for the knob, staring at the opaque glass. I take in another deep breath, trying to force myself to concentrate, but the shift of her feet breaks whatever I had going for me.

"You're not coming in?" I twist around and ask, but she's already halfway down the hall.

"I think you two will want some alone time. And besides, three's a crowd," she raises her voice, "but don't take too long. Shane's plane gets in soon and we're going for dinner after this. He's been going on and on about how important it is, so don't make us late."

I smirk while sneaking a glance at my ring, but quickly pull myself from the thought of Shane down on one knee. I turn to call after her, but she's already gone.

That's just great. I have to do this alone? Maybe I can just walk away and then lie and say they weren't in there.

Shit, I can't do that.

No. I have to do this. I should just get this over with so I can go to dinner knowing I didn't wuss out. It's too soon to do that.

Come on Nova, just open it! I tell myself.

Grabbing the knob, before my courage wears off, I suck in one last breath and swing the door open. My heart almost beats out of my chest when I see who's standing in front of me. And just as a grin starts to curl my lips, I hear the words I didn't think I'd hear again.

"Hey, Kitten."

www.ingramcontent.com/pod-product-compliance
Lightning Source LLC
Chambersburg PA
CBHW010141030826
48979CB00024B/1088